DREAMS COME TRUE AT THE WARTIME HOTEL

MAISIE THOMAS

Boldwood

First published in Great Britain in 2026 by Boldwood Books Ltd.

Cover Design by JD Smith Design Ltd.

Cover Images: Shutterstock and [Paul Thomas Gooney] Figurestock

A CIP catalogue record for this book is available from the British Library.

Paperback ISBN 978-1-83633-262-6

Large Print ISBN 978-1-83633-263-3

Hardback ISBN 978-1-83633-261-9

Trade Paperback ISBN 978-1-80656-360-9

Ebook ISBN 978-1-83633-264-0

Kindle ISBN 978-1-83633-265-7

Audio CD ISBN 978-1-83633-256-5

MP3 CD ISBN 978-1-83633-257-2

Digital audio download ISBN 978-1-83633-259-6

This book is printed on certified sustainable paper. Boldwood Books is dedicated to putting sustainability at the heart of our business. For more information please visit https://www.boldwoodbooks.com/about-us/sustainability/

Boldwood Books Ltd, 23 Bowerdean Street, London, SW6 3TN

www.boldwoodbooks.com

For Denver and Charlane Evans,
with love and thanks

1

JANUARY 1943

'When folk wished one another a happy new year at the beginning of the war,' Kitty Dunbar said as she picked up a plate from the wooden draining board and dried it with the tea towel, 'it felt like wishful thinking – do you remember? But this year – well, it feels like a proper greeting.'

'There's real hope now,' said her mother-in-law, Ivy Dunbar, glancing over her shoulder from where she stood at the big Belfast sink washing up the dishes after the evening meal. Her keen-eyed, shrewd face – razor-edged cheekbones, pointed chin – for once, instead of looking sharp and critical, had softened. That's what hope could do for you.

'Do you think the war will end this year?' Abbie asked, pausing in the act of slotting the knives and forks into their places in the cutlery canteen.

Kitty's heart swelled with love for her precious daughter. Fourteen years old, fair-haired and blue-eyed, with a sunny nature and a loving heart, Abbie was the light of Kitty's life.

'Not this year,' Kitty told her.

'Next year?' Abbie asked.

'Probably not until after that,' Ivy answered.

'There's no knowing,' Kitty added quickly, with a frown for her mother-in-law, in reply to which Ivy raised her eyebrows. 'The end of the war is still a long way off,' Kitty told Abbie. It was important to be realistic.

Returning to her task with the cutlery, Abbie nodded. 'I knew that really.'

The war had gone well for the Allies in recent weeks. At the battle of El Alamein, General Montgomery's brave Desert Rats had driven back Rommel's men. That had been in November and the country had celebrated, showing its pride and gratitude by ringing the church bells all over Britain the following Sunday. It was the first time since the outbreak of war that the bells had been rung. Kitty had wept without shame at the sound and she was far from being the only one. To hear the church bells pealing in thankfulness when, if they had been rung earlier in the war, it would have meant that the country was being invaded, was indeed something to send tingles across everyone's skin. The joyous sound had been broadcast around the world by the BBC.

Then, in December, British, American, Australian and Russian forces had all been involved in various advances and counter-attacks, on top of which the RAF and the American Air Force had conducted numerous raids over enemy territory. It was a far cry from the way last year had begun. 1942 had ended on a strong note of confidence and belief.

It had certainly contributed to a better Christmas, even though more than seven million tons of food had been sunk by Jerry during the year on the dangerous Atlantic crossing, and rationing was biting harder than ever. There were few turkeys to be had and women's magazines had suggested carrot cake as an alternative to Christmas cake. The Ministry of Food had recommended home-made decorations made from dipping greenery in

Epsom salts, and it was true that the result did have the appearance of frost... as long as you didn't scrutinise it too closely.

But, however sparse the traditional trappings of Christmas might have been, the atmosphere in Dunbar's had been positive, Kitty recollected now, as she handed Abbie the small stack of dried plates to put away.

Perhaps Abbie was thinking something similar, because she remarked, 'It was a very quiet sort of Christmas for Dunbar's. Do you suppose the old building minds not being a hotel any more?'

Ivy clicked her tongue. 'You're a bit old for fanciful notions like that.'

But Abbie stood her ground. 'Dunbar's has stood for over a hundred years. How can you *not* think of all the people who have been through its doors? And now it just contains furniture from bombed-out houses.'

'Abbie!' Kitty was astonished to hear her successful business venture dismissed so lightly, but she knew Abbie wasn't criticising. 'There's no "just" about it. Providing somewhere for people who have lost their homes in air raids to store what belongings they still have is an essential piece of war work. And don't forget the wedding receptions we host. We've built up an excellent reputation for ourselves in that area.'

'Not only that, but it's kept a roof over your head, young lady,' Ivy admonished Abbie. 'Over all our heads,' she added. Her own home had been rendered uninhabitable last year, making it necessary for her to move into Dunbar's.

'I know that,' Abbie replied with a blush. 'I was just comparing it to the glories of the past, that's all.'

Kitty smothered a sigh. The 'glories of the past' had been well and truly dashed the day the bailiffs had marched across the threshold, courtesy of her husband Bill's reckless attitude to money. Kitty would have loved nothing better than to run

Dunbar's Hotel, but the chance to do so had been ripped from her that day.

'You want glory days?' Ivy asked drily. 'Go over the road to the Grove and ask Mrs Barnes about glory.'

'Why?' Kitty asked. 'What's happened?'

'She's one of those people who decided to put liquid paraffin in her cake instead of fat,' said Ivy, turning round from the sink and leaning against it as she dried her hands on a towel.

'What's wrong with that?' Abbie asked. 'I thought paraffin cakes tasted the same as ordinary cakes.'

'They do – and the guests at the Grove all thought hers was delicious,' Ivy replied, straight-faced, 'but let's say there were... consequences.'

'Consequences?' Abbie repeated, though Kitty was already smiling.

'Don't tell me,' said Kitty. 'Long queues outside the WC.'

'Ugh!' Abbie exclaimed, pulling a face that transformed her from an office girl to an elementary schoolgirl disgusted at the boys for eating worms.

'Not the Grove's finest moment,' said Ivy.

'Do you think we'll be a hotel again after the war?' Abbie asked.

'That's a good question,' said Kitty, 'and the honest answer is that I don't know.'

'Daddy says we will be,' Abbie said innocently.

Kitty narrowed her eyes, annoyance clenching around her heart. Bill and Abbie were always writing to one another – well, that was fair enough, but did he have to share his dreams with his impressionable young daughter? Shouldn't he square things with Kitty first? She was his wife, after all. But communication between them hadn't exactly flourished since that incident with the bailiffs – and when, shortly afterwards, Kitty had found out about the lies Bill had been telling his mother about her for years, blaming all *his* reckless spending on *her*, that had made their relationship even harder to navigate.

As for Dunbar's one day returning to being the gracious, comfortable hotel it had been built to be, there was nothing Kitty would have loved more – in principle. In practice, well, that was a different story. In practice, Bill would have them all in the bankruptcy court before you could say Jack Robinson.

'We'll just have to wait and see,' was all she could say to Abbie without lying her head off.

'Do you think Daddy will have liked the braces we sent him?' was Abbie's next question. She was a proper little girl where her beloved daddy was concerned, no matter how grown up she aspired to be in all other areas of her life.

'I'm sure he did,' Kitty said warmly and she meant it.

Abbie had found men's leather braces in Ingleby's for eight shillings and thruppence, but they'd been too costly for her, so Kitty had offered to go halves, happy to help Abbie give Bill a decent Christmas present – and, frankly, happy not to have to send her husband a gift that came only from herself. Perhaps it was mean of her, but she felt he didn't deserve that consideration.

'I wish he could have been here with us on Christmas Day,' Abbie said wistfully.

'I know how much he would have loved to see you,' Kitty answered truthfully.

Ivy sat down at the big kitchen table and took out her cigarettes. 'He could have sung carols with us.'

Abbie grinned. 'And "White Christmas". That's the song everyone is singing at the moment.'

'How many times have you seen *Holiday Inn* now?' Kitty asked with an indulgent smile.

'Four,' Abbie said at once. 'Once with some girls from the

office, once with Lily, once with you and Gran, and once with just Gran.'

Kitty looked at Ivy. 'I didn't realise you'd been twice.'

'Gran is Bing Crosby's number one fan,' Abbie said cheekily.

'He has a lovely singing voice,' Ivy said primly. 'Pop the kettle on, Abbie, there's a good girl.'

While Abbie obliged, Kitty sat at the table with her mother-in-law, taking a moment to glance around the large, homely basement kitchen. In the good old days, it had been a busy working kitchen, taking care of meals for all the guests, not to mention the staff. By rights, it ought to be a sad, echoey room now that the hotel was no more, but Kitty, Abbie and Ivy, together with Beatrice Inkerman and Lily Chadwick, who also lived here, had, through their friendship and reliance on one another, turned it into a warm, comfy place.

It was one of the very few parts of Dunbar's that the bailiffs had left alone, so the vast dresser still boasted its extensive collection of china, and pans still dangled from the long hanging racks. The scarred wooden block still housed its array of knives and there was a full set of chairs around the well-worn table.

In the hotel days, the washing-up had been done in one of the vast sinks in the cold scullery, leaving the sink in the kitchen itself for washing the best crystalware. Now, though, all the washing-up was done here in the main room. It contributed to the kitchen's friendly atmosphere.

Kitty lit a cigarette and inhaled, tilting back her head as she softly blew out the smoke. Imagine her and Ivy Dunbar sitting at the same table as friends! *That* would never have happened before the war.

A lot of things would never have happened before the war – such as her running her own business. That had been a real eye-opener. Kitty loved working and she was proud of supporting her daughter. She believed with all her heart that she was setting a good example to Abbie. And it had all happened because of the war.

Without the war, Bill would never have inherited Dunbar's Hotel here on Lily Street in Manchester, not far from the city centre, because it would have gone to his Cousin Ronald. Instead, Cousin Ronald had been run over in the early days of the blackout, and Bill had unexpectedly become Uncle Jeremiah's heir.

Without the war, Kitty would never have been able to arrange for Bill to be called up by the army.

Without the war, there would have been no air raids, no bombed houses, no families desperate to find storage space for what they had left.

And now, thanks to recent advances, the war had turned a corner and things looked brighter than they had done since 1939.

The future looked hopeful.

But what about her? What about Kitty Dunbar's future?

2

Kitty and Ivy set off together for their daytime shift with the Women's Voluntary Service. It had snowed again last night. Over the road outside the Grove, Mr Barnes was leaning on the handle of his spade as he stopped for a breather in the middle of clearing a path along the pavement in front of his establishment. Lily had got up early to clear the pavement and the flight of steps outside Dunbar's, but even so Kitty and Ivy trod carefully. Frost crystals clung to the stone banisters on either side. Thank goodness for stone! The hotels in Lily Street that had previously boasted metal banisters with fancy ironwork had lost their metal to the war effort.

Mr Barnes touched the brim of his cap to Kitty and Ivy, and they each lifted a hand in reply, their breath fogging the air as they called out a good morning. The sky was low, heavy with snow, though at present only a few flakes tumbled to earth.

'At least some fresh fall might brighten up yesterday's frozen slush,' Kitty remarked.

'Frankly, I don't care what it does,' Ivy replied, 'as long as we don't end up with a winter like we had last year.'

'Don't remind me,' Kitty answered with a humorous groan.

The previous January had seen a snowstorm of tremendous proportions that had dragged on for three whole weeks, not merely blanketing the entire country but positively burying it under several feet of snow. Villages had been cut off from the outside world and had relied on the RAF to drop food parcels. Supplies of food and fuel had run dangerously low because the roads were impassable and nothing could be delivered. Trains weren't simply hours late, but days, because of having been stuck fast in enormous snowdrifts. Even when they were finally dug out, they couldn't move because the points were frozen solid.

'At least we had a fine spring after the thaw,' Kitty recalled.

'Oh, you.' Ivy's tone was critical, but that was pure habit, though she didn't sound as judgemental as she would have a couple of years back. 'Trust you to look on the bright side.'

Is that what I do? Kitty silently asked herself. *Look on the bright side? And what's wrong with that, anyway?*

She had certainly always tried to be positive. Throughout the anxious years when Bill had spent money like there was no tomorrow, she had constantly reminded herself of all his good points, especially how much he and Abbie loved one another. Even when it had been hard to feel optimistic or appreciative, she had forced herself to *look* as if that was the way she felt, because she'd been too ashamed to appear otherwise. Her older sister Naomi had known about Bill's shocking spending habits all along, but nobody else had had a clue, and Kitty had been determined to keep it that way.

Things were different now, because Ivy had finally found out the truth the year before last. Up until then, Bill had strung her along, making her believe that Kitty was the feckless overspender, which had given Ivy a fierce dislike of her daughter-in-law.

As for looking on the bright side in more recent times – well, yes, Kitty was aware of doing that, though perhaps not in the accepted meaning of the phrase. In her case, it wasn't to do with seeking good things to concentrate on. For her, the brightness was something she had found inside herself and it stemmed from her work, from the struggle she had gone through to set up her business. Yes, it had been jolly hard work, but so what? It had made her feel good about herself. It had shown her what she was capable of.

She'd married young and become Mrs William Dunbar. Abbie had come along seven months later – and, yes, she really had been premature, not a pretend-premature baby like some women claimed to have had when they produced a whopping nine-pounder with a full head of hair.

After that, as Mrs Bill Dunbar, mother of one, her life had been mapped out. Housework, cooking, passing the time of day with the neighbours in their road. She had offered to get a job once she found out about Bill's debts, in order to make inroads into what he owed, but he wouldn't hear of it. The only women who worked outside the home were spinsters, widows and the unfortunate spouses of men who earned no more than a few coppers or whose nerves had been blown to bits in the trenches. But the wife of Bill Dunbar? Go out to work? Not on your life!

And now, like women the country over, she was holding down a job, thanks to the war. Best of all, though, hers was a job of her own making – a *business* of her own making.

Kitty Dunbar – businesswoman.

* * *

Kitty and Ivy were due to work in the British Restaurant that morning. Ivy was put on carrot-peeling duty and Kitty set to work on the potatoes. The humble potato had become an important war worker, bulking out dinners and stews that were light on meat, persuading soup to stretch further and turning almost anything – meat, fish or veg – into a rissole. Potato pastry made crusts for pies or cases for flans. You could even make potato biscuits.

Today, Kitty's potatoes would go into – she glanced across at the menu written on the blackboard – thick vegetable soup and fish curry. For members of the public who didn't care for curry, there was the option of rabbit pudding with mushrooms.

Kitty didn't even try to suppress a smile. Almost every family kept a bunny or two in a hutch behind the house, rabbits which were destined for the pot – but not the Dunbars, not after Abbie had been old enough to understand.

'You'll ruin that child,' had been Ivy's dire prediction at the time, but Kitty and Bill had simply smiled at one another.

Kitty huffed a little sigh. That tiny child was now a fourteen-year-old office girl, having left school last summer, and her parents were justly proud of her for working in the Town Hall. Kitty wished her dear mam could have been here to see it. It was ordinary for girls to work in the Town Hall offices now, but when Mam was young, the girls had had to earn their positions by scoring a higher mark in the entrance exam than the boys were required to achieve. Mam would have seen this job as a huge feather in Abbie's cap.

At the end of the morning at the British Restaurant, Kitty made her way to the local WVS office for the afternoon. As always, it was busy. As she walked inside, Kitty heard voices, some laughter, the telephone bell. The tap-tap of a pair of typewriters, the whirr of a filing cabinet drawer sliding shut. Hats and gas-mask boxes hung from a couple of hat stands and from a line of pegs screwed to the wall. Noticeboards were covered in lists and timetables. In-trays were full and wastepaper baskets were nearly empty, because paper was used over and over again and once that was no longer possible, it was sent off for salvage.

Kitty hung her coat over the back of her chair. She was on telephone duty. It was here at the desk that she had a late lunch.

'Though, as we all know,' she remarked wryly to a colleague, 'lunch simply means answering the phone with your mouth full instead of empty.'

She didn't mind, though. She loved her WVS work and was proud to do it, no matter what was required of her. The WVS had a well-deserved reputation for getting the job done – and it didn't matter in the slightest what the job was, from running clothing exchanges and staffing nurseries to sewing bandages and driving the mobile canteen; from guiding shocked air-raid victims through the administrative business of claiming compensation for a destroyed house to organising blood donor sessions; from making toys and driving hospital cars to gathering rosehips for rosehip syrup and making special pyjama coats for burns victims.

At the close of the shift, Kitty met up with Ivy to walk home together. The fading light turned the snow a ghostly grey.

'Lily will be expecting us,' Kitty observed. 'She'll have the kettle on.' She gave a theatrical shiver, hamming it up.

'Ah, yes – Lily.'

Kitty's heart sank. She'd known this was coming. Ivy had been certain to start banging on about it once Christmas was out of the way. The only wonder was that she'd left it this long.

'When are you going to tell her to leave Dunbar's?' Ivy asked crisply. 'She has to go before she starts showing.'

'We've got a while yet. She's only just past three months.' Kitty felt a surge of protective sympathy for her young friend.

'Don't stick your head in the sand, Kitty. I know you think I'm being harsh—'

Kitty didn't just think it. She knew it.

'—but Lily needs to make arrangements or she'll end up bringing Dunbar's into disrepute, not to mention the effect on Abbie,' Ivy went on inexorably. 'You can't expose your own daughter to this kind of immorality.'

A flare of annoyance burned the inside of Kitty's chest. 'You know perfectly well I'd never allow anything to happen that was to Abbie's disadvantage,' she said stiffly. It wasn't the first time she'd said such a thing in this context.

The trouble was, her mother-in-law made it sound so straightforward – the other trouble was that it *was* straightforward. If Kitty had heard of any other woman being in her own position, she'd have been as keen as Ivy for the unfortunate girl to move on in plenty of time before her shame began to show. But this wasn't an unknown unfortunate girl. It was Lily – dear, brave, young Lily, who had suffered so much already.

It might have been simpler if Lily intended to have her baby adopted. Then it would have been a simple matter of protecting Abbie from the disgrace of the illegitimate birth. But Lily had decided to keep her baby. Kitty knew full well what Ivy would say: 'That's worse.'

Kitty had nothing but sympathy and affection for the girl whose first baby had tragically died. No wonder she longed to keep this one. In her heart of hearts, Kitty ached to make it possible for Lily to stay on at Dunbar's, and let the gossips make of that what they liked.

Yet how could Kitty keep Lily on at the same time as protecting Abbie's innocence? Or was Ivy right? Was it time to tell Lily to get on with making plans?

And then there was Daniel Chadwick to think about, and the terrific shock to him when he learned what his wife had been up to in his absence. Yes, they'd been estranged at the time, but since then Daniel had made it abundantly clear that he was desperate for a reconciliation and the chance of a fresh start.

Lily longed for the same thing – or she had until she'd discovered she was carrying another man's child. Then she'd been faced with a heartbreaking choice. Give up her baby and return to her handsome young husband, with him never knowing of its existence; or keep her child and sacrifice her marriage.

And she had made her decision.

3

Lily got off the bus, avoiding stepping into a pile of slush, and left the main road, heading for the narrow street where she had grown up. After her parents had died, she'd been taken in by Uncle Irwin and Auntie Nettie even though they barely had room for the five little ones they already had. It had been an act of true generosity fuelled by family feeling, and Lily had never been made to feel superfluous to requirements.

As much as she loved her uncle and aunt and her young cousins, Lily had been thrilled to bits to get a job as chambermaid at Dunbar's when she had left school at fourteen, because it was a live-in position and she had a bedroom all to herself. That same room had been hers almost all the time since.

She had left it when she married, but all too soon she had found herself back there again. Her darling Daniel was in the merchant navy, facing the unspeakably dangerous Atlantic crossing to bring desperately needed supplies to Britain from Canada and America. He had consigned the pregnant Lily to his mother's care, aware that the two most important women in his life hadn't exactly hit it off with one another, but hoping that proximity would nudge them into a better relationship.

It had proved to be a forlorn hope. The formidable Mrs Chadwick had disliked Lily on sight, believing her to be a common little gold digger, who had ensnared the educated, middle-class Daniel into marriage by dropping her knickers and getting herself in the family way. While it was undeniable that Lily had got pregnant and got married in the wrong order, that didn't mean she wasn't deeply and lastingly in love with her husband, and he with her, but Mrs Chadwick had refused to accept that.

Before too long, Lily had moved out of Daniel's family home and returned to her cosy little room in Dunbar's and her mother-in-law hadn't exactly come rushing after her to beg her to reconsider. Lily had stayed at Dunbar's until it was time to go to the mother-and-baby home a few miles away in Sale to wait out the final weeks until her baby came into the world.

Oh, Toby.

Lily and Daniel's baby had been born with a heart defect and he hadn't lived long. It would be two years ago this coming April since he had slipped away, but remembering the trauma of losing him still had the power to rob Lily of the ability to breathe. At the time, hair-line cracks of grief and pain had seemed to shoot along her bones and she had crept through each endless day feeling as stunned as if she'd been bashed over the head with a frying pan.

Daniel hadn't even known he was the father of a son, let alone that the baby had died. When he finally returned to shore, Lily had emerged from the initial weeks of shock and pain and, having once more found sanctuary at Dunbar's, was attempting to claw her way back to something resembling normality. Now it was Daniel who was clobbered by grief. Although Lily had wanted to support him, the enormity of his distress had been more than she could bear on top of her own bereavement.

Eventually the young couple had made the decision to separate.

So much for the happy-ever-after Lily had grown up dreaming of.

As she walked along the road to Auntie Nettie's, Lily smiled and said hello to Mrs Wainwright and Mrs Tilney, who were heading off to the shops with their wicker baskets, and to Mrs Fielden and Mrs Birch, who were brushing snow into the gutter. Lily didn't stop to chat. That would be awkward. Auntie Nettie had never told the neighbours about Lily being separated. She was too upset.

'Your poor mother would be that ashamed,' Auntie Nettie had told Lily, adding, 'I do ask myself how I'm going to explain it to the children. You're their big sister, as good as, and they think the world of you. I don't want them growing up thinking that divorce is somehow acceptable. You've got a lot to answer for, our Lily.'

Parting from Daniel had driven something of a wedge between Lily and her dear aunt. Auntie Nettie was hurt and upset, and not just because of the shame. She loved Lily as one of her own and she grieved over the strain on her young niece's life.

Now, as Lily lifted the polished lion's-head knocker and rapped cheerfully on the door, she couldn't help but be aware that this was one of the final times she would be able to come here before she had to come clean about her pregnancy.

Her baby! No matter how tricky the position she found herself in, nothing, *nothing* could stop Lily wanting this child.

But it might be the end of everything between her and Auntie Nettie. It might cause a permanent breach between her and the good-natured, hard-working, fun-loving family who had taken her in and made her one of their own.

Her family wasn't the only thing she stood to lose. There was her home at Dunbar's too. She had already lost Daniel – not that he had any idea of it yet. The thought of it made her ache with sorrow, but she'd had no choice. Last year, daring to start to live again, she'd embarked on an affair with a charming, attractive doctor. Lily had fought against liking Dr Vivian Shawston, but the feeling he had for her meant that he wouldn't give up. Finally, she had allowed herself to open her heart, something she had never expected to do again.

The secret, short-lived relationship had ended after Daniel had written Lily a long, heartfelt letter wanting to try again. Lily had known immediately and beyond doubt that she wanted this too. Vivian had taken her ending their relationship badly. He had wanted – expected – her to divorce Daniel and marry him. When Lily had proved resolute, he had taken his broken heart to the recruitment office and joined the army. He now worked overseas in a field hospital.

Which meant there was no need for him ever to suspect that he had left a part of himself behind.

At first, when she realised she was expecting, Lily had imagined having the baby in secret and surrendering it for adoption, but she had quickly understood herself better than that. She would keep her baby no matter what – and the 'no matter what' meant giving up all hope of a future with Daniel.

It was just one of many fears she lived with. Above all else, she feared for the health of this new baby after what had happened to Toby. Then there were her fears for the future. She would probably have to pretend to be a war widow. On top of that, she would have to sort out a place to live. She would have to get a job. All she knew how to do was clean.

So many worries, so many fears, plus the dark despair of losing Daniel.

Even so, all that mattered was her baby.

4

Dressed in her trusty old mackintosh, felt hat and sturdy brogues, Beatrice walked briskly along the street to Mrs Chapman's house. It was a decent-sized building in a reasonable neighbourhood and Mrs Chapman must have been as pleased as Punch when Mr Chapman carried her over the threshold, but her life had gone significantly downhill since then. These days, she was a bed-bound invalid and since the death of her husband, she'd been obliged to move upstairs and sublet the downstairs.

The gentleman who had taken up residence on the ground floor, old Mr Trent, was himself an invalid. His daughter, the middle-aged Mrs Williams, dragged herself round here several times a day to do the cooking and cleaning and keep her father, who suffered from double incontinence, clean and dry. Never a day went by without her having to dump a set of soiled sheets into the copper for possing and washing, followed by heaving the lot through the mangle and onto the washing line.

That was how Beatrice had first come to meet Mrs Chapman upstairs. Beatrice used to be the inco lady – the incontinence lady – cycling around pulling a covered trolley and delivering adult-sized nappies. Mrs Williams, worn out by everything she had to do for Mr Trent on top of having a house and a family of her own to take care of, had on occasion taken out her frustration on young Dora Chapman when Mrs Chapman had sent her daughter downstairs to fetch the rent. Beatrice had soon stepped in and put an end to that kind of nonsense and she had taken an interest in Dora Chapman ever since.

When the front door opened, Beatrice automatically smiled, but the pleasant expression almost dropped off her face when she saw not Mrs Williams but Miss Murray, who had taken over her position as the inco lady.

'Oh – Miss Inkerman,' Miss Murray said stiffly, making no attempt to keep her smile in place when she saw who it was.

'Good morning, Miss Murray,' Beatrice replied, locking her own smile in position, determined to be pleasant in the probably vain hope that one day Miss Murray might forgive her.

The trouble was that, back in the days when she had been the inco lady, Beatrice had always spent a few extra minutes at each call, helping the women who, like Mrs Williams, were responsible for the care of the unfortunate invalid. She might help change the bed or she might bring in the sheets from the washing line. At the very least, she would make the overworked lady a cup of tea.

These kindnesses were precisely that – kindnesses – and were unquestionably above and beyond the remit of her job, but Beatrice had cared about 'her ladies' and they had appreciated the attention. Unfortunately, by the time Beatrice had moved into a different position and Miss Murray had taken over as the inco lady, the women had clean forgotten that Beatrice had been doing them favours and they had expected the same assistance from her successor. Poor Miss Murray had taken a lot of stick as a result. Whenever she crossed paths with Beatrice, which fortunately wasn't often, she made sure Beatrice knew how ill-used she felt.

'I take it you're here to see Mrs Upstairs,' Miss Murray said ungraciously.

Beatrice bridled. 'Mrs Chapman, yes. Excuse me,' she added as she slid past and made for the narrow staircase.

At the top of the stairs, she knocked on the door and went in. The room was both parlour and bedroom as well as being where the Chapmans ate their meals, not to mention being the storeroom where bedding, medicine and other supplies were kept. Disinfectant and eucalyptus didn't quite mask the aroma of Mrs Chapman's commode.

'How do? It's only me,' Beatrice said cheerfully. It was important to be bright and breezy with Mrs Chapman. She was the sort who might drag you down otherwise. 'Dora at school this morning, is she?'

A special part of Beatrice's work in the Welfare Department involved 'children with responsibilities', which was the name given to children, almost always girls, who were kept off school to look after everything at home when the mother was too unwell to manage. Beatrice knew all about this way of life because it was how she herself had grown up. Her mother had suffered a stroke at an absurdly early age. Her father had stuck around for a while, but then he'd said bluntly, 'It's up to you now, Beatrice,' and buggered off, never to be seen again.

That had been before the last war. Such children had been called looker-afters back then. 'Children with responsibilities' was a posh new term, but the problem was exactly the same.

Beatrice had come up with an idea whereby the incapacitated mothers, instead of keeping their children at home all the time, would send them to school in the mornings, because this was when the three Rs were taught; then the children were let off school in the afternoons in order to make themselves useful at home. To make this possible for the mothers, women from the Women's Voluntary Service helped with the shopping and cleaning in the mornings.

Some of the mothers were very good about sending their children to morning school in return for WVS assistance; others not so much. Mrs Chapman was one of the latter. Having had Dora at home with her over the Christmas holidays might have given her ideas. She wasn't a bad-hearted creature, but long-term illness had knocked her confidence for six.

More than once she had asked Beatrice, 'What about after the war? What happens to the household help then?'

Each time, Beatrice had been obliged to admit, 'This is a wartime arrangement only, Mrs Chapman,' and each time she could almost see the cogs turning in Mrs Chapman's mind as she clocked the necessity of hanging on to Dora. The poor woman undoubtedly saw the child as her lifeline. The war couldn't last for ever. How much longer? Two years? Three? Four more years? The Allies had had successes towards the back end of last year, but there was still a long way to go.

'I miss Dora... now she's... back at school,' Mrs Chapman said, her breathing shallow and wheezy.

'I'm sure you do,' Beatrice agreed, 'but it's the best place for her. You want her to have a decent education.'

She glanced around the room, trying not to be obvious about it. The place was in considerably better shape now that the WVS were involved. Young Dora, who was coming up to twelve, had done her best, but it wasn't right to foist that much responsibility, that much work, onto such young shoulders.

Having made sure that Dora Chapman was indeed back at school, Beatrice headed back to the Town Hall, sparing a moment, as she often did, to give thanks that the huge, gothic building, with its steeples and splendid clock tower, had survived the Blitz. So many important landmarks hadn't. The Free Trade Hall had bought it, as had Cross Street Chapel, Victoria Buildings and parts of Deansgate. Chetham's Hospital had suffered severe damage. The Cathedral was all but a skeleton.

Beatrice made her way upstairs to the Welfare Department. Another thing to be thankful for was that she was no longer under Miss Brewster's thumb. That highly experienced but basically disagreeable lady had been put in charge of Beatrice when she'd started in Welfare the summer before last. Now, though, Beatrice was considered to have proved herself, and by and large she was left to get on with her duties.

She had arranged to eat in the canteen with Fay Brewer – Miss Brew*er*, not to be confused with Miss Brew*ster*. Beatrice was a great admirer of Fay Brewer, who combined professionalism, knowledge and common sense with a kind heart and a lively sense of humour. Kitty had reason to be grateful to her every bit as much as Beatrice did. Fay Brewer had arranged for Manchester Corporation to have a stake in Dunbar's, namely for Kitty to provide a meeting room, which in turn had prevented Bill Dunbar from selling the building. As for Beatrice, Miss Brewer had been instrumental in getting her the role she loved so much.

Entering the canteen, Beatrice saw Fay Brewer right away. About thirty years old, she was strikingly good-looking with the most gorgeous dark-red hair and hazel eyes.

Beatrice collected her meal and went to join her. Miss Brewer was having the parsnip soup with dumplings followed by a savoury meat roll, while Beatrice, instead of having a starter and a main course, had opted for a main course and a lemon tart for pud. Her main course was devilled fish, devilled meaning curried, and curried being a way of disguising the fact that, whatever kind of fish it was, it wasn't good old cod or haddock.

'How are the clubs going?' Miss Brewer asked.

Beatrice ran a couple of evening clubs for children – the Time Off Club for looker-after kids, and the Gentlemen's Club. This was a group of young lads, tearaways mostly, who had heard about the Time Off Club and had come knocking on Dunbar's doors wanting to join in. Even though some of these boys had previously made her life a misery, Beatrice had put the past firmly behind her and created a separate club with all kinds of rules to do with good manners. The lure of the activities – cards, ping-pong, skittles, jigsaws, tiddlywinks, board games, billiards – had made good manners and politeness seem like a worthwhile price to pay.

'Fine, thanks,' said Beatrice, 'though I'm always on the lookout for more games and what-have-you to entertain the children. Did I tell you we've got a dartboard?'

Fay Brewer shook her head. 'Where from? Or should that be, who from?'

'Do you remember Sergeant Wakefield? The policeman who was in charge when that accusation was made against me?'

'I remember,' said Fay Brewer. 'A decent chap, I thought. Determined to be fair. And he didn't overreact – unlike some people.'

'He donated the dartboard. There's a box as well, with four sets of darts in it,' Beatrice said. 'I thought it was jolly nice of him.'

'Yes, it was,' Miss Brewer concurred. 'I hope you'll let the girls in the Time Off Club have a go as well. No reason why the boys should have it for their exclusive use.'

It wasn't long before, like so many others at present, they got round to discussing the recently released Beveridge Report.

'Have I got it right?' Beatrice asked. 'Is the recommendation that all the various social insurance schemes should be gathered together into one national overall scheme?'

Fay Brewer nodded. 'To cover everybody from the cradle to the grave. There's going to be a family allowance payment for each and every child, and a health service that is free of charge.'

'And all for a single contribution,' Beatrice said wonderingly. She pictured the many private and voluntary payments that people currently made – people who could afford to, that was. Would a free health service mean she wouldn't need to pay into the Hospital Saturday Fund any longer?

'Employers will have to make higher contributions too,' Miss Brewer added. 'Social insurance means social progress. At the end of the last war, the returning soldiers were promised a land fit for heroes. Well, that never happened. This time around, there's far more awareness in all levels of society. This war isn't just about fighting for our freedom. We have to build a better, fairer world afterwards.'

Beatrice nodded, feeling satisfaction creeping through her. Her own world was already a much better place than it used to be. She was sure she would never cease to feel grateful for the way in which her life had moved on after years of being the inco lady, even surviving a false accusation of theft... even surviving Frank's return.

Twenty years ago, she had been engaged to Frank Marsden until it had turned out that they had very different ideas as to what their shared life should be like. Beatrice had regarded children as part and parcel of marriage, but Frank had been adamant that he didn't want to be a father at all. Beatrice had felt torn in two. She wanted children – but she also wanted Frank.

In the end, she had made the heartbreaking decision to end

her engagement. She had loved Frank, but she knew she would never be truly happy without a family of her own.

And after that, no other man had ever come along and taken an interest in her.

Then last year, oh, last year – what a blow! She had bumped into Frank once more and found he was a widower with not one, not two... but *five* children. Five! And he couldn't have been happier. Beatrice had been stunned.

Frank had been keen for them to pick up where they'd left off and had done his best to win her round. His children, Rowena, Les, Herby, Georgie and Josie, were easy to love and Beatrice had thought a great deal about being their new mother... but her heart just hadn't wanted Frank any more, no matter how much she could have cared for his children.

She was too old for love now. She was in her mid-forties. In fact, strictly speaking, and not that she would ever admit it to another living soul, she was ever so slightly closer to fifty than to the forty she had been so valiantly clinging to in recent years.

It was high time she put all silly thoughts of love well and truly behind her. Romantic love had never been her friend.

Her welfare work was her future now.

5

'Please remember, Lily,' Kitty said. 'Only half-fill the punch glasses.'

Lily might look like an angel, with her beautiful blue eyes in a dainty heart-shaped face, but the grin she now directed at Kitty made her look like a naughty schoolgirl. 'Because we've got to eke out the booze for as long as we can.'

It was true. They had been obliged to cut back on the quantity of port they put in the punch, adding a slosh of sherry and a dribble of dessert wine to make up the difference. It was dashed hard for anyone – publicans, hoteliers, keepers of off-licences – to get their hands on alcohol these days, and when they could, it was violently expensive. Only last week a man in a swish suit and a trilby worn at a cocky angle had rung the bell at Dunbar's, clearly unaware it was no longer a hotel, and offered to sell whisky, but Kitty knew a spiv when she saw one and she had packed him off with a flea in his ear. As if she would ever lower herself to make use of the black market!

Besides, you heard tales of illegal alcohol made by crooks who used bottles with counterfeit labels. Such alcohol could be very dangerous, possible effects including blindness or brain damage, even death.

Kitty shook off such thoughts. Together with Lily and Ivy, she was preparing for a wedding reception which was to be held here this afternoon. This had been a new venture for Dunbar's last year and was proving to be a huge success.

They all loved holding the wedding receptions, even Ivy, who had been cautious – which was a polite word for cynical – to begin with. Kitty had worried in the early days that the receptions would prove difficult for Lily after the failure of her own marriage, and had given her the choice of whether to take part, but Lily had been fine.

Since then, of course, Lily's situation had become more complicated – her affair with Dr Shawston, then Daniel's love letter, and now the baby. Kitty thought a lot about what Lily faced, and if she was honest, it wasn't just because she cared dearly about the girl. It was also because it saved her from dwelling endlessly on her own situation.

And her own circumstances made her even more sympathetic towards Lily. Life wasn't clear-cut. If it was, every marriage would be happy and straightforward. Her own was far from that.

When she had first met Bill, she'd been crazy about him and thought all her birthdays had come at once when he proposed. Even in those days, he had spent too much, but she had seen it as a generous man wanting to spoil his fiancée. It wasn't until after the wedding that the truth had started to sink in. It hadn't stopped her loving him, though.

It wasn't until last year that her lingering feelings for Bill had been crushed, when he had refused point-blank to allow her the access she urgently needed to the Dunbar's business bank account. She could pay into it, and she had been doing so since she'd set up her storage business, but she couldn't draw any money out without Bill's permission – consent he flatly refused to provide. Not only that but Kitty had found out that he'd been helping himself to funds from the business account whenever the fancy took him.

For her, that had been the end. Bill wanted her to earn money for him to squander if he felt like it, while she and their daughter were presumably supposed to live on fresh air and with none of the comforts Kitty's hard work might have provided. Well, bugger that for a game of dominoes, as her grandpa would have said!

From then on, as far as Kitty was concerned, the only thing she owed Bill was to ensure his relationship with Abbie didn't suffer – and frankly, she wanted this for Abbie's sake rather than Bill's.

That had been the point when the wedding reception business had started, the profits from which Kitty channelled into a post office savings account in her own name.

Dunbar's also had a third business. Last year, they had started taking in lodgers. Before that, Kitty and Abbie had lived in the family flat that Uncle Jeremiah and Cousin Ronald had occupied for many years. It had been a handsome apartment in those days – much to the satisfaction of the bailiffs, who had emptied it not long after Bill had inherited. After that, Kitty and Abbie had made do with what sticks of furniture Kitty had been able to cobble together.

Then Ivy had been bombed out and Kitty had invited her to move in. Ivy still had her downstairs furniture and that had been moved to the family flat. Not that the Dunbar family had lived in the flat after that, because that was when they started renting it out. The first tenants had come to them via Fay Brewer, and after that – oh, glory – Beatrice's former fiancé and his brood had moved in temporarily. When they moved out, Kitty had left the flat empty for some time while Lily's pregnancy was new. It had felt at the time that the last thing they needed was extra people on the premises.

At the back end of last year, however, Fay Brewer had produced a couple of young women who were at the Town Hall on secondment and in need of a temporary billet, and Kitty had taken them in. Miss Kildare and Miss Egan were pleasant girls who felt they'd really landed on their feet by getting such spacious accommodation. They even had their own bathroom. There was no kitchen in the family flat, and the original tenants had eaten downstairs in the big kitchen, their meals provided by Ivy. She had catered for Frank's family too, though those meals had been sent upstairs via the dumb waiter; and this was the arrangement with the new girls too, so the permanent residents didn't see much of them. They passed on the stairs and sometimes spent an evening together, but generally they operated as separate households under the same roof.

Kitty sighed to herself as she pictured her money-making schemes. The plain truth was that she feared for the future and what would happen when Bill came home after the war. She had no doubt that he would ruin what she had built up. Moreover, he would expect her to return to full-time domestic duties, but she wanted to carry on working outside the home. It was interesting and fulfilling, and she loved every moment of working for herself.

The most, the absolute most, she could hope for with Bill would be if he allowed her to work for him when he tried his hand at re-establishing Dunbar's as a hotel. Kitty desperately wanted Dunbar's to return to its old identity, but she knew Bill would run the place into the ground financially, and that would be unendurable.

In any case, she didn't want to work for Bill. But it was more than that. In recent months, she had gradually come to the realisation that she didn't want to be Mrs William Dunbar any more.

Kitty waited. She actually stopped mixing Dunbar's Wartime Wedding Punch and waited for the inevitable moment when she rejected this preposterous idea, when she set it aside, never to be looked at again.

When that feeling declined to appear, she waited an extra few moments, knowing it would come. Of course it would. It was bound to.

But it didn't.

6

The letter was from Daniel. The envelope had been used three times, each old address carefully crossed out and replaced. Even cramped in a corner, there was no mistaking Daniel's handwriting. A flush cloaked Lily's skin and she had to sit down. She squeezed her eyes shut; then, with a deep swallow, she forced them open. All these weeks, she had been telling herself that she knew what she was doing, that she was prepared for the final split from Daniel, but now it turned out she wasn't anything like as prepared as she was meant to be.

Her eyes settled into an unfocused stare and she pinched the bridge of her nose as indecision rattled through her, jarring her heart. Then she inhaled deeply through her nose and exhaled slowly out of her mouth, pulling determination back into its rightful place. Tightening her muscles, she raised her chin. After all, even though the arrival of this letter had had the effect of an emotional thunderbolt, the fact was that she'd known it would come at some point.

Right, then. Let's see what he has to say.

She opened the envelope and removed the letter. Dry-mouthed, she started to read. It took three attempts before she managed to read it properly and take everything in.

When she finished, she sat motionless for she didn't know how long, feeling shaken. Then she pushed herself to her feet. If there was one thing the past couple of years had taught her, it was the importance of having dear friends to rely on. Kitty and Beatrice had watched over her without intruding, gently letting her know that they were there as they waited patiently for her to turn to them, should she ever decide to do so. And when she did turn to them, she'd received nothing but kindness and understanding.

She felt sorely in need of both this evening. Abbie had gone to the flicks straight from work with her chum Martha, who worked at Ingleby's, the long-established fashion and dressmaking department store on Market Street. And Mrs Ivy Dunbar was out on WVS duty until late.

Lily ran downstairs from the third floor, where they all had bedrooms. Kitty and Beatrice were both in the club room – what had once been the residents' sitting room – at the front of the building, with windows looking out over Lily Street. Just now, the windows were blacked out behind long curtains. There hadn't been any air raids for some time, but nevertheless woe betide anyone who let so much as a chink of light show.

Kitty and Beatrice were busy getting the room ready for a Time Off Club evening. Lily walked across to one of the tall cupboards, which stood open.

'What else should I get out?' she asked Beatrice.

'A selection of comics, please,' Beatrice answered. 'Thanks. And then if you can give me a hand with the bagatelle board...'

Ping-pong and billiards were available at every club evening, for the simple reason that it wasn't possible to put them away, but other activities were rationed so that they wouldn't be taken for granted. That was one of Beatrice's rules.

When the room was ready, there was still half an hour to go before the children were due.

'Time for a cuppa and a ciggie,' said Kitty.

'And – can we talk?' Lily asked.

Kitty had been about to lead the way out of the room. Now she turned back, her hazel eyes gentle and enquiring as her gaze hovered on Lily's face. Beatrice also looked concerned.

'I've heard from Daniel,' Lily said bluntly.

Kitty blew out a sharp breath. 'Well, it was bound to happen. Come on downstairs.'

She looped an arm around Lily's slender shoulders and administered a squeeze, just briefly, before she headed across the foyer to the basement door. Lily was obliged to blink back sudden tears before she followed.

Soon the three of them were seated around the table with tea and cigarettes. Kitty and Beatrice looked expectantly at Lily.

'He's been injured,' she blurted out with no preamble, making the other two gasp in shock. 'Sorry,' she added quickly. 'I'd no idea I was going to blab like that. It just tumbled out.'

'Is he going to be all right?' Kitty asked.

'What happened?' Beatrice asked.

'Yes – and I don't know any details, but I'll tell you what I do know.'

'Actually,' said Kitty, 'it might be better to go back to the beginning. Should we take it that he's back in Britain now?'

Lily nodded. 'Yes. He was in America for I'm not sure how long. There was something official he had to do there. Now he's back.'

'So he's survived another Atlantic crossing.' Beatrice's eyes glanced heavenwards, showing her relief.

Lily felt relieved too. She was almost trembling with it. She nodded again, more vigorously this time, as if the brisk movement could jerk the tears that had suddenly appeared behind her eyelids back inside her head.

'He docked at Liverpool and then he had to go straight to London to see his father at the War Office,' she said in a commendably steady voice. 'That's where he is now – in London.'

'What about his injury?' Kitty asked. 'Did he get it during the crossing?'

'No. It happened here. *They* happened here, I should say.'

Beatrice's brown eyes widened. 'More than one injury?'

'Two. They've had a few air raids down there and he got a broken arm and a damaged shoulder both on the same night.'

'Oh, Lily,' breathed Kitty. 'What rotten luck.'

'He's going to make a full recovery,' Lily hastened to assure her. 'The break is straightforward.'

'What happened to his shoulder?' Beatrice asked.

'He was shot,' Lily said quietly.

'*Shot!*' the other two exclaimed in unison.

'Jerry was strafing everything in sight,' said Lily.

'Poor Daniel,' Kitty said sympathetically. 'Wrong place, wrong time.'

'Or right place,' Beatrice suggested. 'If he took the bullet—'

'Two bullets,' Lily put in, her heart executing a little flip.

'Goodness,' said Beatrice. 'If he was shot twice in the shoulder, then that means six inches in the wrong direction and it could have been his head – or his heart. Sorry to say something upsetting, but it's true.'

The three of them exchanged looks, silently acknowledging the truth of Beatrice's comment. They had lived through enough air raids to know how much luck was involved. No wonder folk always talked about a bomb having your name on it, meaning that when your time had come, there was nothing you could do about it.

'He was jolly lucky,' Kitty said, her voice ringing with sincerity.

Emotion ballooned inside Lily's chest. 'He certainly was.'

'What else did he say?' Kitty asked gently. 'How much longer is he going to be in London?'

'For a while yet. Some weeks. Maybe until March.'

Lily felt stifled all of a sudden. In March she would be six months along. When she had carried Toby, she'd had a relatively small bump compared to other women up until the final few weeks. Even if she remained on the small side this time, she couldn't possibly stay at Dunbar's beyond her sixth month. It wasn't feasible.

Despair overwhelmed her. She felt empty and numb, as if she'd spent days on end sobbing.

Her skin prickled and a quick glance showed her that her friends were watching her closely.

'I'm fine,' she made haste to say, knowing it was essential to ward off the sympathy that would reduce her to a blubbering mess. 'It's silly, really. I've known for ages that Daniel was going to write to me as soon as he could, so it shouldn't have come as a shock.'

'But it did,' Beatrice said softly. 'You've been very strong, Lily, but you don't have to pretend with us. You do know that, don't you?'

'Of course I do.' Lily hung like grim death to her self-control.

Perhaps Kitty realised because she asked in a matter-of-fact voice, 'When are you going to write back?'

'Immediately,' Lily declared. 'I shouldn't keep him waiting. I know what to say – I decided some time ago. I'll give him a few lines about everyday life at Dunbar's – and, of course, I'll express concern for his injuries. But I shan't say anything that might lead him to have... expectations. I'll simply say—' Her breathing hitched in her throat and a fist seemed to squeeze her heart. 'I'll simply tell him that... we have to talk.'

* * *

For such a short letter, it was fiendishly difficult to write, but Lily was determined not to go to bed before she had finished it. Even after it was written, sleep proved elusive. She felt wretched and she had to force herself to stay under the covers because she knew she would end up pacing the floor all night if she got out of bed. As it was, she didn't drop off until the early hours and then was deeply asleep when her alarm went off.

Gritty-eyed and muzzy-headed, she hauled herself from her bed. Her toes scrunched into the bedside mat as if seeking purchase to stop her from toppling over. She went to the window. Twitching aside the blackout curtain and the ordinary curtain behind it, she inserted herself between both curtains and the window, which, after another cold night, had a lacy pattern of frost on the inside. She leaned her forehead against the pane, hoping the chill would jolt her to wakefulness.

By the time she had washed and dressed in her WVS uniform, she felt more herself and went downstairs for porridge and toast.

Beatrice and Abbie were the first to leave after breakfast. Warmly wrapped up, they set off together for the Town Hall. Shortly after that, it was Lily's turn. She had been rostered to collect blood samples from several doctors' surgeries and deliver them to Manchester Royal Infirmary. When she got there halfway through the morning, the sight of the ruins of the nurses' home reminded her of the assault on the hospital during the

Christmas Blitz, when most of the windows had been blasted out. Even so, emergency operations had carried on, and schoolboys, acting as stretcher-bearers, had continued working. Throughout the hospital, even though the building shuddered, nurses had got on with their duties. On one of the men's wards, when an incendiary bomb had come down the chimney and landed in the hearth, the nurses had smothered it, saving many lives.

How brave they had been. Mind you, there were numerous tales of the courage of ordinary folk. Now, facing an uncertain future, Lily would have to dig deep into her own reserves of courage. Sometimes she felt nothing but resolve. At others, she was plain terrified.

Not that it mattered in the slightest how she felt. She had made her decision and had no intention of wavering. She would be as brave as she had to be and would provide her child with the best life she possibly could.

This was the beginning of the year in which her baby would be born. Her second child. Please, *please*, let him or her not suffer from the heart complaint that had ripped Toby from her loving arms. She still ached for him and always would.

Toby would have enjoyed a good life as a member of the Chadwick family – a privileged life, by the standard of Lily's humble origins. As the son or daughter of a lone mother, a so-called war widow, Toby's little half-brother or -sister would have more of a struggle, it was true, but he or she would never want for love. Lily knew how important that was and what a difference it could make, because hadn't she been on the receiving end of the most wonderful act of love when she'd been taken in by Uncle Irwin and Auntie Nettie? Uncle Irwin struggled to provide for his own five, but he and her aunt hadn't batted an eyelid at the thought of number six.

When she returned to the WVS building, Lily found her next

task was netting. This involved making camouflage nets on a huge frame. Lily sighed, but got on with it without a word of complaint. As usual, when she tied the knots, the fluff got down her throat and in her eyes, while kneeling on the floor made her knees sore and her back ache. Well, an aching back would be good practice for later on in her pregnancy. She was well aware that she wouldn't be able to continue tackling arduous jobs like this indefinitely.

Sitting back on her heels and rubbing the small of her back, she made up her mind. It would be excruciatingly embarrassing, but it had to be done. She would tell Mrs Ford, the branch organiser, about her condition. She had to. Mrs Ford could be trusted to be discreet.

Before she could start having second thoughts, Lily pushed herself to her feet and, leaving the dust-filled netting room, made her way through the large office, weaving her way between the desks to get to Mrs Ford's office. The door stood open, which meant she was available.

Standing on the threshold, Lily knocked.

Mrs Ford was seated behind her desk. She looked up from the papers in front of her.

'Can I help you, Mrs Chadwick?'

'Might I have a word, please?' Lily asked.

Mrs Ford put down her fountain pen. 'Of course. Come in. Have a seat.'

Lily hesitated inside the doorway. Should she ask if she could shut the door? But the women in the office might wonder why and the last thing she wanted was to stir up curiosity. Anyway, several women were making a racket bashing away at typewriters, and there was an empty space between Mrs Ford's door and the main body of the office, so if she spoke quietly, she wouldn't be overheard.

Perching on the edge of the chair, she sat up straight. *Head up, shoulders back, don't look ashamed.* Lily's heart gave a great thud. In the calmest voice she could muster, she said, 'I need to ask if you will please put me on light duties.'

'May I ask why?'

'For – for medical reasons,' said Lily.

'I see. If you're unwell, it would be in order for you to take some time off.'

'I'm not,' Lily said quickly. 'Not ill, I mean. But I do need light duties, or I will quite soon. I'm...' *Here goes.* 'Well, I'm in the family way.'

'Oh.' Mrs Ford's eyebrows shot up her forehead, then her expression went politely blank. 'I see. Of course, in that case, I will arrange for the required changes to the rosters. And if you need any further help, Mrs Chadwick—'

Lily jumped to her feet. 'No, thank you, honestly. I don't need anything.'

She was already backing away, desperate now to escape. Later, she might be relieved at what she'd achieved, but just now she wanted to cover her face with her hands in sheer embarrassment.

Swinging round to make her escape, she stopped dead. Outside the office, a few feet from the open doorway, stood Lady Ingrid Campbell, a friend of Lily's detested mother-in-law. Lady Ingrid was turning away, but had she moments earlier been standing there with her ears flapping?

The hairs lifted along Lily's arms and she felt like crumpling to the floor.

Oh, please let Lady Ingrid not have overheard anything!

* * *

Beatrice was busy preparing for a Gentlemen's Club evening. She unlocked one of the tall cupboards to remove some items to keep the boys entertained. Abbie was lending a hand, as was Fay Brewer, who sometimes dropped in on club evenings, just to see how things were going.

Abbie looked pretty in the dark-blue jumper Beatrice had knitted her for Christmas. Usually, girls wore round necks, but something had made Beatrice opt for a pattern with a V-neck and the style looked good on the girl, possibly because the V echoed the dainty point of Abbie's chin. The dark blue had turned out to be a good colour as well. There was so little choice these days. Beatrice had hoped against hope to find a forget-me-not blue to match Abbie's eyes, but she'd ended up having to make do with a blue not far removed from navy, though that, too, had turned out to be perfect. Instead of making Abbie look pale and washed-out, it highlighted her fair colouring.

Beatrice didn't think she'd ever been so pleased with anything she'd knitted. Best of all, though, she knew Abbie loved the jumper, because she wore it all the time.

'Should I get the skittles out?' Abbie asked, standing in front of the cupboard. 'The boys love a game of that.'

'Actually...' Beatrice hesitated. 'Not this evening.'

'Bagatelle?' Miss Brewer suggested.

'Cards,' Beatrice said, making up her mind and, in so doing, finally admitting to herself that she had a problem. 'I think we'll have a whist drive.'

Abbie laughed. 'Good luck!'

'They might enjoy it,' Beatrice replied with a note of obstinacy.

They *might*. They would have, back in the early days, but something had changed and she wasn't sure what had caused it. It was hard to describe. The best she could come up with was that there had been a slight change in the atmosphere. The lads had always been high-spirited, but now they were – or some of them were – more animated, more exuberant... more bold.

It reminded her of where she used to live before she'd moved to Dunbar's. Back then, the local lads used to taunt her by singing the Inky Stinky Stinkerman song.

Inky Stinky Inkerman
Inky Stinky Inkerman
In-KY Stin-KY
Inky Stinky STINKERMAN!

Beatrice had turned hot and cold every time she heard it. There was something in the atmosphere of the Gentlemen's Club now that made her feel a little edgy. Not angry and embarrassed and humiliated and downright miserable, like she'd felt in the old days; but she sensed that this new anxiety, even though it was little more than a twinge, was from the same family of sensations.

That was why she was reluctant to get out the skittles or the bagatelle. Skittles was always a spirited game and recently the bagatelle had been played with greater energy. She couldn't do anything about the ping-pong or the billiards, but she wanted to keep a lid on this new vivacity as much as she could. She couldn't take down the dartboard either, because that would look so obvious, and the last thing she wanted was for anyone to realise she felt discomforted. That was why she held back from speaking to Fay Brewer about it. Miss Brewer had been nothing but kind, supportive and professional, but Beatrice didn't want to share this in case she was mistaken... even though she knew she wasn't. She didn't want to look stupid or as if she couldn't cope.

When the boys arrived, they stood in a line down the front steps, waiting to be admitted. Inside, they went through the usual rigmarole of arriving. As each boy entered the building, he wiped his feet and put on one of the ties that Kitty held out, then he raised his cap and wished the ladies good evening before hanging up his cap and heading into the club room.

'Good evening, Tommy,' Beatrice said to Tommy Abbott with her usual welcoming smile. He was one of her neighbours from the bad old days of the Inky Stinky Inkerman song. So were Malcolm Langton and Joseph Simpson, who were next in line.

'Good evening, Miss Inkerman,' Tommy said before greeting Kitty and Miss Brewer.

'Good evening, Malcolm. Good evening, Joseph.'

'Good evening, Miss Inkerman,' said Malcolm.

'Please, miss, can I be Joe from now on?' asked Joseph Simpson, looking Beatrice straight in the eye. 'If Tommy Abbott can be Tommy, I don't see why I can't be Joe.'

'Yes, I suppose so,' said Beatrice.

She watched as Tommy and Joe said good evening to Kitty and Miss Brewer and then quick-walked into the club room. She had the oddest feeling she'd been taken advantage of, but that was plain daft.

When they had welcomed everyone, Fay Brewer and Kitty hung about in the foyer, chatting, while Beatrice went into the club room and indicated the activities the boys could choose from that evening.

'...and I've got out all the packs of cards. I thought we could have a whist drive. We haven't done that for quite some time.'

Was that a scornful click of someone's tongue she heard? She didn't react. Thank goodness the other two were out in the foyer. Beatrice pretended she hadn't heard – or was that a mistake on her part? But she'd never been a confrontational person. She did notice, however, that a few of the boys dropped their glances and appeared uncomfortable.

Beatrice got her whist drive. That was something, though she didn't get as many takers as she had hoped for. Was that her fault? Ought she to have directed the boys' activities more closely from the start? But she'd always felt that allowing them only some of the possible games and activities each time was sufficient to maintain an orderly atmosphere.

At the end of the evening, the boys hung up their ties and shook hands with Beatrice, Miss Brewer and Kitty as they said thank you and good night. Kitty switched off the lights in the foyer and Beatrice pulled aside the long blackout curtains that covered the front doors. She opened one of the doors a fraction for the lads to squeeze through.

'No running until you reach the pavement,' she said, as she always did.

Just before she shut the door behind them, she heard a jubilant voice from the pavement exclaim, 'Freedom! Next stop – Greasy Lil's.'

Beatrice shut and locked the door and swished the curtain back into position, checking there were no gaps before Kitty switched the lights back on. The three of them went into the club room. One of the rules was that the boys had to leave the room tidy, but Beatrice preferred to put everything away in the cupboard herself.

They made short work of it, chatting as they did so.

'Would you like to join us for a cup of tea before you head off?' Kitty offered, smiling at Miss Brewer.

'I'll make tracks, if you don't mind, but thanks anyway,' she replied and went to fetch her coat and hat from the hall stand.

They went through the rigmarole of opening the door for her and, after she'd gone, Beatrice and Kitty went down to the kitchen, where Abbie was sitting at the table with a film magazine.

'There's water in the kettle for you,' she said.

Kitty put it on the gas and leaned against the sink with her ankles crossed as she waited. Beatrice got out the crockery and sat at the table.

'Did it go well?' Abbie asked.

'Yes, thanks,' Beatrice answered.

'Did they have a whist drive?' Abbie asked with a smile.

'Some of them did.'

'Good,' said Abbie.

As the kettle began to sing, Kitty moved back to the stove. Beatrice rose to fetch the milk jug from the marble slab in the pantry.

'Have you heard of Greasy Lil's?' she asked.

Kitty glanced round, looking startled. 'For a moment, I thought you were saying something about our Lily. No, I've never heard of Greasy Lil's. Why?'

'No reason,' Beatrice replied. 'I heard one of the boys mention it – or her. That's all.'

'It's the chippy down the back street between Caroline Road and Madoc Street,' Abbie told them.

'A chippy called Greasy Lil's?' Kitty asked, her tone laced with a mixture of surprise and disbelief. 'I can't see myself wanting to go to a chippy called Greasy anything.'

'That's not its real name,' Abbie explained. 'It's just what the locals call it.'

Kitty laughed. 'It doesn't sound very appealing.'

Footsteps could be heard on the stairs and then Ivy appeared. She held up a dart, twiddling its body in her fingertips and making the feathers twirl.

'I found this on the floor in the foyer.' She looked at Beatrice. 'If you give me the key to the cupboard, I'll put it away.'

Beatrice held out her hand for it. 'Don't trouble. I'll do it. You sit down.'

'I've just warmed the pot,' said Kitty.

'It'll only take a minute,' Beatrice replied, heading for the stairs.

In the club room, she unlocked the cupboard and reached for the darts' box, but when she opened it, she froze. Three darts were missing. Three – a whole set.

They must have been taken in error, they *must* have. Her Gentlemen's Club boys would never let her down. Never.

7

February opened with sleet. Tiny half-melted balls of ice splattered against windows, and a pebbly film floated on top of puddles. Pedestrians put their collars up and their heads down as they walked, raising their faces only to cross the roads.

On her way to the WVS office with Ivy, Kitty lifted her eyes as they came to the kerb and looked straight across the road to a furniture shop, which had a display in the window.

She grasped Ivy's arm. 'Come and look at this. It's that new Utility furniture. I haven't seen it on display before.'

'It isn't on display now,' Ivy replied drily. 'Those will be pieces that are waiting to be delivered. Just you wait. This time tomorrow or the day after, they'll have gone and the window will be empty again.'

Kitty sighed. 'All the same, it's nice to see them.'

'Nice?' Ivy replied with a laugh that held a touch of scorn. 'You call those pieces of furniture nice? They're serviceable at best.'

'What I meant was,' Kitty answered, 'that it can't be easy choosing furniture out of a catalogue, which is how folk have to choose Utility. It isn't the most handsome furniture, I grant you, but it's good-looking enough.'

'It needs to be,' said Ivy. 'Folk will be living with it for years. It might still be all we have the wherewithal to produce when Abbie gets wed.'

A little shiver of shock rippled all through Kitty. Abbie getting wed! 'Don't wish the time away.'

'It'll fly by before you know it,' said Ivy.

'I know. Sometimes I look back over Abbie's life and wonder where the time went.'

'It's rough on Bill missing out on being with her,' said Ivy.

'She misses him too,' Kitty concurred.

She took another look at the furniture in the window. Her pulse quickened as a thought carefully unfurled itself and she dared to think it. When she left Bill, when she had to set up on her own, would it be simple, sturdy pieces like these chairs and sideboards and dressing tables that furnished her home?

Ivy gave her a nudge. 'Cheer up, you daft thing! You're thinking of Abbie growing up and getting married, aren't you?'

'What? Oh – yes. Silly me.'

Ivy linked arms with her and they resumed their journey.

* * *

Kitty was on duty at the Citizens Advice session in a church hall in Longsite, supporting the advisors in their work by greeting visitors at the door, showing them where to sit and giving them each a number so everyone was seen in the right order. She made tea as well when the advisors had their short breaks.

'Thanks, love,' said Mrs Dewsbury as she gratefully accepted a cuppa in the curtained-off area that passed as a staffroom. 'I've been gasping for this.'

The advisors had tea two at a time. Mrs Dewsbury was chatting with her colleague, Miss Fenton. Kitty, washing up used cups, fixed her mind on other things, but then she caught a word that sent her ears flapping.

Divorce.

'I seem to have done nothing but provide advice on divorce proceedings all day,' said Miss Fenton. 'It makes me glad to be single.'

'Irregular babies?' Mrs Dewsbury asked.

Kitty rinsed the final cup and placed it on the wooden draining board. She had heard of irregular babies. Lily was having one. It was when the mother was married, but not to the baby's father. With her back to the two women, she picked up the tea towel and began to dry each cup and saucer with unnecessary care to spin out the task as long as she could.

'Two or three of those, yes,' said Miss Fenton, 'but I've also had a couple of "I've met someone else" conversations.'

There was a pause. Kitty imagined the two advisors exchanging looks.

'There's going to be a divorce boom when the war finishes,' said Mrs Dewsbury. 'They'll have to make divorce easier. There will be too many unhappy couples for the old "woman unknown" system to carry on.'

Kitty knew about that system. She had come across it in novels. No matter whose fault the prospective divorce was, the husband would go with a woman to a hotel, where the two of them would be 'secretly' photographed arriving together. Officially, this unidentified woman was a 'woman unknown'. The husband would take the blame and the divorce would proceed.

Miss Fenton laughed. 'Every woman who ever earned a few bob by being a woman unknown will be looking elsewhere to earn money. Honestly, after the war it'll be all the authorities can do to shovel the paperwork through as fast as they can.' She stood up. 'Thanks for the tea, Mrs Dunbar. Most welcome.'

Kitty turned to take the cup off her, hoping she didn't look as if she'd been earwigging.

Her thoughts were in a whirl throughout the rest of her shift. Was she really contemplating this? Not just separation but actual divorce? Her heart thudded. Yes, she was. She'd already known it, but listening to the two advisors had made it real.

A frisson of fear passed through her. Would she be allowed to keep Abbie? But by then Abbie wouldn't be a child any longer. All Kitty could do was offer her a comfortable home and hope it was what she wanted. She had to be able to offer a viable alternative to what Bill offered – and he would have Dunbar's. Or he would until he frittered it away.

The thought of that riled her. She had put so much of herself into Dunbar's. She would hate to leave. She loved it.

But she had to think seriously about her future. If she wasn't going to stay with Bill – and she wasn't – what was she going to do instead?

* * *

Evangeline Chadwick walked home along the slushy pavement, wrapped up not just warmly but also stylishly and expensively in her camel-coloured wool overcoat with its large, top-stitched collar and revers, its buckle belt and patch pockets with flaps. It wasn't a new coat, but when one could afford the best, it lasted for simply years. Her hat, a felt one with a shallow crown and a narrow brim, was likewise pre-war. Her brown leather lace-up brogues, by contrast, were just a few months old, and worth every penny and clothing coupon they had set her back. It was essential to be well-shod – and well-corseted. One had to look the part.

As she made her way along Edge Lane, she flicked a sideways glance at every house she passed. The houses were spacious Victorian villas, a mixture of grand detacheds and elegant semis, all with carved gables, bay windows and short flights of steps up to covered porches supported by columns.

The Chadwicks had lived here on Edge Lane in Chorlton-cum-Hardy for years and had brought up their four sons here. The boys were all adults now – although Daniel, the youngest, didn't seem all that grown-up when one considered the complete hash he had made of his life. Honestly! The thought of what that foolish boy had done made her want to throw up her hands in an *I give up!* gesture.

Imagine a son of hers taking up with a girl like Lily. *Lily*, Mrs Chadwick thought with a curl of her lip. Such a lower-class name. And of course she was a lower-class girl, practically an urchin. She'd been fortunate to find a live-in post in a respectable, long-established hotel such as Dunbar's had been in those days.

Of course, there could be no doubt that she had inveigled her way into Dunbar's for the express purpose of chucking herself at the first eligible young fool who had succumbed to her pretty smile – and it had worked. Before that, Mrs Chadwick had considered Daniel to be a responsible young man, but, oh no, he'd had to go and prove himself as susceptible to a pair of fluttering eyelashes as the next chap.

If he'd had to get himself seduced, why couldn't he at least have shown the good taste to get tangled up with a girl of his own class? Instead he'd been taken in by a little tart of a chambermaid, who'd made sure to get a bun in the oven as fast as nature permitted. Slut!

Daniel had been completely taken in. He thought the wretch loved him. Worse, he thought he loved her. Mrs Chadwick had done everything she could to persuade him to wait, to think things over – in other words, to give her the time she needed to prise him from the girl's grasp – but he'd been brought up to be honourable and was set on doing the decent thing. He had sworn blind that he truly loved Lily and nothing would induce him to listen to his mother's words of caution. He wouldn't be swayed by her fury either.

So Daniel had married the gold digger, the harlot, the schemer. Those blue eyes and dainty features might make her look like butter wouldn't melt, but make no mistake, that girl was a Jezebel with the heart of a pickpocket.

And then – and then baby Tobias had died. How shocking and deeply distressing that had been. Lily had come to live with her after that, Daniel being away at sea, and at first there had been a softening in the relationship between the two women, but it hadn't lasted. Well, how could it? They were poles apart in every possible way.

Mrs Chadwick had done her best. She'd been civility itself. Matters had been helped by the fact that both of them had been out of the house much of the time, fulfilling their WVS obligations.

But then Lily had overheard a particular comment Mrs Chadwick had made to her dear friend, Lady Ingrid Campbell, something about how poor Daniel had only married Lily because he'd had to, because she was in the family way. Frankly, Lily had had no business eavesdropping, and she'd certainly had no business taking offence. She'd had even less business telling tales to Daniel in due course. Conniving little piece!

That had been the summer before last, and by the end of that year she and Daniel had been separated, which was jolly good riddance as far as Evangeline Chadwick was concerned. She had wanted Daniel to look into getting a divorce immediately, but he and Lily had decided to wait until after the war. Mrs Chadwick had practically ground her teeth in frustration, but it had made sense, really. It would be better for the family in general if Daniel's divorce was one of thousands post-war when the powers that be would simply have to make the process easier. To divorce now would be scandalous.

Mrs Chadwick had forced herself into a state of acceptance of the situation. The main thing was that, even though it would take time, Lily had been on her way out.

And then... and *then*, last year, Daniel had written to Lily asking for a reconciliation. Not only that, but he'd told his mother – his own mother, mark you – in no uncertain terms that when Lily answered his letter, there was to be no skulduggery with her reply; no 'losing' it.

Mrs Chadwick had fumed at the time, but what could she say? The best she could do was secretly tell herself she had washed her hands of the dire situation, and hope that that would make her feel better.

It never had.

Now, she arrived home and let herself in. The hallway had elaborate panelling and a high ceiling with ornamental plasterwork. As Mrs Chadwick walked into the house, Lady Ingrid Campbell emerged from the sitting room.

'My dear, I hope you don't mind,' said Lady Ingrid. 'I got the maid to let me wait for you.'

'Has something happened?'

Lady Ingrid spoke quietly. 'Come into the sitting room and we can close the door.' She made it sound as though hordes of servants were hiding in the cupboard under the stairs, desperate for all the juicy details.

Mrs Chadwick removed her outdoor things and joined her in the beautifully furnished sitting room, where they both sat down.

'Tell me,' she said simply and with authority.

Lady Ingrid took a deep breath. 'My dear, I've been agonising over whether to say something, and I've decided I simply must. You're entitled to know.'

Mrs Chadwick didn't say anything. She waited, her expression a polite mask, although a knot had started to form in her stomach.

'I had to go to the WVS office in the middle of town not so long ago, and – I shan't keep you in suspense any longer – Daniel's wife was there.'

'Lily.' Mrs Chadwick ground out the name between clenched teeth.

'Lily, yes. I chanced to overhear something she said to Mrs Ford, the branch organiser. She's – well, she's in what my mother would call *an interesting condition*.'

* * *

At the end of another chilly day, Beatrice hurried home from work, quickly ate the stewed kidneys on toast followed by pineapple sponge that Mrs Ivy Dunbar had got ready for her, then went up to her bedroom on the third floor to change into her WVS uniform before she made her way briskly to the British Restaurant. Here, nutritious meals were served at dinnertime and teatime. In the early evening, as well as serving meals and clearing away the dirty dishes, the kitchen staff prepared snacks that would be delivered to the police station, fire station and various ARP posts for supper.

Beatrice was put on washing-up duty to start with. She took off her jumper. There was no need to roll up her sleeves because, for practical reasons, WVS blouses were short-sleeved. The instruction 'Roll up your sleeves, ladies!' was purely figurative.

After that, she helped prepare sandwiches for delivery. Baked vegetable rolls and potato scones had been made earlier and left to cool. Tonight's sandwiches were pilchard-and-cabbage or meat-paste.

'Will you deliver to the cop shop, please, Miss Inkerman?' asked one of the cooks.

Beatrice carefully packed a wicker basket, put on her outdoor things and set off, the basket and her handbag rather awkwardly over one arm while she carried her torch in her other hand. It was essential to have a torch in the blackout, although the mandatory tissue paper over the lens meant no one had a good beam to rely on.

It started to rain – not so much rain as heavy drizzle, sheets of it. Beatrice didn't have her umbrella. Even if she had, she couldn't have managed it. A copper was about to enter the sandbag-fronted police station as she approached and he held the front door for her. Beatrice hurried inside gratefully.

Sergeant Wakefield was behind the front desk. He lifted the flap and came through. He smiled, which made his dark eyes crinkle.

'Miss Inkerman, how nice to see you. Have you braved the elements to bring us our supper? Allow me.' He took the wicker basket and then looked uncomfortable. 'Sorry. I didn't mean to wrench the provisions from your grasp. I just thought the basket might be heavy.' His discomfort vanished as his eyes twinkled.

Beatrice found herself smiling at him; then, all at once, she was the one who felt uncomfortable. 'I'd better head back.'

'Wait for the rain to stop,' said Sergeant Wakefield. 'It won't last long. It's only a shower.'

'No point in getting wet if you don't have to,' added the copper who had held the door open.

'Well – if you're sure,' said Beatrice.

Sergeant Wakefield chuckled. 'We aren't going to sling you out in the rain when you've been kind enough to deliver our supper. I'm due a break. Come through and have a cup of tea with me while we wait for the rain to ease.'

'Thank you,' said Beatrice.

'I'll fetch the tea, Sarge,' the copper offered.

Sergeant Wakefield took Beatrice along a corridor painted brown and ushered her into a room that proved to be an office. It was an interior room with no window. A tall cupboard stood in a corner, with a pair of filing cabinets on the opposite wall. Notice-boards on the walls held various lists, notices and posters, including the ubiquitous CARELESS TALK COSTS LIVES and the one with a picture of a soldier grasping a Red Cross box beneath the words 'A Bit of Home'. Under the picture it said 'RED CROSS & St JOHN needs your help for Prisoners of War'.

Facing the door was a large desk, with wire trays labelled IN, PENDING and OUT. An inky blotter lay in the middle in front of the chair, and there was a wooden tray with a pencil-pot and a bottle of ink, next to a name-plate with SGT C WAKEFIELD on it.

'Home sweet home,' said the sergeant, catching her looking round. 'Have a seat.' He took his place behind the desk.

Beatrice wanted to ask what the C stood for, but that would be impertinent. She settled for, 'You haven't got a window. I'd hate that, myself.'

Sergeant Wakefield glanced over his shoulder at the wall behind his desk. 'If I did have a window, I'd be looking into one of the interview rooms. On the whole, I'd prefer not to have that pleasure.'

There was a knock on the door and the copper appeared with two mugs, which he put on the desk, acknowledging their thanks with a nod before he withdrew. Beatrice hoped she hid her dismay at the sight of the brew, which looked impossibly strong. Undrinkably strong.

'Do you take sugar?' her host asked. 'I have some under lock and key in my drawer.'

'I do normally take sugar,' Beatrice said, 'but please don't trouble,' she added quickly as he leaned down to the drawer. 'I...' She couldn't finish the sentence. It would be so rude.

But Sergeant Wakefield's expression showed he understood. 'Proper builder's tea, isn't it?' he remarked ruefully. 'Let me go and pour some of yours away and top it up with hot water. That might make it more palatable.'

'Oh – no, honestly,' Beatrice exclaimed. 'That would be wasteful.'

'It's more of a waste not to,' he replied genially. 'Either I pour away half and give you something you can drink or else we sit here watching it go cold, and it all goes to waste.'

Beatrice relaxed. What a kind man he was. 'If you put it like that...'

'I'll be back in two shakes of a lamb's tail.'

He disappeared with her mug and returned a minute later. He put it down in front of her. The colour of the tea was now considerably less fierce.

'Is it worth offering you sugar now?' he asked.

'Yes, please.'

Soon they were sipping their drinks.

'Do you mind if I light up my pipe?' the sergeant asked.

'Not at all. I like the smell.'

'We're encouraged these days to reuse half-smoked tobacco by adding small pieces of dried apple, so if you pick up an apply scent, that's the reason.' He produced his pipe and tamped down the contents of the bowl before striking a match. As he applied the flame, he made some soft *puh-puh-puh* sounds as his mouth closed and opened over the stem of the pipe, encouraging the little flame to take root. 'How are things coming along with your clubs, Miss Inkerman?'

'Fine, thank you. The dartboard you donated is being put to good use. We had a little incident recently at the Gentlemen's Club when a set of darts went missing, which was rather upsetting.'

'I can imagine,' Sergeant Wakefield commented, a frown clouding his broad forehead.

'But it had a happy ending,' Beatrice said quickly. 'I said at the next meeting that someone must have taken them by accident and please would everyone check at home and return them if they found them. At the meeting after that, when I tidied up at the end, the darts had been returned.'

'That's good.'

'Yes, it is,' Beatrice agreed, but she felt conflicted.

'You don't sound sure, if you don't mind my saying so.'

She sighed. 'If it had been a genuine mistake, wouldn't you expect the boy concerned to bring the darts to me personally and say, "I'm sorry, Miss Inkerman. I'll be more careful in future"? Instead, the darts were just slipped back into the box. I was glad to get them back, of course, but I still feel uncomfortable about it.'

'Do you have any idea who it could have been?'

Beatrice shook her head. 'None at all. I don't even know for certain that the original intention was to steal. It's only a suspicion, and that makes me feel bad. What proof do I have? None.'

'Let's hope nothing of the kind happens again,' said Sergeant Wakefield. 'But if you think you have a problem, and you feel it might help if I came along one evening and had a word with the kids to make it clear I take an interest in the club, I'd be happy to do so. Just say the word.'

'Thank you,' said Beatrice, 'but I'm sure it won't be necessary.'

She didn't mention the changed atmosphere in the Gentlemen's Club. It would sound silly.

The conversation moved on. They chatted about this and that and then – inevitably – about the war.

'The German surrender at Stalingrad is being hailed as a major turning point,' said Beatrice, 'just like the victory at El Alamein was last year. It gives you hope.'

'It does indeed,' Sergeant Wakefield agreed. 'The Russians used clever tactics. They lured the Germans deep into Russia and encircled them. It was catastrophic for Jerry. It's being called the worst defeat for Germany since the end of the last war.'

'Let's hope we can build on our successes,' Beatrice said in a heartfelt tone.

'Amen to that,' said Sergeant Wakefield.

* * *

Kitty stood outside the reception room's open doorway, smiling as she looked inside. Her gaze skimmed quickly over everything – the snowy table linen, the pretty decorations, the three-tier cardboard wedding cake. Beside it lay a ceremonial sword which the bride's father had provided, and which had made Kitty's hair stand on end when it was drawn from its scabbard. The happy couple would use this to 'cut' the cake for the photograph, after which the real cake, a Victoria sponge whipped to an airy lightness by Ivy, would be served.

Glowing with happiness, the bride wore a suit of cherry-red edge-to-edge jacket and knee-length skirt, together with high heels and a brimless cream hat covered in rosettes.

'Fancy getting married in red!' Ivy hissed in a scornful undertone, appearing beside Kitty.

'Hush,' Kitty warned. 'I think she looks very smart.'

Ivy sucked in her cheeks. 'You know what they say. *Married in red, you'll wish you were dead.*'

'They don't say anything of the kind – whoever "they" are,' Kitty retorted. 'That's just a silly old rhyme.'

They went down to the kitchen to plate up the food. The celery-and-cheese fritters were keeping warm in the oven, as were the fish pasties. Kitty cut the vegetable flans and arranged the narrow slices while Ivy deftly put together the sandwiches. She had made 'fish paste' using mashed butter beans flavoured with anchovy essence.

'If you've got nothing polite to say about the bridal party,' said Kitty, 'Lily and I can take the food up.' She made sure she kept a smile on her face when she said it, but she meant it.

Ivy looked miffed. 'I might not have been married to the brother who inherited Dunbar's Hotel in the previous generation, but that doesn't mean I'm ignorant about how to treat guests. Honestly!' she muttered, not quite under her breath. 'Just because I said red isn't suitable.'

Kitty didn't rise to the bait. Ivy's reference to the rhyme reminded her of her own wedding colour. She had married in white, which supposedly meant she had chosen just right. *Ha!*

She might not have reached any conclusions about how to earn her daily bread once her marriage was officially over, but nothing could shake her resolution about seeking a divorce the moment the war came to an end. If anything, she wondered how on earth she was to hold back until then. Now that she had made up her mind, the urge was growing. At odd moments, her stomach would flutter and the pulses in her throat and at her wrists would jump. She knew that divorce and a fresh start was exactly the right thing for her.

It was increasingly hard to keep the knowledge inside. She

wanted to talk about it. She didn't want to live a lie. What if she told Naomi? Her sister was the obvious choice. Ten years older, Naomi had always watched over her. Discussing it would help it to feel normal. Even though she was in no doubt, Kitty couldn't ignore the prejudice against divorce that she'd been brought up to feel. Divorce was shameful – or it had been before the war; but now, everyone knew there were going to be thousands of divorces after the war, and so it was bound to become normal – wasn't it?

I don't care how shocking or shameful it is. I'm going to do it.

She knew what she must do as a first step. She had to write to Bill. He was entitled to hear it before anybody else. The idea made Kitty go cold. What words could she use?

And was it fair on Bill to tell him by letter? But she didn't know when she would next see him in person. It wasn't as though she was sending devastating news to a soldier on the front line. You heard of women doing that. They were called – what was it? It was a term coined by the Yanks. Kitty had heard it in the club for servicemen from overseas when she'd been on WVS duty. Yes, that was it – 'Dear John' letters. Imagine being on the receiving end of one of those. Imagine a sweetheart or a fiancé or a husband in the Eighth Army getting a Dear John letter on the eve of El Alamein, and having to go into battle the next day. It didn't bear thinking about.

Bill was working in a stores depot on the south coast. He wasn't on the battlefield, but he was doing his duty for King and country. Whatever he'd done in the past to let Kitty down, did he deserve a Dear John letter? Did he deserve to be told that way?

But if she didn't write, he would carry on as normal. He would come home on his next leave, whenever it was, and expect her to sleep with him, and it would damage her very essence if she was obliged to do that.

No, she had to write, had to.

She spent several days agonising over how to express what needed saying.

Dear Bill,

I've got something important to tell you and I know you're going to be angry and upset, and probably confused as well. There is no easy way to say this and so I'll say it straight out. I don't want us to be married any more. When the divorce avalanche takes place after the war, I want our marriage to end.

You have spent recklessly for years, and you blamed the spending on me when you talked to your mother. Things got so bad that the bailiffs came to Dunbar's, the family hotel you were so proud of. Then, after I set up the storage business, you refused to give me access to the Dunbar's bank account. It also turned out that you'd been dipping your fingers in the account.

I know this sounds like a list of complaints. I want you to understand that I have another, more important reason for wanting a divorce. I hope you'll take it seriously.

I have become independent. Women have had to take on a great deal since the men went away. Up to a point, that is what I'm referring to – but only up to a point. My independence goes further than that. I have discovered that I can run a business – I'm now running two. I know how to balance the books and how to speak to people.

Though I say it myself, I'm successful; and that is what I want in my future. I want – I need – a challenge, the chance to do well, the chance to show my daughter what women are capable of. I'm sorry if this hurts you. Truly, I am. But I feel strongly that this is what I have to do.

Having got that far, Kitty went back to the beginning and read it through. She'd thought about it so much that she could no longer tell how good, bad or indifferent her letter was. All she knew was that she'd laid out her case.

Now – how to end it? When Bill had first gone away, she'd ended her letters with *Love, Kitty*. Then it had changed to *Yours, Kitty* because it was less affectionate. But she emphatically wasn't his any longer, so she resisted saying that this time.

Could she just put *Kitty*? But that would look so stark, a real snub. What about *Best wishes, Kitty*? But you could send best wishes to anybody, so it wasn't appropriate to send to your husband, no matter what the circumstances.

In the end, she settled for *Sincerely, Kitty*. Since this was possibly the most sincerely meant letter she had ever written, what could be more appropriate?

After writing it, a couple of days passed before she posted it. Even though this was what she wanted, it was a momentous step to take, but finally she dropped her letter into the pillar box.

Then she went home and waited.

And waited.

8

The feature of the Women's Voluntary Service that made Beatrice proudest was the amount of good they did that could only be described as welfare work. Women learned to drive so they could ferry patients to and from hospital. They made toys because there were precious few in the shops. They worked as volunteers in nurseries so mothers could do war work. They collected clothes for children, for the homeless, for refugees. They ran mobile canteens and mobile laundries. They took care of people convalescing after an illness or an operation, and if the invalid happened to be the lady of the house, they took over her domestic duties until she was on her feet again.

'I feel I have an extra awareness of the importance of this welfare work because of working in welfare myself,' Beatrice remarked to Kitty before adding ruefully, 'But that's probably just me being big-headed because of having a good job.'

'No, it's not,' Kitty answered. 'It just shows you're proud of the Welfare Department as well as the WVS.'

Beatrice thought about that. She was very proud to work for the Corporation's Welfare Department, and not just because it had been a big step up from being the inco lady. She appreciated the opportunity it had given her to help other people and make a material difference to their lives.

'The fact that I get paid to help others during the day,' she told Sergeant Wakefield, 'and then I do more of the same with the WVS, sometimes makes me want to burst with pride – not in a conceited way,' she added hastily.

'Don't worry,' he replied. 'I know what you mean. It's good to feel part of something worthwhile that is bigger than yourself.'

'That's it exactly,' Beatrice said, pleased he understood.

It was a chilly evening and Beatrice, dressed in her WVS uniform, was on her way to the home of an old lady called Mrs Cowell, who was housebound. The WVS helped her by taking meals round and this was Beatrice's first time.

She had bumped into Sergeant Wakefield on her way. He had offered to carry her basket for her, but she'd politely declined. You couldn't ask a police sergeant to walk through the streets with a wicker basket on his arm!

Mrs Cowell lived on a shabby back street in between Caroline Road and Madoc Street. Now where had Beatrice heard those road names before? The street was cramped, with ancient cobbles down the middle in between two cinder paths instead of pavements. Each path was just about wide enough for a single pedestrian. In the intense darkness of the blackout, the constricted road felt pinched and meagre. The tissue-dimmed beam from Beatrice's torch seemed poorer than usual. A faint spicy scent that made the insides of her nostrils prickle told her that the buildings squatting on either side of her were encrusted with soot.

Then another scent twitched its way into her nose – vinegar. From a short way along the street, Beatrice heard voices – young voices, boys' voices. She couldn't see the lads because you couldn't see anything in the blackout, even when it was right in front of you.

Sergeant Wakefield evidently realised what she had homed in on, because he explained, 'That's Greasy Lil's – the chippy.'

Now she remembered. Some of her Gentlemen's Club boys had mentioned going to Greasy Lil's, and then Abbie had said the road names. Beatrice took a gratifying breath of satisfaction at having solved the mystery.

As she and the sergeant drew level with the little chippy, they found a group of lads outside. Beatrice recognised a voice. Smiling to herself, she stopped.

'Good evening, Joseph,' she said.

His back was to her and she saw him start; she actually saw his shoulders bob up and down. Then he turned round.

'Miss Inkerman.' He sounded thoroughly discomforted, but that was probably only to be expected. 'Hello – I mean, good evening, miss.'

'Evening, miss,' said Tommy Abbott.

'Good evening, Tommy.' Beatrice indicated her companion. 'This is Sergeant Wakefield.'

The sergeant took a step forward out of the darkness. He was a fine figure of a man, well-built and broad-shouldered. Beatrice was proud to introduce him – but the next moment, she felt surprised and dismayed. Let down, too. Instead of standing up straight, wanting to look their best in front of a policeman, the boys – not just Joseph and Tommy, but the group as a whole – seemed to drop their chins and slouch. Or was she making something out of nothing?

Sergeant Wakefield nodded to the boys. 'Evening, lads.' He glanced at Beatrice, silently enquiring if she wanted to move on.

They continued up the dingy little street. Beatrice shone her torch on the house numbers, looking for where Mrs Cowell lived.

She stopped. 'Here we are.'

'I'll leave you to it.' Sergeant Wakefield touched the brim of his helmet to her. 'It was good to see you again, Miss Inkerman.'

'Likewise,' she replied and he walked on.

She'd been told what to do – knock and walk straight in.

'The door will be unlocked,' Mrs Taylor, one of her WVS colleagues, had told her. 'Mrs Cowell isn't too steady on her feet, the poor old duck. She's very frail.'

'How she gets up those steep steps to bed, I don't know,' Mrs Neville had added. 'She probably has to crawl up them and come down on her behind.'

'She's one of those poor souls who has really benefited from the war,' Mrs Taylor said. 'She doesn't even live in a two-up two-down. It's a one-up one-down, with a poky scullery tacked on at the back. No cooking facilities aside from what can be cooked in the fireplace. Heaven alone knows how she's managed all these years.'

'But now she's got the WVS keeping an eye on her,' Beatrice had chimed in, pleased. She was glad to feel she was helping.

'When her meal is ready,' Mrs Neville had instructed, 'make sure you take it along right away while it's still hot. There isn't an oven to warm it up in.'

Now, Beatrice knocked on Mrs Cowell's door and opened it, calling clearly, 'Mrs Cowell? WVS.'

In she went, first battling her way past an ancient door curtain made, if she wasn't mistaken, from old sacking. The door opened directly onto what Beatrice was about to refer to in her head as the front room until she remembered it was the only room – and not a large one, either, though maybe it would have felt bigger had it not been crammed full. On the other hand, what choice was there other than to cram it full?

A chintz armchair that had seen better days; an ancient love seat with claw-footed legs and tatty upholstery; a couple of ladder-back chairs with struts missing. An upright piano with yellowed keys stood cheek by jowl with a hefty sideboard, its top covered with ornaments, directories, and bowls overflowing with string, old keys, thimbles and shards of broken crockery. The mantelpiece was awash with china figurines, candlesticks, a jar of spills for lighting the fire, empty bud vases, mugs with the words *Souvenir of...* and not one but two clocks, although only the numbers eleven, twelve and one were visible because of the battered-looking envelopes propped up in front of them.

The table in the middle of the room was equally smothered with old newspapers, scraps of fabric, knitting patterns, a dish of marbles, another of pinecones, a tangled heap of wire, a tottering tower of Ward Lock & Co's *Illustrated Guide Books* with the distinctive red covers, and masses of government leaflets – *Making the Most of the Fat Ration, One-Pot Meals, What To Do Before Going To Your Shelter, A Guide to Woollies by Mrs Sew-and-Sew, Your Household Linen Has Got To LAST!*

Mrs Cowell was a fragile sparrow of a woman, with a small, heart-shaped face and a thin, bony frame. Beatrice instantly felt sorry for her. What a good thing the WVS had taken her under their wing. She obviously needed looking after.

She sat in the ratty old chintz armchair, above which the ceiling was stained yellow with tobacco. From the centre of the ceiling hung an oil lamp of brass and glass, and there were gas brackets with cracked shades on the walls. Mrs Cowell's armchair was pulled up close beside the fireplace. In the hearth stood a contraption with a kettle hanging off one arm and a blackened pot hanging off another. Apparently, these arms could swing across to position the kettle or the pot above the flames. What a way to live!

The room smelled of coal, tobacco, old upholstery, ancient paper and the lingering remnants of something oniony.

Beatrice put on her best smile. 'I'm Miss Inkerman from the WVS. I've brought your meal for you.'

'Pop it on there, love.' With a wavering hand, Mrs Cowell indicated the table. 'The plate's in the scullery.'

Wondering how on earth the plate would fit on the table, Beatrice set down her basket. She had to turn sideways to cross the crowded room to reach a five-foot-high door. As she ducked her head to step through into the scullery, the cold slapped her in the face. Here was a minute room with a deep sink and a few rickety shelves above it. The sink stuck out, meaning that to get a plate from the shelf, Beatrice had to raise herself on tiptoe. As she turned to go back through the door, she banged her forehead on the lintel.

She exclaimed out loud, then immediately added, 'Sorry – my fault,' because she didn't want Mrs Cowell to feel embarrassed about living in such a measly dwelling.

Swiftly Beatrice plated up the meal and gingerly made a space for it on the table.

'Kidney-and-bean pie with kale and a jacket potato,' she said, 'and there's a slice of sponge cake for afters.'

'Thanks, love. You're all so good, the way you look after me.'

'Can I...?' Beatrice stopped, feeling awkward. No one had provided advice about this bit. 'Do you need a hand getting to the table?'

'That's all right, love. I can manage.'

She had her handbag and her gas-mask box on her lap. She looped them over one forearm and, using her free hand to grasp the arm of her chair, she leaned down to put them on the floor. Then she carefully pushed herself to her feet. It was a slow procedure and Beatrice held her breath. When the old lady wobbled forwards and backwards for a moment before she steadied herself, it was all Beatrice could do not to push her way through all the clutter to assist her.

Having balanced herself, Mrs Cowell looked at the things she'd placed on the floor, then she shot Beatrice a rueful glance. 'What an old silly I am. Normally, I put them on the table while I get up.'

Beside her armchair was a table that was piled high with all manner of stuff. How could she possibly place anything else on top without sending the whole heap sliding to the floor?

'It's having you here, love,' Mrs Cowell added. 'I can't help it. I get a bit flustered when I have someone new. No offence.'

'None taken,' Beatrice assured her. 'Should I...?'

'Would you mind?'

Beatrice eased her way through as far as the fireplace. Before she bent to pick up the bag and gas-mask box, she took the precaution of looking behind her to make sure she wasn't going to send something flying. Not daring to put the things on top of the pile on the table for fear of starting an avalanche, she placed them on the armchair.

Beside her, Mrs Cowell fluttered her fragile hands.

'I'm sorry, dear. I didn't make myself clear. I – well, it's daft, I know, but I keep them with me at all times. Air raids, you know. We were told to have our important papers with us in air raids, weren't we? And you have to have your gas mask to hand at all times.'

'It isn't silly at all,' Beatrice said kindly.

'I even take them to the table with me when I have my meals,' Mrs Cowell said as if confiding a great secret.

'You have to do what's best, what makes you feel safe,' said Beatrice.

Mrs Cowell's shoulders sank as she sighed gratefully. 'You understand.'

'Let me carry them to the table for you,' Beatrice offered. 'After you.'

It was a good thing the room was stuffed full of furniture and what-have-you, because it gave the old dear plenty to hang on to as she moved. Beatrice made a mental note that next time she must get her to the table before she plated up.

When Mrs Cowell finally dropped onto the dining chair, she swayed alarmingly. Beatrice took a swift step forward, ready to steady her, even catch her if necessary, but the old lady righted herself. Relief coursed through Beatrice's veins, leaving her feeling quite heady.

Mrs Cowell patted her lap, inviting Beatrice to place the handbag and gas-mask box there.

'I'm sorry I can't stop longer,' said Beatrice. 'I have to hurry back to the WVS office, because someone is off sick.'

'That's all right, love. You run along. And thank you for everything. I do appreciate all the help.'

Beatrice slid behind the door curtain to open the door. Slipping through, she closed it behind her, then stood for a moment, filled with compassion, wishing she'd been free to stay and provide company. She thought of her dear friend Mrs Gates, an elderly lady who had died the year before last. She had been bed-bound, and company had meant everything to her.

Beatrice switched on her torch and made her way back the way she'd come. She could hear the boys' voices again, together with the smell from the chippy even though the frying-room was hidden behind blackout blinds and a door, presumably with a door curtain.

What had brought her Gentlemen's Club boys here? This was close to the middle of town and the boys lived further out. She knew exactly where Tommy and Joseph lived because she had lived in the same road before she'd been chucked out of her lodgings and Kitty had taken her in.

As she neared Greasy Lil's, she stayed on the opposite side, thinking she might slink past without needing to acknowledge the boys again. If Joseph and Tommy were with their pals, they probably hadn't been best pleased she had greeted them earlier – a bit like being fussed over by your mum at the school gates.

An upsurge in the aroma of fried fat and vinegar told Beatrice someone had emerged from the chippy. To her surprise, her mouth watered. Who could resist the delicious smell of fish and chips?

Boys' voices said, 'Thanks, mister... Thanks, mister.'

How kind. Someone had handed out a few packets of chips.

Then a boy's voice added, 'Cor, a real fish supper.'

'Fish suppers all round, lads,' said a man's voice. It was a pleasant voice, rather light, and Beatrice could hear the grin it contained. 'Plenty more where that came from... if you know what I mean.'

'Thanks, mister.'

Beatrice practically hugged the wall as she passed by. No one noticed her in the dark and she hurried on along the cinder-path. Fancy buying fish suppers for those boys. How generous. Beatrice felt warm inside. She always appreciated kindness in others. And it was beneficial for the boys, with their fathers away fighting, to have a good example set by another man.

9

Kitty went to call on Mr Tulip. She did this now and again as a matter of good business practice. He was the owner of three huge warehouses in which he provided storage for the furniture and possessions of people who had been bombed out, the same as Kitty did at Dunbar's, but on a far larger scale. In the early days, Mr Tulip had provided Kitty with masses of information and advice that had enabled her to set up her storage business. He had also – for a fee – provided practical help in the form of his workers' muscles.

Kitty knew she would be grateful to him until the day she died. He'd been a good friend to her in a purely business sense. He'd helped her find her feet and as a result her confidence had grown. He hadn't just explained to her the ins and outs of storage, insurance and the provision of additional services. He'd also encouraged her to pay herself a salary. It sounded stupid now, but that had never occurred to her, though as soon as Mr Tulip had said it, it seemed obvious.

Kitty wasn't going to be on WVS duty that day, so she wore a smart dress she'd been lucky enough to pick up last month at the

WVS clothing exchange. Honestly, the things some people saw fit to part with! This was a wool dress with narrow stripes of bronze and fawn, and collar and cuffs of cream organza. With it, she wore a pill-box hat newly trimmed with a wide bow on the back, and her WVS overcoat to guard her against the February chill.

She and Mr Tulip's secretary, Mrs Carmichael, were old friends by now and they greeted one another with smiles. Mrs Carmichael showed her into Mr Tulip's office.

He was a tubby, well-dressed man whose Burnley accent meant he stressed the letter R in his speech. As Kitty walked in, he was already on his feet and coming round the desk to greet her with a warm handshake, placing his left hand on top of both theirs.

'Thanks for seeing me,' Kitty said with a smile.

'Always a pleasure, my dear Mrs Dunbar.' Still clasping her hand, he looked over her shoulder. 'Mrs Carmichael, would you kindly bring us some tea and maybe a biscuit or two?'

'Of course,' said his secretary.

Mr Tulip released Kitty's hand. 'May I help you with your coat?'

She turned her back and shrugged her coat from her shoulders. Mr Tulip took it to the tall wooden coat stand in the corner and hung it up, along with her gas-mask box. Then he held the back of the visitor's chair for her to sit down. He was a great one for little attentions of that sort, but there was nothing flirtatious about it and Kitty had never felt anything but comfortable and trusting in his presence.

As well as her handbag, she had brought a cloth shopping bag, from which she took a small parcel wrapped in waxed paper. She placed it on the desk.

'Three slices of wedding cake.'

'Your mother-in-law's light-as-air sponge, I hope?' Mr Tulip asked with a twinkle.

Kitty nodded. 'She was asked to make two cakes for our most recent wedding and the bride was kind enough to give us some slices.'

'It's most kind of you to share,' said Mr Tulip. 'Three, you say? One for Mrs Carmichael, and I will take home the other two for Mrs Tulip and myself.'

Kitty smiled. That was why she'd brought three.

The tea arrived, along with ginger biscuits, and Mrs Carmichael withdrew.

'I hope your wedding reception business is flourishing,' said Mr Tulip.

'We have at least two each week from now until Whitsun,' Kitty proudly reported. 'We also lay on funeral spreads and, sad to say, they bring in steady business.'

'A sign of the times,' Mr Tulip replied soberly. 'I hope you are still serving your Dunbar's Wartime Wedding Punch at your receptions.'

'We are,' Kitty confirmed, 'though – strictly between you, me and the gatepost – we've had to adapt the recipe and cut down on the port. Whatever happens, we can't afford to run out.' She smiled. 'But it still has a kick. Apparently, Dunbar's punches have always continued a drop – more than a drop, actually – of brandy. My husband's late Uncle Jeremiah seems to have prepared for war by bringing in a surprising number of bottles of French brandy.'

'Good for him,' Mr Tulip said approvingly. 'There's been no French alcohol to be had since the fall of France. And what about your storage business? All well, I trust. I— what the devil?'

He pushed back his chair and stood up. There were sounds of a commotion outside the office. Alarmed, Kitty twisted in her seat. Mr Tulip came round the desk, heading for the door, from beyond which came the sound of raised voices.

The door flew open so hard it banged against the wall, making the pictures tremble – and Bill burst in. *Bill!*

'You!' he bellowed. '*You!* Are you Tulip?'

Then he threw a punch that sent Mr Tulip crashing to the floor.

* * *

Kitty practically had to trot to keep up with Bill as he marched back to Dunbar's with a face like thunder. At one point she was sorely tempted to stop dead and leave him to storm ahead, but the thought of him erupting through the front doors of Dunbar's and playing merry heck in front of Ivy and Lily kept her hurrying along, determined to stick to his side like glue.

This was the reply to her letter. It had never occurred to her for a single moment that he would do anything other than put pen to paper and write an injured, stinging reply. She had managed to get out of him that his commanding officer had allowed him twenty-four hours of compassionate leave to sort out his marital problems, and here he was.

'How did you know where to find me?' Kitty asked breathlessly.

'My mother told me,' he snapped, anger deepening his voice. 'She said you were out seeing *Mr Tulip*.' He uttered the name with a furious sneer.

'Bill, I've already told you—'

'—that there's *nowt going on*,' he broke in with heavy sarcasm. 'I'm not stupid, Kitty. Pull the other one. It's got bells on.'

She was silenced, though her mind worked at top speed. Bill had punched Mr Tulip – dear, kind Mr Tulip, who had never been anything other than the perfect gentleman – in the belief that he and Kitty were carrying on. It was bizarre. It was ridiculous. If the situation hadn't been so serious and fraught, it might have been funny. No, it wouldn't, not even a little bit. Poor Mr Tulip. What must he be thinking? Kitty was ready to die of mortification. It had been all she could do at the warehouse to prevent a terrified and outraged Mrs Carmichael from telephoning the police.

Bill strode across Oxford Road without noticing if Kitty was beside him, and hoofed it along Lily Street.

Oh no. Kitty groaned inwardly – possibly outwardly as well. She was too het up to know for sure. Mr and Mrs Barnes from the Grove, the hotel over the road from Dunbar's, were coming along Lily Street arm in arm towards Kitty and Bill, with smiles on their faces.

A wild image formed in Kitty's mind of Bill barging past them and possibly even knocking Mr Barnes into the gutter, but instead, as the Barneses smilingly slowed down, Bill came to a halt in front of them and shook hands with Mr Barnes, though Kitty caught the slight wince in her neighbour's features that suggested Bill's fury had swarmed into his handshake.

'Morning, Barnes – Mrs Barnes.' Bill's voice was a little too loud.

'Dunbar, it's good to see you,' Mr Barnes replied. 'On leave? Stupid question. Of course you are.'

Mrs Barnes beamed at Kitty. 'Have you just been to meet him off the train?'

Kitty looked down at herself. In the mad scramble to leave Mr Tulip's office, she had flung on her coat without fastening it, and her lovely dress was on show for all the world to see.

'You made yourself look beautiful for him,' Mrs Barnes said approvingly. She smiled at Bill, inviting him to agree.

Bill flung Kitty a dark look. 'She certainly had good reason to get dressed up.'

'We mustn't keep you,' said Mr Barnes. 'You'll be eager to get home.'

The Barneses went on their way and Bill marched on. Kitty hurried to keep up, pinning a smile on her face in case any other neighbours were watching. Talk about keeping up appearances! Her heart was pounding.

As they entered Dunbar's, Ivy shot out of the reception room, having evidently been on the watch. Lily appeared in the foyer too, though she hung back, looking awkward and worried.

'You found her, then?' Ivy's sharp gaze homed in first on her son and then on Kitty. 'What's going on?'

'That's between Kitty and me.' Bill's blunt tone, laced with disgust, made Ivy's eyes widen as her eyebrows shot up.

Lily edged round them and hovered close to Kitty. 'Are you all right? Only when Mr Dunbar came here looking for you before, he – well, he was rampaging all round the building until Mrs Dunbar got him to stand still and told him where to find you.'

'Everything's fine.' Kitty did her best to sound reassuring, but she was horribly shaken. She couldn't, she just *couldn't* have Bill blurting out that she was having an affair.

He glowered at her. 'Come on, then.'

Without awaiting her reply, he started up the stairs.

'Where are you going?' Kitty called after him.

He turned. Standing up there above them in his uniform, his eyes dark with anger and his features grim, he could have been the image on a wartime poster.

'Where d'you think?' he retorted. 'To the family flat, of course. I take it you don't want to discuss our private business in the foyer?'

'We don't live in the flat now,' said Kitty. 'We've got lodgers.'

'Lodgers – oh yes, I was forgetting,' Bill sneered. 'Another part of your business empire.'

'Bill, please, there's no need for this.' Kitty did her best to sound reasonable. 'Let's go in the reception room.' She hated herself for trying to coax him. She wasn't in the wrong.

Muttering something unintelligible, Bill stomped down the stairs into the reception room. He looked round quickly, taking in its appearance, but made no comment. He waved towards one of the tables, offering Kitty a seat. It was the first sign of courtesy he'd shown.

When they were both seated, Kitty leaned forward.

'I said it in Mr Tulip's office and I'll say it again now. There is nothing, *nothing*, going on between me and him.' The shock was wearing off. Vexation came bubbling up. 'How could you even think it? How *could* you?'

'You send me a letter saying you don't want to be married to me any longer and you expect me to believe there isn't another man in the picture?'

'Of course there isn't!' cried Kitty.

'Of course there *is*,' he hurled at her. 'What other possible reason could there be for you to want to walk out on your marriage? No woman is going to ditch her husband unless she has a replacement lined up.'

'I told you in my letter,' Kitty protested. 'I want to be independent.'

'Stuff and nonsense! What woman in her right mind wants that?'

Kitty's mouth dropped open. It took her a moment to rally. 'Wartime women, that's who! We're all finding out what we're capable of – holding down jobs, spending hours on end doing voluntary work. You have no *idea* what I can do.'

He laughed harshly. 'I know exactly what women can do.

They can take advantage of their husbands' absence, that's what. Don't you dare talk to me about *independence*.' The word came out on a note of disdain as he curled his lip. 'I might have been wrong – *might* have been – about your Mr Tulip, but I know, and you know, that there *is* another man – and you're bloody well going to tell me who it is!'

10

Abbie was going to the pictures straight from work, so Beatrice walked home on her own. When she popped downstairs to the kitchen for a cuppa, she sensed the atmosphere even before she reached the foot of the stairs. She could hear Lily and Mrs Dunbar arguing. Her heart dipped. She'd thought they had put this behind them. At the start of Lily's pregnancy, Mrs Dunbar had been... *forthright* was the politest word Beatrice could think of for it; Mrs Dunbar had been forthright in her view that Lily ought to move out of Dunbar's. There could be no doubting how outraged she had been by the girl's conduct. Beatrice had been proud of Kitty for standing by Lily and she had been glad to do the same herself.

Should she turn round and creep back up the stairs? But it was too late. She was already at the bottom, and the other two, suddenly falling silent, had turned and seen her.

Beatrice felt uncomfortably warm and knew she was blushing. 'I'm sorry. I didn't mean to walk in on anything.' Feeling the need to stand up for Lily, she asked her, 'Are you all right?'

'What?' asked Mrs Dunbar. 'Of course she is. Oh, I see what

you're getting at. Well, you're wrong. We've had...' Her voice trailed off. She huffed a deep breath, blinking furiously. 'We've had an upset here today. Lily and I were exchanging views on the subject, if you must know.'

Beatrice's curiosity might be piqued, but she'd never been a nosy person. She said instead, 'Then I'll make myself a cup of tea and leave you to it.'

'Aren't you going to ask?' Mrs Dunbar demanded.

'Whatever it is, it's none of my business.'

'Well said,' Lily murmured.

'Hark at you!' Mrs Dunbar retorted. 'Well, you're not family, Lily, so you don't care the way I do.'

Beatrice gasped. 'Has something happened to Abbie?' That darling girl—

'No, she's fine,' Mrs Dunbar answered at once. She pinned Beatrice down with a look. 'You might pretend you don't want to know, but I'm going to tell you anyway. It's Kitty and Bill. He came here today. He could only stop a few hours. He's had to go back on the train.'

'Thank heaven,' breathed Lily.

'Kitty wants a divorce,' Mrs Dunbar said baldly.

'She *what*?' Beatrice exclaimed, stunned.

'You heard. She wrote to him, and his CO gave him compassionate leave. He travelled up overnight last night and he has to be on duty again tomorrow.'

A hundred questions streamed across Beatrice's mind. All the reasons Kitty had to feel frustrated with Bill. The money worries. Their entirely different attitudes to their finances. The way Bill had withheld permission for Kitty to have access to the Dunbar's bank account, thereby effectively preventing her from running her business properly.

The latter had left Kitty feeling irked and resentful, but

were things really so bad that she wanted to end the marriage? It was such an enormous step. Beatrice's muscles gave up the struggle and she sank onto a chair, resting one elbow on the table.

Then Mrs Dunbar uttered the words that ripped the breath from Beatrice's lungs.

'Bill says there's another man in the picture.'

'That's what we were arguing about when you walked in,' Lily explained. 'I said there can't possibly be, because we'd know, we'd suspect. Besides, Kitty isn't like that.'

Mrs Dunbar gave a snort of bitter laughter. 'That's rich coming from you, after the way you had us all fooled when you were secretly carrying on with that doctor.'

Lily looked away, but not before Beatrice had glimpsed the hurt in her eyes at having her transgression flung in her face. Trust Mrs Dunbar not to mince her words.

Had she not minced her words with Kitty as well?

Wanting to support the friend who had stood by her in her darkest hour gave Beatrice strength. She stood up.

'Where's Kitty now?' she asked.

'In the club room, dusting,' said Mrs Dunbar. 'Not that it needs it. She's just hiding, if you ask me.'

Quelling the urge to say that no one had asked her, Beatrice went upstairs. She paused to knock on the club room door before she went in, doing so quietly so as not to add to the jangled atmosphere. Kitty had a duster in her hand, but she was sitting by the window, leaning her head against it, one temple pressed to the anti-blast tape. Sorrow and tenderness poured through Beatrice. As she crossed the room, she opened her arms and Kitty rose and walked into them.

'What a mess,' Beatrice said, holding her friend close.

'You could say that,' Kitty answered in a small voice. She

squeezed Beatrice extra warmly for a moment, then stood back. 'You've heard,' she said drily.

'I walked in on Lily and Mrs Dunbar. I'm sorry.'

'Don't apologise. Bill's the one who couldn't keep his mouth shut. I was mad enough to hope he'd keep this between the two of us – though I suppose realistically that ship sailed when he punched Mr Tulip—'

'When he *what*?'

Kitty blinked back tears. 'I wrote to Bill saying I wanted to end the marriage because I want to live independently. He took it into his head that no woman could possibly want that, and that I must have met another man. He came here, found out I was at Mr Tulip's warehouse, went storming round and knocked Mr Tulip to the floor.'

'Is Mr Tulip all right?' Beatrice asked, thinking what a big man Bill Dunbar was.

'He's going to have quite a bruise,' said Kitty. 'It's luckier than I can say that he thinks highly of me. That's the only thing that stopped him sending for the police.' She pressed a palm over her lips, then let it fall away. Breathing unsteadily, she shook her head. 'Quite how well he'll think of me after this is another matter. I must go and see him as soon as I can, so I can apologise.'

'It might be better if you wrote to him,' Beatrice suggested. 'Less awkward – less embarrassing. And you can ask after how he is.'

'That's a good idea,' Kitty agreed. She made a brave effort to smile. 'Besides, if I turned up at the office, his secretary might send for a warehouseman to sling me out. She's devoted to Mr Tulip.' She paused, pressing her lips together in thought. 'I should write to Bill as well and tell him to write to Mr Tulip to apologise.'

'Will he do that, if he thinks you and Mr Tulip...?'

'He will if I tell him that Mr Tulip might take him to court and sue him for assault and defamation of character,' Kitty replied grimly. 'If anything is going to motivate Bill, it's the threat of having to cough up money.'

'I'm so sorry you're having to deal with this,' said Beatrice.

'I did at least think – hope – that Bill would have the sense not to say a word under this roof, but before he left, he told his mother.' Kitty's hazel eyes filled with anguish. 'Oh, Beatrice, what if Abbie finds out I want a divorce? She'll be distraught.'

'No one's going to tell her,' Beatrice said firmly. 'If nothing else, the past few months have proved how good you and I, Lily and Mrs Dunbar are at keeping secrets. We're the only ones who know about Lily's condition – and Mrs Ford now, of course.' After a moment, she added, 'Don't go looking for trouble.'

Kitty gave a half-laugh that brimmed with shock and misery. 'You mean, things are bad enough already without making them worse.'

'Now then, that's enough of that,' Beatrice said briskly but with kindness.

Kitty gave her a watery smile. 'I know. I mustn't wallow. To be honest, who would even want to wallow in something so awful?'

'Come and sit down,' said Beatrice, leading Kitty to the chairs. 'I won't pretend not to be shocked. The thought of divorce... the *stigma*.'

Kitty lifted her chin. 'Maybe there won't be the same stigma after the war. There are expected to be many divorces.'

'It's a big step,' said Beatrice.

'It's what I want,' Kitty answered simply. 'I've shown I can set up a business and run it successfully. That's what I want for my future. I don't want to be under Bill's thumb again. I don't want to be condemned to watching helplessly as the money drains away.'

'I can understand that,' said Beatrice. 'Even so, for a woman to manage on her own...'

'It's going to be hard,' Kitty replied. 'I know that. I'm not kidding myself.'

Beatrice felt oddly breathless. 'I don't know whether to admire you or be terrified for you.'

That made Kitty smile. 'How about both?'

* * *

As Beatrice made her way to the WVS office later that evening, her thoughts were all over the place. She was astonished by Kitty's decision. She'd never met a divorced person in her life, and now she lived under the same roof as two women who were headed towards that state. It was hard enough to picture poor Lily and her baby not having the support of a man to keep them safe, but living alone was the only way for Lily to keep her child. Having longed for a family of her own as a young woman, Beatrice could understand that on an emotional level, though the practicalities of Lily's future made her blood run cold.

Now she was filled with alarm and apprehension at the thought of Kitty's future. Yes, she had set up Dunbar's Storage; yes, she'd set up the wedding reception business; but she'd achieved both these things from the position of having a building to accommodate them. If – when – she divorced Bill, she wouldn't be able to remain at Dunbar's. He'd never stand for that. Kitty would be on her own, in every sense.

Beatrice's heartbeat picked up speed and her mouth went dry. She was scared for her friend.

And what of Abbie? How would she be affected? She might be old enough to go out to work, but she was still a young girl and her parents' separation would be profoundly difficult for her on a personal level, not to mention all the gossip she would have to contend with.

Beatrice pulled her thoughts under control as she entered the WVS office. You couldn't afford to be distracted when you were doing your duty.

She was given the job of delivering the evening snacks to the fire station and the police station. Off she went to the British Restaurant, where the marrow-and-walnut cutlets were cooling on one counter, and the slices of date-and-sultana pudding were cooling on the other. Beatrice helped assemble the corned beef sandwiches and sardine barm cakes while the last woman on the little production line wrapped everything in waxed paper.

Beatrice set off with the wicker basket over her arm. She delivered the snacks first to the fire station, where a couple of firemen jokingly pretended to think all the provisions were for them.

'What – share with the coppers? You're having us on.'

After that, Beatrice headed for the police station. When she walked in, the sweet scent of pipe tobacco welcomed her. Sergeant Wakefield, waving his pipe in the air to illustrate a point, was speaking to a couple of bobbies. He broke off when he saw her.

'Good evening, Miss Inkerman.'

Feeling oddly self-conscious, Beatrice nodded to the group in general. 'I've brought the supper snacks.'

'That's the best news I've heard all shift,' said one of the bobbies.

Beatrice handed him the basket. 'I'll wait here while you empty it.'

'Might I offer you a quick cup of tea?' asked Sergeant Wakefield. 'And don't guzzle anything in secret!' he yelled as the bobby disappeared through a door with the basket.

Seeming to take Beatrice's acceptance for granted, he held open a door for her and they went to his office. After the upset at Dunbar's, it would be nice to have a pleasant conversation with an interesting, well-mannered man. It would give her other things to think about. Besides, he was good company.

Beatrice listed the contents of the supper-basket, then immediately felt she must be very boring company.

But Sergeant Wakefield gave no sign of finding her dull. 'You WVS ladies always take the trouble to provide enjoyable snacks. My late wife loved cooking and baking, and I miss that. She was never happier than when she was in the kitchen.'

'Do you have children?' Beatrice asked.

'Two daughters, both grown up now. Marie is a nurse with the Queen Alexandra's and Hilary works in munitions. She lost her husband at Dunkirk.'

'I'm sorry to hear that,' Beatrice replied.

There was a knock on the door and the tea arrived. This time, instead of the builder's tea Beatrice had been faced with on her previous visit, the brew looked drinkable, she was pleased to see. Sergeant Wakefield produced sugar from his drawer.

'Are you keeping busy?' he asked.

She talked a little about her job, then returned the compliment. 'And are you keeping busy?' She used his own vocabulary. It was a friendly way of asking the same question.

'I wish I could say that, this being wartime, the crooks had given up their nasty ways out of patriotism, but unfortunately that isn't the case. We've had a number of cigarette robberies over the past year or so. Each carton of packets of fags is easy to take, because it's lightweight and the value makes the theft worthwhile.'

'It's a good thing you smoke a pipe,' Beatrice said with a wry smile.

'Do you know Lombard's, the paint factory on the way to Hulme? They suffer from pilfering on a regular basis, and the paint makes its way onto the black market. With all the restrictions on the use of paint, you can see why. I'm pleased to say that when we recently had some Lombard's employees in court for helping themselves, the magistrate refused to allow the defence to call it pilfering. He said it was out-and-out robbery.'

Beatrice was shocked. 'By Lombard's own workers?'

Sergeant Wakefield nodded, his face grim. 'Don't get me wrong. Most folk are honest and respectable, but it's a sad fact that there are some people who, having never put a foot wrong in peacetime, now find themselves, shall we say, taking advantage. There are several local companies having problems – Silver's the road hauliers for one, Porter's the electrics people for another. They keep losing small components, no matter how vigilant they are. It's a damn shame – pardon my French.'

'Of course,' Beatrice murmured. She put down her empty mug. 'I must be on my way.'

'I hope you're not going because I swore. I can only apologise.'

'I understand your frustration, Sergeant. And I do have to go. I'm on duty.'

'I'll see you out.'

He stood up and came round his desk, but no sooner had he opened the door than the telephone rang.

'I know my way,' said Beatrice.

With an apologetic smile, he returned to the desk.

Beatrice closed the door behind her and headed towards the front of the building. When she reached the front office, the bobby who had taken the wicker basket from her was behind the counter.

'Your basket's in the kitchen,' he said. 'Half a mo.'

He disappeared, leaving the door ajar behind him. Beatrice heard his footsteps receding. A few moments later, she heard him on his way back. She moved closer to the door, ready to receive her basket, when she heard a new voice in the corridor on the other side.

'I see you've got the sarge's lady-friend's basket. Come sniffing around again, has she? Well, at her age, anything in trousers will do.'

Beatrice flinched. Humiliation made her skin shrink until it felt a size too small for her frame. Was that how she was seen? As a man-hungry spinster? A husband-hunter?

Tears burned her eyes, but she couldn't let them fall. That settled it. If she had to come here again, she would dump the basket on the front desk and she would not, absolutely would *not*, accept any invitation to take tea.

The bobby appeared with the empty basket. He was trying to smother a grin. Beatrice felt even worse.

She snatched the basket from him and fled into the blackout.

11

Kitty wrote a letter to Mr Tulip, offering her apologies for her husband's conduct. It wasn't an easy letter to write, and it took her three goes, but she managed it in the end. Or so she thought.

But the deep-down truth was that she wasn't happy with it. The deep-down truth was that a letter wasn't enough. Mr Tulip had been good to her. He had given her sound advice and always treated her with courtesy and charm, showing a lively interest not only in her storage business but also in the wedding receptions; and in this shocking situation, he was entitled to more than a few lines on paper, no matter how sincerely they were meant.

No – a visit in person was the only way. Kitty experienced a chilly feeling, but she knew she'd never forgive herself if she didn't do this properly. Mr Tulip deserved it and frankly it would leave a dent in her self-respect if she didn't do it.

Armed with a mixed bouquet that was pretty without being too showy, she went to the warehouse where Mr Tulip had his office.

Mrs Carmichael's eyes narrowed when her gaze landed on

Kitty. Her insides churning with nerves, Kitty went straight to the secretary's desk.

'Mrs Carmichael, I want to apologise to you. What happened last time I was here, my husband storming in like that, must have been dreadfully upsetting for you. You shouldn't have to cope with things like that at work and I'm mortified to think that the incident was linked to me.'

'Mr Dunbar was lucky Mr Tulip didn't send for the police,' Mrs Carmichael said frostily.

'I realise that,' said Kitty. 'I had no idea at all my husband was going to do that. I hope you can accept my apology.'

'It wasn't your fault.' Mrs Carmichael sounded grudging.

'Thank you for recognising that,' Kitty replied gratefully. 'I brought these as a peace offering.'

She held out the flowers. For half a second, everything hung in the balance while Mrs Carmichael decided whether to continue being offended, then she smiled and accepted the bouquet.

'Thank you, Mrs Dunbar. They're beautiful.'

'It's my pleasure,' said Kitty. 'I just wish they hadn't been necessary.'

The two women smiled at one another.

Kitty felt it was safe to move on. 'I'd like to see Mr Tulip, if that's possible.'

'It is indeed possible,' Mr Tulip himself said.

Kitty hadn't noticed the office door was open. Mr Tulip stood in the doorway.

'Please come in,' he said.

He stepped aside to admit her. As he did so, Kitty noticed that he gave Mrs Carmichael's flowers an approving look and she took heart.

Mr Tulip waved her towards the seat at the desk, but instead Kitty turned to face him.

'I'm so very sorry about what happened. I want you to know that I have never said anything to my husband to make him think that...'

'My dear Mrs Dunbar, please come and sit down.'

Kitty perched on the edge of the chair, waiting for him to take his place behind the desk.

'It seems to me,' Mr Tulip said in a neutral voice, 'that it ought to be Mr Dunbar making the apology, not you.'

'I'm sure you'll receive an apology in writing. But I feel so awful about it,' Kitty burst out. 'You've been so good to me and you've always been a perfect gentleman. I'm afraid my husband... got hold of the wrong end of the stick.'

'That must have been quite a stick.'

'I don't want to burden you with my troubles, but I would like to explain, if you'll let me.'

'I'm sure there's no need,' said Mr Tulip.

'But there is,' Kitty insisted. 'Your good opinion is important to me.'

Mr Tulip made a small gesture, turning his palms upwards to convey *Very well*.

'I'm a competent businesswoman, Mr Tulip, but I'm married to a man who is utterly irresponsible with money. That's the truth of it. My husband's attitude towards our finances has brought us – has brought *me* to the point where I wish to end the marriage. I'm sorry if that shocks you, but there it is. I wrote to him a while ago to say I hope for a divorce after the war is over... and you were on the receiving end of his response.'

'I see,' was all Mr Tulip said.

'I'm sorry,' Kitty added.

'It really wasn't your fault, Mrs Dunbar,' Mr Tulip replied. 'I suggest we don't refer to the matter again.'

'Thank you.' Kitty hesitated before asking, 'Does that mean we can continue – *I* can continue to come here for advice? As bad as that incident was, it would be even worse if I lost such a stalwart business associate because of it.'

'You haven't lost a business associate,' Mr Tulip replied. He looked at her for a few moments before adding, 'Neither have you lost a friend.'

It was all Kitty could do not to burst into tears.

* * *

Kitty worked on her accounts in the reception room, using one of the larger tables to spread out the various bills and sheets of paper. The accounts were a lot more complicated than they used to be when all she had to think about was Dunbar's Storage. Now she also had her wedding reception business and the rent from the lodgers, *and* she had to keep track of which money went into the Dunbar's bank account and which she put into the post office account that she operated as her own business account.

The door opened and Ivy appeared. Expecting to be offered tea, Kitty was all set to say she could murder a cup, but instead of staying put in the doorway and making the offer, Ivy shut the door behind her and walked into the room.

'Sorry,' she said. 'I know you don't want to be disturbed.' Clearly, however, she wasn't about to let that stop her. She sat down opposite Kitty. 'I want to talk about this divorce nonsense.'

Kitty stiffened. 'It isn't nonsense.'

'That's the war speaking,' Ivy replied. 'Because of the war, and Bill being away, you've had to do all this work and – well, maybe it's given you the idea that this is what your life is really like, but it *isn't*, Kitty. This isn't your life the way it's meant to be. This isn't the way *any*body's life is meant to be. All our boys away fighting instead of being at home, going out to work and providing for their families. And the women doing war work, delivering milk, driving lorries, operating machinery – building bombs, for heaven's sake – when really they're supposed to be at home, cooking and cleaning and taking care of the children. Kitty, don't misunderstand me. This war has turned everything upside down, and it has to be that way. But I think... I think it's turned your head.'

Kitty's mouth dropped open in astonishment.

'What you've done here at Dunbar's is nothing short of wonderful, and I admire you for it, I honestly do,' Ivy ploughed on. 'You're good at running the business and you obviously enjoy it, and there's nothing wrong with that...'

'But?' Kitty's voice was tight.

After a moment, Ivy said, all in a rush, 'But you've taken it into your head that it's *real*, and it isn't. The war will end, the men will come home and the women will go back to being housewives. It's what happened last time. There were plenty of women who worked for the war effort back then. Afterwards, did they carry on ploughing the fields, driving taxicabs, working as bank clerks, being bus conductors and dustmen and dog-catchers? No, they didn't. The men took back their old jobs and the women went home and looked after their families. That's real life, Kitty, and the sooner you realise it, the better.'

* * *

Ivy's tirade left Kitty so taken aback that for the rest of the day, she had to keep reminding herself to breathe. Could her mother-in-law be right? Was Kitty kidding herself?

No. She wasn't. She knew she wasn't. It would be a huge

mistake to let herself slide into a mire of perplexity, questioning and second-guessing herself. She *knew* she was doing the right thing.

She knew something else too. She must tell Abbie sharpish. She didn't want to. She couldn't bear to hurt her daughter. But Bill had already blabbed to Ivy. What was to stop him pouring it all out in a letter to Abbie? He would want to get her on his side.

Reluctance made Kitty's chest feel tight, but she couldn't leave this to chance – not if that meant leaving it to Bill.

How on earth did you go about telling your little girl that you didn't want to be married to Daddy any more? That you intended to break up the family?

Well, she would have to find a way, and it wasn't just in case Bill got in first. There was also the annoying fact that he'd told Ivy and *she'd* told Lily and Beatrice. Not that Kitty imagined for one moment that any of them would tell Abbie, but if Abbie wasn't told soon, and then, when she was told, realised that the others had known all along, that would make it even worse for her.

Kitty dredged up a deep sigh. Ideally, she would have preferred to wait. It would have been so much better not to be rushed into speaking up until her plans were in place and she could talk confidently about the future and how she would be in a position to provide for Abbie and herself; but as things had turned out, that was a luxury she no longer enjoyed.

With a heavy heart, she took Abbie into the reception room that evening and sat her down.

'What is it?' Abbie asked, looking concerned. 'I can see it's something.'

Kitty had hoped to build up to it gradually, but now she felt pushed into explaining.

'I've got something sad to tell you,' she began.

'Has someone died?' Abbie asked at once.

'No, nothing like that,' Kitty replied. She reached across to place her hands on top of her daughter's. 'It's to do with Daddy—'

'Daddy!' Abbie exclaimed. 'Is he all right?'

'He's fine,' Kitty answered. Sounding as calm as she could, she continued. 'It's about Daddy and me. The thing is...' Her heart beat so hard that all she could hear was the blood thrashing in her ears. 'I'm very sorry, Abbie, but... I've decided I don't want to live with your father any more – after the war, I mean, when he comes home. I – I won't be living with him any more.'

Abbie's face paled. Instead of making her eyes seem bluer, they looked grey. 'What d'you mean?' She sounded like a scared little girl.

'I've got used to being on my own,' said Kitty, 'and I like it better this way.'

'That's nonsense,' Abbie declared, suddenly sounding remarkably like her grandmother. She yanked her hands free from Kitty's. 'If that was true, then every service wife wouldn't want her husband back.'

Shock jolted through Kitty, making her bones vibrate. Abbie was more grown up than she'd given her credit for. She would have to speak more honestly. Her daughter deserved that.

'Abbie, darling, I know how much you love Daddy. He and I have always done everything we can to give you the best possible life. But I don't want to be married to him any more.'

Abbie looked stricken. 'You mean... Are you talking about *divorce*?' The word came out as an anguished whisper.

'I'm afraid so.'

'Does Daddy know?' Abbie asked sharply. Was she about to leap to her father's defence?

Kitty nodded, at first too overwhelmed to speak, but then she forced the words out. 'Daddy is upset at present, and I'm sorry about that, but I know I've made the right decision.'

'What about our family?' cried Abbie. 'What about *me*?'

'I'll do everything in my power to build a good life for us – for you and me,' Kitty swore.

'What about Daddy?' Abbie demanded angrily. 'What about the vows you made? What about leading a respectable life?'

Kitty tried to take her daughter's hands again, but Abbie leaped to her feet, sending her chair crashing to the floor.

'Maybe Daddy will be better off without you,' she burst out. 'You and your feckless spending!'

If Kitty had been on her feet, she would have stepped backwards in shock. As it was, she pressed herself into the back of her chair. She went cold all over, a cold that seeped into her, deeper and deeper, until it froze her very core.

'My... spending habits?'

'Yes!' Abbie flared back at her. 'I know all about you and your *extravagance*.' The word came out on a wave of scorn.

'What? Why would you think such a thing?'

Lifting her chin, Abbie announced defiantly, 'Gran told me.'

Gran?!

* * *

Kitty didn't know whether to be hopping mad or shocked rigid. She tried to fight her way through the shock and out the other side. Shock would weaken her and the last thing she wanted when she confronted Ivy was to feel weak.

Circumstances were such that there was no chance of collaring Ivy until later that evening when they set off together for WVS duty. Kitty said nothing on the way, but when they were given the task of counting and folding or rolling bandages for delivery to the local hospitals, it provided her with the opportunity she needed. Instead of leaving the door to the stores open, which would have been the normal thing to do, Kitty shut it and stood with her back to it.

Her voice steady, she announced, 'I told Abbie earlier about my decision.'

Ivy looked at her, a bitter smile showing her disappointment – more, her disapproval. 'There was no need for that. She didn't need to know yet. If you come to your senses and change your mind, you'll have upset her for nothing.'

'I've already come to my senses, as you call it,' Kitty replied calmly. 'That's how I view my decision. After everything Bill has put me through, I see it as a reasonable choice.' The skin on her face felt so tight, she could hardly move her mouth to speak. 'You of all people know exactly what Bill did. All that spending. All those debts.'

'Aye, I do.' Ivy's eyes were wary. Something in Kitty's tone must have alerted her.

'And you loathed me for years, because Bill told you I was the one letting money slip through my fingers.'

'I thought we'd put that behind us,' said Ivy.

'So did I – until my daughter informed me that Daddy might be better off without me and my foolish spending habits.'

Ivy's lips parted on a gasp. Her mouth remained open, but she apparently couldn't come up with anything to say.

Behind Kitty, the door opened. Mrs Farrow stood there, startled to find Kitty right in front of her.

'Excuse us,' Kitty said briskly. 'We're in the middle of something.' She yanked the door shut and eyed Ivy coldly. 'How *dare* you?' she said quietly. She wanted to shout from the rooftops, but she knew instinctively that a low voice would be more compelling. 'I don't blame you for lapping up Bill's lies, but how *dare* you repeat them to Abbie? To a child, for heaven's sake! How *dare* you make *my daughter* think badly of me?'

'Kitty.' Ivy was flustered. 'I don't know what to say.'

'That's a first,' Kitty retorted.

'I never meant any harm—'

'*Never meant any harm!*' Kitty's voice rose. 'You shared grown-up business with a schoolchild.'

'Well—'

'If you'd known it was Bill doing the spending, would you have told her?' Kitty demanded.

'I – I don't know.'

'Yes, you do. We both do. You'd never have uttered a word against Bill to Abbie – and you'd have been right not to – just as you were completely wrong to tell tales on me.'

'I couldn't help it!' Ivy burst out. 'I was so angry with you for wasting Bill's hard-earned money.'

'That's no excuse and you know it,' Kitty replied, showing her scorn. 'As if that wasn't bad enough, it clearly never occurred to you to set Abbie straight once you knew the fault lay with Bill.'

'I hoped she'd forgotten all about it,' said Ivy. She sounded sullen. Ivy liked having the upper hand and dishing out the criticism. Now the boot was on the other foot and she hated being in the wrong.

'That would have been very convenient for you, wouldn't it?' said Kitty. 'I'm disgusted with you.'

'I'll set her straight,' Ivy said quickly.

'You'll do nothing of the kind. *I'll* do it. That's my job, because I'm her mother. Your job...'

'Yes?' Ivy's eagerness was almost painful to watch.

'Your job is to keep your trap shut and not poison my daughter's mind by sharing what you think of my divorce – because, mark my words, there *is* going to be a divorce.'

'Kitty, I'm sorry—'

'Everyone is when they get caught out.' Kitty opened the door. 'I'm going to find a different job to do. You'd best get a move on. Those bandages won't roll themselves.'

* * *

Before their shift was over, Kitty had a quiet word with Ivy. 'I've said my piece and that's it as far as I'm concerned. I'm not going to give you the cold shoulder. I don't want the others realising something has happened. We all have to live together and I don't want any ill-feeling.'

Ivy nodded, a flash of colour appearing in her cheeks.

That was that. Now, Kitty needed to find the best way of telling Abbie. The girl would be glad to know her mother was trustworthy, but the price would be finding out the truth about her father. Kitty didn't underestimate Abbie's adoration of Bill. She'd always been a daddy's girl, something he'd been only too happy to encourage.

If Kitty dropped Bill in the soup, would that give Abbie a fresh reason to detest her?

Kitty experienced a deep, aching need for her beloved mam. She had always known what to do. Mind you, she'd never known about Bill's extravagance. Kitty had protected her from that.

Well, she didn't have Mam any more, but she had her sister, and Naomi knew all about Bill, and had done from the start. Kitty felt brighter as hope unfurled inside her. She now knew exactly how to approach Abbie.

She went to see Naomi. Derek and Naomi lived in a house that had been built a few years after the last war. It was no secret that, with her three sons away fighting, Naomi now found the house empty even though she had taken in a lodger.

'Come in. I'm in the middle of writing letters to the boys,' Naomi greeted her, 'but I'm happy to stop for a while. We can have a chat and then I can tell the boys all your news.'

'Actually, I hope you won't,' said Kitty as she removed her outdoor things. 'I've got something important to tell you and I want to keep it as private as possible.'

'My goodness, that sounds worrying.'

Naomi led Kitty into the parlour – she called it her parlour, but really it was bigger than that. Posher, too.

'Don't tell me,' Naomi said as they sat down. 'One of your businesses has collapsed, hasn't it? Which one? Kitty, I'm so very sorry, but you know how I've always warned you against taking on too much—'

'It's nothing like that.' Kitty was shocked that Naomi would immediately leap to that conclusion. 'It's – I hardly know where to start.'

'Oh, sweetie,' Naomi said soothingly. 'How about at the beginning?'

Which one counted as the beginning? Her decision to divorce or Ivy's high-handed treachery in spilling the beans to Abbie?

She settled for the former. 'The news I want kept secret is that...' Kitty drew a breath and jumped in. 'After the war, I'm going to leave Bill. I want a divorce.'

Naomi's mouth fell open and stayed open.

'Pick your jaw up off the floor, Naomi.' Kitty tried to sound calm even though her heart was beating hard. 'Yes, you heard correctly. My marriage is over. It can't come as a complete surprise.'

Naomi's hand flew to her chest. 'Actually, it does.'

'You know everything that's happened between us,' said Kitty.

'People don't leave one another just because they feel like it,'

Naomi answered. 'All marriages are under strain at some point, but couples press on.'

Kitty wanted to ask if she and Derek had ever had to press on, but she said, 'That's what you do when you don't have a choice. I *do* have a choice.' Forestalling what she dreaded might be a question about her having met another man, Kitty hurried to say, 'I can work for myself. I *want* to work for myself. I've shown I can set up and run businesses and I'd like the opportunity to do that without my husband dipping his fingers in the till.'

'But, Kitty... *divorce.*'

'I know,' Kitty replied sombrely. 'It shocks me as well if I think about it too hard, but it's the only way for me to achieve independence. After the war, the divorce rate is going to go through the roof. Mine will be just another one in a very long list.' She spoke bravely, but she knew it wasn't going to be as easy as she made it sound.

'I know how hard you've worked,' Naomi said, 'but we're talking about wartime ventures. It's going to be a very different world afterwards. I know you've had problems with Bill all along, but you've always coped and you'll cope again.'

'I don't want to,' Kitty said lightly.

'Sweetie, you know as well as I do that that's what women do. Whatever life throws at us, we get on with it.'

'Life threw Bill at me,' said Kitty. 'Lucky me.'

'You can't give up on your marriage,' Naomi insisted. 'That's not what decent women do.'

'Then I can't be decent, can I?' Kitty retorted. 'I've already given up. Actually, that's not how I see it. I'm not walking *out* on something I don't want. I'm walking *towards* something I do want. Instead of just accepting that wives tag along obediently behind their husbands, I'm going to make my own way.'

'Kitty, you *can't.*' A pleading note entered Naomi's voice. 'I know how difficult things have been with Bill, but you can't walk out, you just can't. Mam isn't here to say it, so I'm saying it for her.'

Kitty bridled, shame flooding through her. 'That's not fair.'

'And what about poor little Abbie?'

Kitty pounced on the chance to move things along in the direction she needed. 'That's another reason why I'm here – to talk about Abbie.'

'Poor little lamb,' said Naomi.

'After I wrote to tell Bill—'

'You've already told him?' Naomi broke in.

'I felt I had to prepare him,' Kitty explained. 'I thought it was the honest thing to do.'

'I thought...' Naomi huffed out a sharp breath and blinked away a tear. 'I thought I was the first person to hear this. More fool me.'

'Oh, Naomi, please don't make this even harder for me.'

'That's the last thing I want to do,' said Naomi. 'You know that. I've only ever had your welfare at heart – yours and Abbie's.'

'That's why I'm here now,' Kitty told her. 'I need your help with Abbie. We both need you.'

'Tell me what to do,' Naomi said immediately.

'Bill told his mother about the divorce and that made me worry he'd tell Abbie as well, so I felt I had to do it.'

'You've told *Abbie*?' Naomi's shocked tone suggested that Kitty had threatened her daughter with the carving knife.

'I had to,' Kitty insisted. 'Then it turned out that before Mrs Dunbar knew the truth about Bill's feckless spending, she told Abbie that we had money troubles and they were all my fault.'

Naomi's lovely blue eyes widened. 'She did *what*? That's outrageous.'

'I've had words with her,' said Kitty. 'Now I need you to help me talk to Abbie and set her straight. She – well, never mind what she said to me. It was the hurt speaking. I need you to tell her that you've known about Bill's spending all along. It's a lot to ask, but please will you do it? I need you to back me up.'

'Poor Abbie,' said Naomi. 'What a mess. Of course I will. In fact, I'll do it on my own.'

'There's no need—'

'Yes, there is. It'll be easier on Abbie,' said Naomi. 'She must be dreadfully upset. Leave it to your big sister. I'll meet Abbie from work this evening and take her to one side. Just you wait. It won't be long before your little girl thinks kindly of you again.'

Kitty surprised them both by bursting into tears.

* * *

Kitty was on pins all evening, waiting for Abbie to come home and silently cursing Ivy for interfering. She would clock her mother-in-law over the head with the frying pan if matters didn't get put right with Abbie. She placed her hand on her chest, filled with gratitude towards Naomi for the way she had immediately stepped in to help. Her sister had never let her down.

At last, from where she sat in the reception room with a book she'd been too preoccupied to look at, Kitty heard the front door open and close – then nothing. Had Abbie headed downstairs to the kitchen to find her? Did Abbie even want to see her? Could Naomi's intervention have gone horribly wrong? It didn't bear thinking about.

Then, putting her sensible head on, Kitty realised it could be something as mundane as Abbie simply having gone upstairs to remove her outdoor things. Should she follow?

Oh, stop fretting and just get on with it.

She went upstairs. She entered the third-floor landing in time to see Abbie had been looking for her and was now stepping backwards away from her bedroom door.

Abbie glanced round. 'There you are. I was just seeing if you were in your room.'

Kitty went towards her, aching to hug her and stroke her hair. She made herself stop out of reach. She had to gauge Abbie's mood first.

'Have you been with Auntie Naomi?' she asked.

'You know I have. Let's not talk out here.'

Abbie opened the door to Kitty's room and they went in. Kitty assumed that Abbie would sit on the bed, but instead she sat on the chair on which Kitty laid out the next day's clothes each night before she went to bed.

Kitty sat on the bed, crossing one knee over the other. 'Is there anything you want to ask me?'

'Not really. Auntie Naomi explained everything.' Abbie's voice sounded strained and hurt.

Kitty answered carefully, 'I'm sorry if this has left you feeling disappointed with Daddy—'

'Are you?' Abbie challenged. 'Are you really?'

'Of course I am,' Kitty replied, feeling a surge of emotion. 'I know how much the two of you mean to one another and, whatever you think, I would hate that special bond to be spoiled.'

'It's a bit late for that, isn't it?'

'What d'you think I should have done?' Kitty asked. 'Let you go on believing I was the one frittering away the money?'

'Of course not,' said Abbie.

'It's all rather a mess, isn't it?' Kitty answered softly.

'Only because Gran stuck her oar in.'

'She was wrong to do that, but at the same time, your father shouldn't have lied to her about me.'

'You don't have to rub it in.' Clearly, Abbie was in a very

scratchy mood. 'I'm sorry for what I said to you that time. I was upset.'

'I know.'

'And I had no reason not to believe Gran about the money.' After a pause, Abbie took a breath and added, 'I still shouldn't have said it, though. I only said it to hit back at you because I felt so hurt.'

Tears came into Kitty's eyes. 'Thank you for saying that. Thank you for *realising* it.'

Abbie pressed her lips together so hard that wrinkles formed across her chin. 'I don't want this to be happening. I don't want you to leave Daddy. I don't want to lose my family.'

Kitty pulled back her head in shock. 'You won't ever lose either of us. The two of us won't be together any more, but we'll always love you and do everything we can for you. You are the most important thing in our lives. You're the best thing we ever did. Come and sit beside me. Please.'

Kitty waited and after a moment, Abbie did so. Kitty didn't hesitate. She budged up closer and slid her arm around her daughter's shoulders.

'I know that what I've decided to do has come as a great shock. It wasn't a decision I made lightly, believe me. But my main concern at present is to help you through this upset over finding out the truth about Daddy and the money.'

Abbie let go of a deep sigh. 'It really hurts to think of him doing that. It hurts a lot more to think of him doing it than it ever did to think the same thing about you.' She turned her face towards Kitty. 'Auntie Naomi said that's because I grew up knowing you were the so-called spendthrift, but with Daddy, it's come right out of the blue. Do you think she's right?'

'It makes sense,' Kitty answered, keeping her tone mild.

'Also, I'm older now,' Abbie went on, 'so I understand it better.

When Gran talked to me, I was only little so I just accepted it without question.'

Quashing the urge to run full tilt in her slippers to the WVS office and give Ivy what for at the top of her voice, Kitty gently pulled Abbie closer and kissed her temple.

'It's a lot to take in, isn't it?' Kitty murmured. 'Me wanting to leave Daddy, and now this.'

Abbie nodded. She gave Kitty a little peck on the cheek, stood up and went to the door. She opened it, then paused and looked back.

'Even when I thought you were stupid with money, I still loved you. I just want you to know that.'

12

March started with the appalling news of the tragedy at Bethnal Green tube station, where not far off two hundred people lost their lives in a dreadful crush. Evangeline Chadwick was as shocked as anyone, her first concern being to ascertain that her husband and Daniel hadn't been involved. There was no reason to suppose they might have been, but the thought was still terrifying, and when she got through to her husband on the telephone in the flat where Daniel was staying with him, she sobbed for ages after she hung up.

It was nothing new to worry about her husband, given how badly London had been hit by air raids, but she wasn't supposed to have to worry about Daniel when he wasn't at sea. Even so, she seemed to have done nothing but worry about the boy ever since the day she'd realised the truth of Lily's background. Daniel had said she came from humble origins. Humble? A squalid little back street! Mrs Chadwick didn't know that for an absolute fact, but it was no hardship to imagine a dreary, tumbledown lane, stinking of the glue factory at one end and with smoke-blackened railway arches at the other. She had no trouble at all picturing

Lily being dragged up in a diseased, louse-infested place of that ilk.

But now, at long last, she had the chance to dispose of Lily for good.

She'd been thinking about it, relishing the knowledge, ever since Lady Ingrid had called on her. Of course, she hadn't relished it to start with. Her initial reaction had been to feel hopping mad. She'd always known Lily was a trollop. Hadn't she got herself in the family way to force Daniel's hand and make him marry her?

But now this – another bun in the oven – and it couldn't possibly be Daniel's. Part of Mrs Chadwick was outraged on her son's behalf. He deserved so much better than this – better than Lily. But another part of her was pleased and relieved. Even Daniel, as besotted as he was with that damn girl, couldn't put up with this.

Another man's baby.

Evangeline Chadwick's mouth settled into a complacent line, not a smile, but a mark of grim satisfaction. Lily had done her best to ensnare Daniel, but it was true what they said. Blood will out. And Lily had been unmasked as the dirty little tart she was.

The complacent line widened and formed a slight curve. Mrs Chadwick had given the matter a great deal of thought since Lady Ingrid Campbell's visit and she knew exactly how to proceed.

She summoned a taxi and made her way from her gracious home in Chorlton-cum-Hardy to Dunbar's, where the front door was opened by a sharp-faced woman of mature years.

'Is Lily Chadwick available, please?' Mrs Chadwick enquired.

'I'll fetch her for you. Who shall I say it is?'

'Mrs Chadwick senior – her mother-in-law.'

'Oh – I see.' Something flickered in the shrewd eyes. 'Would you like to come in?'

'No, thank you.' Mrs Chadwick glanced towards the pavement. 'I'll wait for her at the foot of the steps. Please tell her to put her hat and coat on.'

Without waiting for a reply, she turned on her heel. As she headed down the steps, she heard the front door shut with a loud click that said the sharp-faced woman had felt like slamming it but had restrained herself.

A minute later, the door opened again and Lily looked out. She wasn't dressed for outdoors. She looked at Mrs Chadwick as if she couldn't believe her eyes, then she pattered down the steps.

'Why are you here?' Her voice was little more than a whisper. 'Has something happened to Daniel?'

The girl's blue eyes were wide with fear. No wonder Daniel had fallen for her. She had the vulnerable look off to a T.

'He's fine. Recovering well from his injuries. This has nothing to do with him. I'm here to see you – about the baby.'

Lily gasped audibly, her hand flying to her throat.

'Yes, dear, your secret is a secret no more.' Mrs Chadwick employed a light, cynical tone as she made the most of the moment.

There was a tremor in Lily's voice as she asked, 'Does – does Daniel know?'

'Go and put on your coat and hat and we'll go somewhere private where we can talk about it.'

'But—'

'Please do as you're told, Lily.' Mrs Chadwick showed her impatience with a sigh. 'I'm not in the mood for games.'

Lily stared at her, obviously not daring to glare. Mrs Chadwick looked right back at her. She was reminded of her sons having staring contests when they were boys. Whoever blinked first lost.

Mrs Chadwick did not blink. Lily tore her gaze away. She looked nonplussed. She ran up the steps and disappeared indoors, returning shortly in her outdoor things.

'We'll walk to the Claremont and sit in one of the alcoves in the foyer,' said Mrs Chadwick.

And that was all she said until they were doing precisely that. Even then, the first words she uttered were to the waitress.

'How did you find out?' Lily asked, her voice quiet.

'You were overheard telling your WVS branch organiser.'

'Lady Ingrid,' Lily said in a flat voice.

'I couldn't possibly say.'

'And does Daniel know?'

'Not from me – and apparently not from you either.'

Mrs Chadwick let a long silence fall. She didn't break it. Finally, Lily was impelled to.

'I know I have to tell him.'

'And that will be the end of everything between you.'

'I know.'

'What are your plans?' Mrs Chadwick asked. 'Is it your intention to sponge off him?'

A fierce blush flooded the girl's cheeks. 'No! Of course not. I'll – I'll manage… somehow.'

Mrs Chadwick nodded. 'Somehow,' she repeated.

Lily sat up straight. 'Why am I here? What do you want?'

'To solve both our problems,' Mrs Chadwick replied and received a look of surprise in return. 'Yes – both. You have a child to provide for and I have an inconvenient daughter-in-law I want to see the back of. I have a proposition for you that will work to our mutual benefit.'

* * *

Lily sat in the train, her face tilted towards the window. She probably looked as if she was taking in the scenery, but the truth was that she was aware of nothing except what was in her head. Kitty had come with her, having refused point-blank to let her make the journey on her own. Lily's eyes prickled with tears. No matter how difficult things were for her, she still had reasons to be grateful. The unwavering support she'd received from Kitty and Beatrice was one.

She turned her head to look at her friend. For the first part of the journey from Manchester Victoria, they had shared the compartment with an elderly couple, but they had got out at the last station, so now it was possible to speak freely.

'Thanks for coming with me, Kitty. I don't think I could have faced it on my own.'

'Don't be daft. Of course you could,' Kitty replied. 'You're stronger than you think, Lily. We all are – we have to be these days.'

'I'd much rather do this with you than with Mrs Chadwick,' said Lily.

'Did she offer to come with you?' Kitty asked.

Lily nodded. 'Only to make sure I actually went.' A tiny shiver went through her. 'I couldn't possibly have done this with her watching me like a hawk and making me feel I couldn't back out.'

'It has to be your decision, Lily,' Kitty said softly, 'but I have to be honest. I think this is the best outcome you'll get.'

Lily knew she was right. Mrs Chadwick had made what was, in financial terms, a generous offer. Of course, she hadn't done it out of generosity. She'd made it because it was expedient, which was galling for Lily, but she couldn't afford to get riled up. The last thing her baby needed was misplaced pride.

Mrs Chadwick had offered to pay for Lily to go to a mother-and-baby home. Lily's first reaction had been pure panic at the thought of being sent to Rookery House in Sale, where Daniel had paid for her to go to have Toby. But Mrs Chadwick had very different ideas. She had found out about a place called Maskell House, which was tucked away in the Lancashire countryside.

'You can go there, all expenses paid, to have your child and recover afterwards. Then you can start again wherever you like, as long as you promise not to return to Manchester. I am prepared to purchase a cottage for your use and give you a small allowance, as long as—'

'As long as I stay away from Manchester,' Lily had finished for her. Her heart had been as heavy as a boulder, but at the same time she'd known this was better than what she could provide for her child.

Now, she and Kitty were on their way to Maskell House for Lily to meet the owner, Mrs Ayrton, and have a look round. Mrs Chadwick was footing the bill for the trip.

Lily looked down at herself. Later this month she would hit the six-month mark. To hide her rounded tummy, she was wearing some of Kitty's clothes. Kitty was slim, but Lily's frame was daintier, so wearing the slightly larger clothes preserved her respectability without making her look swamped in the way Beatrice's clothes would have made her appear.

But she couldn't stay on at Dunbar's for much longer, she knew that – which was another reason for taking Mrs Chadwick's offer seriously.

The ticket inspector slid open the door to their compartment. Ticket inspectors these days were either elderly men brought out of retirement or else women doing a man's job. This one was a woman of around thirty with shingled hair showing beneath her peaked cap with its LMS badge.

After she had punched their tickets, Kitty told her where they needed to get off.

'Don't fret,' she answered with a smile. 'I'll pop back and tell you when we're nearly there.'

Alighting at the right station was a challenge these days, ever since the station names had been painted over so as not to provide information for invading troops.

When they got off the train and handed in their tickets, Kitty asked the station manager if they would be able to get a taxi.

'Oh aye,' she replied. 'Old Jimbo has been running the local service since Adam was a lad. His motor will be parked outside. If it's not there, just wait and he'll be back soon.'

They walked out of the station, emerging into a cobbled square, in the middle of which was a gigantic horse chestnut tree around which was a circular bench that had seen better days. An old motor stood outside the station. An old boy leaned against it, smoking, one ankle crossed over the other. His red nose and cheeks suggested that he was fond of a pint.

'Mr... um, Mr Jimbo?' Kitty asked. 'Could you take us to Maskell House, please?'

The journey took them out of the village and along a winding lane bordered on both sides by high grassy banks, then through a hamlet built around a crossroads with an ancient stone cross. After that, there was another lane. Finally, Jimbo steered the motor through a gateway and up a short driveway, along the side of which was a long line of lavender plants, which Lily thought must smell glorious in flowering season. At the top of the drive was a large house covered in ivy.

Jimbo climbed out of the vehicle and went up the steps to ring the bell. He had obviously been here many times before. Lily looked away, embarrassed. Kitty paid him and he pattered down the steps.

A motherly-looking middle-aged woman in a dark uniform opened the door. Kitty introduced them and they went in through a lobby with built-in bench-seats, into a hall with a tiled floor and a table in the middle.

'This way, please.'

The uniformed woman opened a door and smiled an invitation to them. They entered a large, pleasant room with a green-tiled fireplace and a glass-fronted display-case over the mantelpiece. A lady of around sixty came forward to greet them.

'Mrs Chadwick?' she asked, looking at Lily.

'That's me,' Lily confirmed. 'And this is my friend, Mrs Dunbar.'

'Welcome to Maskell House. I am Mrs Ayrton and I've been here for many years, providing comfort, reassurance and discretion to young ladies who find themselves in a difficult situation. Tea and biscuits will be here in a minute and we can talk about Mrs Chadwick's stay. I gather the intention is that you should be here with us for some weeks.'

The motherly woman brought in a tray and put it on the table they were sitting round. Mrs Ayrton did the honours and soon they were all sipping – well, the others might have been, but Lily wasn't. She was too nervous. This was like being in a dream. She hoped she didn't look as scared as she felt.

Mrs Ayrton described daily life in Maskell House.

'I'm a great believer in fresh air and I encourage our girls to go out for walks.'

'You certainly have some beautiful countryside for them to enjoy,' Kitty remarked.

'We do indeed,' Mrs Ayrton replied. 'I'll show you around the house in a while. The principal rooms downstairs are the dining room, the sitting room and what we call the busy room.'

Kitty glanced at Lily as if expecting her to say something, but Lily left it to her friend.

'The busy room?' Kitty asked.

'Lots of board games and a billiards table,' said Mrs Ayrton.

'It sounds like the club room,' Kitty said to Lily.

'Also magazines, sewing, knitting, jigsaws,' said Mrs Ayrton. 'It's important to keep occupied.' She addressed Lily. 'I have a very nice room for you on the first floor. You'll be able to see our apple trees.'

Lily tried to work out whether she would still be here when the apples were ready to be picked. She hadn't slept much last night, on top of which her worries seemed to have clouded her thinking.

'It's hard for mothers these days,' said Mrs Ayrton, 'especially first-time mothers who don't have a little stock of baby things.'

Lily froze. She wasn't a first-time mother, but she couldn't bear to say so.

Kitty came to the rescue. 'I know what you mean. We've got the *Getting Ready for Baby* government leaflet at home and, my goodness, the things they'd have us believe! Saying you don't need rubber knickers on top of a nappy because rubber knickers are "uncomfortable for Baby". Honestly!' She laughed. 'It suits them to say that, because rubber is in short supply.'

'And when they were designing the range of Utility furniture, they deliberately didn't include a cot,' Mrs Ayrton added. 'Who needs a cot when there's a laundry basket or a drawer?'

Lily finally felt able to join in. 'And being told to make clothes that are significantly too big so the baby has something to grow into – but not so much bigger that material is wasted.'

'And my personal favourite,' said Mrs Ayrton. 'Almost all your clothes can easily be altered for maternity wear. As if!' she added with a laugh. Smiling kindly, she said to Lily, 'I have a store of maternity dresses for my mothers-to-be to borrow.'

'Thank you,' said Lily.

'When is your happy event due, Mrs Chadwick?'

'Late June.'

'And when would you like to come to Maskell House?'

She ought to say – she was supposed to say, 'At once, please,' but she said, 'Well – quite soon, really.'

Mrs Ayrton nodded. 'And you do understand, don't you, that not all the girls who come here take their babies home with them? Some of the babies – well, most of them, frankly – will be adopted.'

Lily nodded. Mrs Chadwick had told her that.

'I want to keep my baby,' she said.

'I wasn't suggesting otherwise,' Mrs Ayrton replied soothingly. 'It's tragic that you lost your husband on the battlefield,' she went on, repeating what she had been told by Daniel's mother, 'but your baby is a part of him and I sincerely hope that brings you comfort.'

After they had been shown round the house, it was time for Lily and Kitty to leave. Jimbo's ancient taxi drew up outside. They shook hands with Mrs Ayrton and thanked her, praising Maskell House.

'Let me know when to expect you,' Mrs Ayrton told Lily.

Kitty climbed into the taxi. Instead of following, Lily paused with the door open. She looked up at Maskell House – and felt an overwhelming homesickness for Dunbar's.

* * *

Evangeline Chadwick kept herself busy with her WVS commitments, but her mind strayed constantly to Lily and the likely progress of her day. Had she and her friend arrived at Maskell House? Had they been shown round? Heard what they needed to hear from Mrs Ayrton? Were they on their way home yet? Mrs Chadwick had even provided the opportunity to stay overnight in a hotel should they wish to, so that Lily could go to Maskell House tomorrow as well for extra reassurance, if necessary. Mrs Chadwick had made it sound as if she was offering Lily a favour, but really she'd done it for her own benefit. She needed Lily to agree to this.

Not that the chit had any option. Realistically, this was far and away the best future she could possibly achieve for herself and her bastard. And it would get rid of her for good without allowing Daniel any say in the matter.

That was the crucial part. Daniel was the weak link in all this. Before he had sent the letter to Lily last year seeking a reconciliation, Mrs Chadwick had confidently anticipated the inevitable divorce. But that letter had changed everything. Daniel had spoken to her in a way he never had before in all his life, informing her in no uncertain terms that she wasn't to intercept or interfere with any reply Lily might send.

That was why, even though she was sure Daniel would be appalled and humiliated by Lily's pregnancy, and that it would spell the end of the marriage, there was nevertheless a part of Mrs Chadwick that feared that her kind-hearted, honourable and, let's face it, gullible son would take pity on his slut of a wife and end up making her some sort of offer. Not the continuation of the marriage, of course not, but maybe an offer of financial support. Once he had recovered from the shock of being cuckolded, he was soft enough to want to keep a kindly eye on Lily from a distance.

And Mrs Chadwick wasn't having that.

She arrived home from her WVS work to find a letter waiting

for her on the hall table. She recognised her husband's shocking handwriting.

She started to read, then found herself reading at top speed, so quickly, in fact, that she didn't take in the words properly and she had to go back to the beginning and reread at a moderate pace while her heartbeat clanged and jolted in every pulse-point.

Daniel had decided to complete his recovery at home and would arrive in a day or two.

Mrs Chadwick's heart settled into a steady thud. Her nerves ceased their jangling and turned to steel.

Lily had to be disposed of *now*.

* * *

Lily stared in dismay at her mother-in-law. It had started out as what was, for them, a pleasant conversation. They were in the reception room. Mrs Chadwick had asked all about the visit and, without exerting the pressure Lily might have expected, had sought her opinion of Mrs Ayrton and Maskell House, really seeming to listen to her answers, nodding along without interruption. In fact, Mrs Chadwick had paid her more heed than she'd paid her in the whole of their relationship previously.

But then something had changed and Lily wasn't sure what. Was there an extra layer of scrutiny in Mrs Chadwick's keen eyes? Something a fraction more insistent in the pleasant tone?

'So you're happy to go to Maskell House? That's good. Normally, girls who go there leave as soon as they've recovered from giving birth, but I've arranged for you to stay for up to two months. You are aware, of course,' Mrs Chadwick said firmly, 'that you have to move on, but the additional time at Maskell House will remove the feeling of being rushed. If you find it difficult to make your own arrangements, I am happy for you to find somewhere to go.'

Like the Outer Hebrides, thought Lily.

'I'm sure I'll manage,' she said with what she hoped came across as quiet dignity. 'I appreciate the generosity you're showing me and I'll uphold my side of the bargain.'

'Of course you will.' Mrs Chadwick spoke in the tone of one placating a child. 'To that end, you shan't object to signing a legal document attesting to it.' It wasn't a request. 'Now we have one final detail to sort out and that is, when are you going to leave Dunbar's?'

Having it put to her so bluntly was like having cold water dashed in her face. The baby apparently thought so too, because he or she delivered a hefty kick.

'Well...' Lily managed to say, feeling prickly all over. 'Obviously...'

'Obviously it needs to be as soon as possible,' said Mrs Chadwick. 'You know this is the right thing, Lily. I can see you're scared, and that's one reason to go immediately – tomorrow. Mrs Ayrton has a room ready for you.'

'But...' Lily hated herself for sounding helpless, but she was overwhelmed.

'Besides, I've seen girls like you before – I don't mean girls who are free with their favours. I mean girls who are small, small, small for months on end and then they grow huge practically overnight. Unless you want to slink out of here hanging your head in shame, you must go at once.'

'I know,' Lily whispered. She'd known all along, of course, and she ought to be ready for it, but she wasn't.

Mrs Chadwick touched the pearls at her throat as she said casually, 'And then, of course, there's the other reason.' She met Lily's eyes and held her gaze captive. 'The child.'

'My baby...?' Lily didn't understand.

'Not *that* child. The one here in Dunbar's – Mrs Dunbar's daughter. This has been kept secret from her, hasn't it? Of course it has. I'm surprised Mrs Dunbar has permitted you to stay this long, but since she has, you now owe it to her to leave before she finds herself holding an awkward conversation with her daughter. I'm sure you wouldn't want to be responsible for that – would you, Lily?'

* * *

Lily laid her clothes on the bed in neat piles. Not for the first time she acknowledged how generous Daniel had been. When they were young newlyweds – *young* newlyweds? They were still young now, especially Lily, who had been a bride at eighteen. She didn't feel young these days, though. Losing Toby had left her feeling as old as the hills.

Anyway, when they were newlyweds, Daniel had bought clothes and shoes for her. That lemon-yellow wool dress and that silky rayon blouse – she hadn't let him buy her real silk – and that pretty dress with the polka-dots. He'd bought her a couple of maternity dresses too, because you could still get them in those days.

This wasn't the first time Lily had packed to leave Dunbar's. She'd left when she married, and she'd left again when it was time to go to Rookery House, the mother-and-baby home. Now here she was packing again, but this time she was going to Maskell House to have a different baby. No child could ever make up for losing Toby. This baby had his or her own place in Lily's heart and would grow up knowing about the dear older brother who hadn't lived.

She had already said her goodbyes, having first taken the

precaution of telling Kitty she couldn't face a big group send-off and wanted to say her farewells to one person at a time.

She'd said goodbye to Mrs Ivy Dunbar first, wanting to get that one over with in case Mrs Dunbar took it into her head to say something cutting. But Mrs Dunbar was kindness itself, giving her a hug and wishing her well.

Beatrice had also held her close.

'I know how much it's costing you to give up Daniel,' she said, her brown eyes swimming, 'but before long you'll have a wonderful baby to devote yourself to. However hard the road ahead is for you, having your child will give you purpose and strength.'

'Things would be a lot harder without the help Mrs Chadwick is providing,' Lily had acknowledged.

'Good luck,' Beatrice had whispered emotionally.

After that, Lily had gone to find Kitty, fully aware of the enormous debt she owed her dear friend.

'Thank you for everything.' Lily's voice rang with sincerity. 'You took me in when I needed it most and I'll never forget that.'

'Lily, I'm just glad to have been able to provide you with support,' Kitty answered. 'It's been a pleasure having you here in Dunbar's. You've been a huge help to me. I'd never have been able to set up the wedding reception business without you. You're the one who knew about the china, the linen and the decorations.'

'And the punch bowl,' Lily added with a watery smile. 'I'll never forget Dunbar's Wartime Wedding Punch.'

'There are certainly plenty of wedding guests who'll never forget it,' Kitty said, clearly trying to keep the mood as light as she could.

But Lily had something serious to say. 'I haven't been over to Auntie Nettie's for ages. I was scared in case she realised about my condition. I want you to know I'm going to write her a long letter and tell her everything.'

'She'll appreciate that.'

'I don't think "appreciate" is the right word,' Lily replied drily, 'but she's entitled to know. Then she can decide if she wants to cast me off for ever.'

Lily's heart ached when she thought of the dear uncle and aunt who had taken her in after she was orphaned. She'd let them down so badly.

And she'd let someone else down too – Abbie.

'I'm sorry to go away,' she'd told the girl, 'but you know how hard things have been for me here – my baby dying and my marriage ending.'

'I know all that.' Abbie's voice was tight with unshed tears. 'But for you to go like this, without warning…'

'I have to do what's best for me,' Lily had told her, 'and that means having a fresh start.'

'I thought we were friends,' Abbie burst out, her hurt and bewilderment clear to see. 'I thought you were my big sister.'

Those words had almost broken Lily's heart. It had been tough to say goodbye to the others, but at least they'd known the truth. Abbie had no way of understanding why Lily needed to go.

Now, Lily took a deep breath and picked up the suitcase from her bed. There was a painful, dragging sensation deep in her belly. The case must be heavier than she'd thought.

Then she realised—

13

When Lily didn't come downstairs, Kitty went up to find her, imagining her submitting to a final bout of tears. As she walked into Lily's bedroom, that was indeed what she thought, but only for a moment. Lily's legs had crumpled and she was on the floor, her upper half slumped on the bed, her head in her arms on the edge of the mattress.

Lily turned terrified eyes on her.

'I'm... I'm bleeding.' She gulped. 'Oh, Kitty, it *hurts*.'

Shock streamed through Kitty, turning her cold. Lily couldn't lose this new baby. It just wasn't fair.

Kitty pulled the suitcase off the bed and stood it on the floor.

'Right.' She used a firm voice in the hope it would make her sound as if she knew what she was doing. 'Let's get you into bed with towels to soak up the blood, then I'll send for the doctor.'

'But I'm meant to be going to Maskell House,' said Lily.

'I think we can kiss goodbye to that for now,' Kitty answered, brisk but kind. 'You stay put a minute while I fetch the towels.'

She closed the door softly behind her, then ran like mad to find Ivy.

'Lily's bleeding,' she announced without preamble. 'Send for the doctor, then come and help me.'

Soon Lily was in bed, looking pale and scared. To Kitty's infinite relief, the bleeding wasn't bad. She'd prepared herself for a flood and instead had found smears, but Lily was obviously in pain.

Dr Pitman prescribed bed rest. He looked at the suitcase and raised an enquiring eyebrow.

'Mrs Chadwick isn't going anywhere, Doctor,' Kitty said decisively.

When the doctor had left, Lily tried to protest, but her heart wasn't in it.

'Maskell House will still be there next week,' said Ivy.

Kitty made up her mind. 'Lily shan't be going to Maskell House. D'you hear that, Lily? You're stopping here.'

'Until the danger is past,' Lily said weakly.

'No,' said Kitty. 'You're not going there at all.'

Ivy gawped. Her mouth fell open, her eyes widened and she honest-to-goodness gawped. 'Kitty, think what you're saying.'

'There's nothing to think about,' Kitty replied. 'What matters is doing the right thing and that means keeping Lily here with us. We'll look after her.'

'But...' Ivy's voice dropped to a whisper. 'She's about to start showing. Everyone will know – and they'll know she's part of Dunbar's. The *shame*, Kitty.'

'What about the shame of sending away a young girl, a precious friend, who needs our help and support?' Kitty asked. 'Lily, if you can face the gossip, so can I.'

'Oh, Kitty.' Lily began to cry.

'Now then, no more tears,' Kitty said softly. 'You need to rest and be calm.'

'It's all very well, you two facing the gossip,' Ivy said, starting to sound like her usual sharp self, 'but what about Beatrice and me? Don't we get a say?'

'No,' Kitty answered. 'I know Beatrice will agree with me. She hates to think of Lily going away for good. It'll be a big help if you stand by us, Mrs Dunbar.'

Ivy jerked her chin as if tossing the idea over her shoulder. Then her blue eyes went flinty. 'What about Abbie? Is she to be part of your grand scheme of pandering to Lily?'

Kitty faltered, but only for a moment. 'Abbie will be thrilled that Lily is staying.'

'And when she twigs that Lily is in the family way?'

'She isn't going to be left to realise it, because I'm going to tell her.'

'Oh aye?' Ivy taunted her. 'And how do you propose to do that? Abbie might not be old enough to know where babies come from, but she isn't stupid. She knows that Lily is separated.'

'I'll gloss over the details,' Kitty said, trying to sound matter-of-fact and not as though she was wondering what on earth she was going to say.

Ivy gave a harsh laugh. 'She's still reeling from the idea of her parents getting divorced – and you want to embroil her in *this*?'

'Kitty, are you sure?' Lily asked in a small voice. 'I promised Mrs Chadwick I'd leave. It's all arranged.'

'Can Mrs Chadwick wave a magic wand and stop you needing bed rest?' Kitty answered. 'You entered into that arrangement when you had no other choice, when you thought you wouldn't have a home here. That's changed now. I want you to stay.'

'But Mrs Dunbar is right. I'm going to bring shame on Dunbar's.'

'Lily, Manchester currently has more pregnant women than I've had hot dinners,' Kitty said bracingly, 'and you can't tell me that every single one of them has led a blameless life.'

'Exactly,' Ivy muttered. 'Lily's just another fallen woman.'

Kitty turned to her mother-in-law. 'And that, Mrs Dunbar, is the last time you say anything of the kind.' To Lily, she said, 'You're stopping here with us at Dunbar's – where you belong.'

* * *

What on earth had she let herself in for? Kitty felt the throb of her heartbeat as apprehension flooded through her. How was she supposed to hold such a delicate conversation with Abbie? At the same time, she had no doubt whatsoever that she had made the right decision regarding Lily.

But – how to tell Abbie? Wartime children had grown up quickly in all kinds of ways. They could recognise the type of aeroplane by its silhouette. They knew the difference between the sound of a falling bomb and that of a stick of incendiaries; and when the incendiaries landed, they knew how to extinguish them. They knew first aid and how to maintain the blackout. In daylight raids, they'd learned when there was time to make it to the shelter and when to dive under the desk for safety. Children as young as twelve or thirteen had cycled around in air raids, delivering urgent messages. Bigger boys acted as stretcher-bearers. Boy Scouts and Girl Guides aimed to win a War Service Badge for each year of the conflict.

And yet... they were still children. Younger ones collected and swapped pieces of shrapnel, and still believed in Father Christmas. They played at catching German spies, and slept with their teddy bears.

For all that Abbie had all kinds of knowledge about life on the home front, she was still an ordinary, innocent girl in many ways, and she certainly had no idea where babies came from.

The morning after Kitty had told Lily she could stay, Naomi turned up at Dunbar's. Kitty greeted her with a big hug.

'Thank you for talking to Abbie about the money.'

'I hope it helped,' said Naomi.

'You have no idea how much,' Kitty answered.

'Good. You know I'd do anything for you and Abbie,' Naomi told her. 'I've come in the hope of spiriting you away for a cuppa, a bun and some sisterly chat.'

'Would you mind if we stayed here instead?' Kitty asked.

Naomi looked dubious. 'If you like.'

'But?' Kitty asked.

'It's not as though you still live in the family flat,' said Naomi. 'I miss that privacy.'

'Abbie and Beatrice are at work,' said Kitty. 'Mrs Dunbar has gone to the grocer's, so she'll be queuing up for ages, and Lily...' What should she say?

'Cleaning, I suppose,' said Naomi.

'Actually, she's in bed.'

'What's the matter with her?'

'Nothing now, I hope,' said Kitty. 'She's under orders to rest.' She hesitated. 'I never said anything before, because it was private to Lily, but now that I've decided she can stay here, it's time to tell you.'

'Tell me what?'

As Kitty explained, Naomi's eyebrows climbed up her forehead and her blue eyes cooled. 'I can see why you never spoke up before. I'm surprised at you, Kitty, for lending yourself to something so disgraceful.'

'I'm sorry you take that view.' Kitty hung on to her calmest tone. 'Lily isn't just an employee. She's a friend – and Abbie loves her,' she added, hoping to play on her sister's soft spot for Abbie.

'That makes it worse,' Naomi declared. 'How can you do this to your own daughter?'

'I'm going to be very careful how I tell her,' Kitty replied.

'You'll need to be,' Naomi retorted. 'As if it isn't bad enough that she's got your impending divorce to contend with!'

'Naomi!' Kitty's eyes widened. 'What a thing to say. I know you don't approve of my plans, but you're the one who talked to Abbie about the money and helped her to understand.'

'And now you want her to understand that it's acceptable to condone loose behaviour?'

'Of course not,' snapped Kitty. 'I care about Lily and so does Abbie. She'll want to help her every bit as much as I do.'

'Well, you shouldn't,' said Naomi. 'You should pack her off to the mother-and-baby place.'

Kitty felt winded. 'Where's your compassion?'

'I'm saving it for Abbie,' Naomi answered, 'and for you,' she added, looking upset. 'What's happened to you, Kitty? What's happened to my little sister? You've changed since you came to Dunbar's. You aren't the sweet little thing you used to be.'

'I can't afford to be sweet any more,' Kitty said drily. 'I've got businesses to run.'

'That's what I mean,' replied Naomi. 'I wish you'd go back to how you used to be.'

'If I'd had a better husband,' said Kitty, 'maybe I'd never have needed to change.'

* * *

Kitty wanted to get Abbie on her own to talk about Lily and the coming baby. When Abbie arrived home from work shortly after six, she went straight upstairs to get changed. Kitty gave her a few minutes, then followed her up.

As she walked along the landing towards Abbie's room, she heard voices coming from Lily's bedroom. The door stood half-open. Kitty was about to walk past when she heard Lily say Abbie's name.

'Abbie, sweetheart, I've got something to tell you.'

'Is it about why you're poorly and stuck in bed?' Abbie asked.

On the landing, Kitty stopped moving, almost stopped breathing. Should she intervene?

'I've been worried about you,' said Abbie.

'I know you have,' said Lily. 'Come and sit down.'

A brief silence ensued. Kitty pictured Abbie taking her place on the bed beside her 'big sister'.

'I know your mum was going to tell you this,' said Lily, 'but I don't think it's her job. I think it's mine, because it's about something that's happening to me. Will you listen while I tell you a story?'

That made Abbie laugh. 'I'm too old for stories.'

'You're never too old for a story about someone you know... someone who cares about you.'

'Is it about you?'

Lily didn't answer aloud, but presumably she nodded.

'Go on, then,' said Abbie in a good-natured voice. 'I'm listening.'

'You know I'm separated from Daniel.'

'Because you were both heartbroken over baby Toby,' said Abbie.

'That's right. Separating was very sad, but it was for the best.'

'Are you still sad?'

'I'll always be sad about Daniel,' said Lily, 'and now I have even more reason to be. I need you to listen carefully and try to understand.'

Another short silence. Did Abbie shuffle closer? Were they

holding hands? And what did Kitty think she was doing, standing outside earwigging?

'Last year,' said Lily, 'I... well, I met another man.'

'Who?' Abbie asked at once.

'No one you know,' Lily replied calmly, and Kitty's heart was in her mouth. 'We liked one another.'

'Liked – or loved?' Abbie asked, with an awareness that took her mother by surprise.

'Loved,' Lily said frankly.

'How romantic,' said Abbie, 'and how scary. What about Daniel?'

'When I got the letter from him saying he wanted to try again, I knew it was what I wanted too. I'd wanted it all along, only I'd never realised it before.'

'Oh, Lily. That's *really* romantic.'

'I told the other man I'd changed my mind about him.'

'Good,' said Abbie.

'That's what I thought too,' said Lily, and Kitty heard the smile in her voice. 'But then, something else happened.' She went quiet for a minute. 'I found out that... I'm having a baby.'

'*Lily*.' Abbie's voice, as soft as it was, nevertheless carried through the open door. 'A *baby*.'

'Yes, and—'

'Were you wearing your wedding ring when you were with the other man?' Abbie asked.

'Beg pardon?'

'Ladies with wedding rings have babies, and ladies without them don't,' Abbie answered matter-of-factly, 'so if you wore your ring when you were with the other man...'

'Yes, I did wear it,' said Lily. 'He knew I was married to Daniel.'

'But you never wanted to take off your wedding ring,' Abbie

breathed in a dreamy voice, 'because deep down you knew Daniel was the only man for you.'

Kitty listened in open-mouthed astonishment. In common with many, if not most, brides, she herself hadn't known where babies came from before she got married. Now the same innocence – or ignorance, call it what you liked – in Abbie had allowed her to sail through Lily's vague explanation without having to learn any unnecessary facts about adulthood.

Kitty drew in a breath, knocked on the half-open door and walked in. Abbie was sitting on the bed.

'There you are, Abbie. I thought I heard voices. How are you feeling, Lily?'

'Fine, thanks. Abbie has been keeping me company.'

'Go and get changed, Abbie,' said Kitty, 'and come downstairs for something to eat. Gran's making cheese-and-vegetable cutlets.'

Abbie bent to kiss Lily, then got up and left the room.

Kitty, following, stopped in the doorway, looked back and mouthed, *Thank you.*

14

Evangeline Chadwick's heart threatened to burst with joy the first moment she set eyes on Daniel. She loved all four of her sons, but Daniel had always been her favourite – or he had been until he'd lost his mind and taken up with Lily. That was one of the reasons why Lily's intrusion into the Chadwick family had been so hard to bear – because she had stripped away Daniel's perfection. Even though Mrs Chadwick had now got rid of the girl for good, Daniel would never again be the person he'd been before she'd come along.

But the most important thing was that Lily had disappeared out of their lives for good. Oh, the temptation to pour out the shocking tale to Daniel! To tell him of Lily's pregnancy, to make cynical remarks about the affair she must have had, to declare she'd gone off to have a new life with her illegitimate baby and they would never hear from her again. Oh, the satisfaction!

She forced herself to hold her tongue. It would be so much more effective if Daniel were to find out for himself. If he heard it from his mother, he would very likely suspect she'd had a hand in it. Mrs Chadwick gave her head a little shake. She couldn't have that.

She didn't want Daniel to think about *her*. She wanted him to concentrate on, and preferably be horrified and humiliated by, Lily's betrayal. Even though Lily had played right into her hands, Evangeline Chadwick was furious and disgusted that the little tart had spread her favours around, thereby insulting the entire Chadwick family. Daniel's response, his own shock and anger, would restore him to the Chadwick ranks and ultimately all would be well. The sooner Lily could be erased from the family's collective memory, the better.

When he arrived home, Daniel's handsome face was grey and drawn.

'Arduous journey?' Mrs Chadwick asked. She desperately wanted to make a fuss of him, but she had never been one of those needy, cuddly mothers, and now wasn't the moment to start.

'Long,' Daniel answered. 'The train kept having to shunt into the sidings to make way for troop trains and goods trains. At one point, we sat there for two hours.' A sudden smile made him look younger. 'Could have been worse.'

'And how is your shoulder? Recovering well, your father says.'

'It's much better, thanks,' Daniel replied. 'I manage without the sling most of the time. I've been given a regime of exercises to do every day to build up the muscles and to aid with movement.'

'Go and unpack,' said Mrs Chadwick. 'Your room's ready. Then we can have a proper chat.'

She saw his hesitation and made sure her own expression didn't change in even the smallest way.

'Would you mind if I disappeared for a while?' he asked. 'I want to see Lily.'

Knowing he would expect it, Mrs Chadwick allowed a flicker of vexation to cross her face. 'Very well. If you must.'

'I must,' he replied.

'You have to do what you believe to be right,' she said in the cool voice he would expect.

But inside she felt all puffed up. She felt like preening in front of the mirror. Her belief in herself had never been stronger. Let Daniel go to Dunbar's. Let them tell him Lily had gone for good.

She sent him on his way with supreme confidence.

* * *

Kitty's insides gave a lurch of dismay when she opened the front door to find Daniel Chadwick on the step. Daniel! She'd known he was due to come home but hadn't known exactly when, and surely his mother should have kept him away from Dunbar's. Surely his mother had told him about Lily...

Maybe she had. Maybe it was a storm of emotion that had brought him here – the shock of learning of Lily's pregnancy and of her leaving Manchester for keeps. Maybe he needed to see with his own eyes that she really had gone.

'Mrs Dunbar.' He raised his hat to her. 'I'm here to see Lily.'

'I heard you'd been injured,' said Kitty, playing for time. 'How are you?'

'Doing well, thanks, but it'll be a few weeks yet before I can return to active duty.'

'I'm glad to know you're going to recover.'

'Thanks.' He hesitated. 'May I come in?'

Kitty didn't budge. 'You've come to see Lily.'

'She's expecting me – well, in a manner of speaking. It's probably more accurate to say she isn't expecting me quite yet. I assume she told you I wrote asking for a reconciliation.'

'Yes,' Kitty confirmed, thinking furiously.

'Then you know I'm here with hope in my heart,' Daniel said softly. With an unmistakeable note of determination in his voice, he added, 'I'm not here to cause upset, but I do need to talk to Lily.'

Crikey. There was going to be no wriggling out of this.

Sounding less sure of himself, Daniel said, 'I hope she wants to see me.'

Making up her mind, Kitty stepped back from the doorway. 'Come in. Let's go in the reception room.'

'Is she in there?'

Kitty didn't reply. She led him in and waved him towards a table. 'Please have a seat.'

He remained on his feet. 'Are you going to fetch her?'

Kitty pulled out a chair and sat down. After a moment, good manners obliged Daniel to follow suit, but he looked agitated.

Kitty sucked in a breath. Should she seek Lily's permission before doing this? But Lily would undoubtedly feel she ought to do it herself, and Kitty was determined to spare her that distress.

'I assume you haven't come here straight off the train,' she said, sounding calm in spite of being awash with anxiety. 'I imagine you've been home to Chorlton.'

He frowned. 'What of it?'

'And you've seen your mother,' said Kitty.

'Of course. What's this about?'

'I need to find out what she's told you,' said Kitty. 'About Lily.'

Daniel's frown deepened. 'Nothing.' He sat forward, looking alarmed. 'Is she all right? She's not ill, is she?'

'I need you to listen carefully and not rush to judgement. Last year, before she received your letter asking for a reconciliation, Lily – well, she met someone else.'

The muscles in Daniel's face slackened and his body seemed

to cave in, then lurched upright once more. Taking shallow breaths, he asked, 'Am I – am I too late?'

Kitty's heart ached for him. He wasn't all that much younger than she was, but right now she felt like his mother. All she wanted to do was hug him.

'Lily was...' She wanted to say *thrilled*. She wanted to say *delighted*. 'Lily was pleased to get your letter. It helped her see everything clearly. She immediately ended things with the other man.'

Daniel pushed himself up from the table and paced about, clearly struggling to exercise control over his emotions. Finally, he turned to Kitty, his eyes over-bright.

'That's a relief. It's made me realise even more how much she means to me. Can I see her now?'

'Come and sit down again,' Kitty urged. 'Please.'

He did so. 'If you're worried I'll give her a hard time, I promise you I shan't. I'm just grateful my letter arrived in time.'

'Well, it did and it didn't.' Kitty braced herself. 'A while later – I'm sorry, but Lily found out she was in the family way.'

Daniel froze. Then he shook his head slowly, looking stricken.

'I thought your mother would have told you,' Kitty said quickly.

'She *knows*?'

'She offered to pay for Lily to go to a mother-and-baby home before her condition could become obvious.'

Daniel stared at her. 'My mother *knows*?'

Kitty nodded.

'She – she didn't say a word,' said Daniel. 'I was with her less than an hour ago and she didn't breathe a word.' He cleared his throat. 'When – when is Lily due to leave Dunbar's?'

'She should already have gone,' Kitty told him, 'but...' How did you talk about spotting and bleeding to a man? 'But there was a little complication and the doctor ordered bed rest. There's no danger now.'

The young man scrubbed his face with his palms. 'I can't believe this. I can't take it in.'

Kitty sat up straight. 'I know it's a shock, but as far as I'm concerned, Lily comes first. You said you wouldn't give her a hard time. Does that still apply? Because if it doesn't, you'd better leave right now.'

* * *

Lily lay in bed, her heart beating hard. Daniel was here at Dunbar's – and he knew. Kitty had told him.

'I hope I didn't overstep the mark,' Kitty said. She was sitting on the edge of the bed, holding Lily's hand. 'I know it wasn't my story to tell, but I wanted to spare you the distress.' She smiled, her eyes warm and affectionate. 'You need looking after.'

'I don't mind at all that you told him,' Lily said honestly. 'I'm grateful. I know it's cowardly, but I'd much rather you did that than that I had to.'

'It isn't cowardly at all. There's something else you need to know,' Kitty said quietly, and Lily wondered what could be coming next. 'His mother gave him no warning before he came here. She must have thought he'd find you gone.'

Lily couldn't face thinking about that just now. It felt too complicated. Was she going to be in trouble with Mrs Chadwick for not fulfilling her side of the bargain? But it hadn't been her fault.

'What do you want me to do?' Kitty asked softly. 'I can send Daniel away, tell him to come back in a few days – or not at all. It's up to you, Lily.'

'I should see him,' Lily answered. 'It's the very least he deserves, especially after the wonderful letter he sent me.'

'Only if you feel up to it,' said Kitty. 'I could tell him to give you a day or two, if you like.'

As tempting as that was, Lily was quick to see the downside. 'No, I need to see him now. If I don't, and he goes home, his mother will be in control of what he hears. I can't take that risk. This will be hard enough on him without that. I have to... I have to make this as easy for him as I can.'

Her insides gave a little lurch. Make it easy for him? Who did she think she was trying to kid? He must already be in the depths of shock after hearing what Kitty had said, and nothing Lily could say would lessen that.

If only she hadn't had that bleed, she would have been in Maskell House by this time, with her Manchester life well and truly behind her. But, with Daniel downstairs, it was difficult to picture Maskell House.

Kitty fetched some extra pillows and propped Lily up. She also manhandled a small armchair out of the little sitting room across the landing, forcing it through Lily's doorway so Daniel would have a comfortable seat.

Then she went to fetch him. Lily's heart pitter-pattered as she waited.

He appeared in the open doorway and stopped dead. They stared at one another while Kitty hovered behind Daniel on the landing. Lily's face burned, then she felt the colour seep away. It was a good thing she was in bed because all her strength had vanished.

At last Daniel walked in, but instead of taking the armchair, he sat on the bed. His hazel eyes, which had always looked at her with warmth even when they were losing one another, now contained a bleakness Lily had never encountered before.

'Daniel—'

'Lily—'

Silence.

From the doorway, Kitty said quietly, 'I'll come back in a while.' She turned away, then turned back and addressed Daniel even though his back was to her. 'I expect Lily would like to hear how you got injured.'

It was a lifeline and Lily grabbed it with both hands. 'Yes – tell me.'

Her hand automatically crept towards him. She pulled it back, sticking both hands under the bedclothes.

At first it looked like Daniel might not answer, but then he began to speak.

'Forty or fifty enemy planes were flying low over London, firing their guns not just in front but all around. Then they released their bombs. Molotov breadbaskets, actually.'

Lily shivered. She knew what that meant. Huge quantities of incendiaries.

'There were fires everywhere,' Daniel continued. 'The area was surrounded by fire on three sides, the fourth side being the river. We were conducting rescues by water while around us barges were burning. There was strafing fire and I caught it in the shoulder and was knocked off my feet. I went flying straight down a flight of steps and ended up with a broken arm.'

Lily had a hundred questions, but Daniel's tone made it clear he wasn't interested in expanding on his account. Besides, if she probed, it wouldn't just be out of concern. It would be a means of postponing what had to come next.

She settled for, 'I'm sorry you were injured.'

He shrugged. 'I survived. Plenty didn't.'

Another silence. He stood up and paced the small room.

Swinging round to face her, he exclaimed, 'I can't believe this.

I don't know what to say. I... You're so lovely. I can't blame the other man for being attracted to you. With you on my arm, I always felt like a king.'

A pain, a soreness, grew in Lily's throat. She couldn't have spoken even had she wanted to. There had been a time when she and Daniel had been such a happy, loving couple.

'I suppose I can't blame you either, Lily. Just because I've never looked at another girl doesn't mean you were in the wrong to meet another man. We were separated. We were going to get divorced... until I chucked a spanner in the works by wanting to reconcile.' Daniel shook his head, eyes cloudy, brows drawn together. 'The things I heard downstairs... While I was on my own waiting to come up here, I realised there were holes in the story. I was so shocked to learn that you're expecting, and that my mother knows...' His face hardened as he demanded, 'Where is he now, this man of yours? Isn't he standing by you? Is that why my mother was going to send you away?'

Lily swallowed hard, forcing the constriction in her throat to give way. 'He doesn't know.'

Daniel stared. 'How can he not know?'

'I never told him. I received the letter from you and I ended it with him at once. I knew I wanted you. Then I found out about my condition.'

When she stopped, Daniel said, 'Go on.' His voice was uncompromising. 'Did you go back to the father? Did he spurn you?'

'He would never have done that. I... I never told him, and in the end, I heard he'd joined up. At first... I thought of giving up the baby so you and I could get back together. It seemed the only way. I wanted so badly for us to have another chance and obviously that meant... no baby. Then I realised...' Her voice trailed away. When she tried again, all she could summon up was a whisper. 'I knew with all my heart that I could never, *never* part with my child. Your mother found out and gave me the chance to go away.'

'To disappear?'

'Yes.' Lily lifted her chin. Maternal love burned inside her, flooding her with strength. 'I'm sorry for hurting you, Daniel, but I made my choice some time ago. I chose, I *choose* my child.'

15

Beatrice had been back to Mrs Cowell's with a cooked meal several times.

'It's good to get a proper dinner,' the old lady said, sniffing the air when Beatrice put the plate of thick vegetable stew and dumplings on the over-full table. As always, she had her handbag and gas-mask box on her lap. 'Many a time I've made do with a bag of chips from Greasy Lil's.'

'Is there really a Lilian?' Beatrice asked.

'Not that I know of. I don't know where the name Greasy Lil's comes from. It's run by a brother and sister and they make the best chips you'll ever find anywhere.'

'Maybe I'll treat myself,' Beatrice answered with a smile.

'Don't be fooled by what a cramped little place it is,' said Mrs Cowell. 'They've got this huge cooking range, all black with mother-of-pearl inlay. She keeps it beautiful, she does.'

'I'll definitely treat myself,' said Beatrice, liking what she heard.

'Now, him, he spits in the oil and if it sizzles, it means it's hot enough to cook the chips.' Mrs Cowell glanced at Beatrice. While there was a twinkle in her eyes, there was an assessing look too. 'Not so keen now, are you? They sell eggs an' all, and he spits on the shells to clean 'em.'

'It doesn't seem to put folk off,' said Beatrice, feeling thoroughly put off herself but trying to hide it. 'There's always a queue when I pass by.'

'Told you,' said Mrs Cowell. 'Best chips for miles around.'

'How's your stew?' Beatrice asked.

'Delicious.'

Beatrice was sitting at the crowded table with the old woman. It wasn't just the table that was crowded. The dining chairs were too. Each one, apart from the one used by Mrs Cowell, held piles of ancient newspapers, tatty old boxes and brown paper bags. Beatrice had no idea what the bags contained, as they were all folded over at the top.

The first time she'd sat down, she hadn't liked to move anything in case it was a rude thing to do, and she had perched most uncomfortably on the very edge of the seat, in serious danger of losing her balance and tumbling off. After that, she'd carefully pushed the piles so they butted up against the back of the chair, giving herself a bit more space. She always restored the piles to their rightful position when she stood up. It seemed only polite.

'How long have you lived here?' she asked.

'From the day I was born. My dad was working nights and he told my mam she wasn't to bother him, so she had to have me down here in front of the fire.'

Beatrice was stumped for a reply.

'They had five of us all told, all living here in this one-up one-down,' Mrs Cowell added.

'It must have been quite a squeeze,' Beatrice commented.

Mrs Cowell lifted one scrawny shoulder in a don't-care shrug, her head bent over her meal. 'For as long as it lasted.'

Beatrice immediately pictured childhood deaths. Measles. Scarlet fever. A distraught mother, her heart ripped to shreds.

'The other four were boys,' said Mrs Cowell, 'and they all ran away before they were old enough to leave school. I don't know what became of them. My dad used to tell me they'd run away to join the circus.' Again, that one-sided shrug.

Instinct would have made Beatrice lean closer out of compassion, except that all the detritus between them made it impossible.

Mrs Cowell caught her eye. 'Don't waste your sympathy, Miss Inkerman. Do you hear me complaining?'

Beatrice smiled. 'No.'

Once again she was reminded of her late friend, Mrs Gates. She'd had a similar no-nonsense attitude and had never felt sorry for herself, not even after she became bed-bound. As well as liking her and enjoying her company, Beatrice had admired her friend.

It felt good to be reminded of dear Mrs Gates. It felt good to think she might be edging towards a new friendship.

* * *

Beatrice was worried about Lily – well, there was nothing new in that. Ever since Beatrice had known her, Lily had been going through a difficult time, to put it mildly. She'd lost her baby and her marriage. Then she'd tried to rebuild her life with someone else, though Beatrice had been unaware of that relationship at the time, because it had been a closely guarded secret. After that, she and Daniel had finally worked out what they truly wanted –

each other – only for everything to come crashing down around them once more.

It couldn't be good for Lily in her condition. The situation brought old memories flooding back into Beatrice's mind. How much harder, how much more painful, this must be for Lily after all the turmoil she had gone through – was still going through.

'I'm glad you're letting her stay here,' Beatrice told Kitty as they had a quiet smoke together after preparing the club room for a meeting of the Gentlemen's Club. 'I know it's going to be hard for her once the locals realise there's a baby on the way, but I still can't help feeling this is the best place for her. I know the lady at Maskell House would have taken good care of her, but...' She smiled sadly. 'This is where she belongs.'

'It's where we all belong,' Kitty concurred. 'I couldn't let her leave, Beatrice. She's been through so much and she needs special looking after, and this is where she's going to get it.' Her hazel eyes were troubled. 'Am I a bad mother for letting her stay under the same roof as my young daughter?'

Beatrice inhaled on her cigarette to give herself a moment to think. 'It's tricky. I can see that. But in wartime, *everything* is difficult.'

'Abbie isn't old enough to understand the ins and outs of Lily's affair,' said Kitty, 'but one day she will be. I worry about what she'll think when she looks back.'

'What she'll think of you, you mean? She'll think how kind you were to a friend in need,' Beatrice answered staunchly. 'She loves Lily, that's the main thing. When she's old enough to understand fully, she'll appreciate what a good and brave thing you did.'

'I hope so,' said Kitty.

'You're setting Abbie a good example,' Beatrice replied. 'You're helping a dear friend to weather the storm. If wartime teaches us anything, surely it teaches us the importance of that.'

Kitty's eyes brightened as she smiled. 'When Abbie is old enough to understand, can you please ensure you're there to discuss it with her?'

'I hope I'll always be a part of Abbie's life,' Beatrice said quietly.

Tears rose in her eyes and she hastily blinked them away. She didn't want to go all mushy. Living with Abbie and watching her grow up, being her auntie, was something she was deeply grateful for.

She crushed the stub of her ciggie onto the saucer they'd put on the table, and stood up. 'The boys will be here any minute.'

'No rest for the wicked,' said Kitty.

When the boys arrived, Kitty draped the ties over her forearm and offered the array to the lads for them each to choose one and put it on. Beatrice caught the distinctive whiff of vinegar clinging to Joe Simpson and Tommy Abbott when the boys lined up to say their good evenings. It made her smile.

'Been to Greasy Lil's, have you?' she asked cheerfully.

Instead of grinning at her, they shuffled their feet and didn't meet her eyes.

'No, miss.'

As they moved away, heading for the club room, Beatrice had the uncomfortable feeling she ought to have challenged the lie – because it was a lie, wasn't it? If not, why the awkward behaviour? If they'd been to a different chippy, why not say so? It wasn't as though they'd done anything wrong. Before this, Beatrice would have said she'd built up a good relationship with them, a mixture of formal and friendly, but that seemed to have fallen by the wayside at some point. Certainly the friendly part had. Was it because the boys were getting older? Or was she just a foolish old spinster who didn't really know anything about children?

She tried to push the discomfort aside, but it remained hovering in the background. All of a sudden, she wished she had Sergeant Wakefield to talk to, to share her concerns… to enjoy a nice chat.

But that was no longer possible, not after the way that bobby at the police station had sneered at her behind her back.

'At her age, anything in trousers will do.'

Until that moment, Beatrice had enjoyed Sergeant Wakefield's company, but not any more. Never again.

* * *

Several days had passed since Daniel had returned from Dunbar's. Evangeline Chadwick had sent him there so confidently, knowing he would return hurt and angry and none the wiser. Instead… instead that little *tart*, that little *hussy*, that gold-digging viper had still been in residence, and she and Mrs Dunbar between them had poured out the shameful story.

He had come home stunned. He'd been angry with her, his mother, for withholding the truth from him while he was in London with his father. There hadn't been much need, however, for Mrs Chadwick to justify her actions, because Daniel was altogether too churned up to pay much heed.

Mrs Chadwick had felt like storming into Dunbar's and giving Lily a good slap. According to Daniel, there had been some sort of complication with the pregnancy that had kept Lily from leaving Dunbar's. But the good thing, as far as Mrs Chadwick was concerned, was that Lily had hung on to the baby, so there was no need for Daniel's turmoil to wind down. The more agitated and perturbed he was, the better. Whatever happened, he mustn't be allowed to soften towards Lily. There could be no doubt, of course, that everything was at an end between them, but even so Daniel must be steered well away from doing anything gallant, like offering that Jezebel a financial helping hand. Mrs Chadwick wouldn't put it past him if that little trollop caught him in a soft mood.

After all the trouble she had taken in the matter of making Lily disappear for good, Evangeline Chadwick now found herself having to come up with a new plan, one that couldn't go wrong at the last minute.

In spite of the atmosphere of emotional turmoil that had descended upon her gracious home, a feeling of calm settled on Mrs Chadwick. She felt steady and certain, and at the same time poised, ready to spring.

There could be no doubt as to what must happen next.

Divorce.

* * *

April brought longer, lighter days and milder air. The trees filled out with young leaves and the sight and scent of blossom lifted the heart. To those customers of her storage business who didn't pay for a monthly clean, Kitty offered a spring-cleaning service. Normally, Lily would have been heavily involved in this, but this year Kitty refused to let her lift a finger. Even though the doctor had declared her fit and healthy, the spring cleaning was done by Kitty and Ivy.

After everything that had taken place, Kitty had managed to shove that final conversation with Naomi to the back of her mind, but no matter how hard she tried not to think about it, it was still there and it niggled away at her. She had *never* been in her sister's bad books before and the apparent withdrawal of Naomi's approval hurt. Kitty had a strong urge to apologise, to put matters to rights. After all, she'd been pretty outspoken.

'I can't afford to be sweet any more. I've got businesses to run... If I'd had a better husband, maybe I'd never have needed to change.'

Naomi only had her best interests at heart, same as always. Usually, when Naomi had cautioned her, as she had done many times since Kitty had set up the storage business, Kitty had simply murmured something noncommittal or said she'd think about it, all the while appreciating her sister's concern for her; but this time, she'd flat out answered back.

Answered back? That made her sound like a child. But it was what she'd done, and Naomi hadn't deserved it. As always, she'd simply been showing how much she cared. This situation with the prospective divorce was upsetting for everyone. It was only natural for Naomi to wish she could turn back time for Kitty.

So, yes, maybe Kitty should apologise – but she hadn't done anything wrong. She wasn't the one who had gone through money like a dose of salts. That was Bill. Because of him, she'd had to work darned hard to stay afloat, and it was her good fortune and his bad luck that running successful businesses had given her confidence and the desire for independence.

If only Naomi could see it that way.

'What are you looking so thoughtful about?' Ivy asked.

There were four of them in the basement kitchen – Kitty, Ivy, Beatrice and Lily. Kitty was buffing up the crystalware to a high shine in readiness for a wedding reception tomorrow afternoon. Ivy was de-furring the kettle with borax. Beatrice had made a start of cleaning the packs of cards from the club room with a tiny drop of eau de cologne, but when Lily had insisted on being allocated a task, Beatrice had surrendered the cards to her and turned her own attention to refreshing her shabby old umbrella with warm diluted ammonia. The smell had made them all blink madly at first, but then they got used to it.

When Ivy asked her question, Kitty looked up, feeling oddly guilty. Then she realised the question might not have been directed at her. Lily looked strained, Beatrice… well, uncomfortable was the only word.

After a silence, Kitty said, 'Which one of us were you asking?'

'Well, I was addressing Beatrice, but apparently, looking at your faces now, all three of you had something particular on your minds.'

Another silence.

Beatrice gave a little sigh. 'I don't mind saying. I was thinking about the Gentlemen's Club boys – not all of them, just Tommy Abbott and Joseph Simpson, or Joe as he now insists on being called. They don't seem to be such nice lads any more.'

'They're growing up,' Kitty observed.

'That needn't stop them being nice,' Lily pointed out.

'I feel as if they're beyond my control,' Beatrice admitted, her frown showing she was choosing her words carefully to be sure of saying precisely what she meant. 'I never felt that way before with the Gentlemen's Club. I always felt that even at times when things got a bit boisterous, I was still in charge and could rein things in.'

'And you don't feel like that now?' Kitty asked, concerned.

'Well… no, not always.'

'What are you going to do about it?' Ivy asked. It sounded more like a challenge than a sympathetic show of support. Kitty could have crowned her.

'I haven't got a solid reason to ban them,' said Beatrice, 'but the atmosphere has changed and I worry that it'll affect the other boys.'

'Reinforcements,' said Lily. 'That's what you need. I know

Kitty sometimes does the clubs with you, but you'd feel better if there was always someone, maybe even two people. I'm happy to help.'

'Thank you,' said Beatrice.

'Maybe one of us will spot something you've missed,' Kitty suggested, 'and then, between us, we can get the situation sorted out.'

'If there's a problem with some of the boys,' Ivy declared, 'no matter how vague it seems, you should tell 'em to sling their hook. You're under no obligation to them.'

Beatrice looked a little flustered. 'But I am. I let them join the club. I ought at least to *try* to deal with this.'

'If that's possible,' Ivy replied darkly.

'Anyway,' Lily chimed in, 'would you like to hear what I was thinking about?'

'Your baby, I expect,' Kitty said with a smile.

'Yes – but not the one you mean.' Lily's voice was calm, but there was a flush in her cheeks and she didn't meet anyone's eyes. 'It's Toby. His birthday would have been this month. I'd like to visit his grave. I promised him I'd take him lily-of-the-valley every year. But... supposing I go, and it's too much for me, and I start bleeding again?'

'Oh, Lily,' Beatrice murmured.

'What if I visit my first-born and end up losing my second child?' Pain showed, raw and bleak, in Lily's blue eyes.

Kitty felt her heart would break for her young friend. Her arms ached to wrap Lily in a warm hug, but the girl looked as if that might tip her over the edge. But then, so what if she tipped over? She'd have Kitty's strong arms to stop her from falling.

Before Kitty could make a move, Ivy piped up. It was all Kitty could do to stifle a groan. Instead of crossing the room to hug

Lily, she wanted to leap over and clap her palm over Ivy's mouth to stop her saying whatever it was.

'Now then, Lily.' Ivy's voice was as matter-of-fact as always, but there was an unexpected note of kindness in it. 'The doctor thinks you're all right, but I can understand you feeling iffy. The baby was buried in Sale, wasn't he? I think you should go, but, to use your own word, you need reinforcements – namely, me.'

'You?' Lily exclaimed, and she wasn't the only one. Kitty did too.

'Kitty and Beatrice are too soft-hearted for their own good and might end up blubbing all over the show. You don't want that. You need someone who'll let you get on with being sad or tearful or just plain heartbroken, somebody who'll watch you like a hawk and make sure you're coping. And you know what I'm like, Lily: hard as nails.'

Lily, Kitty and Beatrice all gaped at her.

Ivy tucked in her chin and gave a little snort. 'Just because I'm of the opinion that Lily should have kept her legs crossed when she was with that Dr Shawston, doesn't mean I'm completely heartless.'

'Of course it doesn't,' Beatrice said quickly.

'You'd do that for me?' Lily said wonderingly.

'Aye.' Ivy's voice was back to its crisp self. 'Any decent body would. You've lost a baby, and there's nowt worse than that. Whatever's happened since, I'd never take it out on you over the first baby.'

'Thank you,' Lily whispered.

'We'll get a taxi both ways,' Ivy decreed.

'That'll cost a fortune,' Lily protested.

'We'll get a taxi both ways,' Ivy repeated. 'I'm not taking you on public transport. How many buses would it be? I'll sort out the taxis. All you need do is get your little lad those lily-of-the-valley flowers you promised him.'

* * *

Later, when Beatrice had left for her WVS duty, and Lily had gone to lie down with a library book, Ivy turned to Kitty.

'And what was it you were thinking about? You had something on your mind just like the other two.' She gave Kitty a challenging look. 'Or don't you want to say in case I blab it to Abbie?'

'I hope you know better than ever to do that again,' Kitty answered coolly.

'Don't fret. I've learned my lesson. I ought to have set Abbie straight as soon as I knew the truth.'

'You ought never to have told her in the first place.' Kitty sighed. 'Let's not drag it all up again. It's water under the bridge.'

'Just one thing,' said Ivy. 'I want you to know that I apologised to Abbie.'

Kitty's jaw all but hit the floor. '*You* did? You *apologised*?'

'There's no need to sound so surprised.'

'Yes, there is. Ivy Dunbar saying sorry – that's a big surprise.'

Ivy bridled, then took a moment to calm herself, but Kitty wasn't about to let her get a word in.

'I thought I told you not to speak to Abbie about it.'

'But apparently you didn't tell *her* not to talk to *me*. She said you got her Auntie Naomi to tell her the truth, and that gave me the chance to say I was sorry.' Ivy tilted her chin almost defiantly. 'I told her I was wrong to have told her when she was a little girl and that I then made it worse by keeping the truth to myself when I found out.'

'And what did she say to that?' Kitty asked.

'Nothing, really. Just that she didn't want it mentioned again.'

'Let's hope that's the end of it,' said Kitty. After a moment, she added, 'Mrs Dunbar, I'm glad you said sorry.'

Ivy nodded. 'So am I. Now then, are you going to tell me what it was you were thinking about earlier? Whatever it is, it can't be worse than what Lily's struggling with.'

True enough. That made Kitty decide to confide. It would be a step towards rebuilding her relationship with Ivy.

'It's Naomi. She's upset with me and I feel bad about it.'

'Why's that?'

Kitty explained about Naomi's reservations over Kitty's plan to get a divorce.

'Well, we all have reservations about that,' Ivy stated bluntly.

'And don't I know it,' Kitty muttered. Then she went on, 'Naomi has always been on my side. She tries to stop me working so hard, is always worried when I take risks. She's a real mother hen.' She smiled warmly. 'She has my best interests at heart even more than I do.'

To her surprise, Ivy didn't reply. There seemed to be a crackle in the air.

'You really can't see it, can you?' said Ivy.

'See what?'

Another silence.

'Can I say something without you flying off the handle?' Ivy asked.

Kitty half-laughed even though laughing was the last thing she felt like doing. 'When do I ever do that? If you're referring to that business with Abbie, I was entitled—'

'Perhaps I'd better say nowt,' Ivy cut in.

'No. There's obviously something,' said Kitty. 'Let's hear it. What is it that I *can't see*?' She added a touch of mockery to the words, showing how little importance she attached to them.

Ivy gave her a narrow look. 'Your Naomi. She's as jealous as sin of you.'

'She's *what*?' cried Kitty.

'And you can't see it.'

'Of course I can't – because it isn't there.'

Ivy breathed out a long sigh that blurred her sharp features and made her look old. 'Believe you me, Kitty, I know all about jealousy. I married the younger brother out of the two Dunbar boys, and at the time it never mattered to me that Jeremiah was going to inherit the hotel. But when the time came, and Jeremiah and Miriam took over Dunbar's, well, that was a different story. I was so jealous of Miriam that I could have spat in her eye.'

'Oh, Ivy.'

'Aye, and she knew it an' all. My Bertie, he could have made every bit as good a job of this place as his brother did, but he never got the chance. Jeremiah was the oldest, so he had all the training, all the opportunities.'

Kitty pictured Bill's pride in the family hotel back before Cousin Ronald died. The pride had been real – but had there been jealousy too? Was that the Dunbar curse? That the oldest son got the big prize, leaving everyone else to drool with envy?

Kitty remembered, too, Bill's jubilation when he'd become the heir. He'd hidden it from the rest of the world, but she'd seen it just the same.

'How rotten for you,' she said to Ivy.

'The point is,' Ivy replied, 'that I recognise jealousy when I see it – and I see it in your sister.'

'Don't be ridiculous,' Kitty protested. 'Why on earth would Naomi feel jealous of me?'

She fully expected Ivy not to be able to answer that, but instead Ivy launched into a speech with the confidence of someone who knew exactly what she was talking about.

'Because of your success, of course. Answer me this, Kitty. Does your Naomi know about Bill's spending habits?'

'Yes.'

'Since when?'

'She's known all along – and she's been nothing but kind and supportive.'

Ivy snorted. 'I bet she was. Listen, Kitty. It's easy to hand out support when you're feeling superior. But once the war started and you moved into Dunbar's, that brought you up in the world. Then the bailiffs came, and down you went again.'

'And I've spent all my time since then hauling myself back up.'

'Aye, and you've made a fine job of it – in spite of your sister constantly trying to talk you out of it.'

'She's never—'

Ivy waved a dismissive hand. 'She does it all the time. You said it yourself. She doesn't want you to work so hard. She doesn't want you taking risks.'

'She cares about me—'

'She doesn't want you doing the things that will make you more of a success,' Ivy said bluntly. 'She wants to return to the days when you were poor little Kitty with the extravagant husband, in need of big sister's loving care and advice. Face it. She wants to hold you back.'

* * *

Kitty felt stunned. She couldn't believe it of Naomi – she *didn't* believe it... except that deep down some things now made sense. Or did they merely *seem* to make sense because of what Ivy had poured into her ears?

Kitty had no doubt that Ivy believed every word she'd uttered.

She wasn't averse to stirring up trouble, but she did it using the truth, not rumours and lies or things she'd made up for the heck of it. And just think how honest she'd been about her own jealousy.

As little as Kitty wanted to acknowledge them, she couldn't help but remember certain things...

Naomi urging her not to work so hard.

Naomi not wanting her to take in lodgers.

Naomi telling her she'd just have to carry on with things the way they were, after the fiasco of Kitty not being allowed access to the Dunbar's bank account.

Naomi claiming that the wedding receptions would be too much to take on.

As well as memories associated with Kitty's work at Dunbar's, other recollections surfaced, much to Kitty's discomfort.

Naomi moving to a bigger house when Kitty and Bill got engaged.

Naomi telling her she wouldn't be able to celebrate her and Bill's wedding anniversaries, because the date of the wedding, coupled with Abbie's early birth, made it look like Kitty had had a bun in the oven when she walked down the aisle.

Could it be true? Had Naomi, her beloved sister, the person she had always trusted most in the world, truly spent years holding her back in small ways?

16

Taking her courage in both hands, Lily wrote to Auntie Nettie. Needing reassurance, she talked it over with Kitty first.

'I have to tell her everything,' said Lily. 'To start with, I intended to get in touch with her after I'd gone away, but now that I'm staying, I can't put it off.'

'I think you're right,' Kitty said quietly, her tone approving. 'She needs to know.'

Lily sighed. 'It's going to be horrible. It was bad enough last year when we talked about Daniel and me getting divorced. She was horrified at the example I'd be setting for my cousins. Look at me now,' she added ruefully. 'This is much worse.'

'Why not ask her to come here to see you?' Kitty suggested.

'You wouldn't mind?'

'Lily, sweetheart, you live here. You're entitled to have visitors.'

'It's not exactly going to be a happy visit,' Lily murmured.

'All the more reason to hold it here in Dunbar's,' Kitty said baldly. 'I'm sorry if this sounds hard on Auntie Nettie, but my responsibility is to you, not her, and I'd rather you talked to her here than that you went traipsing off to her house.'

As always, Lily was profoundly touched by the care and concern that surrounded her at Dunbar's. Even Mrs Ivy Dunbar had relented sufficiently to offer to accompany her to Sale to visit Toby's grave. Although Mrs Dunbar had made a point of returning to her normal brusque self after making the offer, Lily couldn't help thinking that she wasn't quite as 'hard as nails' as she claimed.

'Write to your auntie and get her to come here,' said Kitty. 'Pick a day when we don't have a wedding reception or a funeral meal, and you can have the reception room.' She smiled. 'I'll set up a nice tea for you.'

'Thanks,' Lily said appreciatively.

She settled down to pen her letter. *Easier said than done*, she thought, after two or three false starts. To invite Auntie Nettie, letting her believe it was an ordinary visit, wouldn't be honest and would leave her auntie feeling she'd been dragged to Dunbar's under false pretences. What could she write, then? *I want to tell you my news before it's born*. Although she grinned to herself at the joke, she felt shaken and saddened too. Auntie Nettie was going to be dreadfully hurt and ashamed.

In the end, she found a middle way, telling her aunt, *I've got something to talk to you about and I'm afraid it's going to upset you.*

There. That was the best she could do. It gave Auntie Nettie fair warning at the same time as obliging Lily to confess in person.

Not that much confessing would be needed, though, not now that she was showing.

Lily posted the letter at teatime and, the next morning, she imagined Auntie Nettie reading it. What would she think? Would she imagine that Lily was about to get divorced instead of waiting until after the war? Of one thing Lily felt certain: her aunt wouldn't keep her waiting long for a visit.

When Lily looked out of the reception room window the following day and saw her darling auntie walking up Lily Street, her heart quaked. She was all too aware of how badly she had let her uncle and aunt down, and now she was about to make things even worse.

It was a bright spring day and Auntie Nettie, dressed in her faithful old gabardine on which the wide revers screamed 1930s, walked along the road, looking with interest both right and left, admiring the hotels.

Torn between nerves and delight, Lily went to open the door to her much-loved auntie. She had barely drawn her indoors before Auntie Nettie's expression changed. There was an audible gasp as her mouth gaped. Her eyes widened as she blinked rapidly.

'Oh my God... oh my God...' she whispered. 'Oh, *Lily*.'

Auntie Nettie planted a palm on her chest and rubbed it in circles. Tears spilled over. Instinctively, Lily stepped forward to hold her, but she skittered away.

Making an obvious effort, she said in a breathy but determined voice, 'This is what you wanted to talk about – so let's talk.'

Soon they were seated at a table in the reception room. Kitty had taken the trouble to set it nicely with pretty china and she brought a cake stand. Then, after being introduced, she quietly withdrew.

Auntie Nettie clearly didn't give a hoot about the attractive table. 'I assume it's not Daniel's,' she said. 'Had it been his, your visits to your old home wouldn't have stopped. You'd have told me ages ago.'

'It doesn't matter whose it is,' said Lily.

The reply was an angry snort worthy of Mrs Ivy Dunbar.

'It's *mine*,' Lily said quietly but with some force, 'and I'm keeping it. It's important for you to understand that right away...

so that you can be careful what you say,' she added, a warning in her voice.

'*Care*ful!' Auntie Nettie exclaimed.

'Yes,' Lily replied. 'You can say whatever you like about me, but I won't have you or anyone saying bad things about my baby.'

'That's bound to happen, Lily, and you shouldn't kid yourself otherwise,' Auntie Nettie said stiffly.

Tears filled Lily's eyes as she whispered, 'I lost Toby and I couldn't bear to lose this one as well.'

Her aunt leaned forward. 'Where did I go wrong, Lily? Just tell me that.'

Lily was startled. 'You didn't do anything wrong. What are you talking about?'

'Well, I must have done summat. Me and your uncle, we're the ones that fetched you up once your parents died.'

'Auntie Nettie, you were both wonderful to me and I'll always be grateful to you.' Lily hesitated before saying honestly, 'I'm sorry to have let you down. I'm not sorry to be having this baby, but I'm truly sorry to have let you and Uncle Irwin down.' She bit her lip. 'Can I tell you what happened?'

Silence. Was Auntie Nettie going to shove back her chair and storm out?

Instead, she sagged.

'Oh, Lily, what am I going to do with you?'

* * *

'They're saying there's been no spring to compare it with in the past fifty years,' said Mrs Ivy Dunbar.

Sitting beside her in the taxi, Lily appreciated her companion's attempt at conversation, but, honestly, chatting was the very last thing she felt like. But it really was shaping up to be a beautiful springtime. White puffs of cloud were feathered by the wind and the sunshine brightened everything it touched. On the WVS allotments, after the weeding, digging and manuring that had been done to prepare the ground, sowing had begun, always in drills; seed was never broadcast because of the possible waste. Crops were sowed in succession to avoid gluts – broad beans, beetroot, leeks, lettuce, peas, spinach, cabbage, French beans, celery.

'Hark at me,' said Mrs Dunbar, 'trying to get you talking. As if anything could take your mind off what today means.'

'I don't know if it's good or bad that it's such a lovely day,' Lily said softly. 'It would be such a *happy* day if Toby was still here. Part of me thinks the sky should be black and there should be thunder, and another part of me thinks that babies are all about sunshine.'

In her hands, she held the posy of lily-of-the-valley, its little blooms dainty and fragrant. They were unspeakably precious because they were a link with Toby, representing the time of year he'd been born, and then died. At the same time, Lily wanted to chuck the flowers out of the window to be crushed beneath the wheels of an oncoming vehicle. What was the point of them? Nothing could bring her little boy back.

It was some miles to Sale. The taxi drew into the kerb outside the cemetery and Lily got out. She made a move to pay the fare, but Mrs Ivy Dunbar set her firmly aside.

The baby wriggled and did a quick tap-dance, making Lily smile in spite of her sadness. No matter what difficulties lay ahead, this new life was the greatest gift imaginable. He or she would never replace Toby but would be a little person in their own right and Lily would cherish every moment.

To her surprise, Mrs Ivy Dunbar linked arms and they walked along quiet, leafy paths. Part of Lily absorbed the serenity of the setting even as another part of her wanted to howl like a wild animal.

'He's just along here,' she said as they turned a corner in the path.

There was someone at a grave further along – a man, bare-headed, his hat in his hands. Lily hoped he'd be quick at the grave where he was paying his respects, and leave. She'd imagined having this moment entirely to herself. That made her feel mean and guilty. She of all people knew how important these times were.

The thoughts flitted across the landscape of her mind in a single moment. Then her eyes registered and her feet stopped dead.

Daniel.

There was a small tug on Lily's arm as Mrs Dunbar took another couple of steps before she too halted.

'Oh,' she said.

Daniel must have sensed he was being watched. He turned his head. He and Lily stared at one another. At last, Lily stirred. Glancing at Mrs Dunbar, she indicated a bench.

'Let's sit down until he's finished. There's no hurry.'

Before they could sit, Daniel appeared beside them.

'Lily...'

'Hello, Daniel.'

He turned his hat round and round, feeding the brim between his fingers. His hazel eyes showed concern and the deepest sorrow. Lily remembered how he used to look when he smiled, the suggestion of vulnerability that showed only when he smiled at her. He wasn't smiling now, but the vulnerability was there, though perhaps she was the only person who could see it beneath the mask of pain.

'His birthday,' said Daniel. 'He'd have been two years old.' He shook his head wonderingly. 'Two.'

'I've brought him lily-of-the-valley.' She hesitated before she added, 'I don't mind waiting until you're ready to leave.'

He continued to look at her. 'If you like... only if you want... we could visit him together. If you like.'

Lily's heart delivered a massive *whump*. Then she nodded.

Beside her, Mrs Ivy Dunbar stirred. 'Are you sure, Lily?'

Lily glanced at her. 'Yes. Yes, thanks.'

Together, she and Daniel walked to their son's grave. Lily's hand crept into Daniel's as they stood side by side, and his fingers curled protectively around hers. Lily felt a tightness inside her that refused to loosen.

Oh, Toby.

'I wish...' she began.

She moved slightly away from Daniel so she could turn to him. Her right hand and his left hung clasped between them.

'I wish you could have seen him,' she said.

'So do I,' he answered quietly.

In his expression, Lily could see all the love he had for her.

Then his gaze dropped to her swollen figure and his face hardened.

* * *

The end of the month brought Abbie's birthday. Kitty was proud of the young lady her daughter had grown into, but at the same time she boggled at the thought of her baby girl turning fifteen. Fifteen! She'd been going out to work for almost a year now.

Kitty wrote to Bill, expressing these sentiments, and he replied, agreeing. Their shared love for Abbie was the one thing that had never faltered between them.

May began with a Wings for Victory Week that, it was hoped,

would raise a hundred and fifty million pounds nationwide. Living so near to Manchester city centre made it easy for Kitty and the others, though not Lily, to go along and watch everything. THE BOYS IN BLUE LOOK TO YOU proclaimed all the banners in salute to the brave men of the Royal Air Force, the Fleet Air Arm and the Allied Air Forces. A Lancaster bomber stood on display in Piccadilly, the dings and dents in its fuselage proud reminders of its wartime mission.

A parade took place to get the week started, with marching bands and columns of men followed by equipment displayed on open-topped lorries. Bringing up the rear were the bombs, some of which weighed as much as eight thousand pounds. Imagine! Afterwards, folk queued up to purchase wartime savings stamps to contribute to the fund-raising drive. Many wrote messages on their stamps before sticking them to the bombs. *This one's for you, Adolf*, things like that. Other people wrote the names of loved ones who had lost their lives, and fought to conceal their emotions as they stuck their stamps on the deadly bombs.

The Dunbar family returned home feeling proud and invigorated.

As the days went by, Kitty was aware of Ivy dealing her a sharp glance now and again. She knew her mother-in-law must be wondering if she'd said anything to Naomi. Well, not yet, but she knew she would have to in the end. It was so hard to believe that Ivy could be right, and yet... and yet...

It was all very well telling herself that she would tackle Naomi 'in the end', but Kitty knew that wasn't right. Her sister deserved the chance to tell her side of it. Would it look confrontational if she went to Naomi and Derek's house? Or, if she waited for Naomi to come to Dunbar's, would Naomi feel like she'd walked into a trap?

No contest. Kitty went round to Naomi's. Her pulse jumped about as she stood on the step waiting for the door to open.

'Kitty! What a nice surprise. Come in.' Naomi wore her WVS uniform. 'I'm not on duty for another half hour. Time for a cup of tea with my favourite sister.'

In spite of the misgivings that had brought her here, Kitty laughed.

'Peter used to say that – do you remember?' said Naomi. A little cloud of distress passed across her pretty features at the memory of the brother she'd grown up with. 'He used to call me that when it was just the two of us. Then you came along and I became his favourite fair-haired sister and you were his favourite baby sister.'

Dear Peter. He had copped it during the last war. Now the country was fighting again. If you weren't careful, you could find yourself wondering what the Great War had been for. It certainly hadn't been the war to end all wars, which was what it was supposed to have been.

Naomi started to lead the way to the kitchen. Kitty stopped her by touching her arm. Given what she wanted to discuss, it wouldn't be fair to let Naomi make a friendly cuppa.

'Let's have a seat,' Kitty said softly.

'If you like.' Naomi looked a little startled. 'What is it?' She laughed, smiling indulgently. 'What have you done now?'

'Me?' It was Kitty's turn to be startled. 'Nothing. I just want to ask you something.'

There. Now she was committed.

Naomi waved her to an armchair and sat in the other one, looking expectantly at Kitty.

'I'm sorry,' said Kitty. 'There's no tactful way to say this. Why do you always try to talk me out of doing things?'

Clearly surprised, Naomi said, 'I've never tried to talk you out of anything.'

'Yes, you have,' Kitty replied. 'Every time I have a fresh idea for the business, you're on at me not to take on more work, not to stretch myself.'

'Well, excuse me,' Naomi said indignantly. 'I care about you. I don't want you wearing yourself out – and I don't want you setting yourself up for a fall either. And now you accuse me of – of – I'm not sure what you're accusing me of.'

Kitty curled up inside, wishing she'd never started this. At the same time, though, something made her not want to give in. There had been enough in what Ivy had said to make her want to pursue this.

'I'm not accusing you of anything,' she said firmly. 'I'm just asking you to think about *why* you react like that.'

'Why? *Why*? I've already told you – because I care. I've always looked after you.'

'I know that, and you know how much it means to me.'

'Do I?' Naomi demanded. 'It doesn't seem right now as if it means all that much to you.'

'Well, it does.' Kitty knew she had to be much more blunt. 'I love you, Naomi, always have, always will. But I'm concerned that it might not be so straightforward on your side. I worry that you might be – well, you might be a little envious.'

Naomi's mouth fell open. 'Envious? *Me*? Of *you*? You with your spendthrift husband?'

'I'm not talking about Bill. I mean the success I've had at Dunbar's. The storage business. The wedding receptions. The lodgers. I've done very well, even though I do say so myself.'

'I never said you hadn't,' Naomi replied in a tight voice.

Kitty tried again. She changed tack. 'Maybe I was wrong to call you envious.'

'*Maybe*?' Naomi queried.

'But I've realised you always try to talk me out of new things.'

'Like getting divorced, you mean?'

'Work things,' Kitty answered, stung. 'You always have a good reason why I shouldn't pursue something new, and never mind that I *need* to work, I *need* to generate an income. Someone said to me that maybe you—'

Naomi drew in a great gasp. 'That maybe I what? And who said it? Who, Kitty?'

'It doesn't matter.'

'I think I'm entitled to know.'

Kitty could see no way of keeping it quiet. 'Bill's mother,' she confessed.

'Bill's *mother*?' Naomi looked almost dazed with shock. 'Oh, that's rich, that is! Bill's mother! Not that long ago, you couldn't stand the woman. She was awful to you for years, but now all is forgiven and the two of you gossip about me behind my back.'

'It wasn't like that. She told me how jealous she used to be of Uncle Jeremiah and Aunt Miriam, and she wondered if – if you might be jealous of me.'

Naomi laughed, a rather high-pitched sound. 'Why on earth would I be jealous of you? Your marriage wasn't exactly made in heaven, was it? Whereas Derek and I have been happy for years.'

'I know,' said Kitty. 'You're very lucky.'

'Yes, I am,' Naomi replied, 'and I certainly have no need to be jealous of my younger sister. The very idea! And you and your precious mother-in-law can put that in your pipe and smoke it.'

17

May brought yet another drive to inspire civilians to work towards the war effort. This month, it was aimed at salvage, which was now an essential part of everyone's lives. It was more than make-do-and-mend, it was providing leftover things that could be made into items for the war effort. An enamel saucepan could be made into a bayonet; cardboard became part of a fuse assembly or the outer container for a shell. Even old rags could be made into charts for submarines and maps for bomber crews and tank crews.

Children were heavily involved in collecting salvage and there was healthy competition between schools and the groups of Scouts and Cubs, Guides and Brownies as to who could collect the greatest quantity of salvage locally – paper, string, metal, rubber, scraps of fabric, the few inches at the end of a ball of wool. It was one of the ways in which a child could be a 'cog' – a small cog in the vast war machine. Newspapers ran a special 'cog' page every week specially for children and there was a song called 'There'll Always be a Dustbin' which was sung to the tune of 'There'll Always be an England'.

The current salvage drive was focused on books. Children, known as book commandos, delightedly pushed barrows round the streets to collect books door-to-door. Some of the lads from the Gentlemen's Club had taken on this coveted role and Beatrice was proud of them, not least because Joe Simpson and Tommy Abbott were among their number, which made her feel better about them. Maybe their high spirits would settle down. There was due to be a club meeting that evening, so she would soon find out.

The doorbell rang much earlier than expected. Beatrice and Kitty were in the middle of getting the club room ready. Beatrice put down the ping-pong bats on the table and went to open the door. It might be Miss Fay Brewer; she sometimes dropped in at club time.

Sergeant Wakefield was outside. Beatrice felt the colour flow into her cheeks and hoped he wouldn't notice.

'Sergeant Wakefield! Sorry, that was rude. I thought you might be someone else.' She took a breath. *Stop babbling*. 'What brings you here?'

'I was passing and I thought I'd look in... if that's all right.'

'Of course.' Kitty had appeared behind Beatrice. 'Come in, Sergeant. We're busy getting the club room ready.' She laughed. 'Come and see your dartboard in pride of place.'

'Thanks, Mrs Dunbar,' he replied. 'How are the lads getting on with it? Are you going to end up with your own darts team?'

'Maybe one day,' Kitty answered good-naturedly, leading the way into the club room.

The sergeant looked round approvingly. 'Maybe I should come along if my time off coincides with a club evening, and give a few lessons.'

Beatrice wanted to say, 'Yes, please.' She wanted to say, 'There's no need.' She wanted to say, 'What a good idea.' She wanted to say, 'Thank you, but it's not necessary.' She *wanted* to say, 'The boys would love that,' but what if she said, 'I'd love that,' by mistake?

Her hesitation must have been obvious because Sergeant Wakefield said, 'Let me know if you'd like me to,' and Beatrice blushed all over again, but at least he sounded genial and not offended or embarrassed.

No, she was the one who was embarrassed, and it served her right for taking a shine to a handsome man. The young copper's words rang in her ears as clearly as if they'd just been spoken.

'Come sniffing around again, has she? Well, at her age, anything in trousers will do.'

Oh, the shame, the ignominy. It was more than time to put this idiocy behind her.

But still... seeing him again felt good in a butterflies-in-the-tummy kind of way... in a hopelessly self-conscious kind of way. That didn't sound as if it should feel good, but it did. Hopeless and foolish, but good.

As for her heart, it seemed to be doing its own Morse code. There were Vs everywhere you looked these days. Kitty had a shiny V for Victory to put on top of wedding cakes. And some girls did their fringes in a fancy way, with three small, tight curls followed by a long one. Dot, dot, dot, dash. The letter V in Morse code. There was even a victory dance, where the steps went short, short, short, glide... short, short, short, glide.

That's what Beatrice's silly old spinster heart was doing now. Bop, bop, bop, *dum*... bop, bop, bop, *dum*.

Only, in her case, V didn't stand for victory. It stood for vacuous... valueless...

Vulnerable.

* * *

Sergeant Wakefield didn't stay long. Beatrice told herself she was grateful to see the back of him, but she knew it was a lie. Still, if she told herself the lie enough times, she would start to believe it (wouldn't she?) and then, at some point after that, it would stop being a lie.

Anyway, it was time to concentrate on the Gentlemen's Club. The boys arrived and soon the evening was in full swing. Some of the boys read comics, others played bagatelle, which was always popular, and others queued up to play darts, which made Beatrice feel guilty for not having jumped at Sergeant Wakefield's offer to give coaching.

Joe and Tommy were over by the windows, heads close together as they talked. Joe took something from his pocket to show Tommy. More whispering followed, accompanied by grins and chuckles.

They looked pleased with themselves, not in a cocky way, but in a good-natured way that made Beatrice feel that this wasn't going to be one of those evenings when the atmosphere was highly charged. It made her want to reward them with some adult attention. She crossed the room.

'What have you got there, boys?' she asked with a smile.

Tommy looked taken aback, but, of course, that was only because he hadn't realised she was there.

'Nothing,' said Joe. Then, with a small shrug, he held out his hand in which lay a glass tube, maybe three inches long, with something or things metallic inside it – thin, flat discs, maybe? Held together by... something?

'What is it?' Beatrice asked.

'Nothing,' Tommy replied. 'Just a piece of shrapnel Joe found. It's lucky it didn't get smashed.'

Beatrice had never seen a piece of shrapnel like it – but then, she hadn't ever gone scrambling around bomb sites in search of the stuff, so what did she know?

* * *

May had brought the astonishing story of the 'bouncing bombs' that had destroyed the Möhne Dam, causing extensive flooding, and the Eder Dam, which had resulted in a tidal wave thirty feet high; but June opened on a sober note with the death of the film star Leslie Howard when his plane was shot down.

'He was wonderful in *Gone With the Wind*,' said Lily.

'I liked him in *Pygmalion*,' said Ivy. 'He was Henry Higgins.'

'I remember him in *The Scarlet Pimpernel*,' Beatrice added.

'Not a happy start to the month,' said Kitty, 'but,' she added, deliberately brightening her tone, 'we have something *very* happy to look forward to.' She smiled warmly at Lily, who smiled back.

'*Yes*,' said Abbie.

She was thrilled to bits at the prospect of having a baby in the house, which was very sweet to see.

'She's asked me if she can be the baby's big sister,' Lily told Kitty when it was just the two of them. 'She said that I'm her big sister and now she can be a big sister too.'

That struck a chord deep inside Kitty. She loved Abbie for making the connection between her own cherished relationship with Lily and her intentions towards the coming child.

She loved Abbie even more when, later, Abbie repeated to her the short conversation she'd had with Lily.

'Do you think it was all right for me to say that to Lily?' Abbie asked anxiously.

'Why wouldn't it be?' Kitty replied, puzzled.

'Because of Toby. Because the new baby will never know his or her real big brother, and there's me offering to be a big sister.'

Kitty hugged her. 'I'm sure it's absolutely fine. It's dreadfully sad about Toby, and always will be, but that doesn't mean it's wrong for the new baby to have other attachments, other people to love. If anything, it makes it more important.'

Abbie nodded, tears sparkling in her blue eyes.

'You're very important to Lily,' Kitty added, 'and it will mean the world to her that you want to be important to her baby.'

'I want to be as good a big sister to the baby,' Abbie declared, 'as Auntie Naomi has always been to you.'

That was the moment when Kitty knew she had to patch things up with her sister. They hadn't seen one another since the day they'd had words.

But before Kitty could go to see Naomi, her sister turned up at Dunbar's.

Ivy and Kitty were in the reception room, preparing it for a wedding reception on the following day, when the doorbell rang. Ivy went to answer it while Kitty continued laying the tablecloths and checking the lengths were the same on each side of the tables. It was a job she could have done in her sleep after so many successful receptions.

A movement in the doorway made her look round and there was Naomi, looking elegant and flustered at the same time. She hurried across and hugged Kitty.

'I can't stand it a moment longer,' she said, pressing her cheek against Kitty's. 'I had to come and make peace.'

As they stepped away from one another, a click announced that Ivy had closed the door to allow them some privacy.

Kitty drew Naomi to a table and sat her down before pulling a chair around so they could be close together. Naomi caught hold of Kitty's hand.

'I *hated* you for what you said to me, and even now I swear that before I leave, I'm going to bop Mrs Dunbar on the nose for what she said that started you questioning my actions.' Naomi drew a breath before she continued. 'But she was right. I have been... envious of you. I was so used to you being the young one who needed my support, my advice, because you'd married a man whose behaviour left a lot to be desired.'

'Being able to lean on you was a big help,' Kitty put in.

'Then Bill inherited Dunbar's and the two of you went up in the world, but before you could get your feet under the table, Bill was called up – and then the bailiffs came. What a shocker that was.'

'You were a brick,' said Kitty.

They looked at one another, sharing the memory. Kitty waited. She wanted Naomi to carry on speaking, but didn't want to prod her, though when Naomi stayed quiet, Kitty felt impelled to say something. If she didn't, that might spell the end of the conversation.

'After that, I had to have an income from somewhere, so I set up the storage business and turned it into a success, with Mr Tulip's help.'

Naomi bit her lip.

Kitty ploughed on. 'You've never cared for the storage business – or the wedding receptions – or the lodgers.'

'Oh, I never minded the lodgers,' Naomi answered breezily, 'not once I found out it was Mrs Dunbar doing all the work. I just didn't want you being overworked.'

'I'm sure you didn't,' Kitty said softly, 'but there was more to it than that, wasn't there?'

A flash of stubbornness crossed Naomi's face, replaced an instant later by contrition. 'I didn't like you having all that success.' In a rush she went on, 'I didn't want you to overdo it; I didn't want you to get your hopes up unwisely; I didn't want things to go badly for you... but I didn't want them to go well either.'

Even though it was what Kitty had thought, it still shocked her to hear it.

'I wanted you to carry on being the needy little sister,' said Naomi.

'Needy?' Kitty repeated. 'I never thought of myself as *needy*. No matter how bad things got with Bill, I never once thought that.'

'Didn't you? I did. And while I didn't want you to be hurt or upset, I also... well, truth be told, I also quite liked it. I liked being the older sister with the better life and the better husband.'

'Naomi,' Kitty whispered and then had to stop because she couldn't think what to say.

'You've no idea,' said Naomi. 'When you were born, Peter and I had no notion you were on the way. We didn't even twig that Mam was wearing bigger dresses. We just came home from school one day and there you were. When Mam said she was going to call you Catherine, I couldn't believe my luck. It was my favourite name, only I'd never told anyone, yet that was the name Mam chose. It was as if I'd named you myself.'

'I never knew that,' Kitty murmured, intrigued and touched. 'I remember you always had time to play with me.'

Naomi looked pleased. 'I loved you,' she said straightforwardly, 'and I loved the way you looked up to me, though it did annoy me that Mam and Dad made allowances for you in a way they never had for me. They were much stricter with me. But you – you seemed to have a charmed life.'

'Me?' Kitty asked, surprised.

'Yes, you. Mam was always on about what hard work Peter and I had been and how much she was enjoying you. Then, in the next breath, she'd say it was because she had me to help her.'

'That's only reasonable, isn't it?' said Kitty.

'I s'pose so, but it gave me the feeling that everything always landed in your lap. When I got engaged to Derek, we were both young and we had to wait and save up, like all couples do. But when you met Bill, he'd already done his saving because he was so much older, so, lo and behold, you could get wed right away *and* move straight into a nice little house. You got what other girls have to wait years for.'

'That was just how it was. I didn't plan it.'

'It was why – it was why I talked Derek into moving into a bigger place shortly before you got married.' Naomi huffed out a breath. 'There. I've said it. My little sister had a charmed life and I felt – well, I wasn't pleased.'

'Oh, Naomi.'

'Don't "Oh, Naomi" me,' Naomi replied briskly. 'Believe me when I say I've only ever wanted good things for you, but the good things seemed to happen to you so easily. They flocked in your direction.'

'I wouldn't call Bill's spending a good thing,' Kitty said wryly.

'God forgive me, I thought it served you right,' Naomi admitted, her cheeks flushing with shame. 'I'm sorry, Kitty, but you did ask if I'd been envious, and the truth is that I was. When everything went wrong here at Dunbar's, and the bailiffs descended, I was all set to support you through whatever tribulations followed... only they never did follow, because you were so quick off the mark setting up your storage business, and your wedding business, not to mention taking in lodgers.'

'Did you want me to *fail*?' Kitty whispered.

'Of course not. I just wanted you to... struggle.'

'I've done that all right,' said Kitty. 'Everything's been a struggle. It still is.'

'But you win through every time,' said Naomi. 'You've embraced the new wartime world and made a place for yourself. You've even looked to the future and decided to ditch your husband.'

'Naomi!' Kitty exclaimed.

'Well, you have,' Naomi replied with a touch of obstinacy. 'You've stopped being the put-upon little housewife with the extravagant fool of a husband, and you've... blossomed. That's the truth, Kitty. You've grown. You've adapted. You've *survived* – more than survived. You've flourished.'

'I can't tell whether you think that's good or bad,' said Kitty.

'It's good,' answered Naomi. 'It's better than good. It's marvellous. But it does leave me feeling as if I've been left behind, as if I'm... Well, it's the oldest who's meant to lead the way and set the example, and the younger ones are meant to follow and copy, but instead of that, you've forged ahead.'

'And that's put your nose out of joint?' Kitty asked gently.

'You've done nothing but put my nose out of joint since I don't know when,' Naomi said with exasperation but also with a trace of humour. 'You and your charmed life!'

'If I have a charmed life – which I don't, but if I did – do you know what the biggest charm in it would be?'

'No,' said Naomi. 'What?'

'You,' said Kitty, and leaned forward to kiss her cheek.

* * *

After what had happened with Toby, the doctor had made arrangements for Lily to give birth in hospital. She would far rather have had the baby at home in Dunbar's, because that would have felt normal and natural, but at the same time she understood why a hospital birth was necessary, not to mention the problems caused for home births when either the blackout or an air raid made the midwife late for the delivery.

The doctor decided that Lily must be in hospital for a whole week before her due date.

'Just in case Baby puts in an early appearance,' he said. 'This isn't your first, so the birth shouldn't take as long. We can't afford to be caught on the hop.'

This isn't your first. How matter-of-fact he made it sound, how clinical. Lily went cold inside, but she knew she had to shake off the feeling and concentrate on how this prolonged stay in hospital would be of benefit to her child... just in case.

Mind you, if she had spent her entire first pregnancy in hospital, it wouldn't have made a blind bit of difference to the tragic outcome.

'It's good to know your previous experience is being taken into account,' Kitty said encouragingly. 'Everyone wants your baby to have the best possible chance.'

Determined to do what she could to support Lily, Mrs Ford at the WVS arranged for the WVS hospital car service to take her.

'And there'll be a parcel of baby clothes for you to come home to when you return to Dunbar's,' she added.

Lily wasn't sure what to feel about that. What if the promise of the WVS parcel caused a jinx? It was no use telling herself not to be foolish. She couldn't help it.

And what was she meant to say in the maternity ward when the other mums-to-be asked, 'Is this your first?'

'If I say it's my second, I'll get asked how old the first is,' she told Kitty, 'and what am I meant to say to that?'

'You've always been very private about Toby,' Kitty replied

sympathetically, 'and I know what a difficult situation this is going to be for you, so let's decide what you're going to say. I know this will sound daft, but I think you should practise it on me.'

Lily felt overwhelmed. Most people would have shied away from such a hard subject, but Kitty had set her heart on helping her through it.

At last they settled on, 'This is my second. I lost my first.'

'Not so much short and sweet as short and blunt,' Kitty observed, 'but the main thing is it's *short*, which might make it that little bit easier for you to say. And you know what, Lily? I bet you don't have to say it more than once, because the woman you say it to is going to make sure everyone else knows so they don't put their foot in it.'

Lily felt shaky inside, which made her voice wobble. 'Do you think so?'

'I know so.' Kitty's voice rang with confidence. 'Think about it. In that situation, wouldn't you pass it on so as to save the bereaved mum's feelings?'

Lily nodded.

She was thinking a lot about Vivian Shawston these days. She couldn't help it. She didn't for one moment regret not having told him about the baby, but at the same time she felt a deep sorrow for what he was going to miss out on. He would have loved to be a father and he'd have made a good one. But if he'd known, if he'd *known* – oh my goodness, she'd never have heard the end of it. He'd have put her under enormous pressure to divorce Daniel and marry him. The pregnancy would have been a dream come true for him. He would have embraced it as the means by which to insist she married him, but she could never have done that, not loving Daniel as she did.

Ah yes, Daniel. That ship had well and truly sailed. There had been that fleeting moment of closeness they had shared at

Toby's graveside, but what Lily mainly remembered was the look on his face immediately afterwards when his gaze had dropped to her swollen stomach.

Recalling that, she felt more alone than she ever had in her life.

18

Beatrice sat in the Town Hall canteen, enjoying vegetable fritters with salad. Opposite her sat Fay Brewer. She had already eaten her meal, but she had seen Beatrice come in and had waved to her, inviting her to join her. Beatrice was flattered. She liked and admired the younger woman, as well as owing her a great debt that she would never forget as long as she lived.

Miss Brewer smoked and sipped a cup of tea while Beatrice ate, not feeling at all rushed.

'What do you make of the "holidays at home" advice?' Fay Brewer asked, tilting her head to blow smoke up into the air.

'It seems like a good idea,' said Beatrice. 'They need to give priority on the railways to troop trains and goods trains. The fewer ordinary passengers there are, the better.'

'And many of the traditional seaside holiday spots are out of bounds anyway,' Miss Brewer added, 'because their beaches are covered in barbed wire.'

'Abbie says her friend Martha's family are going away for a week,' said Beatrice.

'Where to?'

'I don't know.' Beatrice smiled. 'All I know is, they're taking the rabbits with them.'

They both laughed, but really it was quite a serious matter. Plenty of folk did this these days. It was preferable to coming home and finding that Bunny and Hoppety had vanished from the hutch in the back garden. Tame rabbits were an important source of meat.

'Anyway,' said Miss Brewer, 'this is shaping up to be a beautiful summer, and I'm sure all the towns and cities are doing everything they can to make it worth everyone's while to stay at home.'

'The military band concerts in Albert Square are a great treat,' Beatrice agreed.

'And sports are allowed in the parks on Sundays now,' Miss Brewer added. 'It all helps.'

'Especially for the boys,' said Beatrice, thinking of her Gentlemen's Club.

'People always think sports are more important to boys than girls,' Fay Brewer said.

Her tone was good-humoured, but Beatrice took her point. She held up her hands in pretend surrender. 'Of course. I was forgetting you have a twin brother. You of all people must be aware of the different expectations folk have for boys and girls.'

'Don't get me wrong,' Miss Brewer answered with a smile. 'Randall's a good sort and I wouldn't be without him, but I remember various occasions when we were growing up when he was automatically allowed to do something interesting or exciting that I had to clamour to be allowed to join in with.'

'That must have been frustrating,' Beatrice said. 'I used to wish I had brothers and sisters when I was a child. Mind you,' she added drily, 'if I'd been the oldest, I'd have ended up looking after them as well as my mother.'

'It's the way of the world,' said Miss Brewer. 'Sad but true.'

'Do you have any other brothers and sisters?' Beatrice asked, not wanting the conversation to move on to more serious grounds.

'A sister – half-sister, to be precise. She's older than we are. Her name is Hope.'

'I like that,' Beatrice said approvingly. 'A very appropriate name in wartime.'

Fay Brewer smiled. 'The hope we have these days is on far more solid ground than it was this time last year. You can see it in people's faces, no matter how tired they are.'

'It's good to see,' Beatrice agreed.

'How are things going with your Time Off Club children?' Miss Brewer asked. 'Still attending school regularly?'

'Yes, I'm pleased to say.'

'Roping in the WVS to help out with household tasks was a stroke of genius on your part,' Fay Brewer said, and Beatrice was delighted to catch a note of admiration in her tone.

'It solves the problem until the end of the war,' she replied. 'After that, we'll have to think again.'

The smile Fay Brewer gave her verged on being a grin. 'Plenty of time for you to come up with another wizard idea.'

'I hope so,' said Beatrice.

* * *

Beatrice was once more on her way to deliver a hot meal to old Mrs Cowell, a duty she very much enjoyed and which didn't feel like a duty at all. She felt sorry for the elderly woman for having to live in such severely reduced circumstances.

Usually, on her way to Mrs Cowell's, she had to walk past Greasy Lil's, but this evening she decided to go the longer way round and enter the grubby little street from the other end, specifically to avoid the chippy. Too many times now she had come across Joe Simpson and Tommy Abbott hanging about outside and, even though she couldn't put her finger on the real reason why, she would prefer not to have to walk past them, especially now that the days were longer and it would be too early for her to have the blackout to hide her.

She turned the corner into Mrs Cowell's road and, yes, there was a motley little group of lads loitering outside Greasy Lil's. It made her glad to have gone round the long way. Walking past those boys, not knowing whether to smile, whether to speak, would have made her feel self-conscious.

As she drew close to her destination, a ripple of movement in the group made her glance their way. A man had appeared – young, twenties, slim build. The boys clustered around him, which made him laugh. His words carried up the street.

'Steady on, kids. I've told you before. Keep 'em in your pockets until I'm ready. Now then, how many is it for a fish supper this evening?'

Outside Mrs Cowell's, Beatrice stilled for a moment, listening. She was sure she knew that voice – yes, she did. She'd heard him outside Greasy Lil's before, offering treats to the boys. As if he could feel her eyes on him, the young man turned and peered along the narrow road. Feeling caught out, Beatrice hastily knocked and let herself in. She felt better as soon as she was indoors.

'Evening, Mrs Cowell,' she said cheerfully. 'Kidney pie today. I'll have it ready for you in a minute.'

'By, it's a hot day to be given a plate of pie,' Mrs Cowell said.

'Not that I'm complaining, mind. I've never eaten so well in my life as I have since the WVS took me under their wing.'

'No, you never complain, do you?' said Beatrice. It was one of the things she liked about the old woman.

'Even though I have plenty to complain about, you mean?' Mrs Cowell asked with a shrewd look.

'Of course not,' Beatrice answered at once. 'Well, actually...' she added, wanting to be honest without giving offence.

'Well, actually, what?' Now the old woman's eyes were amused. 'You mean I could complain about living in a one-up one-down in a grotty little back street, with the stench from the glue factory when the wind's in the wrong direction?'

'Did you never have the chance to move elsewhere?' Beatrice asked, thinking that Mr Cowell could perhaps have made more of an effort for his wife and family.

'Are you suggesting that there's something wrong with this?' Mrs Cowell's voice was bland, but her eyes missed nothing.

Beatrice flushed. Had she really just asked a condescending question, as if she was Lady Bountiful? Quite apart from not wanting to sound patronising, she kicked herself for professional reasons too.

'You meet all sorts of people living in all sorts of circumstances,' Fay Brewer had warned her when she started with the Corporation. 'Don't sound judgemental.'

'Is that a Welfare Department rule?' Beatrice had asked.

'No, it's a Fay Brewer rule.'

'I'm sorry,' Beatrice said now to Mrs Cowell. 'I didn't mean to suggest—'

The old lady gave a cackle of laughter. 'Don't get yourself in a flap, Miss Inkerman. If you really want to upset me, stay here talking and let my pie get cold.'

Beatrice smiled, relieved, as she went into the scullery.

Soon Mrs Cowell was tucking into her kidney pie while Beatrice sat opposite.

'Any news of your young friend yet?' Mrs Cowell asked. Beatrice had told her about Lily going into hospital.

'Not yet,' said Beatrice. 'I'm going to visit her this afternoon.'

'Give her my best,' Mrs Cowell responded.

'Thank you,' said Beatrice. 'I will.'

But she knew she wouldn't. She had overstepped a line when she had told Mrs Cowell about Lily, even though she hadn't provided any details, such as the reason why Lily needed to be in hospital for such a long time. Nevertheless, she oughtn't really to have said anything, but it was sometimes difficult to remember that when in the company of someone she genuinely liked and felt comfortable with.

Mrs Cowell finished her meal and Beatrice took the dishes and cutlery into the scullery to wash up.

The front door opened and a man's voice said, 'All right, Nan?'

'Very,' Mrs Cowell replied. 'I've got the lady from the WVS here.'

It would be ridiculous to pretend she couldn't hear. Beatrice stuck her head round the door and saw the young man from outside Greasy Lil's.

'Oh,' she said and then hoped she wouldn't be asked why she sounded surprised.

'This is my grandson Denver,' said Mrs Cowell. 'Denver, this is Miss Inkerman, who kindly brings me my tea.'

Denver Cowell nodded. 'Miss Inkerman.'

'Good evening, Mr Cowell,' she replied.

'Evans.'

'Beg pardon?' said Beatrice.

'I'm Denver Evans, not Cowell.'

'Sorry,' said Beatrice.

'I've seen you before,' he said. 'A couple of the Greasy Lil's boys know you. You run a games club.'

'Yes, I do,' said Beatrice. 'I've seen you too. You treat the lads. It's very kind of you.'

Denver Evans shrugged. 'It's nothing. You hear that, Nan? I'm a – what's the word? – a philanthropist.'

'Well, I think you are, in a small way,' Beatrice said with a touch of stubbornness. Honestly, couldn't the man take a compliment?

'He's a good lad, my Denver.' Mrs Cowell smiled at him. 'I couldn't ask for a better grandson. Looks after me proper, he does.'

'I'm pleased to hear it,' said Beatrice. 'You deserve it.'

* * *

Just what she needed! The letter from Bill trembled in Kitty's fingers and her stomach executed a little flip as she huffed out a breath that was pure nerves. The last thing she wanted was a visit from Bill. Yes, she knew they had to discuss her intention to end their marriage once the war was over. Common sense demanded that she face up to the reality of that, but that didn't mean she had to welcome it. Talking it over with Bill was... well, frankly it was pointless, because she'd already made up her mind.

Nevertheless, he was entitled to a full explanation. She needed to persuade him to accept things the way she saw them. She needed him *not* to contest the divorce. No judge in his right mind would grant her divorce simply because she wanted to be independent and run her own life. A judge would probably think she'd lost her senses and needed a husband to keep her in line.

She reread Bill's letter. It was short and to the point. He'd posted it yesterday to let her know he'd be on his way today. Kitty glanced at the clock. If he'd been travelling all day, he could be here any minute now. She ought to stay in and not visit Lily. Ivy or Beatrice would be happy to do the evening visit in her stead.

But something inside her baulked at that. Why should she change her arrangements because of a last-minute letter? A happy wife would be only too glad to, but she wasn't one of those. If she stayed at home, would it give Bill the impression that he had a chance? She didn't want that. It wouldn't be fair to either of them.

What it boiled down to was the way that her nerves were jumping and her body had tensed. She didn't want Bill to walk in any minute now and expect her to be reasonable. She wasn't ready to see him. It might be cowardly – it *was* cowardly – but getting out of Dunbar's and visiting Lily would give her a bit of extra time to get used to the idea.

She sought out Abbie, who was engrossed in one of the film magazines she loved. She tore her gaze away from a photograph of Errol Flynn.

'I've had a letter from Daddy,' Kitty told her. It irked her sometimes that Bill was darling Daddy while she was plain old Mum, and all at once this became one of those times. She pinned on a smile. 'He's on his way home right now.'

'Is he coming to make you see sense about the divorce?' Abbie asked bluntly.

Kitty almost stepped backwards in surprise, but why should she be surprised? Abbie was no longer the eager little girl whose delight at the prospect of seeing Daddy would wipe out the possibility of thinking more deeply about what was going on. It stung Kitty, too, that Abbie still wanted her to 'see sense'.

'He's coming to talk to me, yes,' she said more sharply than she'd intended, 'and I don't appreciate being spoken to by you in that tone of voice.' She wanted nothing more than to give Abbie a hug and have a heart-to-heart with her, but this wasn't the moment. Would there ever be a moment? 'Will you stay here and look after your father? I have to go and see Lily.'

'Of course you do,' Abbie said in an undertone.

Kitty chose not to rise to the bait.

'Tell Daddy I'll see him later.'

19

When the bell rang and the maternity ward doors opened for visiting, Kitty walked in and saw at once that Lily's bed was empty. She hurried to the desk.

'Mrs Chadwick?' she asked.

'She went into labour this afternoon,' said the nurse. 'You might as well go home.'

Kitty left the ward, feeling excited and concerned and she didn't know what else. The next stage of Lily's life was about to start. It was both wonderful and scary. That poor baby not having a father – but there were so many children now whose fathers were gone for good. War was a terrible thing.

She asked for directions and made her way to the delivery room, although she suspected she could have found it anyway by following her nose. As she walked along the corridor, the smell of stale tobacco grew stronger, telling of anxious fathers waiting for news.

Kitty rounded the corner into an uninviting area with green-painted walls and a couple of wooden chairs – and there, pacing up and down and smoking his head off, was Daniel.

He looked startled to see her, then his shoulders slumped and he shook his head.

'Sorry,' he said. 'For one moment, I thought you were bringing news for me, which is utterly stupid because you've come from the wrong direction.'

They both glanced at the door to the delivery room, which remained resolutely closed.

Kitty struggled to find the best words.

'I… didn't know you'd been visiting Lily. She never said.'

'I haven't.' Daniel blew out a stream of smoke with such force that it almost hit the opposite wall. 'I've been – well, I've been keeping an eye on her from a distance. I rang the WVS office every few days to ask if Mrs Chadwick would be on duty tomorrow, and then one day I was told she wasn't due in for a while.'

'And you knew what that meant,' said Kitty.

He nodded. He walked up and down, then made himself stand still.

'I made myself known to the nurses on the maternity ward. I told them I'm Lily's husband but we're estranged, so please would they not tell her I'd been asking after her. I prevailed upon Matron to arrange for me to receive a telephone call once the baby was on the way.' He shrugged. 'They all assume I'm the father, so there was no problem about that.'

'And here you are,' said Kitty.

'Here I am.'

'Why?' Kitty asked gently.

Daniel turned anguished eyes on her. Was he on the verge of tears? Dragging his gaze away, he chucked the spent cigarette on the floor and ground it out beneath his heel, then immediately produced another and lit up again.

Kitty assumed he wasn't going to answer her question and vowed to press him no further. Poor chap. He looked like he'd been twice through the mangle and then hung out to dry in a howling gale, and who could blame him?

He blew out a couple of long breaths, but either he'd forgotten to put his cigarette to his lips or else he was trying a new way of battling with his nerves.

'Why am I here?' he asked almost brusquely. 'I'll tell you why. Because Lily's in *there*.'

He jabbed his cigarette in the direction of the closed door, then inhaled on it so urgently that a quarter of it turned to ash.

'You still care about her,' Kitty said, making sure not to put a question mark in her tone.

Daniel went dead still. 'Of course I do. How can I not? She means the world to me – *meant* the world to me, *meant*. I know I have to stop caring, but how exactly am I supposed to do that? Except that I have to, don't I?'

Before she realised what she was doing, Kitty reached out a hand to him. 'Daniel—'

The door opened and a nurse looked out. She was smiling.

'Mr Chadwick? Congratulations. Your wife has had a girl.'

Daniel stared.

Kitty said, 'Are they—?'

'They're both doing fine,' the nurse answered cheerfully. 'It'll be a little while before you can come in, Mr Chadwick.'

The door swung shut.

Kitty gazed compassionately at Daniel. It was a moment before he could meet her eyes. Even then, it was only for a second.

'Good.' He nodded distractedly. 'That's good. A girl – doing fine. That's good.' He ground out the cigarette and shook himself. 'Good,' he said again. 'I'll, um, I'll leave you to it.'

And he walked briskly away.

Kitty gawped. Then she ran to the corner, calling, 'Shall I tell Lily you were here?'

But there was no reply except for a door further along banging shut.

* * *

Evangeline Chadwick was completely accustomed to everything smelling of tobacco, but when Daniel arrived home, he smelled like he'd been rolling in it. She wrinkled her nose and waved her hand delicately in front of it.

'Honestly, darling, no one would imagine there's a cigarette shortage.'

'Lily had the baby this evening,' he replied.

Alarm skittered through her. 'You were *there*? At the *hospital*?'

He nodded. In mid-nod, his chin jerked sideways, turning his face from her.

Mrs Chadwick waited for him to speak. When he didn't, she said cautiously, 'And... is she...? Do you know what she...?'

'A girl,' he replied in a harsh voice. 'Mother and baby doing well, apparently.'

'I see,' she answered. She used a measured tone, but her thoughts were racing. 'Did you—?'

He cut her off immediately. 'See her? No, I didn't.' His tone said, *Not on your life.*

He walked up and down the drawing room. Mrs Chadwick sat still, watching, letting him pace, pondering when exactly to make her move.

Daniel swung round and faced her. 'It's real, isn't it? That sounds stupid. I knew it was real. I knew she was having this baby, of course I did. But now that it's here...' He seemed to struggle for breath. 'Well... it's real.'

Mrs Chadwick thought her heart would break at the sight of her son's pain. In the next instant, she was consumed by fury at Lily for bringing Daniel to this point. She gave no sign of either emotion.

In a calm, steady voice, she said, 'I'm so very sorry all this has happened to you, Daniel. I hope you can see that the time has come to put an end to it.'

He looked at her.

'Divorce,' she said, keeping her tone neutral even though a fire was raging inside her.

Daniel looked away and then brought his gaze back to her. His expression was impenetrable. At last, he sighed and shook his head.

'I suppose it's the only way,' he said.

* * *

Kitty arrived home from the hospital, thrilled and energised, but the moment the front door shut behind her, her spirits plummeted. Bill. Yes. The discussion. Damn and blast. Not tonight. Please, not tonight.

Abbie emerged from the reception room, wearing her dressing gown, with a book under her arm. She frowned at Kitty.

'Where have you *been*? You've been gone for *hours*.'

Kitty blinked. Abbie, who had been the sunniest little girl imaginable, sounded like a stroppy child.

'Lily has had her baby.'

The change was instantaneous. Abbie's lips parted on a gasp of delight and her blue eyes widened.

'What did she have?'

Kitty smiled. 'A girl.'

Abbie beamed. 'I wanted a girl. When can I see her? When are they coming home?'

If Kitty had entertained any lingering doubts about allowing Lily to remain here at Dunbar's in the presence of young, innocent Abbie, they vanished in that moment. Abbie's joy was worth any price.

'All in good time,' said Kitty. She didn't add that the hospital wanted to keep a close eye on the new baby after what had happened to Toby. 'Has your father arrived?'

'Arrived and gone again,' said Abbie.

'He's left?'

'Yes. When you didn't come home, and didn't come home, and didn't come home...'

Kitty longed to ask if he'd gone back down south to where he was stationed, but she couldn't possibly ask that. 'He's not staying here, then?'

'No,' Abbie replied. 'He said it wouldn't be appropriate, under the circumstances.'

There was a note of accusation in her voice, but Kitty was too surprised and grateful at Bill's thoughtfulness to let it bother her. She simply looked at her daughter. 'It's for the best,' she said softly.

'What is?' Abbie demanded. 'The divorce – or Daddy feeling he's not welcome in his own home?'

* * *

The next morning, Bill arrived at Dunbar's during breakfast. Abbie flew into his arms. He gave her a hug, then held her away from him.

'Let me look at you.' He sounded proud and indulgent. 'My

daughter, the office girl.' He shook his head wonderingly. 'Little Abbie, all grown up.'

'Oh, *Daddy*,' she groaned, but the sparkle in her eyes made it clear she loved being made a fuss of by him.

Kitty had to avert her gaze. She swallowed hard. How could she possibly break up this family?

After Abbie and Beatrice had set off for work, Ivy very deliberately and obviously left Bill and Kitty alone. They rolled their eyes at one another in an unexpected moment of closeness, though Kitty feared that might be as near as they would come to agreeing all day.

They went into the reception room. Kitty chose a medium-sized table. A large table would give the impression she didn't wish to be anywhere near him – which she didn't, but she couldn't afford to make it obvious. A small table, with its suggestion of confidences, was equally inappropriate.

'Where did you stay last night?' Kitty asked.

'Not on Lily Street,' Bill answered, 'so you needn't fret about the neighbours knowing our business. I don't want that any more than you do. If things go the way I intend, there's no reason for anyone to know.'

Kitty let that pass. 'How much leave do you have?'

Last time, he'd travelled up overnight, stayed long enough to floor Mr Tulip and cause ructions in Dunbar's, then had to go straight back.

'If you're asking if I've got to set off this afternoon,' said Bill, 'you can think again. I'm here until tomorrow morning.'

'I see,' said Kitty.

'So we've got plenty of time to sort things out,' said Bill. 'I have to say I wasn't best pleased to arrive here yesterday and find you'd gone out. You should have stayed at home. You weren't on WVS duty.'

'Lily had her baby.'

'Did you know that was going to happen before you set off?'

'No, but she was expecting me to visit.'

'You could have sent someone else,' said Bill.

It was time to fight back. 'I didn't want to give you the wrong impression.'

'Or,' Bill replied, 'you could have stayed here as a matter of simple courtesy. I am still your husband and that's how I'd like things to stay.'

'Bill—'

'Please, Kitty, hear me out. I've had letters from my mother assuring me that there isn't another man in the picture.'

Kitty pinched her lips together. Oh, the temptation to say bad words under her breath. Honestly! Hadn't Ivy learned anything about sticking her oar in?

'She says you've got this barmy idea that you want to work for yourself,' Bill went on.

'Was "barmy" the word she used?' Kitty asked coolly.

'No. Yes. No. I can't remember. Does it matter?'

'I s'pose not,' said Kitty.

'Can't you wipe that look off your face, Kitty?'

'What look?'

'As if this is all a great fag for you.'

'I don't look like that!' she exclaimed, immediately forming her features into a more relaxed expression.

'That's better,' Bill said approvingly. 'I want to be certain you're going to listen.'

She gave him a dazzling smile. 'Oh yes? The way you listened to me when I tried to tell you there was nothing going on between me and Mr Tulip?'

'Yes – well – you can't blame me for that,' Bill said at once. 'It's a lot easier to believe than that you want to strike out on your own. No judge will ever grant you a divorce for that. He's more likely to have you committed.'

'At this point,' Kitty said crisply, 'I'm more interested in your thoughts on the subject. I need you to accept that our marriage is at an end and that I have my own plans for the future.'

'You can forget your plans, Kitty, because I don't accept any such thing.'

She fought for composure. 'We have such different ideas about money.' To her dismay, there was a pleading note in her voice. 'I simply can't go back to living like that.'

'No one's asking you to, least of all me.' Bill leaned back in his chair, looking at ease and in control. 'I've thought about this long and hard. The main thing is that you haven't met another man and done the dirty on me.'

'How could you even entertain the idea?' Kitty asked scornfully.

'Because how can a wife end her marriage without having another man to take care of her? That's how I know we can still sort out our problems.'

'I can't live that way, always worrying about money.'

Bill leaned forward. He reached across the table and covered her hand with his. She was too late to withdraw.

'I know you can't,' he said. 'I've led you one heck of a dance all our married life. I know that and I'm sorry, more sorry than I can ever express.'

'Thank you for seeing it.'

'You don't have to wonder about the future, Kitty. I'm going to turn over a new leaf, starting now. No more spending, no more debts, no more buying you and Abbie lovely things on account. From now on, I'm going to be a model of financial responsibility. So you can forget your silly ideas about divorce and working for yourself. We both know you never meant it. You just wanted to pull me into line. Well – it worked.' His handsome face settled into lines of complacent amusement. 'Congratulations, Mrs Dunbar. From now on, I'll be the perfect husband. Your little ploy has got you what you wanted.'

* * *

In spite of Ivy's valiant attempts to be permitted to do Kitty's WVS duty for her, Kitty insisted on donning her uniform and hurrying off to do her shift. Bill accepted her departure with unexpectedly good grace, as if, following his promise to reform, he was willing to concede anything. His urbane amiability made Kitty even more uncomfortable and when she went down the front steps to the pavement, she felt like taking to her heels.

She didn't get home until gone six. Evidently, Bill had been over to Congreve's, where he used to work, as well as spending time with Ivy. Kitty imagined them plotting to keep her locked in the marriage. Then he had gone to the Town Hall to walk Abbie home. Beatrice had happened to leave the building at the same time and Bill had insisted on escorting her as well, Abbie on one arm, Beatrice on the other. Oh, he knew how to be charming. Kitty remembered it well from their courting days.

Kitty expected to spend a long evening in discussion with Bill, but instead he announced there was to be a Dunbar trip to the flicks while Beatrice went to the hospital to meet Lily's baby.

While it was a relief not to have another painful conversation, Kitty didn't feel she'd been let off the hook. The four of them going out together was bittersweet. Abbie's delight was both a joy and an ache to Kitty. Abbie was torn between pushing her parents together and wanting to walk in the middle between them, holding hands with both of them.

At the end of the evening, Bill walked them back to Dunbar's and kissed his mother and Abbie on the cheek. Kitty was all set to be disgruntled if he dropped a kiss on her mouth, but he kissed her cheek too before disappearing into the blackout.

Then, this morning, he had arrived during breakfast, complete with his kitbag, so he could walk Abbie to work.

No sooner had they left than Ivy hauled Kitty to one side.

'Mrs Dunbar, really, not now,' Kitty protested.

'It's summat that wants saying,' Ivy declared. 'It's to do with what I said to you before.'

'About getting swept away by everything that women are doing for the war effort,' said Kitty. 'I remember perfectly well, thanks. You don't need to rub it in.'

'No, it's something I *didn't* say that time,' Ivy pressed on, 'and I want to say it now. I've been wanting to say it for a while.'

'Go on, then,' said Kitty, thinking it best to get it over with.

'I don't want you to leave Bill,' said Ivy.

'You made that clear last time,' Kitty answered, 'what with the war going to my head an' all.'

Ivy frowned. 'I'm trying to say something nice here, Kitty. Stop fighting back.'

It was on the tip of Kitty's tongue to say, 'That's rich, coming from you,' but instead she clamped her lips together. The sooner Ivy had her say, the sooner this would be over and done with.

'I care about you,' Ivy announced. 'That's one of the reasons I want you to stay married to Bill. I know we haven't always seen eye to eye, and we both know whose fault *that* was, but these past two years since we got things straightened out, things have been better between us. Better!' she exclaimed as if it was a derogatory term. 'They could hardly have got worse, could they? What I mean is, I like you, Kitty. I admire you for what you've achieved. I respect you. You're a grafter and a jolly good mother, and that's the highest praise I could give anyone.'

'Goodness…' Kitty murmured, stunned.

'Aye, well, there you have it.' Ivy looked embarrassed. 'I'm not one to wear my heart on my sleeve, as you know, but I thought it needed saying. I don't want you thinking I'm all on Bill's side because I'm his mother. I care about you in your own right. I haven't always, but I do now. You've shown you're worth that kind of consideration, and I wouldn't want to lose you.'

20

Beatrice wasn't sorry to see the back of Bill. He was very gentlemanly and charming, and it was as plain as the nose on your face that he adored Abbie, but no amount of social grace could wipe away what she knew he had done. Beatrice was deeply loyal to Kitty, who had stood by her when others had turned their backs, and she knew how tough life had been for Kitty after Bill had refused to give her access to the Dunbar's bank account. Kitty had been forced to work harder than ever because of Bill.

'It can't have been easy for you to have him here,' Beatrice said quietly to Kitty the evening of the day Bill had returned to his barracks.

They were preparing the club room for a Time Off Club meeting and Beatrice wanted to make sure Kitty knew she'd been thinking of her. Kitty glanced at her wristwatch, then sat down on the window seat. She patted the space beside her and Beatrice joined her.

'I don't want to speak out of turn,' said Beatrice.

'You haven't,' Kitty assured her, 'and you're right. It wasn't easy, but it had to be done. He – he…' She leaned towards Beatrice and said softly, 'He says he'll stop being extravagant. He thinks that means I'll change my mind.'

'And will you?'

'No.' Kitty's voice was firm. 'His spending was what started things off, but there's so much more to it now. I want the chance to be independent, to use all the skills I've acquired. Plus, of course,' she added drily, 'there's the small question of whether Bill could actually keep his word.'

'Did you say all that to him?' Beatrice asked.

'No,' Kitty admitted. 'There wasn't the chance. We didn't spend all that much time together. Not that I'm using that as an excuse. If I'd disagreed with him, there would have been an enormous row, and I couldn't have faced that. Last time he came here, he was convinced I'd met another man, and this time he was convinced he can reform and therefore all will be well. It never occurred to him that it's too late. He can reform until he's blue in the face, but it won't make any difference to my intentions.'

'What are you going to do?'

'I'll leave it for a while, then I'll write and say I've thought things over and I've decided I still want the marriage to end.' Kitty shrugged. 'It's not entirely honest, but at least he'll think I've taken the time to consider it. So will Abbie – and so will Mrs Dunbar.'

'It's going to put a strain on you,' Beatrice observed.

Another shrug. 'That's how it has to be. I'm well aware that I'm the villain of the piece. The very least I can do is let the others believe I've weighed up every consideration instead of rushing in blindly.' She smiled wryly, her hazel eyes sombre. 'I've done nothing but weigh everything up for ages. I just need them to think I've weighed up Bill's new suggestion as well.'

'I hope there won't be the same stigma attached to divorce after the war,' said Beatrice.

'I shall be too busy working my socks off to notice,' said Kitty. 'Even if Bill says no to the divorce, it won't save our marriage. It won't make me stay. It's Abbie I worry about the most. All this has hit her hard.' She squeezed Beatrice's hand. 'She's going to need her Auntie Beatrice to help her get through it and come out the other side.'

'I'll do everything I can,' Beatrice promised, honoured to be asked. 'You know I will.'

'Yes, I do. You're a good friend and I know how much you care about Abbie,' said Kitty. 'She loves you too.'

The words made Beatrice feel weepy. It was a privilege to be an honorary auntie. Sometimes, when she looked at Abbie, she thought of her ex-fiancé Frank and his five youngsters and the life she could have had with them, but she'd had to turn down that chance because she simply hadn't wanted to be married to Frank.

'How complicated it all is,' she said. 'I don't just mean your situation. All three of us are in a pickle – you, me and Lily.'

'It's obvious what Lily's pickle is,' said Kitty, 'but what's yours?'

'I'm a silly old fool, that's what,' said Beatrice. 'After I sent Frank packing, I thought that was my last chance. I steeled myself to devote myself to my work.'

'I know your job is very important to you,' said Kitty.

'And then... well...'

Kitty nudged closer, putting her face close to Beatrice's. 'And then, well, what? Beatrice Inkerman, what have you been up to?'

'Nothing,' Beatrice answered immediately.

'Is there perhaps something you'd have liked to have been up to?' Kitty asked archly. 'There is, isn't there? Or rather than some*thing*, should I say some*one*?'

'Stop it,' Beatrice said. 'Nothing happened and nothing ever will. It was just me being daft, that's all.'

'Do you want to tell me?' Kitty asked gently.

After a moment, Beatrice jumped in. 'Sergeant Wakefield.' She looked anxiously at her friend. She dreaded being thought foolish even though she knew Kitty would never think any such thing.

And Kitty, bless her, rose to the occasion. 'He's a fine man. I was grateful to him when you were under suspicion of theft, because he was so steady and unflappable. He's a good man, Beatrice.'

'I got to know him a little when I had to deliver the policemen's supper.'

'That sounds promising.'

'But then I heard some of the younger coppers poking fun at me. "Anything in trousers". That's what they said.'

'They deserve to have their heads banged together,' Kitty said stoutly. 'Flaming cheek. Have you seen Sergeant Wakefield since?'

'No. If I'm on supper duty, I leave it at the front desk and make a run for it.'

'Oh, Beatrice.'

'Don't "oh, Beatrice" me.' Beatrice made a stab at sounding light-hearted. 'I'm just a silly, middle-aged spinster who's never grown out of girlish dreams of marriage.'

Kitty angled herself to face her. 'I'll tell you what you are. You're a loving, loyal, warm-hearted woman. You're a wonderful auntie to Abbie and you're the best friend I've ever had. Abbie always says Lily is her big sister. Well, you're my sister. I have two sisters – Naomi and you.'

'Oh…' breathed Beatrice.

'You work hard and you do everything you can to make other

people's lives better. You're reliable, honest and true. That all adds up to a special person, Beatrice, and I bless the day Abbie had that accident on the bomb site and you brought her home to me.'

'Oh my,' Beatrice whispered, overcome with gratitude.

'Do you remember how you agonised last year over Frank, and what you ought to do?' Kitty asked.

'You were so patient with me,' Beatrice murmured.

Kitty looked her in the eye. 'Am I going to have to be patient all over again with you and Sergeant Wakefield?'

* * *

Beatrice felt shivery inside when she thought of how she had come clean with Kitty about her interest in Sergeant Wakefield. Part of her was shocked at what she'd done, but she couldn't deny that in the main it was a good sort of shivery. She hadn't felt interested in a man since... well, since Frank the first time around, and that had been a very long time ago. Long enough that, if she and Frank had married and had children, she could be looking forward to being a grandmother by now.

'I see you've got the sarge's lady-friend's basket. Come sniffing around again, has she? Well, at her age, anything in trousers will do.'

Shame and dismay rippled through her, not for the first time. They were familiar feelings by now. Fancy being interested in a man – at her age! Honestly! There was something not quite respectable about it.

And yet, why wasn't it respectable? She was a spinster and he was a widower, and so what if they were in their middle years? Of course, she had no idea whatsoever if he entertained even the smallest interest in her, but if he did, *if* he did, and she was interested in him – why not?

She thought of all the things Kitty had said about her, all those wonderful, generous words she had used. Emotion made Beatrice's heart swell and tears touched the backs of her eyes. Kitty believed in her and had made her feel worthwhile. Kitty had said they were sisters, which was the greatest compliment Beatrice had ever received. Imagine being chosen as the honorary sister of the likes of Kitty Dunbar, who was strong and capable as well as loving and kind.

Kitty hadn't laughed at the idea of Beatrice and Sergeant Wakefield. Kitty hadn't been shocked. She hadn't expressed even the tiniest shred of scorn or derision.

And if Kitty Dunbar – intelligent, compassionate, gifted Kitty Dunbar – liked the idea, then why should Beatrice waste her time listening to the mean, insensitive barbs of a young oik of a policeman? All this time, she had let his malicious remarks dictate her behaviour. Well, not any more.

She would try to re-establish what she had sensed she and Sergeant Wakefield had had before, the beginnings of friendship. Maybe something more would come of it or maybe it wouldn't. Even if it didn't, Beatrice knew that in Sergeant Wakefield, she would find the very best sort of friend.

* * *

Beatrice was on late duty with the WVS. The weekly rosters had been pinned to the noticeboard several days ago and she knew what she was due to do. She was to be part of what was called the station team, making and handing out stacks of sandwiches, and topping up urns of tea and coffee, to feed the thousands of men who rolled through Manchester on the troop trains.

Before the team could leave for the stations, Mrs Ford called Beatrice over.

'Mrs Cottrell has had to cry off her duty because her son was rushed into hospital with a burst appendix.'

'I'm sorry to hear that,' said Beatrice.

'He's going to be fine, I'm pleased to say,' Mrs Ford replied. 'Could you please take over Mrs Cottrell's duties for her? She was supposed to be on the supper run.'

The supper run! Beatrice's heart delivered a little bump that could have meant pleasure or could have been panic. Of course, if she wasn't sure about seeing Sergeant Wakefield again, all she had to do was deliver to the police station first and then quickly move on to deliver to the fire and ARP stations. It was as simple as that.

Was that what she was going to do? Was she heck as like!

The suppers that evening included fish pasties, which was a good way of using leftover fish, salad sandwiches, and potato scones. Beatrice helped with the preparation, then with the wrapping. She carefully loaded her large wicker basket and set off.

She called at the ARP station first, then the fire station. At last it was time to go to the police station. Staffing the front desk was a rather old copper, who had evidently been brought out of retirement for the duration of the war.

'Evening, madam,' he greeted her. 'Is that our supper you've got there? A very welcome sight it is, too.'

Beatrice hefted the basket onto the desk. 'If you'd like to empty it in the kitchen and let me have it back, please?'

'Will do.'

'Is – er – is Sergeant Wakefield on duty, by any chance? If he is, I thought I might pop in and say how do.'

'Aye, he's in. Let me sort out the supper and then I'll take you along to his office.'

'No need.' Beatrice was astonished at how casual she could sound, positively breezy. 'I know the way. I'm only going to stick my head round the door. I'll see you back here in two shakes of a lamb's tail.'

'Fair enough.'

The old boy opened the door for her and trotted off in one direction with the basket while Beatrice took her courage in both hands and walked down the main corridor, her chin up. Outside Sergeant Wakefield's door, she paused to draw a soft breath before she knocked.

'Come in!'

His voice was deep and familiar and, even though Beatrice was filled with nerves and second thoughts, she couldn't help enjoying the sound. Smile at the ready, she opened the door.

'Oh!' she exclaimed, taken aback. 'You have a visitor. I'm sorry. The officer on the desk didn't say.'

'I came in via the back door,' the visitor replied. He was in his thirties, narrow-faced with a five o'clock shadow and dark eyes. He wore a tweed jacket and battered-looking trilby, but his shoes were polished to a high shine.

'I'll leave you to it,' said Beatrice.

Then she saw what the man had in his hand. It was a glass tube, approximately three inches long, with thin, flat metal discs inside it – the same as the piece of 'shrapnel' Joe Simpson had taken out of his pocket to show his pal, Tommy Abbott. Beatrice had known at the time that it wasn't really shrapnel and seeing it here, now, in Sergeant Wakefield's office made her even more certain.

'What's that?' she asked.

It vanished instantly into the man's pocket.

'Nothing to see,' said Sergeant Wakefield.

'I've seen one of those before,' said Beatrice. 'The person who had it told me it was shrapnel, but it isn't, is it?'

The stranger's eyes sharpened. 'Which person was this?'

Beatrice addressed herself to Sergeant Wakefield. 'It was one of my Gentlemen's Club boys.'

'When was this?' he asked.

'A little while back.' Beatrice tried to pin it down in her mind. 'Last month.'

'What is this Gentlemen's Club?' the stranger asked, so Beatrice explained and he nodded, looking thoughtful.

She was about to say something more, but she stopped. She didn't want to make a twit of herself. Something was clearly going on here and she didn't want to look as if she was pushing herself in.

Sergeant Wakefield caught her hesitation. 'Miss Inkerman, if you know anything at all...'

'I'm sure it's nothing,' she replied.

Beatrice explained about the change of atmosphere in the Gentlemen's Club meetings. 'It might not mean anything. I'm probably overreacting.' But she knew she wasn't.

'And it was one of these boys who had the so-called piece of shrapnel, was it?' The stranger looked at Beatrice as if he was ready to catch her out.

'Yes,' she confirmed, meeting his eyes squarely. 'And there's something else. Again, it doesn't sound like anything, but I'd better say it,' she added quickly before one of the men could say it wasn't her place to judge these matters. She described what she'd seen outside Greasy Lil's – how the boys hung around and how the man she now knew to be Denver Evans treated them to bags of chips or even fish suppers.

A look passed between the sergeant and the other man.

'What is it?' Beatrice asked.

Sergeant Wakefield started to speak, but the other man spoke over him.

'She doesn't need to know.'

'Who's "she"? The cat's mother?' Beatrice said, stung.

The stranger bowed his head politely. 'I apologise.'

'I think Miss Inkerman does need to know,' said Sergeant Wakefield. 'It's highly probable that she has just provided us with valuable information. If we let her in on this, she can keep her eyes open.' Now it was the sergeant's turn to speak over the other man when he tried to interrupt. 'Miss Inkerman has already managed to provide us with more of a lead than your contact in the factory has managed to do. I think that, without realising it, she has given us the information we have needed all along.'

The stranger held up his hands as if in surrender. 'You're right,' he admitted. 'She has. I think it's time for introductions.'

'With pleasure,' said the sergeant. 'Miss Inkerman, this reprobate is Mr Stoneley. Stoneley – Miss Inkerman.' Sergeant Wakefield looked at Beatrice, and was that admiration in his eyes? 'There is a serious problem with the theft of valves from a factory not far from here. These valves, as you have seen, are small enough to be smuggled out in a pocket. By giving us Denver Evans's name, Miss Inkerman, you have been of great assistance. I must ask you to keep your eyes peeled during your Gentlemen's Club evenings.'

'I will,' she promised, 'although after the way Joe hid away the valve I saw the first time, I imagine he'll be very careful from now on. Can I ask—?' Her heart dipped. 'Do you think Denver Evans is involved in the thefts?' She looked anxiously from one man to the other, but they gave nothing away. Beatrice dropped her head, whispering a soft, 'No,' under her breath as she pictured Mrs Cowell.

That dear lady. Poor Mrs Cowell.

21

When Beatrice and Abbie arrived home from the Town Hall shortly after one o'clock on Saturday, Kitty had a job to contain her smiles. Abbie was excited because she was going to the hospital for afternoon visiting, and Kitty, who had been to see Lily yesterday evening, knew what was going to happen, but not for the world would she spoil the surprise.

The three Dunbars and Beatrice chatted as they ate salad and cold ham with jacket potatoes, followed by date-and-apple layer pudding.

Soon it was time for Abbie to set off. She looked pretty in a linen dress of cream patterned with splodges of light green. Kitty had found it at the WVS clothing exchange and was thrilled to see how the bloused bodice, short puffed sleeves and gathered skirt suited her daughter, at the same time as feeling startled at how grown up her little girl looked.

Kitty knew that Abbie would stay for the whole of visiting time. In fact, they would probably have to bring in a couple of porters to eject her forcibly. She couldn't wait for Abbie to come home. The moment she heard the front door, she went hurrying to greet her.

Abbie walked straight into her arms.

'Oh, Mum, oh, Mum! You never said a word. Lily told me you knew, but you never said a word.'

Kitty hugged her. 'It wasn't my news to tell – though how I managed to keep it to myself, I don't know. It's lovely, isn't it? It's perfect. I'm so proud.'

Abbie extricated herself so she could brush aside a tear. 'I'm the proud one.'

Kitty took her into the reception room. 'Let's sit down and you can tell me all about it.'

'But you already know,' Abbie said with a laugh.

'Pretend I don't,' said Kitty, sitting down. 'I want to share your excitement.'

Abbie's blue eyes shone as she drew in a deep breath and blew it out again. 'Imagine having a baby named after me. It's not her first name, obviously, but it's one of her middle names. She's such a tiny little thing and she's going to have three first names.'

'I know,' said Kitty, delighted by Abbie's happiness.

'Daisy so she has a flower name like her mum, Jeanette after Lily's auntie who brought her up, and Abigail after me. Daisy Jeanette Abigail. Oh, Mum.'

Kitty smiled warmly. 'I told you that you mean a lot to Lily. This means she wants Daisy to mean a lot to *you*.'

'Oh, she will,' Abbie said at once. 'She does. She already does.'

* * *

Abbie's joy at Lily's baby being named after her did Kitty good.

She was thrilled for Abbie as well as deeply touched at knowing that Lily thought so much of her.

When Lily had shared the name with Kitty, she had said she'd chosen Daisy because it was 'a simple name and completely un-Chadwicky', which was what Lily had wanted.

On Saturday evening, Kitty went to see Lily and Daisy. She marvelled yet again at how tiny the baby was.

'You forget how small they are,' she observed, smiling at Lily.

'She's doing well, according to Sister,' Lily said with a touch of anxiety. 'She's to be allowed to go home soon.'

'That's wonderful,' said Kitty, hoping that Lily's worries wouldn't cloud her happiness. 'We're all eager to welcome little Daisy to Dunbar's.'

'You've been so good to me,' Lily whispered.

'And I'm about to be even better,' Kitty answered with a twinkle. 'The lodgers are due to move out shortly. I think that when they do, you and Daisy should have the family flat. I have to give Dunbar's back to Bill at the end of the war, but until then, the flat's yours.'

Lily stared. 'I couldn't.'

'Yes, you could,' Kitty replied firmly. 'It makes much more sense than squeezing a cot into that little room on the top floor.'

'But the flat has so much space,' Lily protested.

Kitty grinned. 'You'll probably have Abbie banging on the door, wanting to move in with you so she can be with Daisy.'

She expected Lily to laugh at that, but instead Lily looked over her shoulder towards the door. 'Auntie Nettie!' she exclaimed.

Kitty immediately stood up so Lily's auntie could sit down, but Auntie Nettie went straight to the crib at the foot of the bed and gazed down at baby Daisy.

'I'd better go,' Kitty said quietly.

Auntie Nettie stirred and looked round. 'Don't leave on my account, love.'

'Aren't you staying?' Lily asked.

'Me? Of course I am,' said Auntie Nettie. 'I just don't want to push Mrs Dunbar out, that's all. Eh, our Lily, she's a little sweetheart, isn't she? Just look at her. Can I – can I touch her?'

Lily nodded. Auntie Nettie leaned down and ran one gentle finger along the side of Daisy's face. Then she straightened and turned to Lily.

'That takes me back. She looks just like you.'

'Does she?' Lily looked surprised and pleased.

'Aye.' Auntie Nettie sighed. 'I remember touching your face just like that when you were new, except you were born at home, so you were in your mum's arms.' She glanced up and down the ward. 'Why mothers in hospital aren't allowed to cuddle their babies beats me.'

'Lily will be coming home to Dunbar's soon,' said Kitty, 'and then she can have all the cuddles she wants.'

Auntie Nettie didn't reply to that. She sat down on the empty chair. 'Have you chosen a name yet?'

'Daisy Jeanette Abigail.'

Auntie Nettie clapped a hand to her mouth. When she removed it, she said in a wobbly voice, 'You put Jeanette in.'

'Of course I did,' said Lily.

'And after I've given you such a rotten time,' her aunt replied emotionally.

'Even if you never spoke to me again,' said Lily, 'it wouldn't alter the fact that you and Uncle Irwin took me in and treated me as your own when I was most in need.'

'Oh, Lily.' Auntie Nettie hid her feelings behind a pretence of exasperation. 'What am I going to do with you?'

'If you don't mind me stepping in,' said Kitty, 'may I say something?' She lowered her voice to say discreetly, 'I know how worried and upset you are about Lily having an illegitimate baby. You're worried what the neighbours will say. You're agonising over what to tell your children. I understand, believe me, because I had all those feelings as well.'

'Did you?' Auntie Nettie sounded sceptical.

'Yes, I did,' Kitty replied, 'because I have a young daughter and the last thing I wanted was for her to be... tainted by anything untoward, but d'you know something? Out of everyone at Dunbar's, the person who is the happiest and the most excited about Daisy is my Abigail. And I'll tell you something else: I wouldn't have it any other way. Once your children have met Daisy, they'll feel exactly the same. As for what the neighbours think – well, frankly, stuff them. Who cares?'

* * *

The evening before Lily was due to come home with Daisy, Abbie asked to speak to Kitty. Kitty turned to her with a smile, assuming this was to do with Lily and the baby, but then she saw the serious look on Abbie's face.

They settled themselves in the reception room.

'Daddy wrote to me,' said Abbie. 'He says that when he came here, he was determined to save your marriage. He promised to stop spending willy-nilly.'

'He did say that, yes,' Kitty confirmed.

'But he says he's now heard from you, saying you still want the divorce.'

Kitty breathed in, then sighed it out, but she did it silently. She wanted to brace herself, not make Abbie think she was tired of this subject.

'Abbie, listen to me. Really listen. Daddy adores you, you know that, and so do I.'

'But not enough to stay married to Daddy.'

'It isn't that simple. Please try to understand that being your parents and being one another's spouses are two different things, two different relationships.'

'I don't think Daddy sees it that way,' Abbie replied.

Kitty tried again. 'Daddy and I have very different attitudes to money and it has always been a bone of contention. *Always*. It was because of Daddy's foolishness with money—'

'It wasn't foolishness!' cried Abbie. 'It was generosity. I wrote to him about it and he told me. He wanted the best for us.'

'It was because of his foolishness with money,' Kitty repeated determinedly, 'that the bailiffs came to Dunbar's. Do you remember what that was like, Abbie? Coming home from school to find the place virtually empty?' She hurried on, wanting it to be clear that she didn't expect or want Abbie to speak against her father. 'But it isn't just that. It isn't just the money, although that was what started it.'

Abbie looked disbelieving. 'What else is it, then?'

'Your grandmother would say it's the war. Women have had to take on so much and we've managed it amazingly well. I've set up two businesses and turned them both into success stories.' Leaning forward, she held Abbie's gaze as she dropped her voice almost to a whisper. 'And I've loved every single minute.' Sitting back, she laughed at herself. 'Well, maybe not *every* minute, but I've learned a lot about myself. I've learned that this is what I'm good at and it's what I want to do.'

'For the duration of the war, yes.' Abbie spoke in the tone of one making a great concession.

'Not just for the duration,' Kitty replied. 'I want to carry on after the war.'

'You could do that and still be married to Daddy.'

'No, I couldn't.'

'If you think he'll spend all your earnings—'

'I keep telling you, this isn't to do with the money, not any more. Now, it's to do with me and what I want to do with my life,' said Kitty. 'And what I want to do is work. Regardless of what your father does or doesn't do in the future in terms of spending, I can assure you that he wouldn't want me working outside the home.'

'He's the man,' said Abbie. 'It's his job to support us.'

Kitty sighed and this time she made no effort to hide it. 'Abbie, my lovely girl, ever since the outbreak of war I have wanted you to appreciate everything that women are capable of. I've wanted you to see all the different jobs women have taken on, jobs that were previously seen as being only for men. I've wanted you to understand how capable and flexible and determined women can be, and how downright *able*. I wanted to convince you of that – but I think I've ended up convincing myself.'

* * *

Kitty and Naomi sat at a table in one of the reception room's gracious bay windows, cups of tea and an ashtray between them.

'What have you done with the decorations?' Naomi asked, looking round at the bare walls.

'We're hosting a funeral tea later on,' Kitty told her.

'I hope that doesn't put too much pressure on you,' said Naomi, immediately adding, 'I'm not trying to put you off doing them. I just hope it doesn't upset you, that's all.'

Kitty smiled at her. 'It's an important service to provide and I'm proud to do it. It's a very special thing to be able to help people on the saddest of days.'

'And there are many of those at present,' Naomi said with a sigh.

'Have you heard from the boys recently?' Kitty asked.

They chatted for a while about Naomi's sons' most recent letters. None of them was a particularly good letter-writer, which made Kitty's heart ache for her sister.

'That's my children dealt with.' Naomi's off-hand tone failed to hide the depth of her emotion. 'Now let's talk about yours.'

'Abbie is... all right,' Kitty said with a touch of caution. 'She'll never be happy with my decision to seek a divorce, but I think that, if nothing else, she has at least started to understand why it matters to me. Sort of. I hope. Fingers crossed.'

'I know exactly how she feels,' said Naomi. 'I just hope you aren't making a terrible mistake.'

'Any husband is better than none, you mean?'

'Not exactly. Well – yes, exactly that. The world in general, and also the world of a woman, won't change miraculously just because of the war. It's all going to go back to normal afterwards.' Naomi reached out and covered Kitty's hand with her own for a moment. 'I don't want you to be at a disadvantage.'

'The way I see it, being married to a reckless spender like Bill is the disadvantage.'

Naomi sighed as she withdrew her hand. 'Damned if you do, damned if you don't.'

'Something like that,' Kitty answered gently. 'As long as I've got you on my side, I'll manage.'

'Yes, you will,' Naomi agreed. 'If there's one thing I've learned about you since the war started, it's that you're more than capable. And you think for yourself,' she added. 'I don't. I do what's expected.'

Kitty's heart softened. 'So might I, if I had a lovely husband like your Derek. That's all I ever wanted, a good husband and a happy family.'

'It's what we all want,' Naomi observed.

'And you got it,' Kitty said warmly. 'You're unbelievably lucky. I've always thought so. Me, well, I got the family part. I've got the most gorgeous daughter in the whole world. It's just my husband who leaves something to be desired. Quite a lot, actually.'

'I know you did your best to make your marriage a success,' Naomi told her. 'I watched you do your best ever since you got engaged.'

'Don't exaggerate,' said Kitty.

'It's true,' Naomi replied. 'Don't you remember how he showered you with gifts when you were engaged? And you kept telling Mam and me that it would stop once you get married.'

'I thought it would.'

'The point is, I remember how uncomfortable you were,' said Naomi. 'I didn't have a crystal ball, Kitty, and I didn't know the spending was never going to stop, but I do remember it made you uncomfortable – and there was a part of me that was glad at the time, because Derek had never showered me with presents. He'd never had the money. We were too busy saving. We're the same age and we knew from the beginning that we were in for a long courtship while we put something behind us. I assumed it would be the same for you when your turn came, and I was all set to help you out with some bits and pieces for your bottom drawer, but it wasn't like that for you, was it?' There was mockery in Naomi's tone, but it was aimed at herself, not at Kitty. 'You got yourself a bloke ten or more years older, an established man with a good job and savings. Nothing was ever going to be hard for you. That's what I thought. *Trust Mam's little golden girl to land on her feet.* That's what I thought.' She took a last puff on her cigarette and ground it out in the ashtray. 'And d'you know what, Kitty? I'd give anything now for you to have the easy life I thought you were going to have, for you to have had the devoted, sensible, worthwhile husband you thought you were getting.'

'So would I,' Kitty murmured.

'I hate to think of my little sister getting divorced,' said Naomi. 'There's going to be shame attached to it – and not just for you. There's going to be gossip too. But shall I tell you what's worse? My little sister *needing* to get divorced, that's what.'

* * *

Baby Daisy was kept in hospital under observation until the end of the month. Lily was sent home sooner than that and she practically had to beg on bended knees to be granted extended visiting hours.

Before Daisy was due to come home, the lodgers, Miss Kildare and Miss Egan, moved out. Kitty, Beatrice, Abbie and Mrs Ivy Dunbar gave the family flat what Auntie Nettie would have called 'a good bottoming'.

'Not that the lodgers left the place in a state,' said Mrs Ivy Dunbar, 'but you can't be too careful when there's a new baby in the picture.'

Lily wasn't allowed to lift a finger.

When the flat was ready, she wandered from room to room, admiring everything and feeling overwhelmed.

'Are you sure you don't mind?' she asked Mrs Ivy Dunbar. 'After all, most of this furniture is yours. It should be you moving in here.'

'Don't talk tripe,' was the blunt reply, and that was that.

The others brought Lily's possessions down from her room

on the third floor. Lily went upstairs and stood in her old bedroom, looking round.

'Don't tell me you're getting nostalgic over this little room when we've just moved you into the flat,' Kitty said with an indulgent smile.

'I was remembering coming in here on my very first day working for Dunbar's,' said Lily. 'If I'd known then I was going to end up in the family flat...'

'None of us has any idea what lies ahead,' said Kitty, 'which is probably a good thing.'

'You won't know yourself,' Abbie teased Lily. 'You'll be too posh to come down to the kitchen with the rest of us.'

'I'll *never* stop doing that,' Lily declared seriously, which made the others laugh. 'And I hope we'll all spend some evenings together in the flat.'

'Try and keep us away,' said Beatrice. 'We'll be knocking on the door so we can be with Daisy.'

An excited tingling started in Lily's chest and spread outwards all through her body. Tomorrow she would bring her beautiful daughter home. She couldn't wait.

'I think we should christen the flat by spending the evening together in it,' said Lily.

'Perfect,' said Kitty. 'I'll nip downstairs and make up a tray.'

'I'll help,' said Abbie.

Mother and daughter disappeared.

'Aren't you going to invite us to sit down?' Mrs Ivy Dunbar asked Lily.

Laughter bubbled up inside Lily. 'You don't have to wait to be invited. You know that.'

She, Beatrice and Mrs Ivy Dunbar settled themselves. Lily sat in the armchair beside a low table on which was a drawer with blankets in it. This was to be Daisy's daytime cot. There was another such arrangement in the bedroom Lily had chosen.

The door opened and Kitty came in, looking serious.

'Lily, Daniel's here,' she said. 'He's waiting in the foyer. Do you want to see him? I can send him away, if you want.'

The happy fluttering Lily had been feeling changed to a different sort. She didn't want to see Daniel. Yes, she did. No, she didn't. Then she remembered how Kitty had described him waiting outside the delivery room, wanting her and her baby to be safe. She ought to see him. Better now than tomorrow when Daisy was here.

She nodded to Kitty. 'Send him up.' Immediately she added, 'Or should I come down?'

'Let him come up here.' Kitty was gentle but firm. 'You'll feel much more private.'

Lily nodded again. Back when she had returned to Dunbar's following Toby's death, and Daniel had come home from sea, Kitty had let them meet in here. There was something scary but inevitable about it happening again.

Beatrice and Mrs Ivy Dunbar got up to leave. Lily felt a hand on her shoulder. She glanced up, expecting to see Beatrice, but it was Mrs Ivy Dunbar who was offering the gesture of support. Mrs Ivy Dunbar! She had been furious and disgusted with Lily for carrying on with Dr Shawston, but her relationship with Lily had come a long way since then.

Left on her own, Lily rose to her feet. Somehow her fingers had got tangled together and she had to drag them apart.

The others didn't close the door properly, just pulled it to. It moved as Daniel gave it a gentle knock.

'Come in,' said Lily.

Such simple words, yet they summed up everything about the

separation. In happier times, there would have been no need to knock. Daniel would have walked right in. Happier times? That made it sound like they'd been married for years and their problems were recent. The truth was, they'd had problems all along, not just because of losing Toby, but also because of Daniel's mother and Lily's feelings of inadequacy.

Daniel walked in, his handsome face marred by – what? Worry? Anger? She couldn't blame him if he was angry with her. Even as she thought it, she knew he wouldn't come here to pick a fight. He would never treat her like that, no matter what.

Lily bit her lip and blinked back the threat of tears. With a slight movement of her hand, she offered him a seat. Ever the gentleman, he waited for her to sit down first.

'How are you?' he asked.

'Fine, thank you.'

'You're looking well. Actually, you're glowing.' After a pause, he asked, 'How is the baby?'

'Doing well.' On the verge of burbling happily all about her darling daughter, she reined herself in. Daniel didn't want to hear about that. 'She's coming home soon.' For some reason, she couldn't bring herself to say it was tomorrow. She couldn't do that to him.

'Good.' Daniel nodded. 'Good. I'm happy for you, Lily – truly.'

'Thank you,' she whispered. 'Her name is Daisy.'

'That's pretty.'

'I like it,' said Lily.

'Have you... have you registered the birth?'

She knew what he was asking. 'I gave her my maiden name.'

'Not the father's surname?'

'He is unaware of her existence and that's how it will stay. Even if I'd wanted to give her his name, I couldn't without his written consent since we're not married.' Lily lifted her chin.

'When I didn't provide a father's name, the registrar wrote *Father unknown* on the birth certificate.' A shudder passed through her. 'It makes it look like I had dozens of boyfriends in tow.'

Silence. Daniel patted his pockets, a familiar gesture. He wanted a cigarette. But instead he sat forward, rested his elbows on his knees and clasped his hands lightly. Lily couldn't take her eyes off them. She thought of her own fingers being tangled and the effort it had taken to pull them apart.

Finally, Daniel spoke.

'I've got something to tell you.'

Chill washed through her. 'What is it?'

'There's no easy way to say it, so I'll come straight out with it.'

Another silence, longer this time. Daniel's brows drew together. He didn't meet her eyes.

'This is you coming straight out with it, is it?' Lily aimed for a light note, but inside she was shaking.

'I'm sorry, Lily. It's time for us to separate properly.'

'Properly? You mean—?'

'Divorce. Yes.'

She was stunned. Yet why should she be? She'd known ever since she had decided to keep her baby that this was inevitable. She ought to be glad of it. Grateful to get it out of the way.

'Divorce,' she said. 'Well – yes.' Unable to stop herself, she added in a tight voice, 'I imagine your mother is pleased.'

Daniel gave her a sharp look. 'You want to know if it was her idea. She was the first to speak of it, yes, but I'd been thinking of it, and trying not to think of it, and knowing I had to face up to it.'

Sadness dragged at Lily's heart, making time slow down. She had thought so much about her future, but now it loomed in front of her – no, not just in front of her, but all around her – in a vast, impenetrable blur.

'You must know that I have the grounds to divorce you,'

Daniel said steadily, 'but I want to assure you that I would never pursue that course of action. We'll get this sorted out the traditional way. My solicitor will arrange for someone to witness my arrival at a hotel with a woman. After that, it will be straightforward for you to bring an action against me. Is that acceptable to you, Lily?'

22

Towards the end of the working day, the telephone rang in the Welfare Department office. There were two telephones, an external one and an internal one, known as the house-telephone, for calls from other parts of the building. It was the house-phone that rang now.

Miss Summers, a shingle-haired blonde with a dainty overbite, picked up the receiver. Moments later, she waved it in the air as she addressed Beatrice.

'It's for you, Miss Inkerman.'

'Thanks.'

Beatrice got up and went to the table where the telephone stood. Miss Summers handed her the receiver.

'Good afternoon. This is Miss Inkerman speaking.'

The call was from one of the ladies on the reception desk downstairs in the foyer.

'You have a visitor, a Sergeant Wakefield.'

'Oh!' Beatrice exclaimed. Aware of eyes turning in her direction, she said in a steadier tone, 'Thank you. I'll be down in two minutes.'

What could Sergeant Wakefield be doing here? She went downstairs, deliberately not hurrying because she didn't want to arrive in the foyer looking flustered. As she came down the final stairs, she saw the sergeant and acknowledged to herself what an impressive figure he cut, broad-shouldered in his smart uniform, with his square jaw and dark eyebrows. But no matter how good-looking he was, what she appreciated more was what she knew of his character: his sense of fair play, his thoughtfulness, his good manners, the insightful remarks that suggested a shrewd mind, the warmth in his eyes that showed a true heart.

He turned just then and smiled at her before she could glance away and pretend not to have been looking.

'Miss Inkerman,' he said, meeting her at the foot of the staircase. 'I'm sorry to drag you away from your desk. Might I have a word, please? It's important. Could we...?' He looked across at an out-of-the-way corner.

'Of course,' said Beatrice. It was impossible not to feel intrigued – or ought she to feel alarmed?

Once they were well away from other people, Sergeant Wakefield said, 'The information you provided about the so-called shrapnel – actually the type 6J6 valve – helped get us on the right track.'

Beatrice felt her skin glow with pleasure. Yes, all right, it was probably a thoroughly unbecoming blush, but it felt like a glow.

'I'm pleased to hear it,' she said.

'I need your help now,' said the sergeant. 'Could you possibly come with me? I mean, right now. I've got a couple of your Gentlemen's Club boys at the station.'

'*No!*' Beatrice exclaimed. 'I don't mean, no, I won't come,' she added quickly. 'I'm just horrified to know you've apprehended a couple of my boys.'

'I'd like your help talking to them.'

'I don't know,' Beatrice started to say.

'It's Joseph Simpson and Thomas Abbott,' Sergeant Wakefield replied. 'I believe you've known them all their lives. You used to live in their road. I think – I hope – they might be more forthcoming in your presence. Mrs Dunbar told me all the Gentlemen's Club boys hold you in high regard.'

Beatrice almost snorted. 'I'm not sure those two do any more.'

'Please,' Sergeant Wake said in a serious voice.

'Very well,' Beatrice agreed, 'if you think I can help – although I don't see how I can.' Even as she said it, she knew she wanted to try. 'I must let the Welfare Department know I'm going out.'

She hurried back upstairs to make her excuses, collect her handbag and gas-mask box, and put on her outdoor things. Soon she was back in the foyer with Sergeant Wakefield.

'Thank you for doing this,' he said, letting her precede him through the front doors.

Soon they were in the police station. Mr Stoneley was in Sergeant Wakefield's office. He stood up to shake hands with Beatrice, then all three of them sat down.

'The lads are in different rooms so they can't confer with one another,' said Sergeant Wakefield, 'but so far they're both playing dumb. That's why we need you here, Miss Inkerman.'

'Heavens,' Beatrice murmured. Did they imagine she could somehow break through the boys' defences? 'Tell me what the situation is. I need to know that, if I'm to be of any use whatsoever.'

It was Mr Stoneley who answered.

'We've tried all kinds to find out who's been pinching these valves from the factory and how they're getting them out, and we've had no luck. We've done random searches on the men as they leave. We've even had shifts where we've had the entire factory workforce line up to be searched before they're allowed to go home. *That* was popular, I can tell you.'

'I can imagine,' said Beatrice.

'But somehow the dashed things are still being stolen. Once you told us of your suspicions regarding the boys hanging about outside Greasy Lil's, we changed tactics. Instead of trying to find the perpetrator as he left the factory, we watched the boys instead.'

'What happened?' Beatrice asked.

'Each time a batch of valves went astray from the factory,' said Mr Stoneley, 'that same evening, the boys congregated outside Greasy Lil's.'

'That could be coincidence,' Beatrice suggested. She didn't really believe it, but the alternative was hard to stomach.

'That's why we need you here today,' said Sergeant Wakefield. 'We want to talk to Joseph Simpson and Thomas Abbott with you here.'

Beatrice started to say, 'If they won't cooperate with you—'

'Your presence might rattle them,' said Sergeant Wakefield, 'and that could be what we need.'

He exchanged a glance with Mr Stoneley, who took up a position near the wall and stood there with his arms folded. Then the sergeant opened his office door and spoke to someone outside.

'Fetch 'em in here.'

He shut the door sharply and returned to his seat behind the desk, taking a moment to give Beatrice an encouraging look that she deeply appreciated. No one spoke as they waited for the boys to be brought in.

When there was a knock on the door, Beatrice expected Sergeant Wakefield to call, 'Come in!' at once, but he didn't. He sat back in his seat, elbows on the arms, and steepled his fingers, resting his chin on his joined forefingers. After some moments, he dropped this pose and sat up straight.

At last he rapped out, 'Come!' in an angry voice.

Behind Beatrice, the door opened and there were footsteps, then silence apart from the sound of breathing.

Sergeant Wakefield looked past her. 'Cat still got their tongues?'

'Aye, Sarge,' said a copper.

And all of a sudden, Beatrice knew exactly what to do. Slowly, she turned in her seat. Joe and Tommy stood behind her, both looking sullen and defiant, but that was an act. She could see they were scared. And when they saw who she was, they looked confused too.

She stood and faced them. Taking a leaf out of Sergeant Wakefield's book, she made them wait. She looked each one of them up and down.

'Well,' she said in the coldest voice she could, 'I suppose I shouldn't be surprised. You were among the boys who used to sing the Inky Stinky Inkerman song. You thought yourselves so clever, didn't you? You made my life a misery. Were you aware of that? Of course you were. You took pleasure in it. Nevertheless, I gave you a second chance. I permitted you to join my Gentlemen's Club. I gave you the opportunity to learn good manners and correct behaviour. I believed I was doing you a good turn – but look at you now. Grubby little guttersnipes refusing to assist the police. Grubby *unpatriotic* guttersnipes. You disgust me.'

'Unpatriotic?' squeaked Joe.

'Shut it, Joe!' hissed Tommy.

'Yes – shut it, Joe,' Beatrice repeated immediately. 'Do as Tommy tells you. Did he get you into this? Is he the one who got you to help Herr Hitler? There's a word for people like that, people like you two boys. *Traitors.* That's what you are.'

'We aren't!' Tommy exclaimed.

'We hate Adolf,' Joe added.

'You've got a funny way of showing it, that's all I can say,' Beatrice replied dismissively. Without removing her gaze from the lads, she tilted her chin to address Sergeant Wakefield. 'I'd throw them straight in the cells, if I were you, Sergeant. It's all they're fit for.'

'Sounds good to me.' Sergeant Wakefield's voice was deep with disapproval.

Beatrice pinned down the boys with a scornful stare, just like she had seen Mrs Ivy Dunbar do. They probably thought she was going to raise the roof, but all she did was whisper, 'Traitors.'

'But we're *not*!' cried Joe. 'Honest, miss, we're not. We'd *never...*'

'You already have,' Beatrice informed him. 'You've aided and abetted a thief. That's the correct term, I believe.'

'Do you know what they make in that factory?' Mr Stoneley interjected. 'Components for radios, that's what – military radios. Our men at the front can't manage without them.'

Joe began, 'The parts we—'

'—steal—' put in Sergeant Wakefield.

'—help with,' Joe said desperately, 'aren't good for anything.'

'Shurrup, Joe!' Tommy insisted in an undertone, as if by lowering his voice he could somehow prevent the adults from hearing.

But nothing was going to stop Joe Simpson now. 'They're faulty. They're broken. They can't be used. They're meant to go for salvage, but...' His voice faded away.

'But you help them find their way somewhere else,' said Sergeant Wakefield.

Mr Stoneley took a step forward. In a clipped voice, he demanded, 'What if I told you they *aren't* faulty?'

'But they are,' said Tommy.

Mr Stoneley turned the edges of his mouth downwards as he shook his head. 'Is that what they told you? And you fell for it?'

'They *are* faulty!' Joe's voice rose. 'We're not doing anybody any harm. The things – the parts—'

'Valves,' put in Mr Stoneley.

'The valves,' said Joe. 'They're only no good for the army. They're not up to standard. But they can be fixed up to mend wireless sets that are on the blink in people's houses. That's all we're doing – isn't it, Tommy? Providing valves to mend wireless sets.'

Another step forward and Mr Stoneley was towering over the boys. 'That's the biggest load of tripe I've ever heard. Pull the other one, son. It's got bells on.'

'It's *true*!' Joe wailed.

'It is,' Tommy confirmed.

'Now listen to me, the pair of you,' Mr Stoneley said in a commanding voice. 'If a valve isn't up to scratch, it can't be fixed, full stop. There's no such thing as one standard for the military and another for domestic use. You've been had, boys. Somebody fed you a load of lies and you believed them – and all for a few bags of chips, from what I've heard.'

The boys hung their heads.

'Look at Mr Stoneley when he's speaking to you,' said Beatrice.

'Not only that,' Mr Stoneley continued, 'but the so-called broken valves aren't broken at all.'

Joe's mouth dropped open in shock. The look on Tommy's face said that he was doing his best not to believe what he was hearing, but he was fighting a losing battle.

'See, we have a test-rig at the factory.' Now Mr Stoneley's tone was almost conversational. 'Basically, what you do is plug the valve into the test-rig and wait for it to warm up. If it gets an orange glow inside, that means it's passed the test and it's working. If it doesn't, it's not working and it's failed. Simple as that. According to you, the valves we took off you earlier shouldn't have shown an orange glow – but they did. That proves they're in good working order. They passed the test.'

A deep silence filled the room. Joe Simpson looked stricken. The last of Tommy's defiance drained away.

Beatrice judged it was time to use a kind voice, sure now that it would provide the boys with a life-raft to cling to.

'It's time to tell Sergeant Wakefield and Mr Stoneley the truth, boys. Answer their questions and don't leave anything out. Remember, first and foremost you are members of the Gentlemen's Club, and that means you always do the decent thing.'

23

It was early evening. Lily was in the family flat, just her and Daisy. Abbie had been here earlier, after she had come home from work. She couldn't get enough cuddles, which was lovely to see. It filled Lily with gratitude that she hadn't been spirited off to Maskell House. Being at Dunbar's with baby Daisy might have brought its own set of complications, but it had brought joy too. Joy and security and continuity.

Beatrice hadn't come home for the evening meal. She had telephoned to say she would be late, but that wasn't a problem as the meal was corned beef with mustard sauce, and a salad.

'Although her jacket potato might well be a cannonball by the time she gets home,' Mrs Ivy Dunbar had declared, 'but she can have bread and scrape if that happens.'

Lily sat in the armchair, with Daisy's cot beside her. The cot might be makeshift, but in Lily's eyes it couldn't have been more special, because of the precious little life slumbering inside it. On the other side of the armchair was a green-baize covered card table, on which was a pile of mending. Lily had volunteered to do minor repairs on items that had been donated to the WVS clothing exchange.

'Otherwise I'll just daydream my days away gazing at Daisy,' she had told Kitty.

'No one would blame you if you did,' had been Kitty's reply, full of understanding.

Lily liked being busy. In Uncle Irwin's house, Auntie Nettie brought up her girls to make themselves useful. Before that, Lily's mum had been the same. Lily smiled to herself. She'd bring up her little Daisy in the same way – but that was ages off yet, and she didn't want to wish away a single day.

Also on the card table were a few reels of cotton, a pin cushion, a scrap of fabric with a couple of needles inserted into it, and a small pair of scissors; plus a saucer that was doing duty as an ashtray, along with a cup of tea Lily was just finishing.

With a satisfied sigh, she wrenched her gaze away from her slumbering baby and plucked the next piece of clothing from the pile. It was a herringbone wool coat with wide revers and an oversized collar, and would easily fall to mid-calf – *very* 1930s, but of the best quality. You could always tell.

On one place on the inside of the hem, the lining had come adrift from the main fabric. It would only take a jiffy to put it right. Lily picked up the scissors and was about to snip off a length of thread when there was a knock at the door.

'Come on in,' she called cheerfully. She'd made it clear she would be happy for the others to walk right in, but they seemed determined to respect her privacy.

The door opened softly and Kitty came in – well, not right in. She stopped just inside.

'Daniel's here again.'

Lily caught her breath. 'He *can't* have. Not already.'

'Can't have what?' Kitty asked.

'Provided the pretend evidence for the divorce.' But he could have, and Lily knew it. 'You'd better send him up.'

Kitty's hazel eyes were sympathetic as she nodded. She withdrew, pulling the door shut behind her.

Dropping the scissors in her lap, Lily twiddled her fingers over the card table to free herself from the cotton that seemed determined to remain attached to her. Should she remain seated? No, not with Daisy sleeping on one side and a pile of mending on the other. This wasn't the moment to look like the picture of domestic bliss.

She scrambled to her feet and the scissors fell to the floor. She bent to retrieve them just as Daniel knocked. She was about to say, 'Come in,' but how would it look if he walked in and there she was, facing him? Would it look confrontational? Stuffing the scissors in her pocket, she almost leaped for the door and opened it, hardly daring to look at Daniel. She knew how handsome he was; she didn't need reminding.

She ought to invite him in, only her throat felt all clogged. A wave of her arm did the job for her. Daniel walked in, holding his hat. Lily's heart pounded in her ears as she shut the door and turned away from it to find Daniel looking at her.

'What brings you here?' she asked – and, 'I'm sorry to barge in,' he said at the same time.

They broke off at the same time too, and stared at one another.

'You don't need to say it,' Lily stated crisply. 'I know why you've come.'

'You do?'

'Yes – so you don't have to stay. You can leave again straight away.' She glanced at the door, wondering why she had bothered to close it.

Daniel didn't speak, not until she'd returned her gaze to him. 'You're chucking me out?' he asked gently.

'No. I'm just saying you didn't need to come all this way just to tell me you've done the necessary and I can start divorce proceedings—'

'Is that what you think? That's not why I'm here.'

Lily's mind stumbled over the unexpected words. 'Then – why?'

'I haven't done anything about the divorce yet. I think it's something I'll have to build up to. Sorry if that makes me sound spineless, but, well, there it is.'

'You haven't been to a hotel yet?' Lily asked, still not quite letting herself believe it.

'Not yet.'

'Then why are you here?'

Daniel's jaw moved as if he couldn't force the words out. Then he brushed a hand across his face – was he dashing aside a *tear*? Without meaning to, Lily took a step closer.

'I just wanted to...' Daniel's voice was husky. There was a silence, then he cleared his throat. 'I just wanted to see you with the baby. I never saw you with Toby. I've never seen you with a baby in your arms. I know it's mad. My mother would *kill* me if she knew, but...' A shrug, a shake of the head. 'I imagined it so many times before Toby was born.'

Lily stood perfectly still. For a moment, her chest caved in, but then she stood up straight. She went softly to the drawer, where she paused to look at Daniel and hold his gaze before she reached down and picked up her daughter, murmuring to her as she stirred and settled again. She held Daisy, looking down at her, drinking in the sight of her as she always did. Then she looked at Daniel. His eyes were filled with moisture.

Lily asked quietly, 'Would you like to hold her?' and was

surprised at herself for offering. Then she realised she wasn't surprised at all. It had felt natural to ask. When she'd been expecting Toby, Daniel had looked forward so much to being a father, to welcoming his child into the world.

He shook his head. 'No. I just wanted to see you...'

Lily rocked Daisy.

'You must be very proud,' said Daniel.

'Yes. Yes, I am. No matter what.'

Gently, she replaced Daisy in the drawer, hovering over her in case she decided to wake up, but she didn't.

'You're happy,' said Daniel. 'I can see it. You're glowing with it.' He swallowed. 'You deserve it, Lily. If anybody deserves to be happy, you do.'

Lily nodded, unable to form any words. Yes, she was deeply happy, it was true, but she'd paid a high price.

Daniel stirred. 'I'd better go. I'm sorry for disturbing you—'

'That's all right,' Lily said quickly, but he wasn't listening.

'I'll get out of your hair. Thank you for humouring my stupid request.'

'It wasn't stupid—'

'Good luck, Lily.'

He turned to go. A few steps brought him to the door. He opened it. Another moment, and he would be gone – probably for good.

Lily hurried towards him. 'Daniel...'

'Yes?' he asked when she stopped speaking.

She drew in a breath. 'I'll see you out.'

'Can you leave the baby?'

'She's fast asleep.'

As they went downstairs, Mrs Ivy Dunbar was on her way up. Although she said nothing, Lily caught the sharp glance she gave them, and felt obliged to explain.

'I'm just seeing Daniel out.'

Mrs Dunbar stopped on the stairs. 'Take your time. I'll go and sit with Daisy.'

'I'd just started the WVS mending,' said Lily and then was astounded at herself for saying something so ordinary and everyday when inside she was in turmoil.

She and Daniel continued to the foot of the stairs and walked across the foyer to the front doors. They both reached for the doorknob and their hands brushed. They both pulled back; they both gave an awkward laugh.

'Allow me,' said Daniel. He opened the door but didn't leave.

'Thank you for coming,' said Lily.

'It felt important,' he replied.

'I'm glad you... That is, I hope it gave you what you wanted.'

'I think it gave me something I needed,' said Daniel.

They stood for a moment.

'Well, I'd best be off,' he said.

The sound of footsteps on the stairs made them both look round. Here came Mrs Ivy Dunbar.

'Scissors!' she said. 'I'd just got myself nicely settled with a cigarette and then I realised there weren't any scissors.'

That sparked Lily's memory. She delved in her pocket. 'Here,' she said, producing the scissors.

The reception room door opened and Kitty appeared. Her glance took in Lily and Daniel, then she addressed her mother-in-law.

'Could you give me a hand for a minute, please?'

'Of course.'

They disappeared into the reception room and the door closed.

'Do you think they shut the door for our benefit?' Daniel sounded amused.

'I don't know,' Lily answered. 'If they did, there was no reason to.'

Was there?

'I'm glad I saw you with Daisy,' said Daniel. 'It's a memory I'll treasure.'

'I'm glad you came round,' said Lily.

'Are you?'

'I know what you did the night Daisy was born. I know how you waited for news outside the delivery room. I was confused when I was told, because I couldn't imagine what made you do it, but I'm glad you did. I didn't know at the time that you were there, but now I'm pleased you were.'

'I just wanted to know you were safe and well,' Daniel told her. 'You and the baby.'

'I'm glad you've seen her,' said Lily.

'We both seem to be glad about an awful lot of things,' said Daniel. 'It's rapidly becoming the most overused word in the English language.'

Somehow or other – Lily had no idea how it happened, but somehow they were standing closer together. She looked up at him. Then the reception room door opened and they automatically stepped apart.

Mrs Ivy Dunbar disappeared up the stairs.

Lily and Daniel glanced at one another. Self-consciousness poured through Lily. She could tell by the flush of colour along Daniel's cheekbones that he felt the same.

An almighty howl seemed to fill Dunbar's from the cellars to the rafters. Mrs Ivy Dunbar! Lily and Daniel both made a dash for the stairs. Lily was dimly aware of Kitty following, and Abbie appeared from somewhere.

Mrs Ivy Dunbar staggered out of the door to the family flat, gasping and choking. The stench of smoke tainted the air and grey tendrils of it wafted onto the landing.

Daniel swung round and shouted to Kitty.

'Telephone for the fire brigade!'

He shoved Mrs Ivy Dunbar out of the way and plunged into the flat. Lily followed, every instinct, every nerve-end propelling her towards her baby. She gasped in terror at the sight of the red and orange flames between her and where Daisy was. The pile of clothes on the card table was on fire and so was the armchair. A huge squeezing sensation inside her throat told Lily she was about to choke. She knew that if she did, her lungs would automatically try to heave air – the smoke – into them.

She was on Daniel's heels when he grabbed Daisy from her drawer, holding her against his body to shield her. He seized Lily's shoulder and steered her back to the doorway and they stumbled onto the landing.

He thrust Daisy into Lily's arms and ran back into the flat. Standing back from the doorway, Lily watched what was happening inside. Mrs Ivy Dunbar, having yanked the bedding free, was about to toss it over the fire. Daniel wrenched the eiderdown and blanket from her arms and, using his greater height, hurled them over the fire in an effort to smother it.

Abbie appeared from the bedroom, staggering beneath the weight of the old coal-scuttle the residents of Dunbar's had cleaned and scoured so it could be used as a baby bath. Daniel hefted it up, swung it back and then forwards, sending water in a wide arc that fell on flames and bedding.

Kitty appeared at Lily's side.

'Is she all right?' she demanded.

Lily was too shocked, too panicked, too distraught to tell. Kitty peeled her hands away so she could lean over Daisy.

'She's moving. I think she's waking up.'

Gratitude swarmed all through Lily. She couldn't have borne it if another baby of hers—

Daisy opened her blue eyes, hiccupped a couple of times and then yelled her head off. It was the sweetest sound Lily had ever heard.

* * *

Beatrice was startled by how quickly things had happened. Once the boys had been reduced to jelly, the truth had started to come out. Joe and Tommy were desperate to throw off the accusation of being traitors. The way the pilfering had worked wasn't how the police and the high-ups from the factory had pictured it at all.

Joe and Tommy had been spirited off into another room in the police station. Beatrice more than half expected to be dismissed as well, but she wasn't. Now that she had helped prise the story out of the boys, should she ask if it was time for her to leave? No, she'd hang on and hope that no one thought of sending her on her way. She was keen to know what happened next.

Sergeant Wakefield and Beatrice sat on either side of the desk. Mr Stoneley had paced about a bit, thinking furiously, judging by his screwed-up brows, but now he sat down so heavily that the chair shunted back several inches.

'Salvage,' he said. 'I must admit, even with all my years of experience, I'd never have thought of that.'

Beatrice shared the men's shock. All the valves assembled in the factory had to be tested. Any that failed were set aside for salvage. Every couple of days, a trolley of boxes of failed valves was trundled along to the nearest salvage depot.

As far as the boys were concerned, the valves they'd been given were failed valves – but they weren't. They were in perfect working order. That meant that someone inside the factory had knowingly put good valves in with the failed ones.

'And then the good valves were handed out to the Greasy Lil's boys outside the factory,' said Mr Stoneley, 'but the boys said it wasn't simply a matter of opening up a single box and dishing out the contents to them. It was one valve from this box and a couple of valves from that. The man who delivers the boxes to the salvage depot is called Scudamore. How did he know which valves had passed and which had failed? How could he tell?'

The two men discussed this, but they seemed to be talking round and round in circles as far as Beatrice could tell.

The telephone rang and Sergeant Wakefield lifted the receiver. He listened, then said, 'Thank you. Put him through.' He held out the receiver to Mr Stoneley. 'It's for you.'

Mr Stoneley stood up and took the receiver. 'Stoneley,' he said. 'Yes, what is it?... I see... *What*?' he exclaimed, making Sergeant Wakefield sit up. 'Great Scott.'

Beatrice exchanged looks with the sergeant as the conversation continued. It wasn't possible to make out what was going on, but evidently something significant had taken place.

When Mr Stoneley hung up, he mashed his brows together. 'Well, well, well.'

'Spit it out, man,' said Sergeant Wakefield. 'What's happened?'

'The chaps in the factory have found out how Scudamore could tell which of the so-called failed valves were actually in working order.'

'How?' Beatrice asked.

'When the valves are tested, failed valves are marked with a tiny dot of red paint on the base, where the pins are. Our chaps spotted that the valves that were in the boys' possession have got *two* red dots. That's how Scudamore knew which valves to hand over to the lads.'

'And then they lurked outside Greasy Lil's, waiting to hand them over to Den the Dodge, who rewarded them with bags of chips,' Sergeant Wakefield finished.

'Den the Dodge?' Beatrice asked.

'He's been involved in various dodgy dealings over the years, since before he was the age Simpson and Abbott are now,' Sergeant Wakefield explained, 'but we've never managed to prove anything against him. He's a sly devil. He obviously learned from a master, though we've never worked out who that master was. He's Den the Dodge because of all his dodgy dealings and also because of the way he's dodged out of the path of the police more times than you can shake a stick at. His real name is Denver Evans.'

'Denver Evans!' Beatrice went hot and cold. 'He's the grandson of a lady the WVS provides meals for.' Her kind heart sank into her shoes as her earlier suspicions were confirmed.

'We haven't actually proved anything against him now,' Mr Stoneley pointed out. 'We can link Scudamore to the good valves on the salvage trolley, but all we've got against Den the Dodge is the word of the Greasy Lil's boys that they gave him their so-called failed valves. Any barrister worth his salt would make mincemeat of the boys in court.'

'But surely the evidence of young lads being taken advantage of would count for something,' Beatrice protested.

'You mean the evidence of tearaway boys who knew full well they were involved in something they shouldn't be doing,' Mr Stoneley countered.

Beatrice fixed her gaze on Sergeant Wakefield, willing him to disagree.

He lifted his broad shoulders in a shrug. 'Reasonable doubt.'

'And that's before the barrister asks the boys so many confusing questions that they don't know which way is up,' Mr Stoneley added. 'We can't rely on the boys.'

Did that mean Den the Dodge was going to get off scot-free? Beatrice felt conflicted. Denver Evans was a thief and a profiteer and he deserved to be punished – but if he got away with it, wouldn't that be kinder on dear Mrs Cowell? Beatrice couldn't bear to think of the sweet old lady being hurt. Even as she thought of it, she knew she was wrong to make allowances, but how could she help it when she felt so fond of Mrs Cowell?

There was a knock on the door. Sergeant Wakefield called, 'Come in,' and a uniformed copper appeared, looking serious.

'Sorry, Sarge,' he said. 'We got to Greasy Lil's too late. There were lads outside finishing their chips, and they admitted it was Denver Evans who'd paid for them, but they all played the innocent when we asked if they'd given him anything. If we'd arrived a few minutes earlier, I'm sure we'd have seen them handing over the goods.'

'Or so we assume,' said Sergeant Wakefield. He looked at Mr Stoneley. 'We still can't prove it.' To the constable, he said, 'Where is he now?'

'In his grandmother's cottage up the road from Greasy Lil's.'

Beatrice caught her breath. She had no idea what was going to happen next, but she emphatically didn't want Mrs Cowell to be involved in it.

'He must have the valves with him,' said Sergeant Wakefield. 'Is the cottage under surveillance? Good. We can't hang about. We have to act immediately. We've got the evidence we need against Scudamore and it's now or never for us to nail Den the Dodge. He'll guess something is wrong because Joe Simpson and Tommy Abbott were missing from his group outside Greasy Lil's.

This is our one and only chance to get him on this matter. We need a warrant to search his nan's cottage.'

'No...' breathed Beatrice. When the three men looked at her, she lifted her chin. 'What I mean is, I know what you have to do and why, but it's going to be desperately hard on his grandmother. She's very frail.'

'You can come with us and look after her,' said Sergeant Wakefield. 'None of this is her fault. It'd be for the best if you could support her through it.'

'Thank you,' Beatrice said quietly.

Sergeant Wakefield stood up, an authoritative figure, his handsome face stern.

'It's time to catch Den the Dodge once and for all.'

24

Lily was exhausted and felt like a wrung-out dishcloth, yet at the same time she was energised with relief and gratitude. Her little girl had been spared and she'd never felt more grateful in her life. The fire brigade had been and gone. They had carried the fire-damaged things out of the family flat – the card table, the pile of mending, the armchair and the rug – and dumped them in the yard behind Dunbar's.

'In case there's a bit of heat left inside that sparks up again,' one of the firemen said. 'It's unlikely, but not impossible.'

Mrs Ivy Dunbar – brisk, judgemental, always-in-the-right Ivy Dunbar – had broken down and sobbed, actually *sobbed*, when she had to admit that the fire was her fault.

'I honestly thought I was helping by saying I'd keep an eye on Daisy. I settled myself down and lit a cigarette, and I was about to get on with a piece of mending when I realised there weren't any scissors, so I went downstairs to find some, and you had them in your pocket, Lily.'

'And then I called you into the reception room to help me,'

Kitty recalled, turning pale, and Lily felt the colour drain from her own cheeks as well.

'If that job had taken us five minutes longer...' Mrs Dunbar whispered, looking ill at the thought. 'Not even five. Just two minutes...'

'But it didn't,' said Daniel.

His voice was firm except for a tiny waver that Lily picked up on because she knew him so well. That knowledge brought her thoughts to a halt for a second. Yes, she did know him. In spite of everything that had gone wrong for them, in spite of the enforced separations caused by his work, in spite of all that, she knew him.

'And then, when I went back upstairs and saw the fire,' Mrs Ivy Dunbar said with a shudder, 'instead of rushing into the room to save Daisy, I panicked and yelled blue murder.'

'Good thing you did,' said Kitty. 'You alerted the rest of us.'

'And you *did* help save her,' Abbie added, putting an arm around her grandmother. 'You got the bedding to help smother the flames.'

'And you filled the coal-scuttle with water,' Mrs Ivy Dunbar replied. 'I'm proud of you, Abbie. You were very brave.'

'Yes, you were,' Lily told the young girl. 'What a tale you'll have to tell Auntie Beatrice when she gets home.'

'I love Daisy,' Abbie replied simply, 'and I love you as well, Lily. I'd do anything for the pair of you.'

'We all would,' said Kitty.

'I'm so pleased and grateful you were here,' Lily told Daniel. She wanted not just to say it, but to say it in front of her dearest friends.

'So am I,' said Daniel.

* * *

Mr Stoneley wasn't at all keen for Beatrice to come to Mrs Cowell's cottage while the search took place. 'Den the Dodge is a criminal. Holding his nan's hand while she faces up to a few home truths is the least of our problems.'

Beatrice threw a pleading look at Sergeant Wakefield and he gave her a nod. To Mr Stoneley, he said, 'We brought Miss Inkerman into this. Now she can help with the old lady.'

Soon they were on their way – Beatrice, the sergeant, Mr Stoneley and three coppers. When they arrived at Mrs Cowell's little one-up one-down, a policeman was standing on the other side of the narrow road. He came forward to report to Sergeant Wakefield.

'He's still in there, Sarge, and he knows I'm here. He looked out earlier, then turned round and went straight back in.'

'Right, then.' Sergeant Wakefield glanced round, gathering eyes to him. 'We go in and search him. If the valves aren't on his person, we search the premises and we don't leave until we've found them.'

The men nodded and shoved their shoulders back, looking determined and keen, but Beatrice felt a shiver of trepidation. Poor Mrs Cowell. This was going to break her heart.

Sergeant Wakefield strode across the road and rapped on the door. Denver opened it.

'Denver Evans,' said the sergeant. 'I have reason to believe you are in possession of stolen goods – military goods, at that. Are you going to hand them over quietly, for the sake of making this easier on your grandmother?'

Denver smirked. 'Dunno what you're on about, mate.'

'Then you won't object to stepping outside to be searched,' said Sergeant Wakefield.

The confidence with which Denver did this said at once that nothing would be found about his person.

'We'll have to search the house,' said Sergeant Wakefield.

'Not my house,' Denver replied. 'I can't give permission.'

'I don't need permission,' Sergeant Wakefield replied testily. 'I have the necessary paperwork.'

'Let me go in first and tell my nan what's going on,' said Denver. 'She's an old lady and this is going to rattle her something chronic.'

The sergeant gave a scornful laugh. 'What, give you time to squirrel away your ill-gotten gains? Not likely! Miss Inkerman here will take care of your grandmother.'

Bringing Denver with them, Sergeant Wakefield and his men marched indoors – or tried to. The small room and its considerable clutter immediately put paid to that. They ended up halting and then edging around everything.

Bringing up the rear, Beatrice made her way as soon as she could to where poor Mrs Cowell sat beside the fireplace, looking scared and confused, clutching her handbag and her gas-mask box on her lap. Kneeling next to her, Beatrice placed a soothing hand on her scrawny arm.

'Try not to worry,' she said. How hopelessly inadequate her words sounded to her own ears. 'I have permission to stay with you.'

'Oh, Miss Inkerman,' the old lady whispered anxiously.

'I'll remain until the police have finished,' Beatrice told her reassuringly, 'and I'll stay beyond that, if you need me to.'

'Thank you... Thank you. Oh my goodness!' Mrs Cowell looked beyond Beatrice to where the men were going through her many possessions. 'What's going on? Do they have to do this?'

'I'm sorry,' Beatrice said, her heart aching for her friend – yes, her friend. 'They're looking for some things – some valves – and they're small, so they could be tucked away anywhere.' She hesitated before asking, 'Did Mr Evans...? What I mean is, did he put something away somewhere, earlier on?'

Was it wrong of her to ask such a leading question? But if it drew this situation to a close more quickly, it would be worth it. Or would it? Poor Mrs Cowell.

The old lady shook her head. 'I don't know what you're on about. My Denver hiding something? You're not making sense.' One hand let go of her handbag and gas-mask box and grabbed at the arm of her chair as if to steady herself. 'Oh, Miss Inkerman...'

Mrs Cowell's home might be tiny but it was crammed full to such an extent that over an hour later, the search was still in progress. Mrs Cowell had succumbed to a couple of bouts of soft weeping that had torn Beatrice's heart in two. She flung a look of anger and frustration at Denver Evans, who was standing with his arms folded.

'How could you do this to her?' Beatrice demanded. 'Why don't you just show the police where you put them?'

'Put what?' he replied coolly. 'I've not put anything anywhere. I'd never do wrong by my nan – would I, Nan?'

'No,' Mrs Cowell answered. 'No, you wouldn't. He's a good boy,' she said to Beatrice.

The search was edging closer to where Mrs Cowell sat. The old lady's eyes widened, showing the whites all the way round. The poor creature was obviously terrified. Beatrice moved nearer, wanting to shield her.

Sergeant Wakefield squeezed through to stand beside them. He squatted in front of Mrs Cowell and Beatrice was filled with the comfortable warmth of gratitude. How kind of him to perform this small courtesy. Plenty of men wouldn't have bothered.

'In a few minutes, I'll have to ask you to move, Mrs Cowell,' he said. 'Do you think you can manage that? Miss Inkerman will stay with you.'

The old lady nodded, flashing a look of appreciation at Beatrice.

'This won't take too much longer.' Sergeant Wakefield's tone was pleasant and kind, but Beatrice, extra alert because of being upset on Mrs Cowell's behalf, heard the underlying note of frustration.

When Sergeant Wakefield returned to the search, Mrs Cowell leaned towards Beatrice. 'Dear Miss Inkerman, thank you for helping me through this.'

'My pleasure.' Beatrice frowned. 'Though "pleasure" is hardly the right word.'

'Could you do something for me? Just a little favour. They've searched the scullery, haven't they? Then do you think you could put my handbag and gas-mask box in there, up on the shelf over the sink, to keep them out of the way? When the police want me to move from my chair, it'll be easier to keep out of their way if I've got my hands free.'

Beatrice took the two items to the scullery, on the way checking with one of the coppers that the search in there was indeed finished. She put Mrs Cowell's bag and gas-mask box on the edge of the wooden draining board while she reached up to shunt the pieces of crockery along to make space. Stretching up, she popped the handbag on the shelf first, but when she dropped back from her toes to her heels, she caught the edge of the gas-mask box and it fell to the floor with a tiny tinkle of breaking glass. That sound wasn't from the gas mask. Mind you, lots of people used their gas-mask boxes these days for carrying all sorts of other things instead – sandwiches, lipstick, you name it. There was no knowing what Mrs Cowell, with her propensity for hanging on to all kinds, might keep in hers. Beatrice's heart dipped. Had her clumsiness caused something special to get smashed?

She picked up the gas-mask box and opened it. A gasp tore at the back of her throat, leaving a scorching sensation. The valves!

Beatrice stood in the scullery doorway, holding the gas-mask box. She fixed her gaze on Sergeant Wakefield, waiting for him to notice her. She couldn't have uttered a word if her life had depended on it. She was too shocked.

Mrs Cowell was on her feet. Sergeant Wakefield cupped her elbow and assisted her towards the table, moving the chair a little with his free hand so she could sit down. He spoke softly to her and she nodded, looking exhausted.

Maybe he felt Beatrice's eyes on him because he looked at her. Whatever he saw in her face made his expression change. Mrs Cowell, noticing this, swivelled to look at Beatrice as well.

The next second, she leaped up and was across the crowded room in a flash. Beatrice was astounded. She'd never seen the old lady do anything but shuffle and totter. Now, though, she was as nimble as a dancer.

She squared up to Beatrice, grabbing the gas-mask box from her. 'Oh, you just had to, didn't you? You had to go and open it, you stupid bitch.'

Beatrice's mouth fell open. This turn of events was too much to take in and her thoughts were scrambling to catch up.

Sergeant Wakefield appeared beside them. He saw what the gas-mask box contained and glared at Denver. 'Oh, very clever, using your old grandmother like that. Very cruel too. What sort of bloke does that?'

He nodded to one of his officers, who grabbed hold of a struggling Denver.

But Beatrice was staring at Mrs Cowell. The speed with which she had moved... the vicious words... the furious tone of her voice. This wasn't a sweet old dear trying to get her no-good grandson off the hook. This wasn't even a sweet old dear. All those times she had shuffled across the room... All those times she had been friendly and grateful... It was all an act.

'He didn't force her to help him,' Beatrice said quietly.

'Don't say a word, Nan!' Denver yelled.

Beatrice's gaze was fixed on Mrs Cowell, but her words were for Sergeant Wakefield. 'It was her idea – the valves in the gas-mask box – and that means she'd known about the thefts all along.'

'Don't listen to her!' snapped the old woman, her soft voice gone now, replaced by a sharp rasp.

Beatrice's throat went dry. 'What a chump I was. You fooled me completely with your little old lady act. I thought – heaven help me, I even thought we were becoming friends.'

Although the men were taken aback by Mrs Cowell's involvement, they were pleased and more than a little relieved to have found the valves. Beatrice felt no satisfaction, though. It must have shown in her face because, as Mrs Cowell and Denver were taken from the little house, Sergeant Wakefield spoke quietly to her.

'This has been hard on you, Miss Inkerman.'

Beatrice made no effort to deny it, not even for the sake of showing a stiff upper lip. 'To be honest, this has left me feeling in need of a good wash. I used to have a dear friend called Mrs Gates. She isn't with us any more. I was daft enough to imagine Mrs Cowell could take her place.'

'Not daft,' the sergeant replied. 'Generous. Good-hearted.'

'Anyway, look how wrong I was about Mrs Cowell. I couldn't have been any more wrong.' Beatrice sighed from her heart. 'And I feel as if I owe Mrs Gates a huge apology for likening Mrs Cowell to her.'

25

July came to an end. The Allies had invaded Sicily and shortly before the end of the month, Mussolini was deposed. At home, a parliamentary White Paper had recommended raising the school leaving age to sixteen. Sixteen!

Abbie gave a theatrical shudder. 'Sixteen! Just imagine. I'm glad I left before that could happen.'

Kitty gave it some thought. 'They can't put it up to sixteen all in one go – can they?' she added, looking at Fay Brewer, who was sitting with them in their kitchen, sharing a cuppa while they chatted round the table.

Miss Brewer shrugged lightly in reply. 'It does seem rather a jump. Fourteen to sixteen: I don't see it happening, myself. Maybe they'll make it fifteen. I'm sure it will go up. There are going to be a lot of social changes after the war.'

'About time too,' Ivy declared.

Following the fire, she had been subdued, anxious to please and generally very un-Ivy-like, but she was back to her normal self now, and Kitty had been surprised by how glad she'd been to see it.

'Your gran can be a difficult person,' she had remarked to Abbie, 'but she's *our* difficult person.'

Abbie had laughed and agreed. 'Our difficult person. I like that. I'm sorry her house got bombed, but I'm glad she came to live with us.'

'So am I,' Kitty concurred.

It hadn't always been easy having Ivy living under her roof, especially when she had treated Lily with such scorn, but overall, the good outweighed the bad.

August looked set to be another fine month. Sometimes there was a shimmer in the air when waves of heat drifted up from the pavement. In the mornings, beads of dew twinkled like crystal in the glow of the early morning sun, and in the afternoons, dogs panted in the shade.

Abroad, after a number of weeks of fighting in Sicily, German and Italian troops started to withdraw.

'It's only a matter of time before we invade Italy itself,' said Ivy.

'Don't jinx it,' Abbie scolded. 'We mustn't take anything for granted.'

Later, when Naomi popped round to Dunbar's, Kitty said ruefully, 'I couldn't believe how grown up Abbie sounded.'

Naomi smiled. 'Well, she is fifteen. Quite the young lady.'

'Do you think the war has matured her?'

'Maybe,' said Naomi, 'although when I see young lads digging like crazy on bomb sites in search of shrapnel, I don't think they're exactly mature. Perhaps it's because Abbie lives with four grown women.'

Kitty liked the sound of that. 'Whatever the reason, I couldn't be more proud of her.' She looked at the clock. 'Sorry, but I have to get ready to go out. I have an appointment.'

'Where?' Naomi asked.

'With Mr Tulip.'

'Has he forgiven you for when Bill punched him?'

'That wasn't my fault,' Kitty answered, 'though I did feel awful about it.'

Naomi snorted. 'Bill was lucky not to get arrested.'

'Anyway, I'm glad to say it's made no difference to my professional relationship with Mr Tulip. I went to see him to apologise for Bill's outrageous conduct, and I got Bill to write and apologise to him too.'

'Why does he want to see you now?' Naomi asked.

'I don't know,' said Kitty. 'Every other time I've been to see Mr Tulip has been at my instigation, but this time he's asked me.'

'Intriguing,' Naomi commented.

'I'm sure it isn't,' Kitty replied with a chuckle. 'It'll be something to do with the storage business – some fresh advice, I imagine. Useful, but not intriguing at all.'

* * *

'I have bought Dunbar's Hotel,' said Mr Tulip.

Kitty stared at him, dumbfounded. It was on the tip of her tongue to say, 'Could you say that again? I didn't hear you properly,' but she knew she hadn't misheard.

'You look shocked.' Mr Tulip's eyes twinkled. He seemed pleased with himself for having dropped his bombshell to such good effect.

'Are you... serious?' Kitty managed to say.

'Entirely,' he replied. 'I never joke about professional matters.'

'You've *bought* Dunbar's?' Kitty felt breathless. '*Dunbar's?*'

'Dunbar's,' said Mr Tulip.

Kitty's thoughts had scattered all over the place. Mr Tulip had *bought* Dunbar's... *Mr Tulip* had.

'Mr Dunbar wanted to sell the hotel a couple of years ago,' Mr Tulip reminded her.

'Yes, but then he couldn't, because I got the Corporation involved. Because they took an interest in the storage business, and the possibility of using the downstairs rooms for meetings, that meant Bill couldn't sell up during the war.'

'Quite so,' said Mr Tulip.

Kitty frowned. 'The war is still in progress, so how can he sell now?'

'Because two years ago, he intended to sell the *hotel* and his buyer wished to purchase the *hotel*, whereas I am happy to comply with the Corporation's wishes regarding the storage business until the war is over and for a further year afterwards.'

Kitty was thinking furiously and trying not to panic. 'When will the sale go through, Mr Tulip? How long do I have to find another home?' Not a home just for herself and Abbie either. For Ivy, Beatrice, Lily and Daisy too. How was she to achieve that? Distress speared her. She couldn't bear to think of her happy household being split up, but it was inevitable. 'And – and what about my storage business? And my wedding receptions?'

'Your businesses will remain intact,' Mr Tulip replied, 'and you will keep running them. And you needn't worry about seeking other accommodation, as I have no intention of making anybody homeless.'

That was a huge relief, but Kitty still felt confused. 'Then, if my businesses remain on the premises, and no one has to move house, what exactly have you bought, Mr Tulip?'

'Why, Dunbar's, of course. The building. The name. Its history – and its future.' Mr Tulip smiled at her. 'Forgive me, Mrs Dunbar. I haven't explained myself very well. I was more interested in catching you by surprise with my unexpected announcement. Let me go back to the beginning. I'm a successful businessman. My warehouses do very well and I have other interests too. You approached me earlier in the war, seeking my advice, and since then I've kept what Mrs Tulip is pleased to call an avuncular eye on you and your storage business.'

'You've been very good to me,' Kitty commented appreciatively. 'I couldn't have managed without you.'

'Nonsense. You're more than capable. I gave you the confidence, that's all.'

Kitty smiled. 'You certainly did that.'

'The tide of the war has turned,' said Mr Tulip. 'The fighting will continue for some time to come, but as a businessman, it is time for me to look to the future – and I see a future for Dunbar's Hotel. It was always the best hotel in Lily Street and it can be the best again.'

Although she knew she would be deeply saddened when the time came to leave Dunbar's, nevertheless Kitty's heart expanded with warmth and pride at the thought of dear old Dunbar's returning to its true purpose, not to mention its former glory.

'Before I continue, I need to ask you a question,' said Mr Tulip. 'It's personal, I'm afraid. After the occasion when Mr Dunbar burst in here, you confided in me your wish to end your marriage. May I ask if that is still the case?'

Kitty lifted her chin. 'Yes.'

'Then I imagine you won't be distressed to hear that my solicitor approached your husband with an offer of purchase, which he accepted.'

'Just like that?' Kitty was shocked. The rat had never said a word in his letters. 'And he didn't mind that the offer came from you – the man he at one time thought had been carrying on with his wife?'

'The offer was made by an anonymous buyer,' Mr Tulip said

blandly. 'Mr Dunbar made no effort to uncover my identity. His sole interest appeared to be in selling the building.'

Kitty's breath caught. Steam started to build up that at any moment would come pouring out of her ears.

But Mr Tulip smiled at her. 'It must be upsetting for you to hear that, but I hope you won't mind it quite so much when you hear my proposition. After the war, you'll need to wind up your storage business. That'll take time. After that, I would like you to refurnish Dunbar's for me and get it ready to resume its true purpose as a hotel.'

Kitty's breath caught once again, but for a completely different reason. 'Oh, Mr Tulip – thank you. I'd *love* to.'

'Good,' he answered. 'I thought you might. And after that, my dear Mrs Dunbar, please would you become the new manager and run Dunbar's Hotel for me?'

* * *

Beatrice was thrilled to bits about the future of Dunbar's. How wonderful to think of the old hotel being brought back to life, and by Kitty too. That was the cherry on the cake – and not just the cherry but the buttercream, sugar roses and the sprinkling of icing sugar all over the top. Dear Kitty wavered between laughing for joy and hardly daring to believe her good fortune.

'You deserve it,' Beatrice assured her when they were together in the reception room. 'You've got the fresh start you wanted.'

'No, I haven't,' Kitty replied happily. 'I've got the fresh start I would never have dared to dream of. Running Dunbar's Hotel – me! It's extraordinary.'

'Have you written to tell Bill?' Beatrice asked.

Kitty shook her head firmly. 'No. Let Abbie tell him – or his mother. He didn't have the courtesy to tell me he was selling up, so I don't feel under any obligation to share my news. He can go and boil his head, as far as I'm concerned.'

'Does selling Dunbar's mean he is coming to terms with the thought of divorce?' Beatrice asked.

'I hope so,' answered Kitty.

Beatrice kept it to herself, but she was dreadfully sad that the Dunbars' marriage had come to this. And just look at Lily and Daniel. Two couples with divorce in the offing. Beatrice's late mother would have been appalled, but here was Beatrice taking it in her stride. Her mother would have been appalled at that as well.

Beatrice sighed so deeply that it seemed to start in the soles of her shoes and work its way up through her body. At least Kitty and Lily had both been lucky enough to get married, no matter how things had soured for them. Beatrice had never had that chance – or at least, she'd had the chance, but she'd chucked it away both times. First time around, she'd mistakenly assumed that another fiancé would come along in due course, and second time she simply hadn't loved Frank any more.

'Come back,' Kitty said with a laugh. 'You were miles away.'

'Sorry,' said Beatrice.

Kitty glanced over her shoulder at the sound of the front door opening. 'That'll be Abbie.' Her face brightened as it always did where her beloved daughter was involved.

The reception room door opened and Abbie walked in.

'Look who I found on Lily Street on his way to see you, Auntie Beatrice.'

Beatrice's heart executed a little stutter as Sergeant Wakefield followed Abbie into the room. She felt the colour rise in her cheeks and tried to conceal it by quickly taking another sip of tea so she could hide behind the rim of the cup. She hadn't seen him since the evening when the valves had been discovered inside Mrs Cowell's gas-mask box. Since then, much to her dismay, Beatrice hadn't been on the supper run to the police station, so she'd had no excuse.

Now here he was. Had he missed her? Had he hoped each evening that she would be the one to deliver the vegetable fritters and carrot scones? Had he been disappointed when it was another WVS lady? Was that what had brought him to Dunbar's?

'Evening, ladies,' he greeted her and Kitty.

'What can we do for you, Sergeant?' Kitty asked in a friendly voice.

'I've come to tell Miss Inkerman about the thefts from the factory,' he replied. 'We've finally got to the bottom of them.'

'Abbie and I will leave you to it,' Kitty offered, standing up.

'Don't go,' Beatrice said at once. She couldn't have Sergeant Wakefield thinking the others were deliberately leaving the two of them together... even if that was what she wanted to happen. 'I'd only tell you myself afterwards,' she told her friends, 'so you may as well have it straight from the horse's mouth.'

She cringed inwardly. The horse's mouth? Hardly the most flattering thing she could have said.

Kitty sat down again. 'Have a seat,' she offered Sergeant Wakefield.

'I won't, if you don't mind. This will only take a minute. It's taken the police a while to get to the bottom of what we most wanted to know, namely who was the brains behind the thefts.' He paused to shake his head. 'I could hardly credit it when we found out.'

'Who was it?' Beatrice asked. Not that it made any odds. If it wasn't Den the Dodge or Mr Scudamore the salvage-trolley man, she wouldn't have heard of them. Perhaps it was Greasy Lil.

'Mrs Cowell,' said the sergeant.

Beatrice stared. '*Mrs Cowell?*'

'The old lady?' Kitty asked.

'The very same,' Sergeant Wakefield confirmed.

'Mrs *Cowell*?' Beatrice said again, struggling to take it in. Then she remembered how the supposedly infirm old creature had flown across the crowded room to confront her. She recalled the distinctly unladylike language too. 'Mrs Cowell,' she said in a steadier voice.

'I'm afraid so,' Sergeant Wakefield confirmed. 'She had her grandson, Den the Dodge, do the work for her and he enlisted Scudamore and the Greasy Lil's boys; but the idea for how to effect the thefts was all down to old Mrs Cowell. It was her idea to sell on the valves to dishonest wireless-repair men. She thought of everything.'

'I was completely taken in by her,' said Beatrice.

'Don't feel bad,' said Kitty. 'I imagine everybody was.'

'That's true,' agreed the sergeant. 'Even when we found the valves inside her gas-mask box, we thought she must have put them there because Den the Dodge had begged her to hide them for him. None of us imagined the gas-mask box was the regular hiding place.'

'No wonder she kept it so close at all times,' said Beatrice. 'And there I was thinking she was a sweet old lady who was scared of air raids.'

'She had all of us fooled,' said Sergeant Wakefield. 'Well, I just thought you ought to know, Miss Inkerman. I'd best cut along, then.'

'Thank you for coming, Sergeant,' said Kitty. She gave Beatrice a little kick under the table. 'Why don't you show the sergeant out?'

Before Beatrice could move, Abbie headed for the door. 'No need, Auntie Beatrice. I'll do it.'

Sergeant Wakefield gave an awkward little bow. 'Good evening, ladies.'

Next moment, he was gone.

Beatrice knew she should try to save face. She should cover her disappointment by saying something about Mrs Cowell.

She said, 'Well, that's that, then.'

* * *

Lily was becoming agitated. Daniel still hadn't provided the necessary evidence for their divorce to proceed.

'I don't know why he's dragging his feet,' she said to Kitty while they enjoyed a cuppa together in the family flat. Kitty had disposed of the fire-damaged furnishings and everyone had mucked in to replace them. The room now had the armchair from Beatrice's little sitting room, Abbie's bedside rug and a table from Ivy's room. Kitty had thrown out Daisy's cot-drawer in case it carried the whiff of smoke, and given up a drawer of her own.

'You sound anxious for it to happen,' Kitty remarked.

'I am,' Lily stated. 'Well, I am and I'm not. It's going to be horrible, but having it hanging over me is horrible too.'

'It won't be easy,' Kitty agreed.

Lily fetched an impatient sigh. 'It's bound to happen, so I wish he'd get on with it, so we can get it over and done with.'

'Perhaps he's giving you time to recover from the scare on the night of the fire,' Kitty suggested.

'It's been nearly a *month*,' Lily said. 'He must think me very weak and feeble if I need that long.'

'He doesn't think anything of the kind,' Kitty replied. 'He's awfully fond of you, you know.'

'And I'm awfully fond of him, too,' Lily answered, 'but it doesn't alter the fact that I'm the mother of another man's baby.'

'Daisy is worth any amount of anyone's trouble.' Kitty's gaze was loaded with affection as she looked across at little Daisy slumbering peacefully in her drawer.

Lily's heart swelled with love. 'Yes, she is. All I want is to concentrate fully on her, but I can't do that until the divorce gets started.' Leaning forward, she confided, 'Every morning I wake up and think, *Is this the day? Is he going to tell me he's done the deed?* You know – gone to a hotel with a woman unknown. He will come here and tell me – won't he? He wouldn't tell me in a letter?'

'I can't imagine that happening,' said Kitty. 'Then again, it might not be up to him.'

'You mean his mother will insist?' Lily asked, trying to sound scornful when really the mere mention of Mrs Chadwick both hurt and rattled her.

'I mean his solicitor might say it's the correct thing to do,' Kitty answered gently.

Lily thought about it. Perhaps the letter wouldn't even come from Daniel. Perhaps it would come from his solicitor. That would be a real kick in the teeth. Another thought struck her. 'It can't be put in a letter, though, can it? Because then there'd be evidence that the whole thing is a set-up.'

'I s'pose so,' Kitty agreed. 'Even though everybody knows the hotel visit is a set-up, it's probably not the done thing to have evidence on paper. All they want on paper is the hotel's registration book and the private detective's statement.'

Lily shivered. 'It's a nasty business, and there's something weird and unsettling about everybody knowing that it's false. It feels... well, it feels dishonourable.' Tears pricked at the backs of her eyes. 'Mind you, who am I to talk? I'm the one who had the affair – the *real* affair.'

'That's enough of that,' Kitty said crisply, but she softened the moment by leaving her seat and kneeling beside Lily to give her a hug. 'Yes, you had an affair, but whether that was right or wrong is beside the point. The point is that, whatever has happened, no matter what you've gone through, you've come out of it with your beautiful, healthy little girl.' Kitty looked at the drawer in which Daisy was fast asleep. 'The whole point is right there.'

26

Beatrice came home from work, feeling drained. Even with the windows open, the office had felt stuffy. Abbie, bobbing along by her side through the dusty streets, hadn't seemed at all bothered by the temperature. Beatrice loved it when Abbie accompanied her home. She cherished their little chats and hoped Abbie would always want her Auntie Beatrice.

Kitty had said that, after the war when Dunbar's was a hotel once more, Beatrice must stay on.

Tears had streamed down Beatrice's face. 'Oh, I never imagined for one moment... I never expected...'

Kitty, dearest Kitty, had hugged her. 'Of course you must live with us. What would we do without you? Lily will have to stay on too.'

'What will Mr Tulip say?' Beatrice had asked cautiously. 'Won't he mind you having all these hangers-on?'

'You and Lily aren't hangers-on,' Kitty had answered firmly. 'You're family.'

'It's funny how things work out, isn't it?' Beatrice had said once the tears had dried and the sniffing was over. 'When Mrs

Gates's daughters made their awful accusation against me, and I lost my job and my home, I thought it was the end of the world – but that was when you invited me to live here at Dunbar's. Now you want me to stay on after the war. Nothing could be better.'

'Good,' Kitty had replied, smiling. 'That's what I think too.'

Beatrice remembered that now as she arrived home with Abbie. *Home*. She might have always been unlucky in love, but she had enjoyed the most magnificent good fortune in other respects.

Mrs Ivy Dunbar was passing through the foyer. She stopped to say, 'I've made a salad of shredded cabbage and grated carrot with chopped-up apple and pear and a bit of finely chopped onion to give it a bit of zing. I thought that would be nice on a hot day like this.'

'*Another* hot day,' Abbie said cheerfully.

'It'll be on the table in forty minutes. Plenty of time for you to freshen up.'

Abbie scampered upstairs to kiss Daisy, and Beatrice made for the third floor. What she longed for was a full bath of scented water – but didn't everyone? Sometimes her bones positively ached for a deep bath instead of the regulation five inches of water that everyone was restricted to.

She settled for a cool strip-wash and a change of clothes.

There was a knock on her bedroom door and Kitty popped her head in.

'You've got changed. Good.'

Beatrice frowned. 'Why "good"?'

There was a sparkle in Kitty's hazel eyes. 'You've got a visitor.'

Beatrice was baffled. 'Who?'

'Sergeant Wakefield, of course.' Kitty's tone suggested this should have been obvious.

If there had been so much as a flicker of breath left in Beatrice's body to allow her to speak, she would have insisted there was no *of course* about it. As it was, her pitter-pattering heart and frozen brain gave Kitty the opportunity to bustle about, taking charge.

'Here, let me re-do your hair for you. It won't take a minute. Abbie has still got some of the rose-scented bath salts my sister gave her for her birthday last year. Shall we pinch some and use it as perfume?'

'I couldn't possibly.'

'Abbie won't mind, if that's what you're thinking. It's in a good cause. A dab of rose scent for an English rose.'

'You're being ridiculous,' Beatrice objected. 'An English rose is the very last thing I am.'

Kitty chuckled. 'Well, that's true when you scowl like that. You're more of a stubborn old crab apple. There, that's your hair done. Stand there. Don't move.'

She disappeared and returned a few moments later, carrying a hanky with a damp edge. She approached Beatrice with the light of determination in her eyes. Beatrice caught a whiff of rose. Before she could object, Kitty dabbed the hanky against her throat.

'Give me your wrists.' Kitty dabbed the inner side of each one, then stood back and looked at her. 'You can go downstairs now. I've put him in the reception room.'

'Don't read anything into it,' Beatrice cautioned. 'He's probably just come to tell me the thieves are going to prison.'

'If he was here on official business,' Kitty replied sweetly, 'I think he'd be wearing his uniform, don't you?' She gave Beatrice a little push. 'Off you go. You can give me all the details later.'

'Very funny,' Beatrice retorted, but her heart soared.

She was still trying not to feel ridiculously happy when she stopped outside the reception room. Taking a breath, she opened the door. Sergeant Wakefield was standing at one of the windows, looking out. His homburg was on a table. He turned round as Beatrice walked in. He looked well turned out in a charcoal grey suit that hung nicely on his broad shoulders.

'Miss Inkerman.' He gave her a nod and a half-smile that made him appear awkward. 'Thank you for seeing me.'

'That sounds formal,' said Beatrice, plunging from happiness to despair and blaming herself for daring to hope.

'Sorry. It wasn't meant to.'

Neither of them spoke for a moment.

Beatrice said, 'You're off duty.'

He glanced down at himself as if realising he wasn't in uniform. 'Yes, I am.' He squared his shoulders. 'I thought it best to come while I'm not on duty,' he added, 'this being a personal call.' He stepped forward, but then stopped. 'I, um, I've been wondering how you are. You haven't delivered the supper to the station for some time.'

'I wasn't rostered to do it.'

'Really?' His dark eyes brightened. 'So it wasn't your choice not to do it?'

'No. We don't pick and choose. I always do what the WVS asks.'

'Of course you do, Miss Inkerman, a decent lady like yourself.' Sergeant Wakefield cleared his throat. 'I – well, I kept on hoping to see you doing the supper run. Then I spent some time trying to dream up a reason to come to Dunbar's and call on you. After that – well, to tell you the truth, my daughter said, "Just get on with it, Dad," so here I am.'

'Your daughter?' Beatrice's voice came out almost as a squeak at the unexpected development. 'You've told your daughter about me?'

'Gave me a right talking-to, she did.' All of a sudden, Sergeant

Wakefield appeared quite comfortable. 'That's Hilary, my married daughter – widowed, I should say. She said, "If you don't go of your own accord, I'll march you down there myself and ask her." She knows her own mind, does my Hilary. She seems to know mine too.'

'She sounds a bit scary,' said Beatrice.

'What, Hilary? Not a bit of it. She's as soft as they come, but she thought I was dragging my heels and she said, "What if someone else comes along and sweeps Miss Inkerman off her feet? Then you'll be sorry." And she was right. I would be.'

Beatrice stared, dumbfounded.

Sergeant Wakefield took another step towards her. 'I'm sorry. I'm making it sound as if I'm doing this at my daughter's behest, which is the very last thing I'm doing. I'm doing this for me, because... because I was married to a fine woman, who gave me two beautiful, clever, loving, utterly delightful daughters, and it broke my heart when she died. I never looked at another woman afterwards, and never expected to... and then you came along.'

'Oh...' Beatrice whispered.

'I like you, Miss Inkerman, I more than like you and I hope you like me too. I very much hope we can start seeing one another. Will you let me take you out for a meal? Now? This evening.' After a moment, he added, 'Unless you have other plans.'

'No, I've no plans,' said Beatrice. In truth, she was meant to go to the flicks with Kitty, but Kitty would skin her alive if she chose Jimmy Stewart on the silver screen over Sergeant Wakefield in the flesh.

'Good. Then please will you let me take you out, Miss Inkerman?'

To hear this handsome, capable, mature man making his interest in her so plain filled Beatrice with pleasure and confidence. 'Doesn't "Miss Inkerman" sound rather formal under the circumstances?' she asked. 'My name is Beatrice.'

'Beatrice,' he repeated, smiling. 'A pretty name. It suits you.'

'If you're going to call me pretty, I shall think you need your eyes tested.' She wasn't fishing for compliments. She meant it.

'You have pretty eyes,' he replied seriously.

'Oh.' No one had ever said that about her before. She stored it away to think about later. 'What's your name? I know it begins with a C. I saw it on the name-plate on your desk.'

'Crispin.'

'That's unusual. I've never met a Crispin before.'

'I hated it when I was a lad, thought it made me sound like a nancy boy. I called myself Cris and let everyone assume it was short for Christopher.'

'Do you dislike it still?' Beatrice asked.

'No, I'm used to it.' He grinned and Beatrice felt a ripple of delight when she saw the twinkle in his eyes. 'Let's face it. I'm a big, burly bloke and no one is going to take issue with me over my name.'

Beatrice smiled back. She couldn't help herself. He might be big and burly, but he was also gentlemanly and kind.

'Does that smile mean I stand a chance?' he asked – Crispin asked.

'Well, we've got our orders from your Hilary, haven't we?' Beatrice replied. 'If I say no, she'll probably tear you off a strip for bungling this conversation, and I wouldn't want to be responsible for that, now, would I?'

* * *

Lily was delighted about the fledgling relationship between

Beatrice and Sergeant Wakefield. She and Kitty enjoyed many a private conversation about it when Beatrice was out at work.

'It's so romantic,' breathed Lily. 'She used to deliver the supper to the police station, and then she helped with that theft investigation, and after that, when he didn't see her any more, he realised he couldn't live without her.'

Kitty laughed. 'Steady on! Not being able to live without her is a bit strong.'

'I don't see why,' Lily replied. 'It's obvious to anyone with eyes in their head that they're completely sweet on one another. I think it's lovely. They're an adorable couple.'

'That's certainly true,' Kitty agreed. 'It's nice to see love happening to people who aren't in the first flush of youth.'

'Especially after the Frank fiasco,' Lily added.

That made her stop and think. Would other people look at her in years or maybe just months to come and make remarks about 'the Daniel fiasco'? It was all too easy to imagine his mother doing that, except she wouldn't call it 'the Daniel fiasco'; she'd call it 'the Lily fiasco'. No, not even that. Probably 'the gold-digger fiasco' or the 'scheming tart fiasco'.

Lily still hadn't heard anything from Daniel about the divorce. Ought she to take herself over to Chorlton and speak to him at home? But what if Mrs Chadwick was there? The idea of facing her was too much. She had a list of reasons as long as her arm for not wanting to see her mother-in-law.

No, she thought. *Stop it*.

She would do better to stop dwelling on the forthcoming divorce and focus all her attention on gorgeous little Daisy. Life would be a great deal simpler, not to mention a lot more enjoyable, if she could do that.

No sooner had she given herself a good talking-to and vowed to do this than Daniel turned up.

As he walked into the family flat, Lily went cold all the way down to her toes. This was it, then. The notice of divorce. Now that Daniel was here, she wished him a hundred miles away.

'Hello, Lily.'

'Hello, Daniel.' Might as well get it over with. 'What brings you here?'

'How's Daisy? Doing well, I hope?'

'Thriving,' said Lily. 'Would – would you like to see her?'

He nodded. 'Please.'

She watched him as he hung over the drawer. After some moments, he glanced up and saw her looking.

'What?' he asked gently.

'Your face,' said Lily. She wanted to be honest because this was to do with her children – both of them. 'When you looked at Daisy, your features went all soft. You never had the chance to look at Toby like that, but now your face has softened for his half-sister.'

Daniel straightened. 'His sister. Don't call her his half-sister. When Daisy is older, tell her she had a brother, not a half-brother.'

'You wouldn't mind?'

'It'll make Toby more real for her. Anything that preserves his memory is good, as far as I'm concerned.'

Tears swam in Lily's eyes. 'Thank you. I feel the same. I want him to be remembered.'

'It's all we can do for him,' Daniel replied. 'To my dying day, I'll regret not having been able to see him.'

'He was a beautiful little boy,' Lily whispered. 'He was perfect – well, he looked perfect.' Her heart twisted. Toby's imperfection had been on the inside.

'And now there's Daisy.' Daniel looked at the sleeping baby once more. 'She's so tiny.'

Lily smiled. 'Actually, she's grown. She doesn't feel brand new any more.'

Daniel looked at her. 'Could we sit down for a minute? There's something I'd like to talk to you about.'

Here it comes.

Lily sat and Daniel did likewise.

'I've been planning how to say this, or at least I've been trying to,' he admitted, 'but I still don't know how to start.'

After the warm understanding between them while they had spoken of Toby and Daisy being brother and sister, Lily suddenly felt a flicker of impatience. 'Then let me start you off. I know you're here about the divorce.'

'The divorce – yes.'

'Why else would you be here?' Lily demanded in her crispest Mrs-Ivy-Dunbar voice. 'Have you or haven't you visited the hotel yet with the woman unknown?'

'What? No! No, I haven't. Lily, listen to me.'

He moved and she thought he was going to sit forward, but instead he slid from the chair and next moment he was on his knees beside her. Lily jerked back in surprise, then she went very still.

'I haven't done anything about the divorce,' Daniel said.

'I'm surprised,' Lily answered. 'I'd have thought your mother—'

'I'm not living at home now,' he broke in. 'I'm staying with a friend. You and I both know what my mother thinks and I had no wish to hear it.'

'Oh...' breathed Lily.

'I haven't been to see her for a while,' said Daniel, 'because I needed to think and I needed to be sure. I don't want to let you go, Lily – and I don't want to let Daisy go either. You're my wife and you mean the world to me, and I love Daisy too. I've known it since the night of the fire. When Mrs Dunbar screamed and I ran up the stairs and smelled the smoke, I knew it would break my heart if Daisy… Getting her out of the room—'

'Rescuing her,' said Lily. 'Call it what it was. You rescued her. You saved her life.'

'Rescuing her was straightforward. I just had to dodge around the fire and grab her.' His voice dropped to an intense whisper. 'But I'll tell you this, Lily. If I'd had to run through a wall of flames, I'd have done it. I'd have done anything to rescue your baby.'

Lily's breath emerged in a little huff of amazement and gratitude… and love. Leaning towards her, Daniel rested his forehead against hers. She felt his breath on her cheek.

'I couldn't bear to lose you, Lily,' he told her. 'I want us to stay together and I want to be Daisy's father. Can we please do that? Can the three of us be a family?'

27

AUGUST 1943

Kitty walked around Dunbar's, unlocking the doors to the old guest rooms. Currently, they were filled with other people's furniture and possessions, but after the war they would go back to being bedrooms for guests, and she, Kitty Dunbar, would have the job, not to mention the privilege, of choosing the furniture. Would they end up with Utility? Mr Tulip had promised Kitty she could purchase from auctions in order to create rooms worthy of the Dunbar name – assuming, of course, there was such furniture to be had.

Happiness settled on Kitty like an extra layer of skin. Dear old Dunbar's was to go back to being a hotel – and she was going to run it. It was a matter of great pride to her that Mr Tulip should have such faith in her. She had always liked and admired him and now he was going to give her the opportunity of a lifetime.

This was the way she had seen herself before that frightful day when the bailiffs had marched in and taken everything, effectively closing the hotel's doors to the public. Alongside the shock and fear of that experience, she had felt that her dreams had been trampled underfoot. But now... now...

She had to smile at herself. It wasn't going to happen any time soon. She knew that. The war would plough on for a long time yet. At the beginning of the month, the Allies had bombed Rome, Turin and Milan, and Sicily had been secured. It was only a matter of time before the Allies landed on the Italian mainland, and surrender was bound to follow soon after. That would mark a big step forward and would add an extra dimension to all the Battle of Britain memorial services that were to take place next month.

On a personal level, Kitty had been deeply heartened by the strike that had recently taken place at the Rolls-Royce factory. She wouldn't normally have had any sympathy for strikers in wartime, but in this case the strike had been for equal pay. Better yet, the men were in agreement and had gone on strike alongside the women – and, together, they had won the day. For a woman to receive the same pay as a man was unheard of, even for doing exactly the same job, so this had made Kitty feel like running a victory lap around Whitworth Park.

She unlocked the final door. It was time to tackle the monthly cleaning. Once, this would have been Lily's job alone. She was back at work now, but Kitty and Ivy weren't about to let her perform this heavy task all on her own. To Kitty's great satisfaction, Ivy was as determined as she was herself to take as much weight as possible from Lily's shoulders.

'I'd be happy for her not to work at all,' Kitty told Ivy, 'and to spend all her time taking care of Daisy.'

'She'd never agree to that,' Ivy replied. 'She's the sort to want to do her share.'

'It's more than that,' Kitty said. 'She wants to work alongside us and feel involved not just in the work but in the friendships as well.'

'I hope you're including me in those friendships,' Ivy answered.

Kitty smiled. 'You have no idea how glad it makes me to hear you say that.'

Ivy flapped a duster at her. 'All right, all right. I know I've been nasty to Lily in the past.'

Kitty swiped the duster aside and caught hold of Ivy's hand to give it a squeeze. 'I'm proud of you.'

'Proud? What are you talking about?'

'The way you've changed towards Lily. You could have kept up your campaign of dislike and scorn, but you didn't. You've softened.' Kitty chanced a grin. 'It took time, but you've softened.'

Ivy jerked her chin, but not before Kitty had glimpsed the light of satisfaction in her eyes.

'Lily's a very good mother,' said Ivy. 'And, of course, she's now a respectable married woman again.'

'And you approve of that,' Kitty observed.

'Of course I do. Don't you?'

'Lily and Daniel being reunited is the best thing that could have happened to them,' Kitty declared. 'You only have to see them together to know that.'

'And little Daisy will grow up with a father,' Ivy added. 'There's a lot to be said for that. There are going to be so many fatherless children by the time the war is over.'

'Daniel adores her.' Kitty felt warm inside. 'You'd never think—'

'No, you wouldn't,' Ivy broke in, 'and that's the whole point, isn't it?'

Kitty looked closely at her. 'It really doesn't bother you, does it? That Daniel has taken on another man's baby? After everything you said to Lily – and about her behind her back – in the past, you're glad now that Daniel has accepted Daisy as his own.'

'Yes, I am,' Ivy answered, her tone ringing with sincerity. 'I'm not too proud or stiff-necked to admit I've changed my tune. I like to think I live in the real world, and in the real world just now, there are heaps of irregular babies, where the mother's husband isn't the father. That'll cause a lot of divorces, that will, but there will be other men who decide to make the best of a bad job and accept the cuckoo in the nest for the sake of keeping the family stable – but Daniel isn't one of those. He worships that baby. He couldn't love her more if he really was her father – and d'you know what that means, Kitty?'

'Tell me,' Kitty invited.

'It means he's her father in the way that matters most,' said Ivy. 'He's going to be her dad. Any old night of passion can create a father, but it takes love and tenderness and a sense of responsibility to make a man into a dad – and Daniel has those qualities in spades.'

'He certainly does,' Kitty agreed.

'I admire that young couple,' said Ivy. 'They've been through so much and now they've emerged at the other end.' She looked at Kitty.

'If you're about to say they've made a better fist of it than Bill and I did, I'll be the first to agree,' Kitty stated flatly. 'Lily and Daniel have got one thing that Bill and I never had.'

'What's that?'

'The same basic values,' Kitty replied. 'We agreed on a lot of things, mainly Abbie. But our beliefs about money were poles apart, and Bill went to such extremes with his extravagance.'

'I don't know where he got that from,' Ivy said sadly. 'Not from me or his father. It shames me to think of all the money Bill has wasted. Still, he's got heaps of money now that he's sold Dunbar's. I just hope he has the sense to hang on to it.'

Kitty didn't hold out much hope, but to make Ivy feel better, she said, 'Maybe the amount will make him see sense.'

'Maybe,' said Ivy.

'How do you feel about Dunbar's being sold?' Kitty asked.

Ivy looked thoughtful. 'Dunbar's has been a part of my life ever since I got engaged to Bill's father. Of course, it was only on the edge of my life, because it was Jeremiah who was in line to inherit. But you can't be connected to a place like Dunbar's without feeling proud. Of course, I felt jealous as well, and left out. When Ronald died, and suddenly Bill was in line to inherit, I felt...'

Kitty expected her to say, thrilled, jubilant, complacent.

'...guilty.'

'Guilty?' Kitty exclaimed.

'After all the bad thoughts and bad feelings I'd had over the years, it was as if I'd made Ronald's death happen.'

'It was a motorcar in the blackout that made Ronald's death happen,' Kitty said crisply.

'It was just a mad thought I had. You asked how I feel about Dunbar's being sold, so I'll tell you. For one thing, I feel ashamed; and for another, I feel glad and relieved.'

'Ashamed? Oh, Mrs Dunbar.'

'Ashamed that after years – decades – of family ownership, my son is the one to part with the old place,' Ivy said, her tone strained. 'And glad and relieved because if Bill had kept Dunbar's, he'd have lost it at some point after coming home from the war. This way, selling to a man who wants to restore Dunbar's to its position as the best hotel on Lily Street, Bill has done the best possible thing for Dunbar's. Not that that was why he did it, but the outcome is the same.'

'It sounds as if you've...' Kitty fought to find the right word, '... accepted it.'

Ivy nodded. 'I reckon I have. I've also accepted that your marriage to Bill is over.'

'Thank you,' Kitty said softly. 'That means a lot.'

'Has he agreed to the divorce yet?'

'Not yet. Even if he never does, I won't stay with him. I'll ask the court for a legal separation if I have to.'

'Something tells me it won't come to that.'

'What d'you mean?' Kitty's ears pricked. 'Do you know something?'

'I know my son,' Ivy replied. 'He isn't the type to stay on his own. He's a charmer, and he'll seem all the more charming now he's got Mr Tulip's money in his bank account. He'll meet someone else. I'd stake my life on it.'

'Heavens.' It was a possible outcome Kitty had never anticipated.

'Let's wait and see,' said Ivy. 'I want you to know that Bill could marry a dozen other women and it wouldn't take away one iota of the regard I have for you, Kitty,' she declared. 'After the war, most women who are currently enjoying their independence and who love going out to work are going to be obliged to return to the kitchen sink, and it won't be easy for them. I'm glad you're not going to be one of those women. I'm glad you're going to have the chance to shine.'

Kitty's heart swelled with gratitude.

'Left in Bill's hands,' Ivy continued, 'Dunbar's would have ended up in financial ruins. Instead, Dunbar's is going to be reborn and I can't think of anyone better than you to make that happen.'

* * *

It wasn't until she and Daniel got back to Dunbar's and shut the door of the family flat behind them that Lily finally felt the rock-hard tension seep out of her shoulders. She managed to hang on until she had settled Daisy, but the moment she'd done that, emotion ripped through her like an electric shock and she began to cry. She couldn't help herself. Daniel held her, which only made the weeping even worse. Soon she was sobbing as though her heart would break.

'It's all right,' Daniel murmured into her hair.

His arms around her were gentle but firm and she clung to him, never wanting to let him go – never wanting him to let her go.

'Shh,' he whispered. 'You'll wake Daisy. If she hears you crying, she won't appreciate the competition.'

That drew a little gurgle of laughter from Lily in spite of everything. She heaved in a gigantic breath and pulled herself together.

'Sorry,' she said shakily. 'Sorry.'

'Don't be,' Daniel answered tenderly. 'Just tell me why.'

Mopping her face with the hanky he pressed into her hand, Lily gave him a watery smile. 'Happy tears.'

'If the strength of the weeping is anything to go by, the sobbing means you must be ecstatic.'

Lily looked into her husband's handsome face and fetched a deep sigh – a sigh that had its origins in the difficult early days of their time together and in their first separation. She felt as if she hadn't drawn breath properly from that day to this.

They had just returned from an appointment with the registrar, where, to Lily's relief, Daniel had done the talking. In any case, the registrar clearly hadn't expected her to utter a word. That was the way of it with men in official positions. They always spoke to the man.

Daniel had told him the story they had concocted.

'I would like you to make a change to my daughter's birth certificate,' he'd said.

'That's a serious matter,' the registrar replied.

'But it is allowed, I believe, given my daughter's age,' Daniel said, sounding serious and well-informed.

'How old is she?'

'She was born in June.'

The registrar had pulled his mouth into an upside-down smile as an indication that Daniel should continue.

'At the time of our daughter's birth, my wife and I,' Daniel began, reaching to take Lily's hand, 'were going through a separation. Hence, my wife, being somewhat distressed and fearful, registered Daisy under her maiden name.' Releasing Lily, he reached into his inside jacket pocket and produced an envelope, which he passed across the desk. 'Here is the original certificate, which we hope to have replaced.'

The registrar flashed what Lily could only think of as a cutting glance at her as he removed the certificate. 'It says *Father unknown*.'

'As I say, my wife had reason to think our separation was permanent and, when she provided the information for the birth certificate, believed she was acting for the best. But as you can see, sir, we are reconciled and look forward to spending our lives together and raising a family. I believe you have it within your power to issue a new birth certificate. Is that correct?'

'It is, given how young the child is,' the registrar confirmed, 'but to do so is no trifling matter.'

'I realise that,' Daniel confirmed, 'but here is an opportunity to put right a most unfortunate wrong. Please will you help us? Will you, to be frank, provide my daughter with the certificate she needs to make her legitimate?'

'Under the circumstances, I will authorise the writing of a new birth certificate,' the registrar answered in such a sombre voice that Lily wondered what his weddings were like.

'Thank you,' said Daniel. 'My daughter's full name is Daisy Jeanette Abigail Chadwick, and I am Daniel Matthew Chadwick.'

The registrar glanced at the original certificate. 'And I take it your address is the same as Mrs Chadwick's? Dunbar's Hotel, Lily Street?'

'Yes,' said Daniel. 'My wife works there and, when I am not at sea, that is my home.'

The registrar looked questioningly at Daniel's suit. 'Navy?' he asked with a slight hesitation. Men from the services generally wore their uniforms when they were at home, and certainly if they had an important appointment.

'Merchant navy,' Daniel replied.

The registrar nodded. 'Keeping the country fed. Essential work – and dangerous.'

'Yes, dangerous,' Daniel agreed. 'Another reason why I want my daughter's birth certificate sorted out.'

After that, Daisy's new certificate had been written up and the registrar had kept the original.

Now they were home again. Home – Dunbar's, where Lily and Daisy would live until the end of the war, with Daniel joining them on his shore leaves.

'This new birth certificate,' Lily said, speaking quietly as she weighed the words. 'It's like... getting married again. That's what it feels like. We got married and we've got the certificate to prove it, but everything went wrong for us and we lost one another. Now we have this new certificate for Daisy and we've got the chance to start again. That's why I was crying.'

'We've been through so much,' Daniel answered, 'but we found our way back to one another in the end, and Daisy has made us into a family. We'll never forget Toby, but we are so very lucky to have Daisy. *I'm* lucky to have Daisy.'

'So am I,' Lily whispered, 'and I'm lucky to have *you*.'

* * *

Kitty was helping Beatrice get the club room ready for a Time Off Club evening when the doorbell sounded. Beatrice went to answer it and Kitty heard voices in the foyer, then Beatrice ushered Fay Brewer into the club room.

'In time to lend a hand, am I?' she asked, removing her jacket and throwing it over the back of a chair.

'You can fix the ping-pong net,' said Kitty. 'The girls love ping-pong.'

'I love to think of them getting a break from their domestic responsibilities.' Miss Brewer smiled at Beatrice. 'I also love to think of them attending school in the mornings. You've made a significant difference to their lives, Miss Inkerman. Those children will remember you for ever.'

'Goodness,' Beatrice murmured, colour rushing into her face.

Fay Brewer smiled, her eyes kindly. 'I didn't mean to embarrass you.'

'You shouldn't be embarrassed to receive praise,' Kitty said encouragingly to Beatrice. 'You should be proud – just like I'm proud of you.'

'Thank you both,' said Beatrice, 'but we can please talk about something else now?'

'With pleasure,' said Miss Brewer. 'That's why I'm here, actually. I've got something to tell you both.'

'We've got a while before the children arrive,' said Kitty, 'so how about a cuppa downstairs?'

Soon, the three of them were sitting around the kitchen table, with tea in front of them and an ashtray in the middle.

'Have you got news?' Kitty prompted.

Fay Brewer nodded. 'I've applied for another job.'

'Oh, *no*,' Kitty responded. Whatever she might have expected, it wasn't this. 'But you're so good at what you do.'

'Good of you to say,' Miss Brewer replied.

'I haven't heard anything about it at work,' said Beatrice.

'It isn't public knowledge,' Fay Brewer answered, 'and I'd be obliged if you could keep it that way.'

'Of course,' Beatrice assured her.

'I wanted to tell the two of you because I've enjoyed my association with Dunbar's and also because it gives me the chance to talk it through. It's a big step.'

'You mean a major promotion,' said Kitty, not doubting for one moment that Miss Fay Brewer was entirely worthy of such a thing.

Miss Brewer tilted her head to one side and briefly raised her finely arched eyebrows. 'Quite the reverse, actually.'

'A step down?' Beatrice asked disbelievingly.

'You must be dreadfully unhappy to countenance that course of action,' Kitty observed, concerned. She wanted to press Miss Brewer's hand, but their friendliness was on a professional level, not a personal one.

'Not at all,' Fay Brewer was quick to assure her. 'I love working for the Welfare Department.'

'Then why…?' Beatrice asked.

'LMS – you know, the railway company – are looking for a clerk to join their women's welfare people.'

'A *clerk*?' Kitty couldn't hide her surprise. That really would be a step down for someone of Fay Brewer's experience.

Beatrice shot a frown at Kitty before saying to their guest, 'Go on about the job.'

'You know how big the railway companies are. Would you believe that each one has just one woman working as a welfare officer for all the other women? And there are thousands of women on the railways these days. LMS is different in that their Women's Welfare Supervisor has a deputy. Both of them travel around the LMS region. Miss Emery is based here in Manchester at Victoria Station. It's in her office that the new clerk will be based.'

'And you see yourself as that clerk?' Kitty asked.

'No, I see myself putting in a marvellous performance in the interview and making them want someone with my experience.'

'Do you mean you hope they'll decide on another welfare officer instead of a clerk?' Beatrice asked.

'Ideally, they'll want both – if they can find the money,' Fay Brewer answered. 'If it doesn't work out the way I'm hoping, fair enough.' She gave a little shrug. 'But if I do get my way...'

'Why this job in particular?' Kitty asked.

'This job that doesn't actually exist yet?' Miss Brewer replied wryly. 'I'm very drawn to the idea of working in women's welfare – the same way you feel drawn to working with children,' she added, looking at Beatrice. 'I'm thinking beyond the end of the war. I'm looking ahead to when all those women lose their jobs. I'm sure there will be those who are happy to return to their roles as housewives, but what about the ones who want to work? I'm sure you can understand that, Mrs Dunbar. Or the ones who need to work because they're unmarried or they're war widows with children to support. Their posts will still be handed back to the returning soldiers, regardless of the women's needs. I want to help these women find places in the world of work. It won't be easy, but I want to do my best for them when the time comes.'

'Very commendable,' said Beatrice.

'I hope you get what you want,' said Kitty. 'For what it's worth, I believe you'd be very good at it.'

'Thank you,' Fay Brewer answered. 'I have another reason for wanting to do it. Years ago, before the last war, my mother worked in an employment agency for women. That makes me feel a particular and very personal interest in having the chance to get women sorted out with jobs after the war.'

'Good for you,' Kitty said warmly. 'And good for your mother for inspiring you.'

28

On Saturday morning, Kitty and Ivy were busy putting the finishing touches to that afternoon's party in the reception room while Lily sat rocking Daisy.

'I could put her down and help, you know,' Lily said. 'Then there'd be three of us getting the room ready.'

'No, there wouldn't,' Ivy retorted, looking up from the silverware she was polishing with a clean tea towel, 'because if you put her down, one of us will immediately pick her up to have a cuddle.'

When they'd finished, the three of them sat around a table with cups of tea.

'There's just time for a breather before the mother of the bride arrives with the food for us to prepare,' said Ivy.

Kitty glanced at the three-tier cardboard cake that would be the handsome centrepiece. 'I sneaked a look at the Victoria sponge you made,' she told Ivy. 'It looks perfect.'

'Thanks,' Ivy replied. 'I added the jam and mock-cream earlier.'

Kitty looked up as the doorbell sounded. 'That'll be the provisions arriving.'

Soon the food was in the kitchen. Kitty sent the mother of the bride on her way with assurances that she could leave everything to them.

'Dunbar's will do you proud,' Kitty promised as she saw her out.

'This time I'm definitely helping,' Lily announced, popping Daisy into a blanket-lined box that lived permanently in the kitchen.

'You can do the cheese-and-semolina rissoles,' said Ivy, 'and I'll make the scones. Kitty, you're on sandwich duty.'

'Yes, ma'am.' Kitty saluted. As she reached for her apron, she asked, 'You haven't forgotten that I have to make a quick getaway at the end, have you?'

Lily's eyes twinkled. 'We haven't forgotten that you're going to dodge the clearing-up.'

'Drat.' Kitty snapped her fingers. 'My plan is foiled.'

Actually, her plan was to call on Mrs Swanson, who had been the housekeeper at Dunbar's for many years in the pre-bailiff days. She had in fact started here as the scullery-maid as a girl. She would have left school at thirteen in those days.

She'd been a huge help to Kitty in the lamentably brief time in which Kitty had been in charge of Dunbar's. Telling the staff she no longer had jobs for them had been one of the hardest things Kitty had ever had to do, and telling Mrs Swanson had been the hardest of all. Mrs Swanson had obtained the position of deputy housekeeper at the prestigious Midland Hotel, and now Kitty was all set to offer her the chance of returning to Dunbar's when it became a hotel once more.

'It'd be lovely to have her back,' said Lily. 'I was terrified of her when I first started here, but I ended up liking her. You always knew where you stood. She wouldn't take any nonsense from anyone.' She grinned. 'She made sure all the maids learned to do things the Dunbar way.'

That made Kitty laugh. 'The Dunbar way – now where have I heard that before? Abbie was always quoting the Dunbar way at me when we were first here – thanks to *you*,' she added, looking at Lily with mock-sternness.

They got on with the preparations, chatting companionably. Then Lily took Daisy upstairs to feed her while Kitty and Ivy changed into their work clothes. Kitty had given everyone a choice of black dress or white blouse and black skirt for wearing in the reception room.

When Beatrice and Abbie arrived home from the Town Hall, they also got changed. It was a case of all hands on deck when there was a wedding reception or funeral tea.

It was a relatively short reception, only two hours, because half past one was the only slot the registrar had had free and the happy couple had to catch a train from London Road at half past four.

While the others started on the clearing-up, Kitty got ready to go out.

'I'll see you later,' she called.

'But not until everything is spick and span, I bet,' Abbie retorted cheerfully.

'Good luck,' said Ivy.

* * *

When the clearing-up was finished, Lily got changed into a smart dress and shoes and re-did her hair. She and Daniel were going to Chorlton to see his mother. Lily had no wish to visit Mrs Chadwick, but it had to be done.

'I can go on my own, if you prefer,' Daniel had offered.

But Lily knew she had to be part of this meeting... this confrontation. It was no use hoping it wouldn't be a confrontation. It was bound to be. Lily's absence would be viewed as weakness by Mrs Chadwick. It was essential that she and Daniel presented a united front.

Besides, with Daniel by her side, Lily could face anything. For the good of her precious daughter, she could face anything or anyone. Thinking of her little family lit a fire inside her. She didn't like her mother-in-law and never would, but that no longer mattered. What mattered now was laying the law down. Mrs Chadwick was normally the person who did that. Well, not this time.

Daniel sent for a taxi. When it pulled up outside, he held Daisy while Lily got in, then handed their daughter to her. He gave Lily a loving smile that filled her with warmth.

When they arrived at Daniel's old home, he asked the driver to keep the meter running and wait for them.

They went up the path. Daniel gently took baby Daisy from Lily's arms as they stood on the step.

'I'd like to be the one to carry our daughter into the house where I grew up,' he said.

The maid admitted them.

'No need to announce us,' said Daniel.

They went straight into the sitting room, where Mrs Chadwick sat reading a book. She looked up, her surprise quickly turning to a stony expression.

'Good evening, Mother,' Daniel said, his tone cheerful but with an edge of steel. 'We've brought your new granddaughter to meet you.'

Mrs Chadwick's mouth twisted into an ugly line before she opened it to speak.

Daniel didn't give her the chance. 'I suggest you should be careful what you say.'

'I *beg* your pardon?' she demanded, clearly outraged at being addressed so bluntly. 'How *dare* you speak to me like that?'

'I dare,' Daniel replied evenly, 'exactly like Father would dare if he felt the need to defend his family. It's important that you understand that, Mother. I'm a family man now. Lily and Daisy come first with me.'

'*Daisy?*' Mrs Chadwick summoned up a scornful laugh. 'What sort of name is that? I take it that it's a family name from your side, Lily.'

Lily's heart beat hard. 'No, it isn't. It's just a name I like.'

'Lily and Daisy,' said Daniel. 'Two flower names.'

'Two common names,' his mother replied icily.

'Two names that you may never had had before in the Chadwick family,' Lily answered, straightening her spine. 'But you've got them now, so you'd better get used to it.'

Mrs Chadwick's mouth dropped open. She shut it with an audible snap and her eyes turned to flint. 'Daisy is nothing to do with the Chadwicks.'

'Oh, but she is,' Daniel replied. 'We've got her a new birth certificate. She is officially my daughter and I couldn't be happier or more proud.'

'You've—' Mrs Chadwick began.

'And if you ever – *ever*, do you hear me, Mother? If you ever talk about what really happened, then you'll never see me again. And, just so you know, I've had some telephone calls with Father and he's on our side, so if you choose not to fall in with what Lily and I are asking, you'll have him to answer to.'

'I refuse to be a party to this deception,' Mrs Chadwick retorted. 'What you've done, falsifying an official certificate, is against the law.'

'Firstly,' said Daniel, 'what I've done is what any decent husband and father would do; and secondly, you have no way of proving it. All you could do would be to bring down scandal and shame on the family.'

'That would make a change, wouldn't it?' Lily put in. 'You creating the shame instead of me?'

'This is outrageous,' Mrs Chadwick declared. 'I don't care for it at all.'

'You don't have to care for it, Mother,' Daniel informed her. 'You merely have to abide by it.' He looked at Lily. 'Time for us to go. Goodbye, Mother. Think about what we've said.'

As they left the house, Lily said, 'She's going to boil over.'

'Let her,' Daniel replied. 'With Father on our side, we're safe from any more plotting. That's what matters. Now, let's take our little Daisy home to Dunbar's.'

* * *

When Kitty arrived home, she found Ivy, Beatrice and Abbie in the kitchen, having a cuppa together and looking relaxed.

'Lily and Daniel are in the family flat,' said Abbie. 'Shall I pour you a drink, Mum?'

'Yes, please,' Kitty said, taking a seat.

'How was Mrs Swanson?' Ivy asked.

'Fine, thanks. Looking well.' Kitty smiled at Abbie as she took her tea and set it down in front of her on the table. 'I'm glad you're all here. I've got something to tell you.'

'Should I fetch Lily?' Abbie offered.

'No. You sit down,' said Kitty. 'We can tell her later.'

'There's hardly any need,' said Ivy. 'She'll be expecting it. We all are.'

'I'm not sure she'll be expecting this,' Kitty answered,

enjoying hugging her secret to herself for these final moments. Her decision was a good one. She was certain of it.

'Expecting what?' Abbie asked.

Kitty looked at the faces around the table. 'I enjoyed seeing Mrs Swanson again and we had a good old chinwag.'

'She must be thrilled at the thought of coming back to Dunbar's,' said Beatrice. 'This was her home for years, the same way it was Lily's.'

'She seems very settled where she is,' Kitty replied, 'and I'm glad of that because – I didn't offer her the post.'

Widened eyes and straightened shoulders greeted this remark.

'Whyever not?' Beatrice asked.

'I thought of offering her the position in the first place because it seemed the right thing to do,' Kitty explained. 'It felt appropriate and right. But over the past day or two, I've wondered about it – and then, when I saw how settled Mrs Swanson is at the Midland, everything slotted into place. I realised it would be more appropriate and right to offer the position of housekeeper at Dunbar's Hotel… to *you*.' She looked at Ivy. 'What d'you think?'

Ivy stared. It took a lot to render Ivy Dunbar speechless, but Kitty appeared to have succeeded.

'I think you'd be perfect,' said Kitty. 'You're organised and you have very high standards… and you're a Dunbar. You've said it yourself. You married the younger brother and it was Uncle Jeremiah who inherited Dunbar's – and you were envious.'

'Envious?' Ivy repeated. 'I was so jealous, I don't think I breathed for five years.'

'Here's your chance,' said Kitty. 'I'm going to manage Dunbar's after the war and I'll need a housekeeper, and the one I'd like is you. Will you accept the post?'

'What would Bill say?' Ivy asked.

'I imagine he'll be astonished and very likely not best pleased,' Kitty answered breezily, 'but are you going to let that stop you?'

Ivy replied without hesitation. 'No, I'm not. No, I jolly well am not.'

* * *

Later that evening, Abbie asked Kitty to help her wash her hair. Kitty was surprised, but delighted too. It reminded her of a younger Abbie needing her for all sorts of things.

But Abbie said, 'I only asked so I could get you on your own. Can we talk in my bedroom?'

'Of course.'

Although taking in lodgers had been a good idea, and although Kitty couldn't be happier to have Lily, Daniel and Daisy in the family flat, all the same there were times when she missed living in it with Abbie and the two of them having their privacy when they needed it.

Kitty had done everything she could to make Abbie's bedroom as attractive and comfortable as possible, with a rose-pink eiderdown, a hinged triple-mirror and china trinket dishes on top of the chest of drawers, and a sweet little armchair with jewel-coloured cushions trimmed with shiny beads.

Abbie perched cross-legged on the bed, leaving the armchair for Kitty.

'Dad's not happy about Mr Tulip buying Dunbar's,' said Abbie, 'and you running it after the war.'

It didn't escape Kitty's notice that Bill had gone from Daddy to Dad. Would that hurt him, leave him feeling taken aback and not ready for the change, the same way it had with her when she'd gone from Mummy to Mum?

'As I understand it,' said Kitty, 'your father made no attempt to discover who wanted to buy Dunbar's off him. He was just happy to sell. As for me one day becoming the manager, that's up to Mr Tulip.'

'I'm glad he's given you the job,' said Abbie. 'It's perfect for you.'

'Thank you, darling. That means a lot to me.'

'And I'm glad Gran is going to be the housekeeper.'

Kitty smiled. 'So am I. There was a time when we didn't see eye to eye, but now...'

Abbie looked serious. 'If you and Gran are both going to work here...'

'Yes?' Kitty prompted, wondering what was coming.

'What about me?'

'You?'

'There's no need to sound so surprised,' Abbie said, miffed.

'I'm sorry,' said Kitty. 'I just wasn't expecting you to say that.'

Abbie perked up. 'So what do you think?'

'What job would you do?' Kitty asked. 'Mr Tulip won't agree to employ you if it isn't a real job.'

'I could be your assistant,' Abbie responded at once. 'Your right-hand man... woman... girl.'

'I'm not sure,' said Kitty. 'Uncle Jeremiah never had an assistant.' When Abbie's face fell, Kitty heart dropped like a stone. Then she had an idea. 'Though, of course, he did have Cousin Ronald, didn't he? I was forgetting that.'

Abbie gave a little gasp of delight. 'Does that mean...?'

'At this point, I'm not sure what it means,' Kitty stated firmly. 'All I can say is that I'll discuss it with Mr Tulip.'

'No – don't,' said Abbie.

'Don't?' Kitty repeated, confused.

'I mean, don't yet,' said Abbie. 'I've been thinking. What if I went to night school and learned shorthand and typing? And bookkeeping?'

'Bookkeeping? That's ambitious.'

'Aren't you the one who's always saying how capable women are?' Abbie retorted. 'If I could get some qualifications under my belt, it would show Mr Tulip how serious I am about this.'

Pride bloomed inside Kitty. 'It would indeed.'

'Could you please help me pay for night school?' Abbie asked.

'Of course I will. I'd be happy to.'

'Thank you. You're the best mother ever.'

'You'd better sign up for some courses, then,' said Kitty.

Abbie grinned at her. 'I already have.'

29

Sometimes Beatrice thought back to the days of the Inky Stinky Inkerman song and marvelled at how her life had opened up since then. At other times, she remembered the scornful *Anything in trousers* comment made by that young copper and pictured how her life had opened up even more since *then*.

'What a dunderhead I was to let that derisive, mocking remark hold me back from being friendly with Crispin,' she said when Kitty was helping her get ready to go out for dinner that evening.

'Crispin,' Kitty said with a little sigh. 'I love to hear you say his name. I bet he does too,' she added with a chuckle.

'Honestly.' Beatrice did her best to appear stern. 'You sound like a giddy girl.'

'The question is, do *you* feel like a giddy girl?' Kitty asked. 'I bet you do.'

And the truth was that Beatrice did. She hadn't felt this happy in years – if ever. It wasn't like when she'd loved Frank all those years ago. This was both more exciting and more solid. *Better.*

'You know what they say,' she remarked airily to Kitty. 'No fool like an old fool.'

'If by that you mean a person with experience of life, a person who has gone through highs and lows and who has learned what really matters, deserves to find true love and be madly happy, then yes,' Kitty said. 'You've waited a long time for this, Beatrice Inkerman, and I hope you're relishing every single moment.'

'Oh, I am,' Beatrice assured her. 'I really am.'

Yesterday Kitty, Abbie and Ivy had marched her down to the WVS clothing exchange, with her protesting every step of the way at what they planned to do. You were only allowed to visit the exchange once a month and you had to take an item of good-quality clothing to donate. Kitty had taken a linen jacket, Abbie a shirtwaister dress and Ivy a tweed skirt – and as a result Beatrice now possessed a dark-red crepe dress with three-quarter-length sleeves and a V-neck; a tailored jacket with a single button at the nipped-in waist; and an oversized beret with a bow on the side, which Beatrice thought should look utterly ridiculous on her, but which she had been obliged to admit looked rather attractive.

Looking at herself now in the long mirror, she was startled.

'The clothes are beautiful,' she said, 'but I don't look like myself.'

Kitty peered over her shoulder into the mirror. 'I'll tell you what you look like. You've got shining brown hair and kind brown eyes. You stand up straight and you carry yourself nicely. You look folk in the eye because you're honest and you want to do the right thing. You've never had the money to splurge on special clothes, but here you are now, decked out in the best the clothing exchange had to offer, and you *deserve* it. You deserve to look smart and attractive.'

'Oh, Kitty,' Beatrice whispered.

Kitty held up a warning finger. 'If you're thinking of disagreeing, you can forget it right now. Your Crispin is a fine-looking fella and he deserves to have a fine-looking lass on his arm, doesn't he? Well, doesn't he?'

Beatrice nodded.

'And that's you,' said Kitty. 'Look at yourself, Beatrice. You're gorgeous and he's jolly lucky.'

Beatrice gave her a hug. 'You're such a good friend.'

'Sister,' Kitty corrected her. 'I told you before. We're sisters in every way that counts.'

Beatrice nodded. Daniel was Daisy's daddy and Kitty was Beatrice's sister. That was how families were made.

Kitty wouldn't let Beatrice go downstairs yet.

'Wait until he's here and then you can come down and make a grand entrance while he gazes up admiringly from the foyer. Trust me. That dress deserves a grand entrance even if you think you don't.'

Beatrice laughed and complied, though she expected to feel a bit of a chump. But when the time came, the sight of Crispin's expression – proud, affectionate, admiring – made her feel like a queen.

They had barely greeted one another before Abbie appeared, carrying flowers – a gentleman's buttonhole of an ivory-coloured carnation and a lady's corsage of two of the same ivory carnations in a froth of fern.

'Abbie...' Beatrice started to say.

'Don't thank me,' Abbie replied. 'Sergeant Wakefield gave me the money to get them.'

While Abbie attached Crispin's buttonhole, Kitty saw to Beatrice's pretty corsage.

Kitty stood back. 'There. Don't you both look splendid!'

'The ivory is perfect with your dress, Auntie Beatrice,' said Abbie.

Beatrice turned to Crispin. 'Thank you. It's such a kind thought.'

He offered her his arm. 'Shall we?'

He took her to the Claremont, where they walked up the curving staircase to the dining room on the first floor. Beatrice lifted her chin. Plenty of the ladies were in full evening dress, complete with jewels and fur stoles. Others wore day-length dresses or skirts, but with a pretty brooch, a velvet evening bag or a shimmering blouse.

In her new rig-out, Beatrice felt as good as any of them and she silently thanked heaven for the dear friends who had made it possible for her to have such confidence. She knew too that part of her confidence came from Crispin, from being on his arm, from knowing he wanted to be seen with her.

And, yes, she took a moment to remind herself that some of the confidence was already inside her. She had grown and blossomed in her job with the Welfare Department. She'd learned what she was capable of and she'd had the satisfaction of contributing to making other people's lives better. She had learned a lot from Fay Brewer and she would always be grateful for that.

The waiter showed them to a table set with snowy linen and shining tableware, and presented them with menus before withdrawing.

'Are we having starters or puddings?' Beatrice asked. 'You choose.'

Crispin consulted the menu. 'I like the sound of the cheese-and-egg tartlets, so will you be happy with a starter?'

'Yes, I think the lentil-and-parsley soup,' said Beatrice, 'and then the braised chops for me.'

'Snap!' Crispin exclaimed with a boyish grin. 'For me too. What is it they say? Great minds think alike.'

They chatted through the meal, which was delicious, as was only to be expected of the Claremont.

'This has been lovely,' Beatrice said when they had finished. 'Thank you for bringing me here. It's a great treat.'

'It's my pleasure,' he replied.

Wanting him to know how much she appreciated it, Beatrice said, 'Coming to the Claremont makes this feel like a special occasion.'

'It's funny you should say that…'

To Beatrice's surprise, Crispin rose to his feet and felt about in his jacket pocket, then he went down on one knee, holding out a ring box in which nestled a twinkling diamond. Beatrice stopped breathing and clean forgot to start again.

'Beatrice, I hope it isn't too soon for me to ask this. I liked you when I first met you, in those unfortunate circumstances. When I started to get to know you, I came to admire you as well. Knowing you has brought love back into my life. You have put my heart back together and, if you'll have me, I'll spend the rest of my days doing all I can to make you feel happy, secure and loved. I have two daughters who are happy for me to provide them with a stepmother, and two granddaughters who are happy to have a new nana. They're also more than willing to be bridesmaids. Will you marry me, Beatrice?'

She realised she had lifted a hand to cover her heart. Her gaze travelled over Crispin's handsome face. Her pulse sped up and she warmed inside.

She nodded. 'Yes…'

Crispin removed the ring from the little box, popping the box on the table. 'I love you, Beatrice,' he whispered as he slid the ring along her finger.

'I love you too,' Beatrice replied.

The ring didn't simply twinkle – it dazzled. It took her a

moment to realise it was because she was looking at it through a mist of joyful tears.

* * *

The reception room was ready. There was no food, because Beatrice and her beau would already have eaten, but the Dunbar's famous punchbowl was on the table in the centre.

'They should be here any minute now,' said Daniel.

Kitty felt a little shiver of anticipation. She hoped Beatrice had enjoyed the perfect evening, and she hoped a celebration gathering in the Dunbar's reception room would finish off the evening in the best and happiest possible way. Crispin's daughter Hilary was here and so were her two daughters. Aged ten and twelve, they were beside themselves with excitement.

Fay Brewer was here too.

'I'm honoured to be included,' she'd said to Kitty.

'Beatrice would want you here,' Kitty had assured her. 'It was thanks to you that she got the welfare post at the Town Hall, and you've always supported her children's clubs.'

Not long after Fay Brewer had arrived, the doorbell rang again and this time it was Crispin's other daughter, Marie, who was a nurse with the Queen Alexandra's, based on the south coast. Hilary and her daughters ran to hug her and then Hilary introduced her around.

'I hope Beatrice said yes,' Kitty whispered to Ivy, though she didn't really doubt it.

'We'll know soon enough,' Ivy murmured back. 'If she slams the front door and goes flying straight upstairs—'

'Don't even think it,' Kitty chided.

At the sound of the front door opening, Kitty shushed

everyone in the reception room and, aside from a couple of giggles from the two children, the room fell quiet.

After a few moments, the door opened and Crispin appeared with Beatrice on his arm. At the sight of everyone, Beatrice looked astounded.

'There are a few friends here who want to congratulate us,' Crispin told Beatrice, then he addressed everyone else. 'Ladies – and gentleman,' he added, looking at Daniel, 'it gives me more pleasure than I can possibly express to announce that Miss Beatrice Inkerman has done me the very great honour of consenting to be my wife.'

'Oh, *Dad*,' cried Hilary.

The next moment, everybody was clustered around the happy couple and Beatrice was passed from friend to friend to be hugged and kissed, and Marie was brought forward to be introduced.

'You came all this way,' Beatrice said wonderingly. 'Thank you so much.'

'No thanks necessary,' Marie replied. 'I've heard all about you from Hilary and I wanted to be here. You can't imagine how many favours I had to call in before I could get the time off.'

'I'm delighted you could come, Marie,' her father said, hugging her.

Abbie slipped her arms around Beatrice. 'Congratulations, Auntie Beatrice.'

'Thank you, Abbie.' Beatrice kissed her. 'I hear that my future step-granddaughters want to be bridesmaids.'

Abbie rolled her eyes. 'It was all they could talk about while we were waiting for you.'

'I'm also going to need a chief bridesmaid, if you're interested.'

'*Oh*, Auntie Beatrice,' breathed Abbie.

'Is that a yes?' Beatrice asked, smiling.

'It's yes a hundred times,' Abbie answered happily. 'I'd love to.'

It was one of those moments when Abbie sounded like a young girl again. Kitty exchanged smiles with Beatrice.

'Thank you for this,' Beatrice said to Kitty. 'I know it was your idea.'

'When Crispin asked for help getting a corsage and button-hole that would tone in with your dress,' Kitty replied, 'I couldn't resist adding to the celebrations.'

'I'm glad you did. Look at him with his daughters and grand-daughters. He's a real family man.'

'They're your family now,' Kitty said, 'or they soon will be. Daughters. Granddaughters. I'm happy for you, Beatrice.'

'I'm very lucky,' Beatrice said softly.

'I think it's time for a toast,' Kitty answered, indicating the punchbowl.

'Don't tell me you've made Dunbar's Wartime Wedding Punch for tonight,' said Beatrice.

Kitty grinned. 'Not exactly.'

Daniel ladled the drink into glasses and Lily handed them round. There was fruit cordial for the three girls.

'The floor is yours,' Kitty said to Crispin.

He looked round at the expectant faces. 'Thank you all for being here to celebrate this wonderful occasion. I'm not going to make a speech because I've already made one speech this evening, when I asked this dear lady to be my wife. I'll be proud to have her as my wife and my daughters' stepmother. Will you all please raise your glasses to – Beatrice.'

'Beatrice!' was the happy echo around the room.

Everyone drank and some of the adults coughed and banged their chests.

'Heavens,' Beatrice said to Kitty. 'That's stronger than usual, isn't it?'

'Of course,' Kitty answered. 'Did you think I wouldn't add an extra slug of brandy and port to my friend's engagement punch?'

Crispin blew out a sharp breath. 'That has a kick like a donkey with a grudge.'

'I hope you aren't casting aspersions on my Dunbar's Wartime Proposal Punch,' Kitty retorted.

His laugh rang all round the room. 'Wouldn't dream of it. Do you mind if I spirit my beautiful fiancée away?' To Beatrice, he said, 'Come and meet Marie properly.'

Kitty gave Beatrice a little push. 'Off you go.'

She sighed happily as she watched Beatrice cross the room to be the centre of attention in her new family.

'It does your heart good to see it, doesn't it?' said Lily, sliding her arm through Kitty's. 'She will hold her wedding reception here, won't she?'

'We won't let her get married if she doesn't,' Kitty replied with a smile. 'I'll be very sorry when she leaves Dunbar's, but also very glad that she's found her happy ending.' She looked into Lily's blue eyes. 'You and Daniel have got your happy ending too.'

'Yes, we have,' Lily concurred, 'and part of it is being able to carry on living here until the war ends. Dunbar's has been my home for a long time. It feels right for Daisy to start her life here.'

'I think so too,' Kitty agreed. 'Lily, you know that if you ever want a job here...'

'I know.' Lily squeezed Kitty's hand. 'You've made me as welcome here as Auntie Nettie and Uncle Irwin made me when they took in a poor little orphan. After the war, Daniel and I will have a home together and I'll devote myself to being a wife and mother, but I'll never forget Dunbar's.'

'I should hope not,' Kitty declared.

'I'll come and see you all the time, and I'll expect you to come and see me too. I can't think of anything better than Dunbar's being a hotel again. I'm so glad you're going to stay here and be the manager.' Lily chuckled. 'I'm even glad that Mrs Ivy Dunbar is going to be the housekeeper. Imagine me saying that!'

Kitty lowered her voice. 'Shall I give you something else to be pleased about? Abbie is going to be my assistant manager.'

Lily caught her breath. 'That's *won*derful!'

'She doesn't know yet, so keep it to yourself for now. But it's what she wants and she plans to get some qualifications under her belt so she earns the chance. I couldn't resist having a private word with Mr Tulip and he says that, if she does well at night school, I can have her as my assistant.'

'I can't think of anything better,' said Lily.

'The day the bailiffs came,' said Kitty, 'I never imagined…'

Tears blurred her vision, but they were happy tears. No one could say how much longer the war would last, but the news was good. And after the war… after the war, Dunbar's would go back to being the smartest hotel with the best reputation in Lily Street, with Kitty at the helm, Ivy as housekeeper and Abbie as the manager's assistant.

The Dunbar family – running Dunbar's Hotel.

* * *

MORE FROM MAISIE THOMAS

Another book from Maisie Thomas, is available to order now here:

https://mybook.to/NewMaisieBackAd

ACKNOWLEDGEMENTS

Acknowledgements generally start with thanks to the editor, but this time I'm starting with thanks and a big hug for my friends, Charlane and Denver Evans. Greasy Lil's, the chippy in this story, really did exist and Denver went out of his way to help me by finding out all he could about it. Thanks to Denver also for letting me use his name – though that is the sole resemblance between him and Den the Dodge. The real Denver is kind, generous and funny and I appreciate his contribution to this story. The cheque's in the post, Denver!

I am grateful to my editor, Francesca Best, who is a delight to work with. Also Shirley Khan, the series copy editor, and Anna Paterson, the series proofreader. And, of course, my agent, Camilla Shestopal. I'm lucky to have you in my corner.

Thanks as always to Jen Gilroy, and to all book bloggers, reviewers and online fiction group administrators who have supported my books, including Beverley Ann Hopper, Vicki Eddison, Helen Hopwood, Meena Kumari, Karen Mace and Nicola Smith. And, of course, Julia Franklin, the best narrator in the world of audiobooks.

To all my readers – welcome back to Dunbar's!

ABOUT THE AUTHOR

Maisie Thomas is the bestselling author of the Railway Girls series. She is now writing a new saga series for Boldwood, set in wartime Manchester.

Download your exclusive bonus content from Maisie Thomas here:

Visit Maisie's website: www.susannabavin.co.uk

Follow Maisie on social media here:

facebook.com/MaisieThomasAuthor
x.com/maisiethomas99

ALSO BY MAISIE THOMAS

A New Home at the Wartime Hotel

Hopeful Hearts at the Wartime Hotel

Dreams Come True at the Wartime Hotel

Printed in Dunstable, United Kingdom

80611777R00188